SARA— I hope this finds you well.

Beards for Life!!

Keep up the [scribbled]. Much love +

BBJ 2016!!

Bushadk cuddles QLTW!!

[signatures]

4/14/14

D0291693

S.A. Bailey

THE
LINES
WE
CROSS

This is a work of fiction. Names, characters, and events are all products of the author's imagination, are used fictitiously, and should not be construed as real. Any resemblance to actual events, organizations, or persons, living or dead, is purely coincidental. That is the God's honest truth and if that's not good enough for you, perhaps you can go fuck yourself.

Credit where it is due

This was a long work in progress. It started before my first book, *And The Rain Came Down*, was even published. It's been said that every book is a labor of love. For many reasons, I'm finding that to be true. I owe the following people immeasurable gratitude.

My dear friend and editor Noël Daley, for sticking it out despite my madness and the long slow march. I can't say enough good things, or thank you enough. If people knew how hard your job was, no one would ever mistake me for a writer. I hope one day I'll be able to pay you what you're worth. The next one won't take so long, promise.

Ryan Lavoie, good friend, scholar, Peace Corps vet, card shark, martial artist, and brother from another mother. One of the things I truly cherish most in this life is our long-going (well over a decade) conversation on politics, philosophy, and everything worthwhile which was no small inspiration in this work..

Lucas Bailey, for inspiration, and being the good brother. Someone had to be.

Rocky Clapp, for picking up his slack.

Jeremy Basore, for always being there, no matter what. The most consistent man I've ever known. Much respect.

Curtis Watson, for rounding us out and always managing to anchor us firmly in reality. Probably the only one that could.

And from another life, Perry Gilliam, Michael Records, Thomas Grove, Ray English, Joshua Schmidt, Eric Pazz, Paul Yoder, and the rest of my Eco 51st family. I miss you, and that damn thing, every day. For what it is.

I couldn't ask for better brothers than you guys. Thanks for the inspiration, motivation, and support. I love you all deeply.

My mother, Jane Bailey. I know it's a struggle, sometimes. I'm working on it.

Marcus Wynne, warrior poet and Jedi knight, for early insight, motivation, friendship and support. Because of him, I met a great many people I now call friend, and am most grateful. Thanks.

Rob Krott, warrior poet of some renown, and an old school war dog, adventurer, and writer like no other. He went above and beyond the call, of his own accord. There is no telling how much red ink he used on my rough draft. His notes were not only helpful, but hilarious.

Dan Kemp, another warrior-scholar of the first order. A Screaming Eagle with a mind like a steel trap, he may know more about military history and weaponry than anyone I know. That is a tall, tall order. Like Rob, he went above and beyond, of his own accord, and the two of them managed to help unfuck the manuscript in places where my addled mind just wasn't firing on all cylinders.

Lori Pudliner, for also going out of her way, and providing me with an extra set of eyes and some late process proofing, as well as insight on the perceptions someone not from Texas might have certain local colloquialisms. I hope there's not so much local flavor people can't keep up.

Mike and Sarah Driscoll, for being themselves. Keep being awesome. Laurie Zieber, of She Speaks to Inspire: Multi-Media Initiative Focused on Women, Culture, and the Arts, for friendship and encouragement. It is much appreciated.

Dellani Oakes, writer and host of the What's Write for Me radio show and podcast, for the same. I feel like I've learned a lot about the craft, industry, and promotion of writing the past couple of years, and much of it came from here. I can't thank you enough.

I have to thank my good friend Caleb Causey, EMT and combat medic par excellence, whose company Lone Star Medics provides emergency, tactical, and basic emergency medical training. I can assure you, any and all mistakes are my own.

Greg Ellifritz, "Beefcake," police officer, tactical trainer, and voracious reader. For encouragement, and checking my six. I was afraid I was stepping way out of my tactical depth, and it was comforting knowing the things I was worried about didn't set off any bells and whistles from someone much more knowledgeable than myself. Based in Ohio, he works with Tactical Defense Institute, and Active Response Training, and training with him would be well worth your time. You may even look up and see my fat ass in class. Just don't hurt me.

Christian D. Orr, for friendship and unparalleled support, I can't thank you enough.

Glen Furtardo, for the chance. You did what you could at a time when I needed it, and because of that I have hope for the future. I hope you know I appreciate it.

Montie Guthrie, for friendship, support, and saving my bacon on some of the finer points of the law and police work. Your nitpicking helped add depth I wouldn't have been able to achieve otherwise. I hope I put it to good use.

I have to thank Shelly Haffly for support, motivation, and schooling me on the ins and outs of website building. Shelly also does a lot with the DIVA WOW organization, introducing women into shooting sports and outdoor activities, both of which I respect and hold dear to my heart.

To Jody Albritton, for more website building advice. I'm a cave man, slowly dragging my knuckles into the modern world, with the help of my friends.

Chris Paul, for encouragement and checking the local vibe. Much love homie.

Ben Westbrook, for friendship and encouragement. Much appreciated.

Bryan Seever, Sherman House, Morgan Atwood, Taylor Mock, Jack "Dubstep Viking" Clemons (thanks for keeping the same vampire hours I do), Ian Wendt, Chris Sanchez, and Aaron Little, for, each in their way, inspiration, support, and motivation. Super special thanks to Aaron, for a term coined and stolen; and to Chris for hard advice and honesty on something, and not being afraid to go against the grain. I appreciate that to no end, my friend.

Eric Cashion of Confederate Forge, for the same. And for forging the finest rebel steel and being his own damn self. Too few live unreconstructed.

Mike Blackgrave, SEAMOK founder and master, for wielding it and passing on the knowledge.

Ed Lawrence for being himself.

Brian Tindle, good friend, boon docking companion on countless nights, and walking, talking encyclopedia of all things DFW, trains, Texas Country music, and terminal ballistics. Brian is responsible for the picture on the front of this book and many others. He is my most reliable sounding-board and occasional thorn in my side. Thank you so much, for everything.

Ellen Fagala, for friendship, motivation, and maybe a little insight. I hope you know it's appreciated.

To my friend and mentor, the late, great Paul Gomez. The nicest compliment I ever got was a look from Paul that said I should know better. There is a Bowie fight in this book that plagued me for years. Rewrite, after rewrite after rewrite. "Uncle Paul" fixed that.

Uncle Paul fixed a lot of things. It's what he did. I know of no person more dedicated to advancing the art and science of self-defense, in a responsible, methodical, well thought out manner, than Paul Gomez. I met nothing but quality people through him, most of whom I now consider to be good friends. The world is a far lesser place without his presence, and he is missed dearly.

Author's note

As I said before, this was a long work in progress. Life, work, family responsibilities, and my own inherently chaotic nature were all obstacles I could have probably managed better. I think I spent the last two years polishing, trying to give it that little bit. I don't know if it worked, but it was my windmill to joust, regardless.

Because of this though, there are some minor anachronisms. Some will only be noticed by people who live in Dallas, like smoking in bars (a city ordinance was passed during the writing of this novel. It is a travesty, and an affront to my religion), and the building of the Margaret Hunt Hill Bridge. It has been completed for some time now, much like this book should have been.

In my attempts to create a series that somewhat reflects reality, and a character that continually ages, I fear I've already started to play with time a little. For those students of the genre like myself, who get irked at protagonists who are forever 35, I apologize. Bear with me, I'll keep it in check. Promise.

During the writing of this book, much has changed while staying the same. As a political junkie in remission, I have tried hard to only touch on politics enough to add flavor for time and place, and help describe the perspectives of various characters. I did so hoping to add realism, and to more accurately reflect the world we live in. I tried to be fair. There is nothing more pretentious than some twatwaffling douchecanoe who thinks they alone have the answers to all the world's ills.

That being said, Jeb's voice is, naturally, much like my own in these matters. Not really all that confused, but often conflicted. A libertarian with a bent toward individual anarchism, and an occasional jingoistic streak.

I am also, without apology, a semi-professional gun nut. Through the magic of the interwebs I met the man this book is dedicated to, Paul Everett Gomez. I discovered his work on a forum, Total Protection Interactive.

I am hesitant, for several reasons, to direct anyone to an internet forum. However, Paul and TPI are forever intertwined. There is a wealth of information there, and the lowest static to noise ratio on the net. One of the things I appreciate the most about TPI is it hasn't been allowed to become some shrine of worship for a personality cult. That Craig Douglas, aka S'narc, of Shivworks fame, has not allowed it to do so speaks volumes of the man. I respect this to no end. If you are interested in any and all things self-defense, you would be doing yourself a massive favor seeking out both TPI and Shivworks out.

There is a book set to be released on 19 August 2013, a compilation of Paul's work and output, titled Paul Gomez: The Traveling Range Bum or Gnomez's Philosophy of Self Defense-- Gun Fighting for Thinkers, collected by Kristen Benson. The proceeds of which are to go to a trust for Paul's kids.

Paul was on point for a lot of behind the scenes, forward thinking in the training community. He wasn't just ahead of the curve, he was one of those rare few who laid the track. Many things that are common place now can be attributed all or in part to his input. Paul, never one to brag, wasn't someone who sought the spotlight, though other, better known but lesser men, certainly enjoyed the fruits of his labor.

If you are a gun guy, a student in the art and craft of the gun and self-defense, this work would be well worth adding to your library. I hope you will look for its debut.

I'm sure there are many wonderful people who helped me along the way who I failed to mention. I apologize profusely.

Dedicated to

Paul Everett Gomez

Friend, mentor, philosopher, itinerant gun bum, and iconoclast.
They broke the mold, sir. They broke the goddamn mold.

"He unfucked us all."

PROLOGUE

A cool wind licked at my scalp with a savage tongue. The smells of East Texas filled my nostrils with a pang of unexpected nostalgia: the scents of pine and cedar and lake water mixed with those of the highway—fumes of sulfur and diesel, dead rubber and worn asphalt. It should have been misplaced, but I had put this off long enough.

The Harley rumbled beneath me, an unsatisfied lover, begging for more. Dallas was ahead, lying upon the night like a diamond on a jeweler's cloth. Thoughts of where I'd been and what I'd done as far behind me as another man's war. Replaced, once again, with those of all the things I wished to find.

With luck, the city's luster would last.

I came in on 175, hit I-20, and took it west around the south side of the city. It was out of my way, but that made me no never mind. It had been a long time since I'd prowled the 'Plex, and I needed to get my bearings, in more ways than one. This had been the route I'd always taken to Dallas as a child. The changing landscape seemed almost emblematic of the differences I found throughout the city and the world I'd known in the East Texas of my youth.

Finally I had to make a choice, and knowing perfectly well all I was doing was working up my nut, I got off at 67 and made my way toward the island of glass and concrete on the Trinity River.

It may have been a long while since I had been to Dallas, but unfortunately, it didn't take long to remember the psychotic selfishness from which every single one of the city's commuters suffered. I was going eighty in the slow lane, and blue haired old women trying to make it home for the late, late showing of Matlock flipped me off. Welcome home, I thought.

I took the ramp behind the southern levee and rolled to a stop at the end of the off-ramp before the light. I was bracketed by three liquor stores, ghetto fabulous pimp rides and various other vehicles—mainly work trucks and vans, clamoring in line at the light—while whores, bums, and just old fashioned lowlifes paraded up and down the boulevard.

Dallas after midnight.

I made my way into downtown, and stopped at a red light beside a high-end, European SUV. Behind the wheel, a man about my age with expensively styled shoulder-length hair talked animatedly into his cell phone. The woman beside him looked painfully bored as she stared out the window. He was one of those cats I could tell had been born whiter than I'd ever cared to be. His wife was beautiful, and I saw an obvious intelligence in her eyes as she stared at me on my bike, a nice distraction, a walk on the wild side.

They reminded me of my ex-wife and her second husband.

I gunned the throttle and ran the light, not wanting to let my mind wander on that reflection.

It took another hour rumbling through downtown until I found my destination almost by accident. Parking the hog and setting the kickstand, I fired up a smoke and listened as the sounds of the city engulfed me. Not exactly rain on a tin roof, but it beat the hell out of where I'd been. I looked at the front door of the club, wondering how it all would go.

Our correspondence had been minimal this time away, and I knew he held going back against me. I'd barely survived the first time; going back for money didn't make any sense. The fact that the money had been ancillary at best couldn't be explained to anyone who didn't understand. Nobody liked guys in my line of work, even when we seem to be needed more and more.

I slid off the beast and tried to stretch the road out. It didn't quite work. Maybe it was the pistol I wore beneath my vest. I killed the cancer stick with a steel-toed boot and walked numbly toward the door, hoping they didn't have a dress code.

Inside I was met by a cranky old bastard with a cigar chomped between his teeth. Others in the crowded lobby looked at me, dressed in my boots, ancient Levis, heavy black leather vest over my wife beater, the dark ink on my swollen arms, and assumed I was lost. The old man didn't bat an eye. He didn't even remove the cigar from his mouth when he spoke.

"You want on the list?" he asked. I almost asked him if I looked like a goddamn comedian. The way the world works, he'd probably known some rougher than me.

"Has Joshua Shaw been up tonight?" I asked. His face lit up as the smile broadened around his cigar.

"Josh-*ua*, Josh-*ua*. Jesus fucking butt-fucking Christ, are you kidding me? Josh-*ua*? Yeah, he's here. Hell, he's about to go up." He waved me on, laughing. He made a crack about rednecks before I was at the bar, but I ignored it. I ordered a shot of Jack Black with a beer back from a bartender with beautiful, gigantic breasts pushed toward the heavens. I rarely drank while working, a fact which hadn't made me popular with the Soldier-of-Fortune crowd—the guys who spent half their time posing for pictures and flexing around the pool for beauty-contestants-turned-network-reporters—but made me loved by both employers and clients, who were the ones that mattered. It had paid many dividends, and led me through the looking glass, and on to other much more meaningful employment opportunities.

When she placed them before me, I thought long and hard about what awaited me at the bottom. I'd been down there before, but then it'd been different. Then, I didn't know who I was; now, I did. And truth be known, I'd been looking forward to it for a long time. The sparse, occasional couple of drinks had done nothing to satiate the urge. The demon warrior rested in the darkest part of my soul, waiting for his chance to rush forward into battle; his most dangerous weapons were every failure I couldn't let go—everything I truly hated about myself.

Still, here and now, in Dallas of all goddamn places, it was different. It felt different. My Spidey-Sense pinged hard and high like an air-raid siren.

Did I really want to tempt him, to put my sanity in peril? Was the momentary comfort, the bolstered self-assurance, worth it?

Fuck it, I thought.

It's the bitch in the car and her soft-ass husband.

"Don't mean nothin'," I said softly and all to myself, and then I dropped the shot smoothly down my throat.

It felt good. Just like it always had, and I had to resist the urge to order another. Instead I pulled on my beer and walked into the theater, making my way along the wall until I found them. Joshua Shaw, my baby brother, sat at a small table with Cornelius Winston Ellsworth III, or C.W., an old friend we'd grown up with. After I'd dropped out of college the first time and entered the army, they'd left home together, coming to Dallas to tackle the big bad city. They made lives for themselves here. Joshua worked as a graphic designer, and had begun illustrating an online comic strip. After college, Cornelius served in the Peace Corps, where he'd kept an online blog about his work. His writing had been praised, and awarded, and that got him a gig with the Dallas Morning News.

They were further away from me than they'd ever been. They'd grown up with real jobs and lives, while I still played soldier. At least I was better paid.

I finished my beer and made my way back to the bar for another round. I knew where they were; now I needed to figure out what I was going to say to them. Cornelius had told me about their weekly sojourn in an email, but I hadn't told him to expect me. I had no idea whether or not he'd told Joshua about our emails. One more drink to get my courage up.

CHAPTER 1

Two weeks later I was once again enjoying the slow suicide of alcoholism in a rundown joint in Deep Ellum. I sat chain-smoking menthols between shots and beers, staring at my reflection in the mirror behind the bar. It was me, the toothless wonder behind the tap, and a regular in the far back corner that kept to himself. Just the three of us. Of course, it *was* ten o'clock in the morning.

It was a historic district with a rich musical history. One that started with East Texas's contribution to the blues, greats such as Leadbelly, John Lee Hooker, and Blind Lemon Jefferson, and ran all the way through the country and blues influenced southern rock and outlaw movements of the 70's and 80's. There had been a great alternative phase in the 90's when we'd snuck into bars to see acts such as Jane's Addiction, Tripping Daisy, Slobberbone, Radish, Bowling for Soup, and The Old 97's perform as teenagers. I often missed those days and that music.

Now the Red Dirt Texas Country set had established itself, and though I liked that genre best of all, it was nearing the point where it needed a good purge to separate the wheat from the chaff. There was a glut of artists flocking to it, and with it they brought polish and business acumen instead of hard-won life experiences. The tradeoff wasn't fucking worth it.

The neighborhood itself was constantly under siege by economic worries, arcane zoning laws, yuppie gentrification, and, worst of all, the brain trust in the City Council, who were bound and determined to make Dallas something it wasn't. Artists and musicians, the heart and soul of the little neighborhood, fought and reclaimed some ground, but its fate always seemed to be a fearful proposition.

Both the neighborhood and the bar fit my mood perfectly. I'd chosen to grace this particular establishment with my presence, not because I liked the company, which I didn't, or because I liked the ambiance, which it lacked, but because no one cared how many times Roseanne Cash sang about a "Seven Year Ache", which was a good thing. I'd fed the juke enough money to keep her going until I was drunk enough not care who was singing about what.

Maybe I was searching for that great oblivion, the one that had never failed to find me, to wrap me in its comfortable embrace, shielding me from the world I hated so goddamn much. Maybe I was nuts, like the shrinks at the V.A. had told my ex-wife, or maybe I would just always be a little lost, but there's something magical about a good ol' high lonesome. I needed to just get drunk every so often and stay that way for a while. Such was the case this late morning.

Our reunion had actually gone pretty well. My mother had even driven in from East Texas one night and everybody ate dinner at my grandmother's house in Oak Cliff, like we were still one big happy family. Of course, she wanted me to drive home and do some heavy lifting. She had retired, and was opening an antique store with a friend. I assured her I would. Strong back, weak mind, that's me. All I'd ever been.

I didn't care. I was used it. It did make me mull over some job offers that were there, though, if I acted quickly enough. That's the way it is in my line of work. Work hard to earn a good rep, work harder to keep it. The good gigs come, and then you work even harder to keep them coming. Nothing lasts forever.

Take the wrong job, cross the wrong line, and you get shuttled to the end of the line or wind up dead. When you're at the top of your game you stay on it. The worst thing you can do, aside from getting yourself or your principal killed, is to drop out of it for too long.

It'd be romantic to say employers worried about you losing your nerve, but the hard fact is that there are more contractors than there are jobs. If you take yourself out of the mix for too long, people have got to know, trust, and want you specifically to let you back in. The pool's filled with both grizzled D-boys who make more in a month than most people in the first world do in a year, and twenty-one year old kids fresh off multiple deployments who were still gung-ho enough to do it for the glory. Like most people in the business, I fell somewhere in between, which meant I was the most expendable, and had to work the hardest to keep whatever place I found. Just the way it is with that kind of work.

There were other jobs available as well in that weird world that exists between the private sector and the Fed, but I didn't particularly want to think about them. Work that was available to me because of my time on the Task Force. Work that, no matter how much good you knew you were doing, caused you to stay awake at night and question the intentions of those signing your paychecks.

It is a hell of a thing when you forfeit your soul for a cause you believe in only to realize the hard way that it is, in the end, useless. That no matter how hard you try, the lengths you're willing to go to, and the horrors you're willing to live with, that you are doomed. That it's nothing but another goddamn windmill.

Sometimes wars need to be fought, evil needs to be vanquished. And sometimes, trying to decide between where right and wrong ends and pure greed begins is a barren wasteland, fit for only the corrupt and the hopeless.

I held the cold Lone Star to my head, and closed my eyes while Toothless behind the bar refilled my whiskey. I thought, I swore, I could hear, just out of reach, that lonesome sound that had founded that place so long ago.

I took another drink and tried not to think.

A razor sharp blade of sunlight pushed open the front door, ruining the bar's perfectly darkened hue, and an extra from a bad eighties movie ambled inside, his leather covered in grime and road dust. I could smell him from the door. His dental hygiene nonexistent, his hair nothing but long thin strings of matted split ends. They didn't make a shampoo strong enough to get the job done. In fact, to say he needed a bath would imply he was familiar with such a concept, giving him a little too much credit.

I knocked back my shot and asked for another, just in case he stopped near me, which was good, because he did, just long enough to ask for a whiskey and coke. I could feel his eyes go over me while Toothless fixed his drink. I didn't feel like talking, but he didn't seem to care.

"Goddamn, you a big'un ain't you?"

"Work at it," I shrugged. Not wanting to be rude, hoping he'd be cool, and leave me the fuck alone.

"Shit, I'll say. Who you ride with?" he asked. Hey you, here's my dick.

"Nobody man, I'm just pass'n through is all. Just want to have a few drinks."

"Lobo, huh? That's cool man, I been there," he said, his voice lazily soft, practiced. He'd grown into his role. Of course, I guess we all have.

"Say bud, looking for a guy named Torres, he around?" he asked as Toothless sat his drink down. Toothless said something more audible than intelligible, and then nodded toward the man sitting alone in the dark corner in the back. The biker took his drink and left. Thank God for small favors.

I sucked on my cigarette and looked at the silent television above the bar, as the President gave a press conference. I didn't know what he was saying, and in truth, didn't care. I'd had more important things to worry about than the election at that time, and even if I hadn't, he wouldn't have gotten my vote anyway. I wasn't sure I would ever vote for any of the fucks ever again.

I didn't like being told I had to choose between the lesser of two evils, and I didn't understand those who went along with the charade. I didn't understand how anyone could live their lives that way.

And I would not accept that progress meant apologizing to our enemies, or turning an ambivalent cheek toward the evils of the world.

Toothless found a dirty, stained rag, with which to wipe a clean glass, and stood nearby, watching the screen along with me, tarring a clean glass, wet brown trails streaking down it.

"You believe people are dumb enough—vote for a nigger?" he asked, shaking his head. I took a drink, turned slightly, and stared at him. Like maybe I might rip his throat out. I was thinking it might be fun. I might've hated the guy on principle, but at least I had meaningful reasons for it. I hated most people anyway.

He caught the look in my eye and backed off, making a pretense of going over the other clean glasses behind the counter. I wondered if they were due an inspection.

I was monkey fucking one menthol off another when the door opened a second time, just as soon as my eyes had finally readjusted. This time Cornelius walked in, all crisp khakis and polished alligator boots, waved at the men in the back, and sat at the corner beside me, smiling. Great, here we go again, I thought.

Since my brother and his wife had recently had a child, I'd been crashing on his couch. This, he thought, entitled him to bug me for an interview, so he could do a story on mercenaries. I'd tried to explain the subtle and not so subtle differences between mercenaries and contractors, but he didn't seem to get it. Mainly because he didn't want to. I probably should've expected that from someone with his particular political outlook. Besides, I had crossed that line in order to do the right thing, the just thing, the thing that someone had to do, that needed to be done, on more than one occasion, and he couldn't know anything about it. No one could.

Still, I hated that word and the things it brought to the front of people's minds, things that made me cringe. I never did anything in my life simply for money alone. There was much, often worse in fact, I'd done for free. Anybody you could pay me to kill I would gladly kill for free. I hoped that made me something besides what that word implied.

He ordered a Shiner and scowled when Toothless informed him they didn't carry it. He settled for a Bud Light, though I know he'd been tempted to ask for a Heineken, just for shits and giggles. He winked at me before taking his first sip.

"Don't you have to work?" I scowled.

"I am working. Right now. My editor's hounding me for an interview. All the shit in the media right now? He wants some straight answers from someone in the *biz*." He pronounced *biz* in the strangest way, as if it were something he both despised yet couldn't live without.

"Keep your liberal spin, pal," I said, smiling, twirling a finger in the air.

"You've got to stop watching Fox News, bro," he said, shaking his head. It's not that I didn't trust him to set his personal politics aside and do a fair story. I didn't trust his editors or journalists in general, though. I'd had bad luck with them before.

"They've got the best looking women."

"You've got me there," he said, taking another sip. "How drunk are you planning on getting, anyway?"

"Why do you ask?" I shrugged.

"It's not even lunch and you're halfway there. I'm not going to leave you to drive yourself, but I've got Tai Chi tonight."

"Tai Chi's gay," I said, trying to bug him.

"Plenty of ass there to be so gay."

"Stupid fuckin' hippy ass that'll hate me for me," I said. I could just see them from my spot at the bar. A room full of females who were all fit, toned, college educated or working on it, in a muted room with soft music playing, going through the positions, and sweating neatly. Afterwards they might go out for a vegan soy lattes or whatever the fuck they drank, maybe talk about how evil capitalism was while hanging out at Starbucks.

"I met my last girlfriend there."

"And I bet she left you for a man that sucks cock on Sunday morning," I said, drawing out the redneck in my voice.

"You can be a real asshole, you know that?" He asked. I shrugged. He shook his head and smiled. "What's up? How about we get some lunch?"

I motioned for another shot. This time I asked him to just leave the bottle. "Maybe in a bit," I told him.

"Sure, sure in a bit," he laughed.

"Let me get drunk. I'll tell you all about machine gunning orphans and torturing innocent civilians in CIA prisons."

"Really?" he asked only half kidding, dreams of Pulitzers dancing in his eyes.

"Sure," I said, tossing it back, holding, and letting it slowly down, loving the burn. As if I'd ever tortured anybody in a secret prison. They'd been in safe houses for the most part. And none of them had been innocent.

Cornelius shook his head. Christ, here it comes, I thought. "Bubba, you know, if you need to talk about anything…"

"What the fuck would I need to talk about?"

"There's got to be a reason you're drinking so much. Might be good to get it off your chest."

"I'm drinking 'cause I like being drunk. That's it," I said, telling him the truth. He was one of those liberals, always needing to find something, some deep, dark secret on which to blame people's problems instead of simply accepting the facts of life. Like how some people, myself included, simply liked the sweet oblivion found at the bottom of the bottle.

"Seriously, if you're hiding from something, you can tell me."

"Sobriety, that's what. Why don't you man up and take a shot?"

"I got class tonight, Jeb."

"Pussy," I scoffed.

"Fine, give me a shot," he said, giving in.

Hell, yeah.

"Outstanding." I motioned for Toothless. He hadn't left the bottle like I'd asked. I was starting to like him even less.

"What n' tha hell ya want now?"

"Shot glass for my *homes* here. We're celebrating."

"Yeah, what tha hell ya celebratin'?" He asked, grabbing a shot glass from behind the bar and setting it in front of Cornelius. I thought about it.

"Rigorous philosophical debate," I told him. Toothless squinted at me and turned around, shaking his head, muttering. Cornelius smirked. Probably the smartest man in the place, at least as far as he was concerned.

I poured us both a shot and had him make a toast. Naturally, it was something about peace. At least it wasn't about global warming. We gunned our shots, Cornelius forcing it down, while I closed my eyes and relished the burn once again. He coughed hard as he slammed the glass against the bar.

"How'd you find me, anyway?" I asked.

"On my way home, Jeb, I saw your bike outside," he said. That made sense. His home was near my brother's in the M streets just a few miles away.

We started a conversation about politics, and Toothless walked over to listen in. He was wiping the dust off a pilsner glass without knowing how to pour one when the door opened for the third time. I listened to Cornelius rebut my statement that the U.S. would be better off we pulled out of the U.N. while I watched Toothless' eyes follow the man that walked in.

An older man, who looked to be in his early sixties, walked past us in the mirror. He was dressed in chinos, running shoes, and an oversized blue tropical shirt. He wore amber yellow shooting glasses that may have been prescription, and a straw, early sixties style hat. He had what may have been the world's most excellent horseshoe mustache. Two feet past us the biker in the back cocked the hammer on a long barreled revolver.

"Stop right there, old man," the biker told the old man. Toothless backed himself in the corner between Cornelius and myself, his hand grasping under the bar.

Everything slowed down, yet sped up at the same time. Cornelius was all eyes; the old man was exchanging words I couldn't hear with the two in the back.

Except for my knives, I was unarmed. I had a Last Ditch custom made by Phil Rose, hanging on a chain around my neck, a waved Spyderco Endura in my front pocket, and Benchmade Skirmish in my backpocket.

Was that the best move? I'd have to roll with it as it played. In the mirror, I saw the old man cup the fingers of his left hand around the bottom of his shirt, prepping the draw.

"You boys is outta luck," Toothless said, shaking his head like nothing could be done about it, and my mind went into overdrive, knowing just what he meant. Cornelius started to ask him why, when the old man brought the front of his shirt up and pulled a small nickel-plated handgun up in a good, solid two handed hold, pulling the trigger faster than anyone I'd ever seen. He might've started firing before the gun was fully raised, his left hand still moving to support it.

A double Mozambique, two to the chest plus a head shot to each one. In the middle of it, one of the two dead men managed to get off a shot that buried itself in the ceiling. As Toothless tried to bring whatever he had up from behind the bar, I lurched up and delivered a cradle blow to his throat instead of fumbling for the knife in my pocket. I was drunk, lurching at a moving target from a bar stool. So I didn't kill him. He staggered back a moment, both hands moving toward his throat, one still clutching a cut-down double-barreled 12-gauge. His eyes were wide for the briefest of moments as recognition crossed over his eyes, then the glass behind him spider webbed and a red dot emerged from the center of his forehead. I glanced over my shoulder to see the old man eye me as he nonchalantly performed a tactical reload without moving his eyes from mine. I paused like a moron, staring briefly at the gun in his hand. It looked like a Devel M39, not a gun you see every day.

Our eyes met again, as he slipped the gun back under his shirt.

I sat back down and poured another shot. Fuck it. Cornelius, who was out of his realm, looked at me like I was insane.

"You okay, bro? Be cool, it's over with," I told him, watching the old man in the mirror, dropping the used mag in his back pocket. I kept my hands visible, non-threatening. On his left wrist sat a huge old Rolex submariner, below a faded rat, fat and smiling. The rat held a flashlight and pistol in his hands. Our eyes met briefly; he gave me a nod then walked to the back.

Cornelius had gained a little color back, which was dangerous because his mind would start working soon, and it wasn't the time for that. Not yet. I poured us another shot. He leaned over to watch Toothless convulse in death. I pushed him back.

"Drink the fucking shot." I ordered. He didn't need much coaxing. I stole a glance at the old man who searched the men in back before he looked back at us, holstered his gun, and walked out a fire door. Next to me, Cornelius took deep gasping breaths, looking relieved though slightly green.

"You need some air?" I asked.

"Yeah," he said, his hand over his mouth. I'd tried, anyway.

"Ok," I said, picking up the Jack by the neck. "Hope you got your cell phone."

We went outside, sat on his tailgate, and drank, while we called the cops and waited.

They weren't very impressed that their two witnesses to the shooting were stone drunk by the time they arrived. Cornelius composed himself pretty quickly, and was in full-blown reporter mode by the time the plainclothes detectives arrived. Only drunker than Cooter Brown. They weren't thrilled that he was a reporter. They were amused at the answers I gave them when they asked for my personal info. What do you do for a living, sir? I'm currently unemployed. What *did* you do for a living then? Independent contractor. So you work construction? Sort of. At least I'd protected some construction magnates.

The two detectives assigned the case were the pair of the century. Morales was a calm, paunchy, older Latino with gray streaking through his hair and mustache, and Conyers, a fidgety, bossy white guy about my age. His hair was thick and combed up and back, a lá Michael Douglas in *Wall Street*, and he wore the kind of semi-expensive suit that men wear when they want to project things they can't name off the top of their heads. They didn't seem to get along, and Conyers obviously didn't like being junior to Morales, though he'd probably never be in his class. I could've told you their respective history without even talking to them. Morales never went to college, might have served in the military, though he was probably a little too young for Vietnam, and far too old for either Gulf. He probably never knew exactly what he wanted to do with his life, but felt the need to help people.

Conyers, on the other hand, wouldn't have served in the military even if there was a draft. He went to college, to as elite a university as his grades and status would allow, B. A. in Soc. or Psych., because Criminal Justice is just so low-brow. He would've have spent the minimum amount of time in a squad car; he hated the street because it scared him.

Morales had grown up in the streets, and enjoyed doing good in the community. He did well there and was promoted because of it. He felt guilty about leaving the position he'd worked hard to cultivate over his 3/5/10 whatever years there, but consoled himself with the fact that he might be able to do more good with his increased rank. Conyers was more than content to shuffle every homicide they encountered in the "hood" to the organized gang task force on the theory that they were better suited for it because of their intel. base.

I'd served on several details with former cops over the last few years and there are things only they could tell you about watching and reading people. No one was better at it. Freud could not hold a candle. The only people who might be better at it are high end, professional bouncers.

Once they knew you, they'd share their experiences with you. Every one of them would have hated Conyers with a purple passion, and I figured they would have liked Morales just fine. Of course, Morales talked to Cornelius, and I got Conyers. Luckily, I was drunk.

"Jesus, pal, you know you're talking to a law enforcement official? Huh?"

"The badge kinda gave it away," I told him, swaying just a little on purpose, just to fuck with him. One of the uniforms, a short, sturdy Hispanic woman with short, dark hair stifled a giggle. Hell yeah, I thought. Conyers waved his hands in the air, flustered, and made a show of putting his hands on his hips and turning his back to me. Probably wanted me to sober up and see the gravity of the situation. I caught the uniform's eye and winked. She blushed. I still had it. Outstanding.

"I can't talk to this biker trash. I'm gonna check out the scene again." Conyers announced proudly before walking into the bar. The uniforms busied themselves on the perimeter. Cornelius took meticulous mental notes. Morales tried to hide his disdain and embarrassment for his partner's lack of professionalism.   Then our eyes met, and I could see the sheen of recognition gloss over his eyes. I'd just overplayed my hand, and he knew I wasn't as drunk as I acted, smelled, or blew on the Breathalyzer. He excused himself from Cornelius and walked over to me.

"Giving my partner a hard time, huh?"

"He's the one calling people trash, officer."

"Why don't you want to cooperate?"

"I have cooperated. I told him everything I know, and he called me trash," I said it low, but let him see me look toward the television cameras at the edge of the lot. He pretended he didn't see it, or the mischievous twinkle in my eyes.

"Why give him a hard time?"

"He gave it first. I told him what happened, and it wasn't good enough. He acts like I'm guilty and I ain't done shit," I said, trying to regain some lost ground.

"What'd you say you did again?"

"I'm between jobs."

"Do you make a habit of being drunk before noon?"

"Just making up for lost time."

"I see. And where are you staying?" he asked. Before I could respond, the Hispanic officer I was developing a crush on bounced gorgeously over and spoke in his ear. He nodded his head.

"Just one moment, please sit back down. I'll be right back," he told me before turning and walking back into the bar. I slipped back onto the tailgate and found my smokes. Cornelius watched me, and decided he was tired of standing by himself. He walked over and bummed a smoke before sliding onto the tailgate next to me.

Morales took his time coming back out. The lovely Hispanic officer caught me leering, and I pretended to look away. I watched her shake her head as if to herself. Cornelius looked ashen, not seeing the beginnings of my brilliant seduction.

I remembered the last time we'd sat on a tailgate together. It had been a pasture party out in the middle of nowhere, and Jamie Sue Navarro decided she was going to put on a show. So, she pushed us off the tailgate, and climbed up, trying to act sexy. Only, halfway through she slid off the end. Which wouldn't have been too bad, except that she was the very first girl we knew to get a clit ring, and she loved showing it off. When she slid off the tailgate it snagged, and she withered on the ground in too much pain for noise to escape her lips. It hadn't been funny at the time, but damn if it didn't get funnier as the years rolled by.

Figuring he needed a laugh, I told him what I was thinking. He enjoyed it. It didn't quite bring him all the way out of his funk, but far enough to nudge his shocked mind away from where we were. With the cops he was a pro working on a story, but without their attention the things he'd just seen wound their way to the front of his consciousness. As we nearly giggled ourselves right off the tailgate, a paunchy Hispanic man in an expensive grey suit clawed his way out of the gathering crowd, only to have a couple of uniformed cops stand in his way. He blustered and yelled, and shook, his eyes wide and angry.

"Jesus," I said, no longer laughing.

"No shit," Cornelius said next to me.

We watched as the uniforms tried to calm him down. It only infuriated him further. He wore a two thousand dollar suit with a four thousand dollar watch on his wrist and a two hundred dollar haircut on his head. He threw his weight around with the bearing of one who was used to being listened to and obeyed. He stammered, yelled, and bandied about like a first class fighting cock. He pointed toward us, sitting on the tailgate, and the cameras in the crowd pointed toward us. I covered my face and leaned back.

Morales came out of the bar, cursing at the spectacle. The man in the suit screamed at him some more, pointing his finger. When he tried to step forth, the uniforms scooped him up and held him at bay.

Morales leaned close to say something in the man's ear and both uniforms pretended to turn away. When he was done, the man seemed to calm somewhat, and Morales took him and led him back through the throng of reporters and onlookers. A couple of moments later, Morales came back through and walked toward us.

"Security camera was on the whole time, caught the whole thing," he told us then turned to the object of my infatuation. "McCrummin, drive these two home then come on back."

"Sure thing, Sergeant."

She helped me off the tailgate, though I didn't need it, as Morales joined his lesser half inside the bar.

"Gonna make it, big guy?" she asked, the twang in her voice far from a brogue. It sounded like a field of blue bonnets beneath a Texas sun.

"You don't sound Irish, darlin'. I mean, officer." C'mon charm, don't fail me now, I thought.

"My grandfather had the brogue. Here, let me help you." Rookie. Second year, maybe third. Could be trusted to ferry drunk witnesses home by herself, yet still not senior enough to lose her enthusiasm.

She put us in the rear of a well-worn cruiser, the doors locked, the cage between us.

She pulled out of the lot and I tried not to go all vertigo. I really should've paced myself. "You're not going to be sick, are you, big guy?"

"No, ma'am."

"You got a name?"

"Jebediah. It's a family name," I told her.

"That sounds like a dog's name," she said, laughing, watching my face in the rear-view for a reaction. Suddenly she was little less cute. But not much. Not much at all.

What did I expect, hitting on the cop who was driving me home from the scene of a shooting? I was too drunk to have much pride anyway. Cornelius, the traitor, laughed with her.

"She hit that nail on the head, didn't she?" he said, laughing. I laughed with him. Maybe that'd help. I'd read once in *Men's Health* chicks liked guys who could laugh at themselves. That's what the Girl Next Door kept telling us.

"So, why you wanna tie one on so early in the day, huh, Jeb?"

"Just making up for lost time, darlin'. That's all."

"Prison?" she asked, not missing a beat.

"No, he was a mercenary\ over in Iraq." Cornelius chimed in, as if he had good sense. Apparently, away from the spectacle of the crime scene, he was less worried about containing the thoughts in his head. I just looked at him. The traitorous little commie. The little pseudo-intellectual, Jimmy Carter-loving pinko.

"Oh really?" she asked, leaning forward, looking back at us through her rearview.

"Security contractor," I said. "My friend here is confused."

"Yeah, the liberal media will do that to people," she said. Cornelius' mouth dropped open. I was in love. I wanted to stick my tongue up her butt and ask for seconds.

"Will you marry me?" I asked, as seriously as I could muster.

"It's a little soon, don't you think?" she asked, laughing, smiling at me in the rearview.

"Not at all. I'm bonafide. I got prospects," I said, imitating a movie. She blushed then made a show of concentrating on the road.

I was doing pretty well for a drunk who'd just left a crime scene. It'd probably be best not to push it, though, I thought. She'd probably appreciate it more if I respected her boundaries, or some such shit. However, I was drunk, and didn't feel like shutting up.

I hadn't just taken a break from the booze but from women as well this last time around. I don't fall off any wagon well.

CHAPTER 2

I woke on the thick, fluffy couch in Cornelius's living room. It was well past dark, and I felt wonderful. The kind of pleasant morning after, when you know you drank just enough. I stretched with a yawn and crept to my feet, less stiff than usual. I had government metal holding me together, as well as some flak from various this and that. Some was from when I'd been riding the roads, and from later after I'd moved up to the protective detail among other things. I smelled coffee in the kitchen, and I could hear Cornelius in his makeshift office, where normal people kept a spare bed.

When the lovely Officer McCrummin had dropped us off earlier in the day, he'd gone straight to work, and I'd gone straight to the bottle. From my bag, I'd pulled a book of poetry I'd been working on for a decade, sat at his dining room table with pen and bottle, and pretended to have a sensitive side. When I realized I was once again writing about my ex-wife, I closed the book and just drank. It seemed more productive.

At some point Joshua had come over with food, and the three of us ate a lunch, him wanting to know every detail about the shooting. Cornelius had plenty to give him, at least about the three we'd seen shot. He didn't know anything about the old man, and kept asking me if I'd caught his name. I had, but I hadn't given it to the cops, and letting Cornelius have it for print didn't sit right. I also didn't tell him about the tat on his forearm, what I knew it meant, the silver bracelet on his wrist similar to the one on my own, or how I could tell by his movements the old man's combat instincts hadn't been in a closet the past forty years.

Now, hours later, well into the night, he was still busy, doing research and writing about the incident at the bar. I knew I couldn't ask him not to write it. I could however, at least ask him not to use my name. I thought about how best to do just that as I made my way to the kitchen.

I fixed a cup of coffee with the pink powdered cancer and some chocolate milk, and drank half of it in the kitchen, getting my wits. I caught my reflection in the window. I could still fit into the gray sweat pants with my high school mascot high on the thigh. The dark ink on my arms was vibrant, almost glowing in the night's soft blue light. I hadn't shaved my face or head since being home, and the stubble was starting to grow. A beard was forming around my standard issue goatee, and the bald spot I'd hidden by shaving my head was starting to peek through. My arms and chest were thickly muscled and well defined, but the six-pack, or in my case, four pack, that I had killed myself developing, was starting to slacken. Time to cut back on my vacation and get back on the program, I thought. There's no one fatter than someone who used to have muscle.

I topped off my cup and walked toward the clacking of keys. His back was to me as I leaned against the door frame, and took a loud sip. He jumped, and then cursed me.

"Goddamn, Jeb, you trying to give me a heart attack?" he said, shaking his head. Beside his laptop, I saw the Luger his grandfather had brought home from his war.

"It's not my fault you don't have any situational awareness," I said. He gave me incredulous.

"You're going bald, you know that? I bet that sweet little number that dropped us off likes it thick and full," he said, and turned back to his computer, smirking. I racked my brain, ran a hand over the stubble, trying to remember how big an ass I'd made of myself.

"How bad was I?" I asked. He just laughed. "Fuck you. How's the story coming?" I asked. He smiled broadly.

"Outstanding, that's how. This is great," he said, turning back to his screen.

"Gonna make a name for yourself, huh?"

"Hell, yeah. Story like this, who knows? Find out who the old man was, his story, what drove him to this, hell, I might get a book out of it," he said, genuinely pleased. It wasn't all selfishness on his part either. There are many great writers no one hears about, and a ton of duds who, through sheer luck, are in the right place at the right time.

"You can't use my name."

"What the fuck you mean I can't use your name?"

"My work's important to me. If my name starts popping up in the papers, then people are going to think I'm a publicity hound. They'll think I do what I do to make the wrong kind of name for myself, for the wrong reasons."

"Your work? Are there good reasons for what you do?" He asked, looking at me with a cocked eyebrow, indignant. I just looked at him. There was no point arguing with him. Though many of his assumptions were true, he had no factual knowledge to base them on. He simply *wanted* to believe certain things.

Eventually he put his hands up.

"Sorry, you don't deserve that. I won't mention your name," he said. "Ok?"

"Better. Been working hard?"

"You damn betcha."

"Learn anything?" I asked. I watched a heavier than slight tension, one hard to put a label on, spread through his shoulders. I listened to his voice pause in search, looking for something to say.

"Nothing much," he said, dismissively.

"That a fact," I asked, watching him for the certain signs, not liking what I saw.

"Yep," he said, matter of factly, my presence growing into an annoyance I could feel. I told myself I was being an asshole, that my time as a contractor, and the contract work I'd done for certain government agencies in particular, not to mention my past dealings with reporters, jaded me.

"Want me to top off your cup?" I asked. He handed me his cup.

"Hell, yeah, my own right-wing, mercenary maid. Just what I need," he muttered, turning his focus back to his work.

I topped off our cups while thinking about nothing but the body language and facial signs C.W. had given away when he'd been searching for an answer to my question about the men we'd seen killed. I told myself he'd been preoccupied, his mind on his work. That he was more family than friend, and that he wouldn't intentionally lie to me.

I told myself these things. A part of me wanted to believe them. But I hadn't survived as long as I had, in the places I'd been or doing the things I'd done, by ignoring instincts honed by my intelligence, experience, and training. I didn't like what they had to say. I listened to the sound of his banging keys on the other side of his house, and stared at the cups on the counter.

I pulled the bottle from the table, now room temperature, and drank straight from it. I took another long pull, and came away coughing, lucky I didn't gag. I took as deep a breath as I could, and then, as soon as my head settled, put the bottle back to my lips.

When I was done, I dropped half my coffee, pink cancer, and chocolate milk concoction into the sink, and replaced it with vodka. The vodka was probably healthier anyway. At least it didn't pretend to be anything but poison.

He thanked me when I handed him his cup. I pushed some pamphlets for various causes, community organizations, and other bullshit liberal propaganda off the end of the twin bed, and sat on the corner. He looked at my cup with his nose.

"So, it's coming along, huh?" I asked.

"Yeah, bro. It's coming along nicely," he said, and took a drink before setting the cup down.

"That's good," I said, going for easy breezy. It probably still came out menacing.

"What's on your mind, Jeb," he asked.

"Is there anything you want to tell me?"

"What do you mean?"

"I don't know my-damn-self," I said.

"That doesn't make any sense," he said, and turned back to his computer screen.

"Are you keeping something from me?" I asked. He didn't answer, just stared at his screen like he was trying to avoid me. Eventually, he let out a breath, conceding fate.

"The reason I haven't told you this, is because I don't want to have to explain myself," he said. I just stared at him and took another drink.

"I knew one of the men we saw get killed. The Hispanic guy, Torres," he said.

"How'd you know him?"

"I didn't really know him. I ran into him a few times around town, on the circuit," he said. The circuit was C.W.-speak for the underground poker tables he had a habit of finding himself seated at. He'd studied the game from an early age, the same way I'd studied the skilled application of violence. He hadn't had a choice. He'd inherited the vice from his father, and it plagued him worse than the bottle plagued me.

"Did you tell the police this," I asked.

"I didn't realize it at first. And even if I had…it's generally not something you advertise," he said.

"That could be a problem, if they find out," I said. He shrugged. If they found out, he'd just call one of his family's platoon of lawyers.

"Any idea what it was over?" I asked. He shook his head.

"Nothing hard, but Torres was planning the Cinco de Mayo parade as a migrant worker's rally. LARO has already put out a statement saying that the parade will go on. Been hearing a lot in the *whisperstream*, about something happening," slipping in a term coined by Andrew Vachss in books we'd devoured and traded back and forth growing up.

"Like what?"

"Fuck, Jeb, you know how *your* people act. Fucking right wing *fringies* come out of the woodwork just to piss on the sunshine these days."

I didn't reply. There were any number of forces that might have a reason to stage an attack of some sort on a parade or rally. Especially one with obvious sociocultural and political influences. Right wing crazies could very well try something. So could Mexican Nationalist groups. Drug cartels openly controlled much of Mexico, and their violence spilled over a border that was little more than a line on a piece of paper. Paper that was almost as worthless as the dollar looked to be soon. The world was changing, as were the wars we fought. But no one in power cared to acknowledge it, and neither did my friend.

I left him, and went back to the living room to lie on the couch. I tried to ignore the thing poking me on my shoulder from another realm, trying to warn me of the path ahead.

CHAPTER 3

Before the sun had risen, I'd run three miles at a medium speed, not wanting to kill myself, not wanting to take it too easy either. Afterward, I spent two hours in the back yard on calisthenics and abdominal work, before finishing up with a kata of my own devising. It incorporated simple, easy to master moves, from different styles. All things I had picked up along the path. Its only application was for life and death. If you looked at me you'd think they were the spastic movements of a punch-drunk has-been.

I finished by cooling off in C.W.'s small kidney shaped bachelor's pool where I floated, concentrating on the nothingness, my eyes closed; a hole in the dark sky behind my eyelids. I tried to pretend I didn't feel the abuses of my body, the wounds and injuries that marked my life. I felt weightless and empty, very nearly Zen, but not quite, not all the way. For some, peace is always just out of reach. The physical symptoms of a violent life are the easiest to live with. At least they'd better be, if you made the choices I had. Other things still clouded my mind. I had worked hard to make my moments empty for a long time. It had been easy at war. And even after I'd moved on to other work, it hadn't been that difficult. The work demanded it. Now, it seemed the less chaotic my surroundings, the more tumultuous my soul.

The Great Mind Fuck.

I wondered if I'd ever outgrow it.

I pulled myself out of the pool and dried off, thinking about breakfast.

When I picked the paper up off the front lawn, I opened it to see the scene from the day before, felt a flash of rage, and folded it back. I went inside, fixed a big vodka and OJ for breakfast, and walked back out to the pool. If the vodka didn't work, I thought I might raid his Mary Jane.

He had gotten his story done in time to make the front page. I wondered how they did it before the Internet. It was a good, well-written article. I noticed he'd managed to stay objective, which was a growing rarity with news people. He even kept my name out of it, though he used my call sign. I couldn't even remember telling him my *nom de guerre*. Tex and Tank had both been taken, so the team leader stuck me with the one he used. I'd been called it before. There are worse names to be stuck with, I guess.

I hoped it was a common enough nickname to keep people certain people from being interested. I had my share of enemies. The vast majority of them, the ones left alive, had no intention of ever leaving their third world shit holes. Still, there were a few men, a precious few in my line of work, who might hold certain things against me.

Most of these men were dead as a matter of course, or at least content not to work with me. At least professional enough, I shouldn't have to worry about them while visiting family. But not all of them were so restrained, and I worried greatly they may see 'Bam-Bam' the security contractor pop up on the radar and come running to settle debts.

The story held other information as well. The bartender had been a nobody, another recidivist loser who had spent his entire life in and out of the system. He'd grown up in foster homes and orphanages and the only people who would miss him were his wife and daughter, if even that.

The bartender had been a man named James Jung. He'd done time for armed robbery twenty years before, and had a few misdemeanor beefs for possession and not paying his tickets. He'd worked at the bar since it had opened a year earlier. His work history showed no previous experience tending bar or serving people in any capacity. His previous occupations had run the spectrum from roustabout, to pizza boy, to pawn shop employee. Though he wore the garb, he wasn't known to be a patch wearing member of any club. He'd never even been licensed to ride a motorcycle.

The biker who'd been shot was named Tommy Halloran. He'd had a long criminal career that stretched back to the early 90's when he'd pulled his first bit, a six year stint in Leavenworth for assaulting his CO when he was in the 82nd Airborne. After that stretch and his dishonorable discharge, he followed it up with a jolt in Huntsville for domestic abuse, along with time spent in a few different county jails for things like check fraud and DUI. The last recorded job he'd held had been as a mechanic. He'd worked there until his probation ended after the Huntsville jolt. He hooked into the Aryan Hounds motorcycle gang sometime after Leavenworth, and had ridden with them ever since.

Though the club was a popular hangout for bikers and general white trash, it did not have a reputation for being a 1% club. Weekend warriors and college kids looking for a gritty, Dirty South-type vibe hung out there for the experience of being in a dive bar, without the risk of actually being in a dive bar.

There was no indication from the text that either man should know each other, except for the bar itself. I did not know how likely it was that a genuine 1% would hang out alone in a yuppie version of a dive bar, but I also didn't know why a man in his fifties with a history of menial jobs, would suddenly try a career as a bartender.

The faux-hawked Hispanic was a former Marine and veteran of Afghanistan. He'd been a gang banger before that. He'd mustered out eighteen months before, had worked briefly as a bartender while going to college, before using his position as a

vet and college student as a means of going to work for a
community organization focused on immigrant rights. His uncle,
a prominent local attorney, and minor celebrity had founded the
organization. Next to the article, was a picture of the man in the
expensive suit that had shown up after the shooting, yelling his
lungs out.

There was lengthy paragraph talking about the work they did,
fighting for the civil rights of illegal aliens, the annual rally they
were planning for the upcoming Cinco de Mayo, and their
opposition to a current bill about to be passed at the state level
that, according to Cornelius, made the Arizona immigration bill
look humane and tolerant. He even managed to get in a swipe at
the Republican state senator who championed it, something snide
about his party girl daughter who had recently dropped out of
college, and into, according to sources, court-appointed and
church-sanctioned rehab. What a spoiled, wayward rich girl
daughter had to do with a bill aimed at curbing illegal
immigration I did not know, but C.W. managed to get that dig in
there.

Nothing in the article made me want to drink less. I turned
away from the front page, and towards the comics, in search of
more redeeming material.

I was still laid out in the porch chair, reading the funnies,
drinking my breakfast, enjoying some menthol refreshment, and
trying not to think when I heard C.W. pull to a stop in front of his
detache garage. The neighborhood was older and a lot of the
homes still had the detached garages reminiscent of another era. I
liked that, though I didn't really know why.

I watched him out the corner of my eye as he emerged from
his truck and walked through the gate, whistling a tune. He was
dressed much the same as he had been the day before, only today
he wore an expensive polo shirt tucked into his slacks. His

clothes had been pressed so tight the creases looked sharp enough to cut, and his boots had been polished. He never polished his boots.

"You're drinking already?" he asked as he walked up, his boot heels clicking on the stone pathway from the driveway to the back porch and border of the pool.

"Just a pick me up," I said, setting the glass back down on the little table. I was thinking a nice long day of lounging at the pool and drinking would be a fitting reward for that morning's exercise. I was doing everything I could not to think about the day before and whatever reasons he might've had for lying to me.

"How many have you had?"

"Does it matter?"

"Well, I was going to see if you'd take a ride with me somewhere."

"Where's that?"

"Run some errands, talk to some people."

"About yesterday?" I asked, stating the obvious.

"Will you roll with me?"

"Why the fuck would you want to do that?"

"Bitch, please. I'm working a story here."

"OK, why the fuck would I want to come along?"

"Because you're my friend, and I asked."

"You gonna tell me how you knew so much about all these people? You sure seemed to get a lot of information pretty goddamn quick to make the front page," I said.

"I'm a reporter, Jeb. I have resources. They allow me to do what I do. Kinda the name of the game, baby."

"That a fact?" I asked.

"Yes, it is. Now would you please sack up and come with me?"

"Why do you want me along?"

"Because I'm already getting death threats from motherfuckers that think I had something to do with what happened yesterday."

"Really?"

"Yes, really. Email was flooded with them, so was my voicemail at work."

"Well, that's just awesome," I said, knocking back another. When the glass left my lips, I was chomping ice and thinking about another one.

"Not really, no, it's not."

"Maybe not for you. For me, it's a riot," I said. He didn't reply, just stared at me wondering if I was going to make him beg.

"You scared?" I asked, and took another drink, just to hide my grin.

"Why is this funny to you?"

"I'm just waiting on you to tell me what else there is."

"There's nothing else."

"Oh, yeah there is. Whatever it is, is the reason you acted the way you did last night when I asked you about it," I said. He rolled his eyes.

"What was I gonna say, Jeb? I was in the groove, baby. Besides, I knew you'd just get pissed, for no goddamn reason, just like you are now."

"I'm not pissed," I said, and took a drink from my glass, and chomped on some more ice.

"You were born pissed, dude. You gonna stop being a little bitch and roll with me, or what?"

"You think this lawyer, his uncle, will talk to you?"

"He's expecting me."

"What about that? He into stealing elections and shit?" I asked.

"He helps the people of his community realize their rights. They're oppressed," he said, as sure of it as he was water was blue. I pulled in some smoke and tried not to roll my eyes at the idea of social justice.

"How very 1975 of him."

"They're still people, Jeb, whether or not you think they should be here. And they have the same rights granted them by the government."

"Rights are natural, not given by the state," I told him. I could feel, more than hear, his chest fill with air.

"I'm not in the mood for one of your bullshit libertarian lectures, Jeb. Besides, if you really believed that shit, you'd want to make sure they were extended across the board, unlike all the other fucking right wing hypocrites."

I thought of a million things to say, but instead took another drink. He had no idea what I thought of it.

"You gonna pick your vagina up off the ground or what?"

"Got any place else you want to check out?"

"Was gonna go by Torres' place. I know this realtor, the building manager, he's going to let us in. Maybe go by his mom's and talk to her."

"Kind of convenient you know the building manager."

"Yeah, well. Lucky me," he said.

"How do you know him?"

"What's with the inquisition?"

"How do you know him?" I asked again. He looked at me, looked away, stuffed his hands in his pockets, and kicked at a rock that wasn't there.

"From the circuit," he said. It came out a mumble.

"What was that, *Boomhauer*?"

"Poker, Jeb, from playing in the underground circuit. That's how I know the building manager. The same way I knew fucking Torres, ok?" he said. His tone soft, his eyes slanted toward the earth, and I felt a pang of regret for forcing him to share something he was embarrassed about.

Poker. His father's disease.

"No way his mom talks to you, day after her baby boy gets waxed. She'll have a house full of *wetbacks* on top of everything," I said, changing the subject, choosing my language to annoy him.

"Do you wake up thinking of new ways to be an asshole?"

"Ten to one, whatever Miguel was tied into, his uncle was tied into it more. We need to gather intel before we brace him."

"We're not bracing anybody. We're talking. I'm talking. You just hang out unless someone gets tough, ok?"

"What? I'm supposed to be your footstool while you talk to the greaser kingpin of Dallas?"

"You just don't like his politics."

"You fuckin' wish."

"That's a filthy habit, fucker," he said, waving a hand in front of his face, waving air that was too far away to carry my smoke.

"Why don't you let me finish my breakfast in peace, then I'll clean up and get dressed, and then we can go run your goddamn errands," I said, and took a long pull off my cigarette. He smirked and spun on one heel then walked into the house.

CHAPTER 4

The office was in Oak Cliff, across the street from what had once been the house where Lee Harvey Oswald had lived. It was located above a trendy taco dive, the kind of place that tried to look low class but catered to the weekend bad-asses who watch too much Food Network. The lawyer owned the taco bar, as well as the lofts next to it. When we parked at the curb we could see the house and the sidewalk in front where Oswald had gunned down Officer J.D. Tippet.

A hard looking Hispanic woman of indeterminate age with cement breasts met us in his shallow foyer, and a moment later she ushered us in to see the man. Outside his windows, downtown Dallas loomed large. Behind him, I could see a rooftop pool, deck chairs, and a bar. He probably entertained clients and business associates out there, while girls trotted up margaritas and gourmet cooked tacos and nachos from downstairs.

His office was done up in southwestern pimp, light pastel colors, shelves of blonde wood, walls of faux adobe, a cactus in a corner, a Mexican flag on the wall. Pictures along the wall highlighted his various efforts, endeavors, and claims to fame. Degrees, certificates, newspaper clippings; the usual, all hung along the wall or sat before the books in his shelves. I wondered if anyone had told him Ft. Worth was just half an hour away, across the great prairie. I thought the Southwestern theme would fit in better over there.

He rose to meet us, extending a hand. He wore a cream colored summer suit, pressed white shirt with a simple black tie, and his coat hung from an oddly placed rack, standing tall near the middle of the room next to a low shelf that appeared to function as a wet bar, and a closed door that, I assumed, would reveal a small bathroom.

"Yes, Mr. Ellsworth, please have a seat," he said standing, reaching a hand over his desk. I hung back out of reach. "I didn't know you were bringing a friend," he said. "This is the gentleman who was with you yesterday, is it not?"

"Jeb, Alejandro Castillo. Alejandro, Jeb Shaw. Yeah, he's an old friend. He does, uh, protective work. Luckily for me he's in town," he said shaking the attorney's hand before he stepped toward the offered chair.

"Yes, well, I must admit, I was pleased to learn it was you who had the misfortune of watching yesterday's events, and writing about them. I'm afraid I didn't recognize you yesterday. I was rather distraught," he said. I stood where I was and stared at the Mexican flag hanging on his wall. It wasn't simply an acknowledgment and respect due his heritage or the state's, it was another statement altogether. The office held no other flags.

"Is your friend going to sit?" he asked C.W. I turned my attention back to them and didn't say anything.

"Evidently not," C.W. said, his voice strained with exasperation. "He's just tagging along with me, keeping me safe."

"Well, if you're looking for the madman that shot Miguel, you need it," he said, and they took their seats. I stayed back, playing the role.

"I'll do what I can," C.W. said, settling into his chair, crossing an ankle over his knee.

"Well, I hope so. The police have already made their speculations. They want to hold Miguel's past against him. Never mind the sacrifices he made for this country, or all he did for the community in his work with me."

"It's a goddamn shame."

"It is, absolutely. Damn right it is," the attorney said, thumping a thumb against his desk.

"It is. Unfortunately, I don't have any leads on the shooter. That's why I hope you'll talk with me now. I know you're probably sick of answering questions," C.W. said.

Alejandro acquiesced with a shake of his head and a hissing sound then said with a wave of his hand, "But I know you, your reputation. We need more unbiased media on our side. I'm sure I can't help you, but go ahead and ask your questions."

"You don't have any idea why anyone would want to hurt him, or why he'd be meeting with a known criminal, a biker, yesterday?"

"None."

"The drug business makes strange bedfellows, Mr. Castillo. You guys do a lot of work with gangs. Is there any chance he might have been meeting the man in that way, maybe as an informant, perhaps? Maybe someone giving him some information, even?"

He shook his head slowly, contemplatively.

"It's possible. Miguel had a habit of doing things on his own. He had a very agile mind. I was trying to convince him to go to law school," he said, his voice that of a weary, disappointed father.

Instead of saying something condescending about just how great a lawyer Miguel would've been, C.W. just sat there, watching Alejandro's face as the moment passed. I saw pomposity, and neglectfulness on the surface and something furtive much deeper, but wasn't sure what. I wondered if my friend saw these things as well, if he caught the attempt at misdirection.

"Do you know if Miguel had any contact with his old crew? The guys he used to hang with before he cleaned up?" C.W. asked. Alejandro sighed, let out a great sigh, and hung his head, swiveling in his chair just a bit, looking down.

"I don't know. I don't think so. Sometimes he took it upon himself to try to help kids on the periphery of that world…those that could still be helped. But no one from his old gang that I know of. When he left, there…it was very bad. I pulled him out of there when he was fourteen. That's a lifetime in that world. He was hanging with college kids. Rich white kids that thought he was hard," he spat, his mouth contorted around a foul taste. I turned away, biting my tongue, and looked at the pictures on the wall.

There was one of him in the restaurant downstairs, embraced by a celebrity chef with a travel show. There were several at various parties, mostly political fundraisers for various local and state Democrats, one with the president, another with a left wing money guy who was perpetually clouded in conspiracy. There was a framed newspaper article about him freeing a Latino man unjustifiably arrested for whatever, pictures of him at rallies and demonstrations, him fighting for the little man and the re-conquest of the South West. I imagined a luxury car sitting just outside of each picture.

"Were you guys working on anything that might've been particularly dangerous?"

"No more than usual. You *know* I've made my enemies. People are so resistant to *change*," he said, relishing his status as cultural crusader. I wanted to puke.

"*Senor Castillo*, I've been hearing a lot of rumors, whispers, the past couple months about something bad coming down. Do you think it might've been political in any way?"

"What have you heard?"

"Just things. It's been crazy out there. Cinco de Mayo is coming up, the rallies."

"Yes, well, who knows? The nutcases come out every year, and every year we still celebrate."

"Yeah, but this year's different. You can't tell me people aren't worried about the bill before the state house."

"Garbage. It makes Arizona's look tolerant. One day, the jackals in Washington and Austin both are going to have to recognize the basic human rights of its workers. It will only get worse until they do so," he lamented, C.W. soaking it up. I tried to keep a straight face, but I must have let out a twitch, some involuntary muscle spasm that betrayed me and drew his attention.

"Did you say something, Mr. Shaw?"

"No, sir. No, I was just admiring your wet bar," I said, pointing it out.

"Please, help yourself," he said. He didn't mean it, but he did say it, so I helped myself…to three fingers of *Don Julio Real*. At four hundred bucks a bottle, it was the sort of thing I'd drink only if somebody else was buying.

Fuck him if he can't take a joke.

"Still, some are already talking about the federal government following suit. It's gotta be on your mind. That's why I think it'll be even more of a shame if something happens, if someone does something to light a spark. I've been hearing these rumors for months now. Little whispers in the air, but they've been building. Now I'm getting death threats. Less than a day after I witnessed Miguel's death. From people whose side I'm on. My answering machine at work was filled when I came in. I don't have any clue how many death threats I got in my work email. That's just in a few hours," C.W. said, almost a plea.

"Yes, well, I am very sorry about that. You're a reporter, Mr. Ellsworth. Surely you've received threats before. And as we said, the white trash crazies have been coming out of the woodwork."

"Most of the calls I've gotten so far are from Hispanics!" C.W. said, his voice hardening. "An act of violence against anyone, especially a member of the media, will be a coup for the right-wingers. What'll happen then?" he said, his voice still rising.

"You sound more like an activist, than a reporter, Mr. Ellsworth."

"The truth needs more activists, Señor Castillo," he said, stone cold fucking serious, and I did my best to hold back a cackle. It came out a smirk. Alejandro Castillo stared at me. Cornelius turned around in his seat and glared. I shrugged and took a drink.

"What do you two care? You're just looking for a story," he asked, staring across the desk at my friend.

"That's a part of it, sure. But you said you know me and my reputation. If so, then you damned well know that's not all I'm about. Help me find his killer. If the cops aren't going to take it seriously, who is? Who is responsible for this?"

"Where would I begin?" He slammed his fist against the desk. "Our people come to this country, land that is rightfully theirs, as basically slaves, and they are shunned for wanting a better life. A young man sees this; it's understandable why so many turn down the paths they do. He was fourteen when I took him in, a child. I pulled him out of that life, me. Kicking and fucking screaming. I got him cleaned up, put him in school. He had such a bright future, and, then he had to go fight in that *illegal* war your friend there," he nodded toward me, "loves so much. And when he came back, I had to do it all over again. And now, years of negligence and oppression are coming to a boil. We should all be shocked it hasn't happened sooner."

"Oh, well, I'm sure it's all Bush's fault, just like everything else," I said, and stared at him while I drank his booze. They both turned, gape mouthed. I shrugged. Cornelius looked ashen, the lawyer's blood boiled just beneath his skin.

"Your friend has an attitude problem, Mr. Ellsworth," he said, running thumb and forefinger through his bushy-to-the-point-of-clichéd mustache.

"Perpetually," C.W. said, shooting me an angry glance.

"He was a good man; he helped people. You two were shitfaced drunk before noon yesterday. *Los barachos*. Everything you saw is suspect. I'm still not sure he wasn't a part of it," he pointed toward me. "Goddamn mercenary, not a big jump to think he might also be an assassin."

I nearly told him to go fuck himself, but managed to stop myself. Too busy drinking his top-shelf booze.

"I'm not looking to give him or you a black eye. I just want to tell the truth," C.W. said. Old Uncle Alejandro just stared past him at me. C.W. looked back.

"Hey, Jeb, go outside. Why don't you go outside and wait for me, ok?" He asked, the tone of his voice neither a request nor a command. I stared at him as I tossed back what was in the glass, set it on the bar, and walked out the door and down the stairs.

CHAPTER 5

The apartment listed under Torres' name was in the refurbished Cliff Tower, a large brick building just over the river, with a view of the city around it, not far at all from *Señor* Alejandro Castillo's office. Built in 1928, it had spent time as a luxury hotel, nursing home, and condemned shooting gallery. Now it held luxury condos. We parked in the shallow guest lot out front and walked through the heat to the locked front doors.

Cornelius hit the buzzer but no one answered back. I stared at him through my sunglasses and smiled. A few moments later, a tall man with about a ton of wavy gray hair walked out to meet us. He was dressed in pressed jeans and polished boots that had never seen a pasture, but hey, that's Dallas. Lot of that here.

"Cornelius, my man, what's happening?" he asked, extending his hand. He had a warm smile and capped teeth and probably sold a lot of real estate. Cornelius shook his hand, and the real estate agent insisted on hanging on to it, shifting it into a modified soul brother, or what middle aged white guys who thought black people melted at the sound of the "N" word thought of as a soul brother.

Cornelius rolled with it for a five count. A long five count; seemed like forever. When he was done he turned to me.

"Is this Bam-Bam?" he asked, grinning, as if I was a goddamn pet. I shook his hand, firm, and skipped the flourish.

"The one and only," C.W. said, and slipped past him through the open door. I followed, and stepped into rarefied air, perfectly chilled.

"So what do you think all that was about yesterday?" the realtor asked as we stepped into the elevator. I pulled off my sunglasses and slipped them in my vest.

"Don't know, dude, that's what we're here for. The cops been by?" Cornelius asked as his friend thumbed the button for the correct floor.

"Not that I know of," he said. "Should they have been?"

"You'd think so," C.W. said, and cast a sideways glance my way. I felt the elevator carry us up and remained silent.

"So what the hell you been up to Corny? I haven't seen you around much," the realtor asked.

"Working, dude. Busier than a one legged man in an ass kicking contest," he said. I noticed the tension spread through his shoulders, the slight rocking movement at his ankles.

"You get to know Torres pretty well?" I asked.

"Not really. He didn't really socialize with everybody else. About like Corny, from the games," he said. I could feel C.W.'s body tense, his eyes roll.

The doors opened to a thickly carpeted floor beneath art-deco gray walls of a smoothly rough texture, and we followed him down to the apartment.

"Tell you the truth, Michael wasn't around that much. He rarely stayed a whole week. Always traveling, working," the realtor said as he led us down the hall. "These lofts really are very nice. Let me know if anybody you know is looking to make a move. The area's really coming out of the dark ages, too," he said over his shoulder, as he swiped the key card and opened the door, leading us into a dead man's home.

Inside, instead of somebody's cozy apartment filled with too much shit, it looked like a minimalist showcase, if you wanted to attract a villain from a Michael Mann movie. Everything was neat and orderly. There were no magazines or other debris left atop the marble kitchen counter, or the just as trendy as IKEA but not quite IKEA breakfast table offset from the kitchen. There were no photographs on the wall, no bookcases filled with books, no knick-knacks or paraphernalia cluttered about. It was almost sterile, a near hermetically sealed environment, one that provided a very specific function.

"Pretty swank," C.W. said from the living room.

"Yep, here it is," his friend said. I went about peeking in the cabinets while I listened to the realtor annoy C.W. in the other room. The cupboards were nearly bare, the dishes within looked to be never used. The refrigerator was nearly as bare as the cupboards, the freezer fully stocked with microwave dinners, pizza, and liquor, but in such a way that suggested people didn't go rifling through either very often.

I found nothing worth noting, unless you counted the obscene austerity of the place meaningful. I pulled a small bottle of vodka from the freezer and left the kitchen, stepping into the living room as they walked down the hall, the realtor jabbering on about where the hell Cornelius had been lately, and how he knew where there were a couple games cooking, or some such shit. I shook my head at the addicts, took a swig from the bottle, and sat down on a dead man's black leather couch to drink booze he didn't need and work through the math. There was danger I needed to be aware of, but it wasn't immediately physical, and thus was harder to find.

I thought about my friend, his nature, dead men, secrets, and everything I wasn't being told. I'd been there before; it just felt sleazier this time. I took another drink, to abate my nausea, and stared out the window.

Outside I could see Oak Cliff, from the area we'd just left Uncle Alejandro in his office, all the way to the furthest edge of it, where I thought I could see the Arcadia Park section Torres had pulled himself out of. He'd made enough money to be able to afford to live across town, with the yuppies and college kids he was known to associate with, but he chose to live here. If he'd chosen a house, among the people everyone insisted he was trying to help, it would have been easier to understand.

What did he see when he looked out these windows? Did he see people much like he once was who needed help? Did he see further opportunity for him to prosper? Businesses he could help open, boards he could chair, charities he could drive? Did he see what he thought of as his people, and the waiting revolution? Or, as is often the case, did he simply see those he could exploit?

These were questions only a dead man could answer.

I took another drink and got back to hating the world. It's what I was good at.

"You guys need anything else?" C.W.'s realtor friend asked as he stepped out of the hallway. He saw me and stopped in his tracks. I shrugged and took another drink.

"Did you take that from the freezer?" he asked. I didn't much care for the tone in his voice. I stared at him without speaking.

What the fuck's it look like?

"Hey, Jeff, it'd be a big help if you'd hang out downstairs and let us know if anyone comes up. It'd be awkward for a family member to catch us here," Cornelius said from wherever he was down the hallway. I stared at him some more and turned back to the bottle and the world outside the window. The realtor muttered an ok and left.

He closed the door meekly behind him, and it echoed anyway. I wondered if my old friend was really hiding something, or if I was just being paranoid.

The couch was black leather with stainless hardware, and the coffee table before it was matching black and made of wood. Across the top was a glass piece that could be taken out for cleaning. Some people placed photographs under it, but Torres hadn't.

There were deep drawers on either end, for storing magazines or DVD's. If it were me, the DVD's would go in the furthest drawer, since it would be the least used. I tried the opposite drawer first. Black vinyl cases. I let the drawer roll closed and checked the one closest me. Inside I found a cigar box, sitting on top of a black leather journal. I pulled them both out.

The cigar box contained an unsealed envelope, a sandwich bag of weed, a small bindle of white powder, a small mirror with half a crumbled line still on it, an ornate glass straw that must've been a headache for the glassblower to make, and a roll of condoms. The envelope contained a little over three thousand dollars. I checked over my shoulder and slipped the envelope inside my vest. Torres didn't need it.

I stared for a moment at the coke, before closing the lid and setting it on the table. I caught myself looking at it a moment later, and put the box back in the drawer, before taking a pull of the vodka, and picking up the journal.

Stuck between two pages were two folded pieces of white paper. I sat the journal face up, and open, so that it stayed open where I'd taken the sheet, and opened it up.

It was a test key, for a pamphlet. Or, what I assumed was a test key for a pamphlet.

It was written in both English and Spanish, and was filled with the type of one sided, proletariat stirring calls-to-action you automatically expect.

Except for one thing.

Across the top, there was a quote, one I recognized because it was one of my favorites, from Max Stirner.

"The State calls its own violence law, but that of the individual crime."

Stirner was a 19th century German philosopher, and one of the fathers of individualist anarchism. He was just obscure enough to be out of the collective conscious of most of the pampered hipsters who walked around college campuses in their Birkenstocks and Phish t-shirts. Which was just as well, since most of them would've hated him if they'd truly grasped what he had to say.

I refolded the page, and stuck it back where I'd found it, and continued thumbing through the journal.

Flipping through it, I found several notes in both Spanish and English, along with several pages starting from the end and working in reverse that looked to be a coded ledger. There were several sketches, and a several more concerning the coming demonstrations. I turned the next page, and found an index card, with more numbers and abbreviations on the back. I didn't think anything of it, until I flipped the card, and felt my heart sink.

I'd drawn thousands of them myself. On my first tour, running recon, making them as detailed as possible for larger raiding parties to clear the objective, and later as a contractor after I'd moved up to PSD and snatched myself a counter-sniper role safeguarding diplomats and oil tycoons. The Task Force, and after that still, doing favors for Yalies who relished laying the patriotic guilt trip on a *ronin* with a cause.

Goddamn it.

I stood from the couch, and walked toward the sound of my friend, rummaging uselessly for a clue.

"The games, huh, *Corny*," I asked as I stepped through the doorway of the office. It looked much like C.W.'s own cluttered home office, and contrasted starkly with the utilitarian grandeur of the rest of the apartment.

"Man, not right now, ok?" He said, concentrating on going through the desk. He looked at me over his shoulder, scowled at the vodka in my hand, and shook his head without speaking.

Torres had a dedicated I Love Me Wall, with photos of him both in the military and out, leading a protest somewhere with Alejandro. There was one, an old one, a Polaroid, of him barely in his teens, in Dickies and wife-beater, in front of a cut down Impala with a crew of hard cases. Everyone in the picture was flashing a gang sign.

There was a large bookcase against one wall, and it was filled with notebooks, binders, and literature. Textbooks, law books, and various books on culture and philosophy (mostly Latin American, and political, with a heavy bent toward Left oriented anarchism) occupied the bottom two shelves. The shelf above was dedicated to the esoteric knowledge of the professional warrior, everything from sniping to vehicular surveillance to ditch medicine to point shooting to lock-picking. There were even a couple of weighty professional texts on Executive Protection, by Kobetz. I'd read most of them, many while still in high school.

"I can't believe there's not a computer right here," he said. On the desk before him, there was an empty spot there where a computer had probably sat. He was scowling at it.

"Did you find something?" he asked.

"Yeah, I did, matter of fact," I said. I brought the journal out from around my back and handed it to him.

He took it, started flipping through the pages.

"This is it?" he asked. Like I should have found a note describing the old man who'd killed him, along with his name and home of record.

"No, no it's not. I also found a cigar box with a dime bag and a nice ounce of powder."

"So? When did *you* start holding recreational drug use against anyone?" he asked. I did my best to ignore his tone.

"I don't. Does that mean anything to you?"

"No, should it?" he asked. He came to the ledger at the back and stared, then frowned, before shaking his head and making his way back to the part about the Cinco de Mayo rallies.

"This thing on the fifth, it's happening downtown, right?" I asked.

"Yeah, of course."

Fuck it.

I pulled the index card from my back pocket and handed it to him between two fingers.

"You know what that is? That's a range card. Soldiers make one for their field of fire when they're on guard duty. Those ones usually aren't very detailed. Recon troops and snipers make more detailed ones. Snipers include wind and elevation."

"Where'd you find this?" he asked.

"It was stuffed in that journal, in that section concerning the rallies."

He started to speak, but didn't. I walked out of the office, across the hall, and into the bedroom. I looked in the bedside table, around it, behind the headboard, under the pillow, between the mattress and box spring, and under the bed, but I didn't find what I was looking for. I looked in the closet, and in the dresser, and then walked out of the bedroom, down the hall, and through the large front room and checked the coat closet near the front door.

Still nothing, most certainly not a sniper's rifle, or related paraphernalia.

I went back to the office and checked the closet there.

"What are you doing?"

"Looking for a gun, or the things that go with it."

"They get lots of threats, Jeb. He was probably looking into one of them. Lots of crazy right wing nut jobs in this state. Oh, wait," he said, grinning.

"Looking into it himself? Not the cops or a P.I.?" I asked.

"He took it upon himself to provide security for his uncle, and personally investigate serious threats. Insisted on it, even. You would've learned that, had you not been such a douche-bag drunk this morning."

"Fuck you," I said, took another drink, and walked back to the couch.

I didn't know many vets in states where it wasn't a hassle to own a gun who didn't. Given his life before the military, I would think he would be particularly sensitive to the criminal mind and the need for self-protection, but there was a lot I did not know.

He'd had a pistol the day before. Maybe he'd only owned one gun. That was a possibility. The only people I knew who owned only one gun were cops that rode a desk and women who never shot, but it was still a possibility. If he was meeting the biker about a threat, then it made sense for him to have it with him.

Except for the old man. If he was there to cover up a conspiracy, it didn't make sense to leave witnesses. I'd made eye contact with the man, a fucking operational no-no if you have to do a public hit, which you shouldn't do anyway. Eye contact focuses your attention on nuance, the little things that are hard to hide.

The man had left us alive, not because he recognized another operator, but because he simply did not want to kill us. He was there for those two men. The bartender would have lived had he remained a bystander.

Something else bugged me, too: the Stirner quote. Although an anarchist, his train of thought did not jive well with the books on Left Anarchism on the shelves, or Torres' life as an activist leading protests and stirring up revolutionaries.

Stirner had thought revolution itself was a statist endeavor.

I stared out the window, thought of Torres, the pictures on his office wall, the books he read and the philosophers he quoted, drank his vodka, and wondered who he had been.

CHAPTER 6

Though Miguel had been born and raised in the Arcadia Park neighborhood of Oak Cliff, his mother, Señora Torres had since packed his younger siblings up and moved them way out to McKinney, out in the sticks, to a nice upper middle class, almost suburban environment.

We sailed over smooth pavement, Cornelius holding onto the steering wheel, a Dr Pepper bottle full of spit between a thumb and forefinger, a fat dip under his lip as he tried to calm down.

There had been a scene as we left Torres' apartment building. C.W.'s friend the realtor had said something to me. I'd said something back. It had gone downhill from there.

"You did not have to act that way. First with Alejandro, and then with Jeff. Fuck man, why'd I even bring you?"

"Because you just saw some shit you can't handle by holding hands and singing kumba-fucking-yah, that's why," I said, and took another sip. I didn't even feel like drinking anymore, really. I just knew it annoyed him.

He shook his head, and spit in his bottle.

"There was no need for any of that, Jeb. None. Now I gotta mend two fences."

"Fences you're better off leaving broken."

"Life's easy for you, isn't it?"

"I fuckin' wish," I told him, and drank the last of the vodka. He shook his head some more as he pulled to the curb in front of a newly built home in a recent subdivision. Everything was new, and spackled with sparkling promise.

"They're probably not even here," I said as he killed the engine. He took a deep breath, not even bothering to look at me. He just drew it in and stared out the windshield. I took one last drag from my cigarette, and tossed it out the window. Along with whatever peace and serenity I expected to find.

Cornelius opened the door and stepped out, slamming it behind him. I watched him walk around the back of the truck and stared at him the rearview, wondering, briefly, if I should leave him to it.

C.W.'s shallow knock was answered by an attractive Hispanic woman somewhere in her forties. She looked tired, but not weak or frail, and she didn't look like she was in the midst of grieving the loss of her only son. He spoke to her in Spanish, in a quiet, calm, soothing tone, and she just looked at him like he had a dick growing out of his forehead.

"Alejandro called, let me know you were coming by," she said, with just enough of an accent to let you know she could hide it if she chose.

"Señora, you have our deepest sympathies. Your son was a blessing to so many people. I hope you'll grant us a few minutes so that we can ask you some questions." Cornelius told her, and she rubbed a hard hand over her face, sweeping away an errant length of long, black hair.

She looked us over a long moment, her eyes looking over my stereotype until C.W. said something I didn't quite catch, and she nodded, opening the door further. C.W. looked over his shoulder, as if to say, shut your mouth. I shut my mouth and followed.

Inside the house was typically Mexican. Tall candles sat on every flat plane available, each one encased in glass with Catholic imagery frosted on the side. A beaded curtain hung in the entrance of a hallway. Jesus, Mary, and various members of her family looked down on us from the walls. Her son occupied a special place on one shelf.

The shelves above it were piled so thick they bowed under the weight. Pulled from the stack, and lying flat, its spine facing out was an ancient copy of the Bible, one that looked like it had been read maybe nine million times.

Around the nearest corner, the kitchen clearly sat. Smoke billowed from one room to the other, carrying with it cilantro and peppers, skirt steak and onion, and beans simmering. It smelled good, like love personified.

She turned to face us, her hands on her hips. Her face was strained and tired, her hair pulled back yet still frazzled. She looked at us, a question in her eyes.

"Beer?"

"That'd be fine," C.W. assured her. She motioned for us to follow her into the kitchen, and pointed us to the chairs around the table there. We sat.

She pulled three cans of Keystone Light from the fridge and handed us ours. I couldn't help but smile at Cornelius, who normally drank Heineken and Shiner while proclaiming to be all about the working man.

He caught my smirk and ignored it, popping the top and turning in his chair. She popped her own, and took a long swallow before setting it on the counter and turning to the stove. She pulled a wooden spoon from a bowl on the counter, and stirred the simmering beans. I drank my beer.

She stirred the beans slowly, absentmindedly, her heart not fully in the long accustomed task. Finally, she sat the spoon down and turned. She stared at us individually a long moment. Taking stock of each of us in a way available to her by our being seated at her table and not at her door.

She was a handsome woman, well built, but not from inside a gym, dressed in jeans, running shoes, and a form fitting red t-shirt. It rode high over her hips, and I could see dark, faded ink, poking out the bottom near her waist, and at her neck. I saw the ink, and watched her move with a certain stiffness, the tension drawn through her muscles like an animal, ready to pounce, and I listened to the emptiness of her home, the absence of family, and I thought about that—what it might mean. Wondering why she was alone, cooking such a big meal in an empty house.

I thought it odd that the day after we'd watched her son shot dead she was cooking a stove full of food in an empty house. I watched her there, slowly stirring the pot, while C.W. spoke to her.

"So, ask your questions," she said bluntly, her tone almost antagonizing.

"Do you plan on going downtown on the 5th?" He asked. She spat a Spanish curse too fast to catch. There was something about the mother of God in there, I think.

"Why would I want to be part of a thing like that?" She asked.

"Miguel was getting it together."

"So?"

"Well, I just thought..."

"What, because I came here from Mexico, I have to like the work you think my son was doing? *Ay, dios mio,*" she said, shaking her head in disbelief.

"Can you tell us when the last time you saw Miguel was?" C.W. asked. She shrugged, staring into the pot as stirred.

"Michael, his name was Michael."

"Oh, I'm sorry," he said, visibly flustered.

Good thing he's not playing poker, I thought.

"When was the last time you saw Michael, ma'am?"

"I don't know."

"Did he ever talk about his work?"

"I didn't want to hear about his work," she said, over her shoulder, her lips puckered with disdain. She lifted the wooden spoon to her lips, as if to replace the taste of a thought.

"Why not?" he asked, the shock in his voice obvious. She looked back over her shoulder at him, her tongue sliding over her lips to collect any lingering sauce.

"What do you know about his work?" She asked, her eyes locked on him between two narrow slits

"That he tried to help people in his community," he said, more of a statement than a question. She sat the spoon down on a small plate in the middle of the stove and turned around, shaking her head.

"His father was a gang banger and a drug dealer. So was my son. He lost his father in a turf war, and that was it for him. Getting him away from all that nearly killed me. Then he joined the Marines, went to war, and came home worse off than before. What else is there?" she asked.

"A lot of people come home from war with problems. That doesn't take away from the things he was doing with LARO," he said, throwing a sideways glance toward me like that should have been my cue to give some perspective to the conversation. I drank my beer and tried not to smile. Cornelius pretended not to notice.

"Nothing in him changed! He just learned to hide it better. He was no better than his father; probably worse," she said. Though she wasn't quite yelling it, she was loud and forceful. She meant every word she said.

"He was much more than that to many people," C.W. said.

"What do you care anyway? You're just looking for a story. And if not, then you're just another rich white boy who cares more about making himself feel better than helping anyone," she said, her back to us. I felt C.W. tense beside me. A wave crossed over his face, one that originated deep within. He was many things, but above all else, he was an idealist. He stammered in response.

"Are you still a *chola* ," I asked, and she shot me a look over her shoulder that could have cut the heart out of a man's chest. Cornelius stared at me gape mouthed. She stepped forward, squared herself to us, and pulled her shirt over her head. Her breast strained the plain white lace of her bra, still supple and youthful.

"You tell me," she said, and then turned around, and we saw the horrible burn scars that covered the top half of her back. When you join a gang, you have to get jumped in. To leave, you have to get jumped out. Voluntarily. If you don't, they might take a harder road to let you leave. Judging from the scarring on her back, she'd taken the harder road.

C.W.'s breath caught and he looked away. I drank my beer, and when she looked back over her shoulder, I caught her eyes and looked for whatever was there to find.

Her eyes welled with tears and she turned away, slipping her shirt back over her head.

"My husband will be back soon with our daughters. If there is nothing else, you should leave. I haven't told them about Michael's death, and I don't want them to learn with strangers in the house."

C.W. stood from the table. He looked back and forth between the two of us trying to find something to say.

"Mrs. Torres," he started, but she cut him off.

"That is no longer my name; you have no idea who my son was. I cannot help you. If you want answers, I suggest that you take a real good look into the men who were also killed yesterday alongside him. Or Father Mitchell. I'm sure you know who he is. Now, good day," she said, and that was that. When she spoke the priest's name, her mouth turned into a cross between a scowl and a pucker.

"Ma'am," C.W. tried to get another foothold, but she cut him off with a hand, motioning us to walk the few steps from the kitchen, through the corner of the TV room, and out the front door.

C.W. dropped his empty beer can in the trash can, and I followed. Before stepping back out into the sun, I slipped the envelope with cash out from my vest, and dropped it on a pile of mail stacked on the table beside the door.

I didn't need anyone else's blood money.

CHAPTER 7

The drive back to C.W.'s house was more or less silent. He was still upset with me over my oafish behavior, and I was still pissed at him for dragging me into the mess, not to mention whatever the fuck it was he was keeping from me. He didn't share with me what he'd talked about with Alejandro after I'd walked downstairs, and I didn't tell him about the pit in my stomach that formed whenever I thought of the sterile apartment we'd visited.

The sun was fading into dinner time when we pulled into his driveway, but neither one of us was hungry. He went back to work in his home office shutting the door behind him, and I stepped to his dining room table. I slipped out of my vest, setting it on a chair, then out of my guns, most of my knives, and my undershirt. I took off my boots and socks and stepped outside, walking around barefoot for a bit in the grass, trying to work the tension out. I have bad feet and ankles. Over pronation and flat feet are hell on wheels for a man in my line of work.

I sat on the bench beside his patio table, took turns massaging my feet, and wondered how much of it was the life I led or fate. I could remember going to the Ronald McDonald House when I was very young, and getting special shoes that didn't correct the problem. My ankles plagued me through football and my hitch in the army. Somehow, I never broke them, though there were several occasions I sprained them so bad a break would have been preferable. I felt old and tired, worn down in a way that I hadn't felt since I'd failed to be the man my ex-wife had needed. And as old, tired, and worn as I felt, my feet felt twice as bad.

Afterward, I pulled the bottle from the freezer and sat at his dining room table in my jeans, pulled out my laptop, and worked on some articles I was in the middle of. They would be submitted to various food and travel magazines under different names. That was a part of what I'd been doing, the path I was trying to decide whether or not I still wanted to go down. Being able to tell people you're a food and travel writer gives you legitimacy all over the world. That was helpful in some of the work I'd done. Since I couldn't remember birds for shit, I had to make do with something I could fake.

I listened to "Closer to Fine," by the Indigo Girls, and cleaned my weapons. Primarily, I tried real hard not to think about very much at all—most especially, of the day's events.

Eventually, his office door opened and Cornelius walked out smoking a joint and shaking his head at me.

"Jesus, dude, you and this Angry Lesbian Hate Folk bullshit. If you decide to blow your brains out, please, go outside first," he said, smiling at the guns and knives on the table, but just barely. All my friends hate my music.

"I like it," I said.

"Yeah, that's 'cause you're insane," he said, sitting down across the table from me. "You afraid an army of uneducated migrant workers that just want to feed their families are going to storm the castle?" he admonished. Or tried to anyway. He was pretty baked, and even if he hadn't been, it wouldn't have mattered. I leaned back and took a pull of my drink.

"You can never have too many books, too much red wine, or…" I said. It didn't really fit, but I'd been reading Kipling and it was the only thing I could think of that wasn't abrasive.

"Don't quote Kipling to me. You massacred it anyway."

"At least I understood what he was saying."

"Let me see that," he asked, pointing to the Glock 19 on the table. "How many guns do you have, anyway?" He asked, racking the slide several times.

"Not many," I told him. He shook his head.

"How many does this hold?" he asked, picking up the 'Happy Stick' I kept in my saddlebag.

"Thirty-three."

"That's just ridiculous," he said, shaking his head. Of course, he'd never needed something like that before.

"You know, sooner or later the cops are going to realize you knew Torres and his uncle. I'm amazed they don't already."

"So, I got people, man," he said, drawing it out like he had a ghetto accent.

"You got your family's money."

"That's fucking low."

"Sorry, you didn't deserve that. Just like I don't deserve you keeping shit from me," I said. He shook his head.

"I'm not keeping anything from you. You know what I know. I didn't tell you about the games because they're not relevant, and because I knew what you'd say."

"I'm not gonna judge a man, or his vices," I said.

"Yeah, well," he said, looking away. "Maybe I do."

I left that where it was and concentrated on my task.

"You hungry yet," he asked.

"I could eat," I said. I knew I needed to eat, but was pretty well content to just keep drinking and trying not to think. I was thinking about having him pass me the joint when someone knocked on the door, and he coughed, nearly falling out of his chair. We both laughed at that.

Our laughter was met by another harsh rap on the front door. Cornelius grabbed the air-freshener off the table and sprayed liberally.

"Just a moment," he shouted at the door, picking up his paraphernalia.

"It's Detective Conyers. I'm looking for your buddy, Shaw," came back at us, followed by more knocks. Cornelius looked at me like it was my fault.

"I'll take care of this," I said, getting up, with a sigh.

I slid a menthol between my lips as I made my way to the door. Stepping outside, I closed it behind me, wondering how savvy he was.

Automatically, I was on guard. Morales was nowhere to be seen. It was just Conyers and the bald headed uni from the day before, McCrummin's partner. I didn't like that. I didn't think a detective would need a uni for a field interview. Of course, I thought he would've called, and asked me to come in.

"Hello, Detective. Can I help you?" I asked, lighting my cigarette, as pleasant as pie. "Can we come in?" he asked, coughing around the smoke.

"Got a warrant?" I asked, swallowing smoke.

"We just want to talk."

"Let's talk out here. It's a nice afternoon," I said. Conyers flushed, clearly agitated.

"I think I smell marijuana, detective," the uni said, using the oldest trick in the book. Now, however, it was dangerous simply because it was true.

"That right? You got weed in there?" Conyers asked, stepping up. I blew smoke out my nose. I wasn't aiming for his face, but he shouldn't have been standing so close. Fuck him. If he was the kind of cop who gave a shit about someone smoking an herb in the safety of their own home, he deserved it. He coughed, I tried not to smile.

"It'd be a helluva thing, you boy's got yo' asses in a crack, you searched this place without a warrant, then didn't have anything to show for it. Wouldn't it be?"

"Fine, that's how you want to play it," he said, nodding his head up and down. It was an oversized head, with too much mousse. I wanted to use it for a basketball. I don't even like basketball. He stuck his finger in my face.

"The Constitution's a beautiful thing," I said. Staring at him, right back down it, as if it was the barrel of a gun.

"You were supposed to come in and make a statement. You didn't show up."

"You were supposed to call. Nobody called."

"We shouldn't have to ask you to do the right thing, though that's probably hard for you to grasp."

"Just what's that supposed to mean?"

"If you're just an innocent bystander, what were you doing making your rounds today, looking into Torres? You think you can just waltz around, interfering with a police investigation?"

"They weren't my rounds, Detective. They were C.W.'s. I was just going along for the ride. We didn't interfere with shit."

"Bullshit. I've been checking up on you, *merc*. Don't you for one second think you're too smart for *me*. If you have anything to do with this shit, I'll find out."

"Do you want me to congratulate you for doing your job?" I asked. Everyone these days wants to be congratulated for simply acting like decent, responsible human beings.

He lost it, and I watched the back of his hand come at me, as hard as he could muster. I took it, right on the lips, thankful he couldn't bolster any more strength or courage than he did. If he had more power, I didn't know if I would've been able to control myself.

I felt my lip split, and blood slip out. I looked at him and grinned, licking the soon to be scab, and put the menthol back in place and took a draw. He looked at me, not expecting my response, and the bald headed uni with him put a hand on his shoulder. There was a mother with a dog on a leash, walking beside her daughter on her tricycle, on the sidewalk, staring.

"Come by and make your statement. Don't make me ask again," Conyers said, straightening himself up, trying to ignore the spectators.

"Wouldn't dream of it, Detective."

"I'll be watching you. Fucking mercenary. You are a person of interest. Don't make any sudden trips."

"Be still my heart," I said, took another drag, and watched them leave. The bald uni looked at me for a long second like maybe he wanted a go at it, and I made sure to look at his nametag. Shavers.

Cornelius had righted his chair, and was drinking a beer when I sat back down and started loading the next mag.

"That was pretty quick and painless," he said, between chugs.

"For you. Conyers wants to make a name for himself, and I'm an easy target. Thanks so much for the press, bro," I snapped.

"Man, I was just doing my job," he said, looking up. "Jesus."

"Yeah."

"That's police brutality," he started in, but I looked up and drew in smoke.

"Leave it," I said. He shook his head.

When everything was cleaned and loaded, I took a shower, dressed, and then we went to dinner.

We ate at Snookies on Greenville Avenue, then walked home enjoying the night, ogling the sorority girls from SMU who were out jogging in the waning yellow light of dusk. Back in his cozy little home, I poured a couple of fingers of Jack and he fired up his bong, and we continued our seemingly endless discussion on politics and philosophy.

We discussed the modern thinkers. He was upset about my continued under-appreciation of Chomsky, whom he considered a personal hero. For my part, I continued insisting that, compared to Thomas Sowell, his "contributions," if you could bring yourself to call them that, were nothing but senile, meandering rants from a radical who missed the revolution. I took a few swipes at people who professed anarchism, but wanted nothing more than one huge, all powerful government. He insisted that I was indeed insane and born several centuries too late. It was a good, long argument, which left us both where we'd started from, which was probably inevitable.

CHAPTER 8

The next day brought us first to the widow Jung, whose husband we'd watched get shot in the head two days before. They lived in a rundown ranch house in Garland, not far from the International plant. The grass needed clipping, and the flower beds beneath the windows where a mess of weeds and dried out potting soil. The door was answered by a chunk of a woman in a tattered robe. She didn't appear to have anything on under the robe, BO radiated off her body, and her breath stank of cigarettes and onions and beer. She had a large, angry mole on one temple that had sprouted hair. Lots of it. A long, slim cigarette hung from the corner of her mouth. I could feel the change in C.W.'s body language through the air between us as he took in the full sight of her.

"You the reporter," she asked.

"Yes ma'am," he said.

"Who's this? Fella that was there with you yesterday?" she asked, missing a day, I assume due to stupor, as she looked me up and down, with no pretense of shame or decency. I felt my stomach turn at what would've normally felt like a compliment, and wondered if it were karma. That shit never comes back easy.

"Yes, it is." C.W. told her. She looked at me another moment like maybe I might just decide I wanted some of that, before turning back to C.W.

"Bring the money?" she asked.

"I need to see what you have first."

"Honey, the money gets you in the door. You can have whatever of that bastard's you want," she said. C.W. looked at her a moment, crinkling his nose slightly like he didn't like the way she smelled, and pulled a folded hundred dollar bill from his pocket.

She took the money and walked back inside, and we followed.

Whatever you could say about her stench at the door, at least we'd been outside where it could circulate some. Inside it hit us like a Dachau oven. All the blinds were closed, there was tinfoil taped to the windows, and elderly Chihuahuas limped and wheezed across the floor. There was piss and shit everywhere. I needed a drink in the worst way.

She plopped herself down in a recliner that had been brought back to life about ten too many times and farted. Then she laughed at her flatulence.

I stayed sober this morning for this shit? I thought.

"His mail is on the kitchen counter. He usually picked it up couple of times a week."

"He wasn't living here?" C.W. asked on his way to the counter. I stayed where I was. What I could see of the kitchen looked to be worse than the living room. I wondered what diseases we were being exposed to in the house.

"He stayed here when he felt like it."

C.W. didn't answer immediately, preoccupied as he was navigating his way to the kitchen counter.

"Where was he staying when he wasn't here?" I asked.

"How the fuck am I supposed to know? You want something to drink, big man?"

"I'll pass."

"When's the divorce final?" C.W. asked as he tip-toed back into the room.

"Divorce? Hell, who can afford a divorce in this economy? Goddamn porch monkey in charge, ruining shit."

"So, he left, but you weren't going to get a divorce?"

"Hell no, 'least not until the housing market picks up some. That is if King Nigger in the Black House will let it."

"I see. Does he have anything else here besides your bills?" He asked. I could hear him wading around in the kitchen. I wondered if I should've brought some rope, just in case. I didn't particularly want to go swimming in there after him.

"Fuck no. Everything in this house is mine."

"I gave you a hundred bucks for a water bill and three credit card bills?" He asked. She smiled, like she was proud of herself and there was no way he was getting it back without a fight.

"Did he have any friends?" C.W. asked. He looked a little dejected. I thought he might feel better if he used the bitch to practice some of his bullshit martial arts moves. A nice, whirling, movie star-style roundhouse kick to the face would've been cool.

"If you'd call 'em that," she snorted, howling with something that might've passed for laughter on Mars after the colony had descended into post-apocalyptic chaos. "I call 'em a bunch of retards that waste money playing dress up," she snorted again, tossing back some more beer.

C.W. stood there, tense, needing a long, deep, cleansing breath, yet not willing to risk breathing in whatever toxicity doing so would've resulted in. She, for her part, took a double long pull on her cigarette, engaged in a coughing fit that resulted in her spitting a wet, yellow lung onto the ancient shag carpet, and waved her little smoking wand toward the entertainment center.

"Green binder there, that's his from their meetings. There's a photo in it, I think," she said, before sitting back in what might've been cardiac arrest.

I kicked my way through the rubble all the way across the room to where the TV sat playing an ancient episode of *Walker,*

Texas Ranger on cable, and pulled the binder off the shelf next to it.

Sure enough, stuck in the slot inside the front flap, there was a photo of him and several other men holding weapons. They were dressed in a collage of army surplus and hunting camouflage that, to someone who knew what they were doing, looked sad, pathetic, bi-polar, and too much like you see rebel fighters all over the world actually dressed. Inside the rings, were a collection of military manuals someone had Xeroxed off.

My heart sank, remembering the mid-90's. Not a good time to be part of the gun culture, then.

"You can't tell us anything about the men with him in this photograph?" I asked.

"Fuck no. He never brought any of them home. Acted like he was something special once he hooked up with them. Shee-it."

We left without thanking her, and enjoyed much deeper breaths of air than either of us had taken inside. We laughed at that, and CW slapped me on the shoulder as we walked to the truck.

"That's your people, son, your people. A rather fine representative of the Grand Old Party. She'll probably run for office," he said.

"Fuck off," I told him. I wondered why I hadn't brought my flask.

CHAPTER 9

Though it was the middle of the day, the parking lot of the apartment complex was filled with vehicles, many of them work trucks that carried the logo of various companies in that Alejandro Castillo either owned outright or had large shares in. Cooking smells did not linger from windows, but seemed to drift lazily along the ether, left over from the day before, as if the air there was permanently saturated with them. In one corner of the large communal area, near the little building that housed the main office, children played on a playground.

Beside it, under a pavilion, sat the man we'd come to see. He was dressed in his customary dark suit and collar, and on the table before him were the tools of his trade. With him was a young man, maybe fifteen, hunched and forlorn on the bench, his body so rigid with tension you wanted to unplug him at the socket just to give him a break.

We walked to the pavilion and stood at the corner, letting the priest know we were there but respecting their space. The priest acknowledged our presence, but it took fifteen minutes and two cigarettes for him to finish with the boy. When he was done, he came to us, and the boy left, his body still filled with tension, his eyes still wet as he looked back over his shoulder at the strange men who had interrupted his search for peace.

"Let me guess. You're the reporter and his friend the mercenary," he asked. He didn't offer to shake our hands. I wanted to punch him for the mercenary comment. Probably not positive for the ol' soul, that.

"Yes, Father, that's right. Could you spare a few minutes?" C.W. asked.

"It seems I can now," he said. He spoke with the soft, almost effeminate accent of the aristocratic south, but his voice did not match the constant anger in his eyes. "What is it you think I can tell you?"

"You're involved with LARO and worked with Miguel Torres on a number of matters. You're a vocal supporter of Alejandro Castillo. Can you tell me why Torres might be meeting with a known member of a biker gang, one with ties to militias and patriot groups, less than two weeks from Cinco de Mayo? There has been a lot of talk about something big, a possible terrorist attack by the right wingers for instance, happening."

"This nation and this state are both hostile to the rights of its immigrant workers. That is the heart of the matter, really. As to why Miguel was meeting with the biker," he paused, taking a deep breath. He looked out at the children playing, and his face softened, but the anger never left his eyes. "I'm afraid that is between them, and the bastard who killed them. Miguel was a bit of a loose cannon, but he had a good heart. His history, both in the Marines, and...before, made him think he was a little invincible."

"You don't think it's strange that a Latino activist got gunned down in the company of a right wing crazoid while there are all these wild rumors going on about the fifth?"

"Do you think people are basically good, Mr. Ellsworth?" he asked. I was glad the question wasn't directed at me. I was busy trying not to vomit.

C.W. stuttered slightly, not sure what to say at the run around. He probably hadn't expected a priest to flip the bitch on him.

"I try, yes," he said.

"Then I think that's your answer."

"You're saying the biker was feeding him information, and they were both killed to cover it up?"

"I didn't say that. I don't know why they were meeting. But, I know many people say hurtful things out of the love for their family and the desire to protect those who they consider to be their people. It's human nature. Those without always look for enemies. For some, these people, here in these apartments are an easy answer. They don't really hate them. They're just scared. And sometimes they lash out. And sometimes, someone has the courage to stand up against it. Oftentimes though, they just have enough courage to send a warning. That's what I would think about, if I were you, Mr. Ellsworth. I would look at those close to the gentleman who was killed along with Miguel."

There was a pause, and I wondered if we were supposed to let the impact of his words sink in before saying anything else. I liked him even less than I thought I would.

"If there's nothing else, gentleman, I need to be on my way," he said.

C.W. thanked him for his time. We turned to leave but he caught my eye. He didn't say anything to me, just stared at me, his mouth shaped like he was working up a bad taste to spit out of his mouth.

"You got something to say to me, Padre?" I asked.

"You're just exactly what I expected."

"The same to you, Father."

CHAPTER 10

The address for the biker was a trailer park on the far side of Waco, a town I never really liked that much. Too many Baptists and a rather boring strip club scene are not my preferred community demographics. In front of the trailer park was the tire shop and wrecker service where he was supposedly employed. Next to that was the clubhouse for the motorcycle gang with which the man we'd seen gunned down with Torres had been affiliated.

The small fringe community where we'd left the priest in Dallas had well-tended and cared for yards, clean buildings and pavement with a fresh coat of paint on everything that carried it. In stark contrast, everything in the trailer park looked to be sagging, rusty, and peeling. Even the work trucks looked to be abandoned wrecks. Many vehicles sat up on blocks, and the yards they graced largely consisted of littered auto parts and dirt saturated by an assortment of vehicular fluids.

Score one for the wet-backs, I thought.

We parked in front of the tire shop and walked through the front door. A rusty little bell rang weakly above our heads. The front room was small, and dark. In the nearest corner, two chairs that looked like they'd seen better days as part of someone else's dinette set sat too large on either side of a short table that sported a three-quarters-played game of dominoes waiting to be picked back up. There was dust on top of the dominoes.

Along the back wall was what appeared to be the rear seat of someone's van, placed there against the wall presumably for the comfort of their customers. Next to it was a door that led to an empty looking shop. A troll peeked above service counter, and I wondered if we'd stepped through the door into Narnia: Meth Edition.

The troll was maybe four feet tall, with a great big belly beneath a leather vest that was stretched tight around him like a busted sausage casing. Beneath it were various layers of clothing that didn't match, but on him they didn't seem so out of place.

"What the fuck do you two want?" he asked.

I hadn't really hoped he would be jovial, but I did not need an attitude out of him after talking to Bertha the Klan Queen earlier that morning. My stomach churned. I was trying not to think about how a shot and a chaser would really be swell right then, just to keep everything in perspective.

"Yeah. We want to talk to somebody about Tommy Halloran, a club member who was shot up in Dallas day before yesterday," C.W. said.

"Is that right?" the troll asked. He ran his stunted hand over his beard, and scratched at the side of his face as if in contemplation.

"Yeah, we were there. We just wanted to ask some questions about…" C.W. said, cut short by the door from the shop opening up, a heavyset man stepping in with a sawed off pump. C.W. put his hands up. I followed suit, watching the barrel of the gun. The moment it wavered, the moment the man holding it looked away, was all I needed.

And then, the man holding it gave me the perfect opening. He racked the shotgun. Slowly, going for that movie star action shot. He might have been looking at his reflection in the window.

I snatched the Glock from the holster above my appendix, but before I could level it, C.W. advanced, grabbing the shotgun and sweeping the man's legs out from under him. He came up, slamming the action forward, planting his lizard skin boot in the man's neck.

The troll stared at him from inside the little office, a Ruger .45 suspended about halfway across his body. I aimed the Glock at him and motioned for him to drop it. He dropped it on the desk and stuck his hands in the air.

I walked over, took the Ruger from the desk, and moved the troll to one of the chairs beside the domino table.

C.W. grinned at me, his smile spread from ear to ear as the second man crawled the three feet across the dirt-plaqued tile, and into the chair opposite the troll.

"Did you like that? Did ya? That's what we call, a moderate response. I didn't have to kill anybody," he said, cradling the shotty.

I ignored him, holstered my gun, and checked the Ruger. When I was done, I slid it behind my belt, and took the shotty from C.W. He gave it a playful tug before relinquishing it.

"Ask your goddamn questions," C.W.'s new best friend grated.

"Touchy," C.W. said. He looked at the two odd men.

"Don't mind him. His vagina has been leaking a lot lately," I smirked with a nod in the direction of Cornelius, the newly crowned Ninja Turtle.

"What the fuck do you want," the troll whined, rocking forward in his seat. "And will you please lock the door and flip the sign? Believe it or not we do have a business here."

C.W. looked at me, and I did it. I thought he enjoyed playing boss a little too much. I also worried flipping the sign could also be a warning signal, but there was no use having some nice person walk in on this.

"Shit jumps off..." I started, but the troll held up a hand and shook his head.

"I know, I know. I get it first. Like I haven't heard that before. Who the hell are you, and what do you want?"

"My name is C.W. Ellsworth; I'm a reporter with the *Dallas Morning News*. This is my associate, Bam-Bam," he told them. I rolled my eyes, but he carried his smirk all the way to the bank.

"Day before yesterday we were minding our own business in a bar and your friend Tommy and a Latino rights activist got blown away in front of our faces. I wrote about it because it's what I do. I'm investigating it further, because it's also what I do. My friend here is with me because…he doesn't have anything better to do."

"I could be drinking," I said, interrupting him.

He ignored me. Then he continued, "Rather strange bedfellows, isn't it? A biker and a Mexican rights activist?"

"Tommy hasn't been patched in six to eight months. We kicked him out. His business is none of ours," said the one C.W. had taken the shot gun from.

"That's not what my sources told me. That's not what his vest said that day in that bar," C.W. told him.

"If that fucker was wearing our patch, then I'll take it up with him in hell!" The troll shouted, shaking with anger. I nearly smiled.

"Why'd you kick him out?" I asked.

In some clubs, true 1 percent-ers, losing your rocker and living through it was almost unheard of. I had a friend in Florida who was in a club. Not one of the ones dentists roll with on the weekends. I'd spent some time with them, rolling through on my great American road trip. I'd needed to lay low and heal up, and they'd taken me in, on just his word. Of course, I'd brought with me goodies…of the automatic and explosive variety.

I could've stayed, but it wasn't for me, so I left on good terms while I was still welcome. There were things I respected about them, things that appealed to me about their way of life, but I had too much respect for the Divine Feminine to ever let myself be fully accepted any place like that.

"Fucker was retarded. Spent too much time at gun shows and shit talking to the crazies. He was just begging the ATF to ream our asses, man."

"He make some new friends in all that?"

"Yeah, the kind nobody with any sense wants. The violent, political type."

"That's funny coming from someone like you," C.W. said, alluding to the gang's name. The troll shook his head like he was retarded.

"Jesus Christ. Do we look political to you? We're a small charter in a small club. We've got maybe twenty members. Still, we've got enough to deal with, trying to stay afloat, keep people out of jail, and not getting patched over the moment someone decides we're a threat to their *corporation*."

"He was too much hassle, too much risk."

"You're goddamn right he was. A true believer. We don't mix colors, but Tommy kept talking about how what this country needed was a more immediate solution."

"You know where he was staying? Who he was hanging with?" C.W. asked.

"No, I don't. Some militia nut-jobs would be my bet. You might try his ex old lady. She might know where he wound up."

"Where would we find her?" C.W. asked. The troll motioned to the little office behind me.

"In the office, on the cork-board, in the corner, there's one of her cards," he said. I stepped into the office and located the card in the corner of the cork-board.

Tricky Dixie, exotic dancer, personal massage therapist, hypnotist, and psychic.

Of course.

I handed it to C.W.

"Is there anything else you can tell us?" he asked the troll.

"No."

"Why'd you throw down on us?"

"Some other shit," he said, waving his hand.

"What other shit?" C.W. asked. The troll stared at him.

"Nothing that concerns us," I said. I held the button down beside the trigger-guard of the shotgun, and ejected the shells into the floor. When it was empty, I broke it down, and dumped the barrel and receiver into a short steel trash bin. Next I took the Ruger, dropped the magazine in, followed by the chambered round, before separating the barrel and slide from the frame. Everything clanged loudly off the bottom metal bottom of the trash bin.

"Oh, wow, I'm fuckin' impressed," the troll said. Everybody is Hollywood these days.

"Shut up," I told him. I didn't like the look in his eyes or the tone of his voice. I was debating, real hard like, taking a step forward and kicking him in his ugly ass face.

C.W. stepped between us.

"Gentlemen," he said, one of his business cards appearing between the fingers of one hand. "My card, if you suddenly remember anything about your friend. If it's useful, there might even be a little compensation," he said. He leaned over and stuffed the card in the troll's shirt pocket.

➤┼◆➤ ┼ ⊙ ┼ ◀◆┼◄

The stripper wasn't in town. She wasn't even in the state. She was in Biloxi, headlining. She was moving up in the world. And she was leaving her scumbag ex-husband and his white trash world so far behind, she couldn't tell us anything. When Cornelius told her he was dead, I could hear her laugh on the other end.

We stopped for gas just outside Waco, in the little Czech town of West, at a famous-in-Texas gas station and food stop known as the Czech Stop. They have to-die-for sausage and cheese kolaches. The sausage and sauerkraut ones are pretty good, too. I went inside and loaded up on whatever they had left while C.W. pumped.

When I carried the heavy sacks outside, C.W. was still standing by his truck, the pump running, looking out over the busy interstate at a mass of dark clouds rolling in from the south.

"I'm surprised you don't drive a Prius, some gay shit like that," I told him. I opened the door and set the sacks on the bench seat and pulled a can of Dr Pepper for myself. I popped it, took a long, satisfying drink, and then propped my elbows on the side of the truck and looked at him over the bed.

"This one's paid for," he said. I figured his mother could've bought him one for Christmas, all the money they had, but he'd always lived with a utilitarian streak despite their money.

"You just don't want to have to collect all those bumper-stickers again," I said, grinning. His rear bumper and tailgate were covered with stickers for causes and musicians he supported. Things like "TEXAS DEMOCRAT!", and "Rednecks for Obama!" littered the rear bumper, tailgate, and much of his rear windshield. Just the type of thing you want to drive around rural Texas in.

"They probably cut down your gas mileage."

"I've heard that. From Republicans that can't come up with any new material."

"I'm not a Republican."

"No, you're an anarchist, and that's worse. We've covered this ground before, my man."

"Least I don't push my God off on you."

"The only God you ever had was violence, Jeb," he said. A looked passed over his face like he wished he'd said something else, so I kept quiet. It bothered him more than me, anyway.

He set the pump and we climbed into the truck.

"I feel like I oughtta start suckin' dick, just riding in this motherfucker. All the gay ass stickers on it," I said, looking through the sacks for another kolache.

"It's a long ride back to Dallas. If you decide to lean over and indulge yourself, I won't tell anybody."

"Nicely played."

"I thought so," he said.

We pulled onto the highway headed back to Dallas. Eventually, we discussed our fruitless trip, but not until we got tired of listening to the highway hum.

CHAPTER 11

On day three, Cornelius needed to go into the office and talk to his boss, and maybe his boss's boss, so I was left, blessedly, to my own devices. I ran in jeans and boots, before doing calisthenics and my own personal kata work in the back yard. In the real world, you don't get to change into sweats before the fight. I finished up with drawing the Glock 19 from concealment, dry firing, and exchanging mags. Practice makes perfect.

Afterwards I turned on the day's news for company while I fixed an omelet for lunch. I'd just added the eggs when my cell rang on the counter. It was Cornelius.

"What are you doing?" He asked. There was frenzy in his voice.

"Making breakfast, what's up?"

"I think I'm being followed, dude. Big guy from yesterday, couple of his friends."

"Call the cops."

"And do what? They'll just drive away."

"Where are you at?"

"Downtown, on my way home."

"Don't come here," I said, "unless you want them to know where you live." It wasn't the real reason he didn't want to bring them home. With today's technology it would be all too easy for them to know where he lived. I didn't have the time to explain the real reason.

"No. What are we going to do?" He asked. I thought about it.

"Call the cops, dude," I said, hoping he'd take the easy out.

"And tell them what?"

"Ok, then. Do what I say. Lead them around for half an hour, then go to the parking garage at North Park Mall. Park on the top level and then go inside. They won't do anything in public."

"What are you going to do?"

"Make it to where they can't drive away," I said, and snapped the phone closed, hurrying to redress and make my way to the parking garage.

CHAPTER 12

I was posted in the far stairwell, watching Cornelius descend the stairs across the lot when a beat-up rust bucket of a ten-year-old white Honda came up the ramp. It stopped just long enough to let the passengers out. There were few cars parked on the top level and the troll from the day before parked near me, where he had a commanding view of the level. I gave it a slow ten count as he shut the engine off and lit a smoke.

I didn't want to make it obvious, so I went for nonchalant, my hand on my key chain, as I stepped out of the stairwell. I slipped my middle finger through the single knuckle titanium Top Popper attached to my key ring, and kept my hands low.

Our eyes met in his rear-view and recognition twinkled in his eyes. The door swung open and his bulk surged out, a battered Smith 9mm in his hand. I took two long strides and drove my fist into his face, again and again, his eye socket and nose cracking as blood spurted from broken bones and cuts.

He howled and forgot about me long enough for me to put a steel-toed boot to the outside of his knee. The cartilage snapped like dry kindling and he dropped, the pistol sliding on the cement. I swept up the gun with my left hand and racked the slide, chambering a round.

"Get up, get back behind the wheel," I said, holding the gun at my side, out of view.

The fat little man whimpered out of shame.

"Do it, or I'll fucking kill you," I told him. He looked at me once before doing what I told him. I had him cuff himself to the steering wheel with some flex ties, and then I tightened down on them to be sure he couldn't twist out of them.

"Man, you do not know who you are fucking with," he growled. My hand flexed around the titanium knuckle.

"Shut up," I told him, hitting the sweet spot just behind the ear, turning out his lights.

I worked the de-cocker on the Smith, and slipped it behind my belt and looked around the clear garage and called Cornelius on my cell.

"Man where are you?" he asked, not quite frantic.

"In the garage, I just took care of the driver. Where are you?"

"Just walking man."

"Do they know you're on to them?"

"I don't think so. It's almost worth it to see these two try to blend in."

"Lead them around a little bit then come on back. I'll be here."

I walked near the elevator and looked down at the walkway on the second level, connecting the garage with the mall. They'd be coming through there. I watched the walkway as I formed two more sets of cuffs. I didn't want to waste any time getting them ready after it went down.

Cornelius walked out with a quick stride. I hid behind the elevator. He walked up the stairs and straight toward his car. The two men followed, and the sound of their steps hurried as they increased their speed up and out of the stairwell, their hands moving under their loose shirts. I brought my Glock up with both hands and yelled for them to stop where they were.

The closest one, the second one out of the stairwell, was drawing a 9mm from his waistband. I shot him four times in the chest so fast it sounded like two shots, a perfectly controlled pair. His body dropped, red pulp hanging in the air, the rattling sound of his handgun clanking against the cement floor louder in my ear than the gunshots.

Without taking a breath, I shifted, my front sight finding the next target, his own gun only half way toward me. C.W. was on the edge of my consciousness, also shifting, moving toward him, racing me even as I forced myself to slow down, focusing at the top the target's nose, right between the eyes, and stroking the trigger just before C.W. leapt for him.

There is nothing in this world like a bullet to the face. It's not as pretty as it looks in the movies. Only the smallest of bullets leave something and only then if they are entry wounds. C.W. stood over the body of the man who had just come to abduct him, his body tense with adrenaline, the air heavy with gunpowder and the red mist clinging to it inside our consciousness. His hands flexed at his side, and he kept looking from the bodies, to me, and back to the bodies.

I holstered my Glock, pulled my cell phone, took a deep breath, and called 9-1-1. I gave the dispatcher our location, and that I had just shot two men with guns, gave our descriptions, and promised not to touch anything. She wanted me to stay on the line, but I told her I needed to check on my friend, and hung up as politely as possible.

C.W. stared at me while I slipped the phone back in my vest pocket and walked toward him. "You ok?" I asked. He shook his head slowly, still taking stock of the scene.

"Fuck no, I'm not ok, Jeb. Goddamn it, you just killed two people."

"Well, yeah."

"That's all you have to say?"

"No, you need to figure out which of your family's attorney's you're going to call, and you need to do that by the time the cops get here," I told him.

"Yeah," he said, his mouth wide as he nodded his head up and down. "I-magine so, since you just killed two people," he said, almost to himself, shaking his head slowly from side to side.

I no longer felt like talking or listening to him, so I lit a smoke and waited for the cops.

CHAPTER13

I was leaning against the trunk of their car, enjoying some menthol-y goodness when the first squad car arrived. Cornelius spit a wad of Copenhagen into an empty Dr Pepper can, and continued mocking the one asshole who had survived their merry little kidnapping. He'd been doing that the whole five minutes we waited. You can take the redneck out of East Texas, educate him, send him to the Peace Corps to save the world, but you'll never be able to take the redneck out of the boy. Just the way it is. East Texas stays in you forever that way. It kept him from annoying me with his shit.

We held our hands where they could see them, but they didn't seem to care. I had expected to be handcuffed, or at least separated, but all they did was take positive control of the guns. Them not doing these things stuck in the back of my brain like a frozen ice pick whose owner had taken the cork handle with him after he rammed it in. I didn't like the feeling, or the images it conjured.

They were taking our statements when Morales and Conyers pulled up. Morales seemed almost cheerful; Conyers just seemed like an asshole.

"Trying to do our job for us, huh, *merc*?" He strutted, snapping a piece of gum in his mouth. I wanted to snap his neck, but I thought it might look bad, circumstances being what they were.

"I'm not a merc," I said, not quite lying, because his definition of the word and mine were far, far apart.

"You are in my book."

"Well, in my book, you're an asshole," I said. I had been wondering when my temper would get the better of me.

"What did you say, you piece of shit?" He said, jumping up, getting my face. I felt my hands clench at my sides. I saw the monster in the box in the back of my brain wink at me. I took a deep breath.

"Conyers!" Morales snapped. The unis ignored them, giving respect to the rank. I remembered one of the many reasons I'd left uniforms behind me. Conyers looked at him like he'd just slapped him.

"And this looks like you're interfering with police business," he persisted, ignoring the senior detective.

"Get over here," Morales ordered. I lit another smoke and breathed deep, taking the nicotine all the way down to the third chamber, for all it was worth. I already wanted a drink—so goddamn bad.

Morales was scolding Detective Asshat behind their unit when the senior uniform, a huge black guy who'd spent more time under the iron than I had, hung his mike up and pulled himself from the cruiser. When he did, the springs uncoiled. Massive.

He handed us our IDs from the clipboard in his huge paw.

"Where you lift, man?" he asked, killing time.

"I'm new in town. Haven't found a gym yet. Know any good ones?"

"Sure. If you wanna drive to Arlington," he said with a smirk. Arlington was sort of an unofficial lifting Mecca in the Lone Star State. Ronnie Coleman trained there, as well as several other successful bodybuilders and power lifters. This cop was obviously serious enough to ignore the drive.

"We'll take it from here, *patrolman*," Asshat said, strutting back. According to his uniform, he was a sergeant with more than a dozen citations in ribbons underneath his badge. He invariably had more experience and probably had far more influence with anyone who mattered than Conyers would ever achieve, but Conyers insisted on insulting him in front of both perp and civilian. The big cop just rolled his eyes, no doubt filing his anger away for motivation. Morales tried to squeeze the migraine out of his head by pinching the top of his nose. I wondered if it worked.

"I know you're involved in this, Shaw," he started in.

"Really? Are you fucking serious? What fucking planet are you from anyway? I've been home two weeks, genius. I'm gonna help a bunch of dirt-bags I've never met try to kidnap someone whose couch I'm living on, only to shoot them as they try to pull it off? Fucking brilliant."

"Keep running your mouth, biker boy."

"Actually, I don't think I have anything to say until I confer with my lawyer."

"Who's your lawyer, tough guy?"

"The same one mine is," C.W. said, finally.

"Think you're smart? It's illegal to provide protection without a license. I could arrest you for that alone," he said, confident. I started to inform him that for that to stick, I'd have to get paid for it, but decided to let him step on his dick.

"*Detective*," the huge black cop called out from behind a hidden grin, "he's got a P.P.O. license, as well as a concealed carry permit." Dick meet foot. When I trained up before going back to the sandbox, one of the places I'd trained had offered P.P.O. certification in their training package. I took it, just to have it, in case. Didn't think I'd ever use it, but training is training, and you can never be too knowledgeable. My line of work, you never know what'll pay the bills. I would've thought someone who had bragged about checking up on me the day before would know those things.

I could see the blood boil just beneath his skin. It gave me a grin. These were all things he should've known had he done even the most cursory "checking up" on me. What a fucking idiot.

"That doesn't mean anything. You still need to come in for questioning. Why didn't you come in and give your statement? What are you trying to hide?" He sputtered, everything rushing out of his mouth so fast he didn't have time to breathe. I started to explain that I hadn't had time, I was too busy doing dangerous, nefarious, mercenary things to be bothered with a petty little thing like his statement, but Morales stepped in.

"You guys follow us to the station. Can you do that?"

"We'll take my truck and be right behind you," Cornelius said, spitting again into his spit can.

"Good." Morales put his hand on Conyers' shoulder and turned him around.

CHAPTER14

The interrogation room was the nicest I'd had the pleasure of experiencing. I'd seen many different kinds, some outfitted with advanced, beyond state-of-the-art equipment that could read your pulse, brain wave patterns, and probably your goddamn astral signature. Manned by psychologists with advanced degrees and years of experience so far in the black they got six figure salaries and government pensions to be little more than technicians.

And I'd seen the kind of rooms I'd worked in, the kind procured and equipped as the need developed, often with little more than jumper cables and a battery. Maybe a pair of pliers or a bucket of water. The people who worked in the first kind of room generally didn't like those of us who worked in the second. Which was fine, our paths rarely crossed anyway.

This time I even had a can of Dr Pepper to drink while I stewed. I'd been on the other side of the equation, in worse places, in worse situations, talking to men that, if they were smart, accepted the fact that they probably wouldn't make it back outside. That considered, I was pretty goddamn comfortable.

I sat, sipped at the Dr Pepper, and I thought about what a stupid mistake I was making not lawyering up from the start. The thing was, I wanted information, and if I lawyered up right away, I wouldn't be likely to get it. I hoped if I played ball they'd give me something, anything, about just what the hell we'd stumbled into. I could always shut the fuck up and play the lawyer card if it didn't work, but I couldn't go back after I did so. I'd come back to Dallas to reconnect and stay drunk, not….this. Whatever the fuck this was.

On the table before me was my statement. It was the second one I had written out. Conyers had come in and started the idiot dance before he'd even read it. Possibly the worst interrogator I'd ever seen. It was so bad I laughed several times through it. He didn't even bother sticking to the facts or my statement. He asked the same questions repeatedly about my work as a contractor, and veered off on tangents that sounded like a conspiracy theorists wet dream. I don't know how long I sat through his drivel, but when he left he did so making sure to leave paper and pen in case I wanted to revise my statement. The one before me matched my first one exactly.

Conyer's idiocy was not the only thing that troubled me. What really bothered me was just how easily everything had gone since the shooting. Not only had we not been taken into custody, we had been allowed to drive ourselves in the procession, between a patrol car and the detectives, to the station house. Both things that, to my knowledge, were out of the ordinary. Unheard of, even. So much so that I doubted C.W.'s family's money and influence by themselves constituted a plausible excuse.

That weighed on me, and I was debating how cooperative I wanted to be, come round two, when Morales stepped through the door and smiled.

"You ready to lawyer up, or you think you can handle me, too?" he asked, a devilish twinkle in his eye.

"Better you than your goddamn partner," I said. He smiled, and closed the door behind him before taking a seat across from me. His partner had stood and paced the whole time, occasionally stopping to spew his idiocy.

He was wearing half-framed reading glasses and they made him look older, wiser. He probably cultivated the look to put suspects at ease with the grandfatherly appearance. I didn't see any reason to risk being uncooperative with him. It didn't take a genius to figure out he was the better cop, even if it meant he was also far more dangerous than his partner. He sat his stack of papers on the table and peered over his half rims at me.

He slid the paper I'd written my second statement on a little closer to him. He looked over it, and then pulled the original from the thin manila folder he'd brought with him. He placed them side by side, and looked over them both. There might've been a slight smirk across his lips.

"You know, usually, someone writes a second statement, they change something, even if they don't mean to. Even if it's just a punctuation mark, there's almost always a change, of some kind," he said.

"I've written a lot of after-action reports," I said, and then wondered if it was a poor choice of words.

"I'm sure," he said. "Security contractor, huh?"

"Yes sir, that's right," I said, somehow managing not to groan.

I hoped this wasn't going to be a replay of the conversation I'd had with his partner. I thought more of the man than that. "Army before that?"

"Airborne all the way, sir," I told him. He leaned just far enough back to appear comfortable and relaxed. I took a sip from my can.

"What company was that you worked for downrange?" he asked, pen ready. I told him the name of the biggest, the one I'd spent most of the time with. We didn't need to get into the others. He nodded his head.

"That's a good company, got a good reputation. Unlike some of the others," he said. I nodded my head in agreement. The industry was grossly under-appreciated, with more than one black eye because of a few select dirt bags. Self-regulation was slow, and didn't catch everybody. It was hurting the professionals while the ass-hats everyone thought of as the face of the industry kept douching it up.

"You follow the war?" I asked.

"My middle boy's an MP with the Third Marine Division. He worked pretty closely with a lot of contractors when he pulled PSD duty."

"He must be pretty squared away. The Marines don't let just anybody pull that duty," I said, not having to lie. He nodded his head slowly. I had no idea what was going on in his head.

"I just got off the phone with a Sheriff's department in East Texas. They had some interesting things to say about you."

"I can't imagine what it would be."

"It was positive, for the most part. You do seem to have a long history of violence, though."

"You know how us country boys are, detective. Get drunk, get in a fight. Seduce a goat. Small town Saturday night," I said, flashing him my best shit-eating grin, like a proper good ol' boy.

"Don't play bumpkin with me, boy. *I'm* no idiot," he said, looking at me over his half rims—telling me he felt the same way I did about his partner without actually saying it.

"I'm not shitting you, detective. You know everything I know. I've been home two weeks. The last thing I want to do is to get caught up in some *bull*-shit," I said, drawing out the last word. He looked at me through his half glasses.

"You used to work for a bail bondsman?"

"I just stood around and looked mean. It wasn't any kind of life," I said, dismissively. I didn't care for the fact that we were talking about my personal history instead of the events of that morning.

"So you became a contractor?"

"It was there. A friend offered to vouch for me. My marriage was over. I didn't fit in back home, and trying to was making me nuts."

"Yeah," he said, nodding slightly, as if he might know something about that. "You're lucky. Sooner or later you're going to step in it, someplace there aren't security cameras watching to vouch for what a good citizen you are."

Like you'll fucking know.

"The age in which we live," I said, trying to focus on the man across the table, and not the one in the back of my head.

"That was a pretty nifty move with your key-chain," he said.

"You liked that, huh?" I asked, pretending to be a selfish bastard, in need of positive reinforcement.

"So you've been working as a contractor how long, now?" He asked, changing subjects. So much for the positive reinforcement angle.

"Four years and some change."

"Almost five," he said.

"Yeah, I guess that's about it," I said. I tried to look thoughtful, but not too much so. It was the difference between reviewing your math and looking for a lie.

"You work for the same company all that time?"

"For the most part, we had a crew that liked to stay together, so we tried to get the same contracts. Made getting some jobs easy and others hard, but we had a tight team," I said, reminding myself not to get agitated. I told myself he just had to cover his bases, and that we'd get to that morning's events in good time.

"And the past couple years?"

Ah, fuck. Someone had done his homework.

"I moved around a lot, kind of a vagabond. Some K&R work here, some EP work there, wherever the opening was," I said. It was true enough.

"K&R? Like Kidnap and Ransom? Like the movie?"

"Not me, no. I worked retrieval, not negotiations."

"Just a gun hand, huh," he asked.

"I'm a professional, sir," I said. I didn't get pissy, but I wanted him to know I didn't care for the label. He didn't give a shit.

"You're not really built like a guy that has breakfast in a bar you know," he asked, leaving the rest of it hanging in the air. And all I'd wanted out of Dallas was to reconnect with my little brother and stay drunk awhile. Goddamn it.

"I've been dry a long time. I was playing catch up. Why is that so hard to believe?"

"Maybe we're having trouble finding the shooter."

"I thought you had a video. Surely Big Brother's got some facial recognition software you can run it through."

He didn't say anything to that, just looked at me a long silent moment sizing me up.

"You're having trouble finding the shooter, so you assume I just had to have something to do with it, because I'm a contractor? Seriously," I asked, shaking my head.

"I didn't say that."

"You didn't have to, that goddamn idiot you're partnered with said it for both of you," I said. He looked at me, his head cocked to the side, like a bulldog who couldn't decide if he should play nice or eat me for lunch.

"Watch your mouth," he said flatly. I looked at him, sizing me up behind his half rims, trying to decide what to say next. I sighed and looked away.

I figured he said it for two reasons. One, obviously to set boundaries. He still had a job to do, and when you're on that side of the table, you only have one side. Two, it wasn't just for my benefit. We weren't alone in the conversation.

The thing is…I didn't care. I'd assumed both those things from the get go.

"What the fuck is this shit? Giving me the third degree? I just kept three men from kidnapping my friend. You know what happened, you watched it on candid fucking camera, and instead of talking to me about the men I just *popped*, or what kind of danger my friend might still be in, or even arresting me, I just get henpecked. What the fuck over?"

I was angry, and I let it show. I hate games and I wasn't going to play his. If I needed to do the smart thing and lawyer up, I needed to know. I was getting nowhere fast with the current tac and I was already sick of watching him take a long trip around a hard map dot. For fuck's sake.

He waited for me to calm down. I took a breath, and had another sip of Dr Pepper.

"Gotta admit though, it looks bad. You, with your history, personal *and* professional, being in a biker bar when three people get whacked," he said.

"You're smart enough to know that if I really was what your partner wants to think, and had anything to do with this shit, I wouldn't have been there with a civilian. One, who, on a personal level, is family to me, on top of being a reporter with a bleeding goddamn heart," I said.

"A bleeding heart, lots of family money, and connections," he said.

Shit, I thought.

C.W.'s family had lots of money, much of it made, and all of it beginning in Dallas and East Texas. An hour and a half away, if the Metroplex had grown toward it instead of every other direction, our hometown would damn near be little more than just another suburb now. His Uncle Jack had been a fixture in local, state, and occasional national news for nearly four decades. He'd even served a couple of terms in Congress in the 80's, before a messy divorce had bankrupted him with the religious right. He was a Libertarian in everything but defense and foreign policy, so I loved him. His nephew was convinced he'd been a part of the Kennedy assassination, while still a college student.

"Don't say it like that to him, he'll take it personally."

"What, he can't handle the truth?"

"He's probably got some liberal angst about it. He's got the shit about everything else," I said. He nodded his head like he understood.

"So… you two talked to one of these guys yesterday?" he asked.

"Yeah, that's right," I said, before he interrupted me.

"About the biker you two saw killed?"

"Yeah, that's right," I said. "Cornelius got a line on his club, and his last place of employment, and we rode down to Waco yesterday to see what we could find. That's where we talked to them."

"And what happened there?" he asked. My eyes flicked to the side in thought, but I wasn't worried about it. I didn't have anything to hide. All I had to do was tell the truth and it would show.

"They drew down on us, we handled the situation, we talked to them for a bit, and then we left."

"And what'd y'all talk about?"

"What the fuck you think we talked about? We talked about a friend of theirs getting whacked in front of us, and why it might've happened."

"They say why?"

"No, they didn't. They didn't say anything useful."

"What'd they say?"

"Nothing,...bullshit. I didn't know whether they were giving us the run around or just fucking stupid. Judging by how things turned out, I'm guessing it was a bit of both."

"I guess it was, wasn't it? What exactly did they say?"

"They told us he wasn't welcome around there anymore. They said he lost his rocker, said he was drawing too much heat. Said he was...overly political. They gave us a phone number for his ex old lady, who just happens to be out of town, and never wants to see him again."

"You say they pulled guns on you yesterday?"

"Yes sir, that's correct," I said.

"And you handled it?"

"Yep," I said.

"How?" he asked.

"We were just better than they were."

"We? As in both of you?" he asked, the disbelief in his eyes purposefully obvious, as if we were in on the same joke, and that joke was my friend.

"C.W. can handle himself," I said. I thought I could feel an unconscious snarl forming at the corners of my lips. I didn't like my old friend's political disposition, but I didn't pretend to equate that with his masculinity. At least not completely, and not to his face.

"Then why does he need you?" he asked. I shrugged.

"I guess…just in case."

"In case what?"

"In case it goes to that next level."

"The one where you have to kill people?" he asked. I looked at him a long moment and let out a long exhale and shut my goddamn mouth.

"Relax, Shaw. No one's looking to jam you up. You've got video backing your story. Plus, the driver is already talking."

"What's he saying?" I asked.

"Oh, that's the good part. He's not exactly bright. I'm surprised he managed to get a driver's license. He won't shut up about the coming race war, and the mixing of the races, how the wetbacks are stealing the country, and what he thinks America was really founded on. Basically, he's a living, breathing talking point for the Democratic Party. I mean, if you've got to shoot a couple people, you want them to be friends of his. Hell, the mayor'll probably give you a medal," he said. The smirk on his face didn't fit, like he was trying it on and knew we both knew it didn't belong.

"Does he know why his brother in arms was meeting Torres the other day?"

"Why do you think they wanted your friend?" he said bluntly, indicating the obviousness of it. I shut my mouth and nursed the chip on my shoulder.

"They thought we knew the answers to the questions we drove all the way down to Waco to ask them yesterday?" I asked.

"Yeah. He's not exactly a molecular physicist."

"How many more are there in this little band of merry men?" I asked.

He shrugged.

"Don't know. Don't know who else they might be hooked up with, either. Militias, paramilitary groups have been popping back up left and right the past couple of years. We've put in calls to ATF and the Feds to see if they have anything on these yokels. If the driver gives us something you need to be aware of, we'll pass it on."

"I'd appreciate that," I said.

"What's your opinion on all this?"

"Man, I just stumbled into this shit. To be honest with you, I'm a little goddamn depressed I'm sober right now," I said. Maybe if I wore a shirt that said I was on vacation, someone would eventually believe me.

"That right?"

"Yes, that's right," I said. He didn't say anything back.

We sat and stared at each other in the frigid cacophony of the sterile room for what seemed like an hour. It was probably only about thirty seconds.

"What is it you're not telling me?" I asked. He didn't say anything. I didn't know if he was playing games, or trying to decide what I should know.

"I really don't think you need to worry about a bunch of white trash that can barely tie their shoelaces," he said.

"That a fact? Who was Torres? What exactly was he into?" I asked, cutting to the chase. Probably a little stronger than you should ask a cop when you're sitting in an interrogation room. Perhaps especially so when they've been taking it easy on you. He smiled at me behind his half-rims. I thought about how he'd been taking it easy, wondered just what that meant.

"Now that guy, he was an interesting guy. But you know that already, don't you?" he asked. I nodded. In the whole misbegotten cast of characters, Torres was the only common denominator.

"I don't know shit. I just want the people I care about to be safe," I said. It was the truth. I would do whatever I needed to do to ensure it.

"Torres mustered out of the Corps three years ago. He was going to school, but only part time. He worked for his uncle's organization, the Latino American Rights Organization, but you knew that. He was heavy in the club scene. Knew every bouncer and bartender in town."

"He was a drug dealer," I said, completing his thought.

"Was he?"

"It'd be my guess," I said. He shrugged, in that paternal way people do when they aren't going to explain themselves, and figure you will figure it out eventually.

"Probably a good guess."

"Doesn't fit well with his public image," I said.

"Not really," he said. He didn't say anything else, just kept looking at me, searching for a chink in the old chain mail.

"Does his Uncle have a piece of that shit?" I asked.

"No...I don't think so, anyway," he said. Momentarily, I watched a brief wave of sadness pass, not over his face, but just behind his eyes. Something small and fleeting, something he probably didn't talk about even though it was profound enough to carry always.

"So, Torres came home from the Marines and hooked up with his old crew, dealing drugs, and started teaching them all the shit he'd learned overseas, did he?"

"I don't know, did he?"

"How the fuck should I know?" I snapped, forgetting myself.

"I never said he was hooked up with his old gang."

"That happens. Gang members join up all the time just to get skills they can bring home and pass on," I said.

"We don't have any reason to believe he was hooked back up with his old crew. He was trying to go corporate. He hadn't hung with that... *demographic* in years."

"If he was dealing drugs, he had to get them from somewhere. You say it's not his uncle. I say his uncle looks like a prime candidate for scumbag shyster of the fucking year."

"I think I need to show you something," he said. I stared at him like I couldn't wait. He brought a manila folder atop the table, and opened it up.

"See this, this girl here," he said, holding up the picture of a pretty girl in her twenties. White, blond hair cut short to avoid fuss, sexy librarian glasses, a nice figure, even though she was a little on the lean side.

"Just out of college. She worked with Torres at LARO. Somehow, I don't know what, or how, but she pissed off the wrong people," he said, spreading 8x10's out across the table. "And this is what happened. Poor little white girl. Just wanted to save the world."

I didn't want to see what was inside, no man ever does. But I did. I looked at the pictures, and saw things I couldn't forget. I saw things you can't take back. A young woman at another's twisted pleasure who obviously thought mercy was weakness. If they thought about it at all. I saw her in pictures. I saw her in pieces. I saw her on a spit.

I saw her ravaged by forces I would not describe after. I inhaled deeply, trying to get the psychosomatic stench out of my nostrils. It did not dissipate very well.

"See this shit," he said, filing through the pictures. "Who's gonna do this to somebody?"

"You tell me. You're the one with the pictures," I snapped again, forgetting to keep my cool.

"Looks like Cartel handiwork to me, but that's not the official story."

"Of course not," I said, somehow knowing just where he would be going with that. It might sound cliché, trite, but stereotypes often exist for good reasons. Government bureaucracies and the political machinations of those involved only ever really exist to meet their own ends.

"Six months ago someone broke into her apartment and kidnapped her. We suspected it might've been someone she'd come into contact with at LARO. Every community that's ever existed has had its fair share of psychos. Immigrant communities are no different, it's just that…," he said, thinking about what to say next. Or, more appropriately, maybe just how to say it. "It's just that because of the organic nature of the communities, and the mobility necessary for them to exist and function the way they do, it makes your job nearly impossible," I said, finishing the thought. He cocked his head to the side, as if he were re-appraising me.

"I told you I was a goddamn professional," I said, drawing out the redneck.

"Well, that's it exactly. We tried looking into LARO, and the connections Alejandro and Torres might have with the cartels, but someone, somewhere, has juice with the mayor and the city council. Nobody wanted a story to get out about a cartel faction doing something like this to a pretty little white girl. The border's in flames. Cartel gangs, some with shooters we trained, are operating a guerrilla war for fun and profit who knows how far into this country. You might want to think about trying to talk your friend out there into backing off this shit."

"Let me get this straight, you couldn't find a connection between a civil rights lawyer, the community organization he founded, his drug-dealing-cum-former-gang-member nephew that worked for him, and the cartels?"

"It's harder than you think, Shaw. It's easy to find lots of circumstantial evidence. I nearly drown in it every day. Getting enough of it to form a case the suits can't turn away from is another thing entirely."

"So what's the official story with this girl that got barbequed? It go in the unsolved stack with every other psycho wetback you can't find because our immigration policy is goat fucked?"

"No, it got picked up by a special task force, one that reports directly to the Chief," he said.

"The Chief, who was hired by the mayor and city council, both of whom are big fans of Old Uncle Alejandro and LARO," I said. And then, the brief flash of great sadness I'd noticed earlier just behind his eyes, was replaced, with pure, unadulterated anger.

"Yeah," he said. He thumped a thumb hard against the tabletop twice, trying to gain control.

"Yeah, and why are you telling me all this?"

"I just hate to see decent people get hurt because they can't mind their own business," he said. He looked honest and thoughtful, the anger already dissipating, however slowly.

"Well, to be someone you suspect of having ties to Cartels, you sure seemed to be real cozy with Alejandro the other day," I said. He was far too much a pro to take the bait.

"We've known each other a very long time. I don't like everything he does, but I don't know for a fact what his involvement with the cartels consists of, or how deep it is, if it's even there at all. I know he cares about his people. Him making a spectacle that day would've made my job a lot harder."

"Why'd you say you were having trouble id'ing the guy in the video from the bar?"

"I didn't."

"No, I don't guess you did," I said. We looked at each other another moment, not really sizing each other up, but not not doing that either. Wondering what was going to be the next question asked, and who was going to ask it. Finally, he stood, and opened the door behind him. That was my cue. I stood and walked out the door.

"Anyway, you can sign for your property at the front desk," he said.

"My gun too?"

"What do you think? Fuck no."

"Sweet. That way you guys can lose it just like you lost the video of the shooter. Oh well, I'm sure I won't need it anyway," I said, and caught the confirmation in his eyes before he could hide it.

"Somehow I don't think you'll have a problem when it comes to finding a weapon," he said. I shrugged, and walked silently with him toward the front desk.

CHAPTER 15

Cornelius was sitting on a wooden bench near the front door, using a new can for a spit cup, talking to some uniforms. He looked up as I stepped into the foyer, the large brown envelope containing my crap heavy in my hand.

We stepped out into the sun, Cornelius explaining what a hit I was.

"They showed me the video. That was some pretty smooth shit. People want to know if you can teach 'em, maybe tell them what they need to do to score some work," he said, spitting in his can. They wouldn't believe me if I told them. My military pedigree wasn't that impressive. They were probably more qualified than I was when I first went back over. You'd be surprised what you can do when you just stop sitting on your hands and do it.

"Conyers one of 'em?"

"Fuck that guy. He's about to get his, *sumbitch,*" he said, sliding into the vernacular we'd grown up with.

"What's that mean?"

"That motherfucker is about to be immortalized in print for all the wrong reasons."

"It's probably a bad idea to piss off a detective. Even if he deserves it," I said.

"The only reason that fucker has a job is because his uncle's brass. Let him get pissed. Every other cop in town will fucking love me. That will pay dividends, my friend."

"That's a little devious isn't it?"

"You never could gamble worth a shit."

A patrol car slid to a stop at the curb next to us, and Officer McCrummin smiled up at us from the shotgun seat. I knelt down, just to be on her level. Less intimidating that way.

"Trying to show up the police, tough guy?" She asked, smiling.

"Just a concerned citizen doing my part. Your job's too tough for me." I made eye contact as I spoke, trying not to be too cheesy. Her eyes twinkled. Giggity.

"That was a pretty smooth move you pulled on the big guy. What do you study?" Shaver asked from behind the wheel.

I reminded myself not to be a dick. It hadn't been that smooth. Just a couple power punches with a cheater.

Everyone wants to know the latest ass-kicking fad. When I was a kid, it was karate, everyone wanted to be Ralph Macchio. Then Van Damme made kickboxing cool. That was a little better. Then Brazilian Jujitsu was all the rage. That was even better, except most people were too lazy to stick with it long enough to be effective with it. Now everyone wanted to be MMA fighters. Something else would be popular tomorrow. For most people it will be just another fad. My advice? Take boxing or kickboxing. You'll learn the basics, and more importantly, you'll learn how to take a punch, which is a lost art in the age of the metrosexual male. The fact is, if you want to learn a technique for saving your bacon, almost any art has something useful. If it takes more than five minutes for the average person to master, it's useless in combat when your heart is about to explode from the adrenaline dump, and you've turned feral.

"Little of this, little of that. I pick up whatever I find to be useful. Ya' know?"

"Yeah man," he said, nodding in agreement, like he knew just what I was talking about. I decided not to mention the day before. Water under the bridge and such.

"Do you two need a ride?" she asked.

"We're cool. I don't suppose I could interest you in dinner though?" I asked. She blushed. Shaver scowled.

"Stay out of trouble," he said as his foot pressed the accelerator, pulling them away before I got an answer. I waved good bye, her scent lingering. Not worried about his warning at all.

"You're going to get your dick cut off. C'mon, Romeo. Jeezus," he said, walking on. I caught up to him and he asked if I'd learned anything from Morales. I thought before speaking, and saw that recognition flash through his eyes as I debated what to say.

As he drove me to North Park to pick up my bike, I told him what Morales had shared, and watched him salivate behind the wheel. He dropped me off at my bike, anxious to get home and get to work on his next piece.

By the time I made it to his house in the M streets, he was already half baked, the air heavy with the pungent smell of his drug of choice, this time sitting in his love seat, banging away at his laptop, instead of the desktop in his office. His grandfather's Luger sat in the built in cup holder in the armrest.

"You smoke too much of that shit," I said.

"It's better for you than booze. Fuckin' drunk."

"Yeah, yeah," I said walking past him to the kitchen. I pulled off my vest and t-shirt, nearly gagging on my own ripe musk. I was sure that had been a hit with Rosie. Sure, it really impressed her. I picked up the Jack and a short glass, and walked back into the living room. I snatched the Luger out of the cup holder before taking my seat on the couch.

"Jesus, dude," he said, pinching his nose.

"Yeah, I'll shower in a second," I said, pouring my first taste of the day.

"I thought you said you were going to stop."

"I said I was going to slow down. And I have," I told him, putting the glass to my lips, my thoughts heavy and dark, worried about so much.

I closed my eyes, and searching for the fleeting peace all addicts find in their sustenance. The deafening silence in their heart of hearts that makes their choice so sweet. When I found my fix, I set the glass back down, and picked the Luger back up off the table. I dropped the mag, checked the chamber, slid the magazine back in, and then worked the dinky little collapsing slide mechanism, chambering a round.

"Why the fuck did you just chamber a round?" He asked.

"You're joking, right?" I asked. He just shook his head some more. "You call Joshua, tell him what happened?" I asked. He took a deep breath, and stared at his laptop.

"No," he said, concentrating on whatever was on his screen.

"Well, would you, and ask him to bring my guns over," I said, and took another drink. C.W. didn't say shit, just stared at me out the corner of his eye, his head tilted down, the light from the laptop reflecting off his face.

"What?"

"You didn't have to kill them, Jeb."

"Well, it was taking all goddamn day for you to stun them with your chi. If you want me to leave, I will," I said, as if I'd ever run from a fight in my life.

"Goddamn it, Jeb. Sometimes, a moderate response is called for. Like the way we handled those two yesterday. We could've tried a little harder to take those guys alive."

"A moderate response?" I asked.

"Yes, a moderate response. Not everything's the full tilt boogie, babe," he said.

"That's the most idiotic thing I ever heard. Call Joshua," I said, dropped the last swallow down my throat, and stood. "Get him to bring my guns over. I'll take a shower."

"Thank God for small favors."

CHAPTER 16

I turned the heat on full bore and undressed while it picked up steam. I pulled my ditty bag from the towel closet, sat it on the sink, and placed the tools down near the sink, ready and waiting. It didn't take long, and by the time I slipped a foot in the tub the water was scalding. I adjusted it before slipping in.

I soaked and scrubbed, and tried unsuccessfully to wash away something unseen that knocked about inside my head. I ran through the day's events, the conversations I'd had with Morales and C.W., but nothing came. And then I realized, it didn't have to, because I knew. I had been ignoring it for two days.

Cornelius' family had money. Moreover, his mother's family had money. They owned lumber mills in East Texas, steel mills in Dallas, Houston, Shreveport, and San Antonio, and land all over hell and gone. His father, however, had been a degenerate gambler with a wandering eye, lazy zipper, and a perpetual run of bad luck.

No matter how often his father-in-law tried put him in various nothing positions in any number of sundry business ventures, he'd take off, wind up in Vegas or Shreveport or Oklahoma, broke and lying in a pool of his own piss.

Finally, he pushed someone too far, and they came to see him during a rare father/daughter moment. C.W.'s sister had played sick, just to stay home from school and be with her father. When Cornelius came home from school he found his father bound and bleeding in the bedroom, almost dead, a ransom note stapled to his chest. He was ten, she was eleven. There were always rumors that he'd given her up himself, before he disappeared, and I tended to believe them, because he was that big a piece of shit, but we never gave them credence out loud. C.W. deserved better than that. At least in spirit.

The ransom was paid, but his sister never came home. After a couple months, his father went missing, for good. Everyone in town knew his grandfather was responsible for that, and the glances cast his grandfather, for the rest of the old man's life, were not those of righteous indignation. No one gasped in his presence and asked, *How could you?* No, the only question their eyes held for him was simply *What took you so long?* The good townsfolk who spent more time in church than I ever cared to think about, who gave and gave to their faith, knew his father for what he was, and would've gladly turned a blind eye to his loss. I think maybe, maybe, in that respect it was a little better then. At least when it came to children. Some lines you just don't cross. People don't seem to know that anymore. People don't know a lot of things, anymore.

Every once in a while they'd get a letter or postcard or phone call from someone who would claim to have seen her, or even to have taken part in her kidnapping. Somehow C.W. got it in his head that she was still alive. Thus ensued a series of Mulder-esque adventures in which he took off looking for her. The first time he went missing, it was for five days. A cop picked him up for truancy in Shreveport, watching the entrance of a casino, and shit his pants after he put his name on the wire. Cornelius never explained how he'd made his way, or why he'd thought she'd be in Shreveport.

Six months later, he was off on another adventure. He had many over the course of our adolescence. The last time he'd taken off, so far as I knew, had been the summer after I graduated high school. I was out on the salt, chipping paint on an oil platform, which was why I heard about it second hand. Joshua and Bear had forced themselves onto his little road trip, and rode with him all the way to an Indian Casino in Michigan. Someone had sent him a letter with picture of a nineteen year-old girl who worked there as a waitress. Everyone else in their grade was spending the summer hauling hay and practicing for football, and they were headed to damn near Canada in search of his long dead sister.

They spent five days camped out in the parking lot, watching the employee lot for anyone who looked like her. Finally, Joshua and Bear had enough, and gave C.W. one more chance to go in and see if someone would talk to him. A week in a van, far from home, living off fast food was enough. He was inside for a while, and when he came out, he had a slip of paper with an address on it.

It took them another day to find her apartment, and when they did, she wasn't there. So they waited. When she finally returned home, she was with a big Indian whose eyes were wide with reservation meth. He wore one of those awful short black leather jackets with a belt and thick black Johnny Depp hair.

C.W. stepped out of the van, determined, and called her name. She didn't understand who he was, and her boyfriend got pissed. Then C.W. pulled the letter from his pocket and showed her the picture.

She held it, her face ashen and quizzical, and then her boyfriend grabbed it and laughed hysterically.

He'd seen the story on Unsolved Mysteries, realized his girl would be able to pass for Cornelius' sister seven years later, and decided to have some fun. Joshua and Bear watched C.W.'s blank face as the big Indian laughed at his pain, the clouds rolling beneath it indiscernible. His first strike had been a high sweep to the thigh. It had been well placed, but he was still a novice. The big Indian laughed some more, and punched him in the face. He fell back, his eye blackening. He rolled quickly, trying to get back up, but the Indian stepped in and put the boots to him.

Bear stepped around the back of the van, a bat cocked back. The big Indian pulled a Buck knife and laughed some more, until he heard the bolt slam forward on a Remington '48 "Sweet Sixteen" gauge shotgun, and looked up and through the sliding door of the van to see my baby brother staring at him behind it.

"That's about enough, Tonto," Joshua said. The first load was rock salt. He didn't want to shoot him, even with the rock salt, but he figured it should be enough to scare the dumb *sumbitch* off. He hoped it would. Everything else was #4 buck.

"What are you gonna do with that?" the Indian scoffed, a fountain of originality, and stepped forward. Joshua was taking up the slack on the trigger when Cornelius yelled, a low, pain-filled rumbling thing that Joshua and Bear only spoke of once. Then there was the sound of wet vines in a howling wind snapping against a thick tree, and then the big Indian crumpled to the pavement.

They watched as C.W. climbed atop him, a chunk of brick clenched in his hand so tight the skin around it looked like a white glove, and went to work. They stared, in silence as he let go. They said the Indian looked like a side of raw beef when they finally worked up the nerve to pull him off. They loaded C.W. up and hurried out of the parking lot. They left the big Indian there, broken, bloody, and wheezing tiny bubbles with each breath.

Joshua and Bear took turns driving while C.W. lay in the back, shaking beneath a blanket. They didn't speak, didn't turn on the radio. They just drove south the way they'd come, and didn't stop for anything but gas until Kansas, where C.W. got out and carried a change of clothes to a truck stop shower stall.

It took him over an hour, and Bear and Joshua ate in silence. He came out with only the fresh clothes on his body, and asked if it was his turn to drive.

They never found out what happened to the Indian, if he'd died outside that apartment, or hung on for a few days, or lived the rest of his life as a deformed cripple. For all they knew, he might've made a full recovery, seen the error of his ways, and become a social worker, guiding misspent youth down a more righteous path. No one knew, no one cared, and most importantly, no one ever talked about it.

I didn't know if it still kept him up at night, his moment of abandon. The blood on his hands. His father had been a degenerate piece of shit, and he'd spent his life trying to prove to the world he was not his father's son, that he was better than that. My father had been a loving man, all too willing to shield my brother and I from the harsh realities of the world. However, I'd never wanted to do anything but burn it the fuck down. I was comfortable with the blood on my hands.

I thought about that as the water went cold, and I reached for the drain.

CHAPTER 17

I took longer clearing the stubble from my scalp and around my goatee than necessary, but I felt like avoiding C.W. until I heard Joshua come whistling through the door. I finished up, cleaned my mess, slipped on a pair of gym shorts, and went to meet old friends.

When I stepped out of the hallway, Joshua was sitting in the recliner opposite the couch, on the other side of the coffee table and C.W.'s love seat. On the table were my old .45, and .38 Bodyguard, along with a shoe box full of ammo. I had to move little the Mossberg Maverick to take back my seat on the couch.

"You killed two people?" Joshua asked as I opened the Mossberg's breech and checked its chamber.

"Yep," I said, setting it aside, and scooping up the .38, still in its pocket holster the way I'd left it when I went back downrange.

"And evidently, he wants to kill more," C.W. said his voice dripping with snark. I shot him a look that told him to fuck off, and popped the cylinder, closed it, and dry fired it couple of times, just to check the action.

"What are you involved in?" Joshua asked, staring at me. I shoved the .38 back in its holster and dropped it on the table.

"I'm not involved in shit. Not a fucking thing. I'm trying to keep this asshat," I protested, pointing a thumb toward C.W., "alive and well! Only nobody seems to respect that!"

"You don't have to yell," Joshua said. He almost looked hurt. I shook my head, muttered something about them being worse than my ex-wife, and picked the .45 off the table, sliding it out of its leather.

I'd bought the gun with hay hauling money when I was seventeen years old, from one of my father's drinking buddies who didn't want to lose it in a divorce. Over the years, I added to the basic package an ambidextrous safety, a beavertail, slotted Commander-style hammer, Novak night sights, titanium slide stop so rare a Screaming Eagle drinking buddy tried to tell me they didn't exist, and finally a match bushing to tighten up my groups. All the after-market parts except the slide stop were stainless Wilson's, giving the gun a nice, subdued two-tone look. It was a classic old school gun for another generation, a generation I identified with more than my own.

In the years since I'd left home again, I'd worked hard to change my mindset, to be professional, to strive toward the mythical Todd, to view guns simply as tools, nothing more. Doing contract work I'd used almost exclusively Glocks and Sigs, the occasional Browning and Beretta, a Makarov, the occasional locally produced pot-metal nightmare, and even once an old battered Webley revolver when I'd gotten in this bind in Africa, but never a .45. Though many still used them, I never seemed to find myself in a position where I had both the option, and a specimen available worth trusting my life with. Moreover, I never really thought about it at the time, but always forced myself to focus on the job at hand.

And when I wrapped my hand around the old King's Gun Works skip checkered cocobolo grips of my old friend, my hand sliding into a perfect position beneath the stainless beavertail, my thumb riding the thumb safety as if it'd never left, something clicked, deep inside. I was no longer that stone professional. I was once again the little macho redneck kid who didn't know better. I was a gun nut, an enthusiast, a weapons spiritualist, and this was my fetishistic totem.

"You enjoy that a little too much," C.W. said, putting the joint back to his lips.

"Just shut up and smoke your weed, hippy," I said, going through the functions check, the sound of slightly oiled metal filling the house.

"You ever take it out and shoot it?" I asked Joshua.

"Naw dude, I spend too much on my shit to shoot your Neanderthal crap."

"You want to go to the range tomorrow? I need to give this thing a workout," I said, putting the gun back on the table and pulling the cartridge boxes and magazines out of the shoebox.

"Maybe, I gotta check with the wife."

"You ask permission to take a piss, too?" I said, not really thinking, pulling bullets from the container to thumb into my magazines.

"We'll see, I'll give you guys a call tomorrow," he said, and left. His absence left a heavy stillness, an aching in my heart, and I regretted what I'd said. Hated myself for it, even.

"Wow. You really are a piece of work, you know that?" C.W. said. I tried to ignore him as I thumbed rounds home. "You know, he still looks up to you, right? He was scared to death for you every day you were gone."

"I know," I said, my voice low, trying to stay calm, wishing I could turn the dial back and not be a raging, macho, asshole. Basically... myself.

"Why be that way?"

"I just snapped, ok? Not really in the mood for a lot of shit, from either one of you. I just killed two men to save your life, and instead of gratitude, I get shit on from all sides."

"I didn't think you cared about killing them."

"Yeah."

"Joshua didn't say shit to you."

"I know," I said, more of a growl than anything else, and he shook his head, pulling his laptop back toward him.

When I was done, we ordered Betty's Best, which C.W. insisted was the best Chinese food in the Metroplex, after which I sprawled out on the couch and he tucked himself into his massive love seat, each with our poison of choice, and pretended to watch a documentary in our never-ending debate. The events of the day hung heavily in both our minds, but he didn't want to talk about what he'd seen, and I didn't really feel like arguing with him about the necessity of what I'd done.

He chose *Man From Plains*, which was a vast improvement over his last choice, which had been a Michael Moore piece of shit I'd had to get drunk and stoned just to watch without tearing the television into pieces. My last choice had been *Lake of Fire*, about abortion, and it had left us both crying drunk.

CHAPTER 18

I was sprawled out on the couch, my hand wrapped around the .45 in its holster resting on my chest, slightly buzzed from both the booze and occasional toke. My gut pleasantly filled, my eyes heavy with the day's strain, as well as the leftist propaganda it had been C.W.'s turn to subject me to.

"Hey, Jeb," he said, nestled in the cave of his love seat.

"Yeah, *Corny*, what's up?"

"About earlier man, thanks," he said.

Took you long enough.

"Don't mention it."

"You gonna stick around a while?"

"Don't really have much choice, right now. Have to get cleared for the shooting first, no telling how goddamn long that'll take. Hopefully Uncle Jack's lawyers can keep me out of prison and my prime virgin ass tight and nubile."

"Guess that's as good a reason as any," he said. He had a far off, distant look in his eyes but I couldn't tell how much of it was the effect of the shooting, the differences in our natures, or his weed.

"I think so. Besides, I don't like leaving loose ends."

"You really worried about it?"

"I try not to waste time with worry. I'm aware of it, that's for goddamn sure."

"You were defending my life. The security cameras recorded the whole thing."

"Yeah, and the world is filled with liberals and lawyers," I said, and left it at that. I thought it pretty much explained everything, and much of what was wrong with the world.

"What does being a liberal have to do with anything?" He asked. I didn't answer.

"I still think we could've taken them alive. At least the second man," he said, his voice rising just a little. He didn't feel like arguing, but he felt someone should.

"Kinda my point," I said. We both left it at that.

"Hey, bro, what did you mean about not leaving unfinished business?" Cornelius asked on the inhale, before handing the joint over to me.

"Pretty much just what it sounds like."

"You can't be serious," he said, the questions concerning my morality obvious upon his face.

"When have you ever known me not to be?"

"Well, I don't think I like the sound of that."

"What's not to like?"

"Oh, I don't know, everything?"

I ignored him, taking my turn, and then another, just to be sure I'd get it.

"Ok, why don't you tell me just what you're thinking about?" He kept at it.

I knew I shouldn't, knew it was only asking for trouble, but he was one of my oldest friends. And I was both drunk and high, so my judgment was probably a little impaired.

"Well Bubba, these guys want to hurt you. They probably want to hurt me too, but that don't matter much." I took a big drink from my glass, while he rolled his eyes. "And if they suddenly just disappeared, like, off the face of the earth, then the world would be a much better place anyway, and you'd be safe."

"You can't do that, Jeb," Cornelius said, exhaling a trail of sweet smoke through his nostrils.

"Why not?" I asked, accepting his offer as he handed it to me.

"Because you just can't go around killing people, just because you think they need to die."

"I don't think; I know. There's a world of difference."

"You don't get to decide what someone deserves."

"It's not about what they deserve," I said with a cough, and handed back his joint.

"So you want to start a war?"

"I'm not talking about starting a war so much. More like a preemptive strike," I said, smiling.

"You can't be serious," he said. I watched him shake his head while he put the joint back between his lips.

"Why not?"

"You're talking about becoming a vigilante, that's what you're talking about, Jeb," he said, handing it back as he exhaled.

"I wouldn't say that."

"That's what it is. You're talking about circumventing our entire legal system, just because you want to. All our laws, our courts, everything."

"Most laws are bullshit."

"Jeb," he started in, the righteous indignation liberals know so well setting in.

"This is illegal," I said, cutting him off, holding up the spliff, before handing it back to him.

"Ok, this is a bullshit law," he admitted, putting it back to his lips and sucking down. "But going around killing people's not."

"Some people need killing."

"Maybe so, but cold, calculated murder is another thing entirely."

"Not necessarily," I told him.

"You wanna talk about that?"

"You fuckin' wish."

"Damn, there goes my Pulitzer," he mocked, snapping his fingers.

CHAPTER 19

We smoked and drank in silence, not quite watching the documentary on the screen. I was thinking about everything he'd told me, and then everything he hadn't.

"You ok, bro?" He asked, in response to the heavy quiet.

"Yeah, why wouldn't I be?" I asked.

"I know you're in pain, dude. I can see that shit on your face," he said.

"Dude, if you wanna talk about it, I'll listen to you. I know you're not used to that shit," I told him.

"That's it, bottle that shit up," he said, shaking his head side to side while he took another puff.

"You know what I'm bottling up, motherfucker?"

"I was there, Jeb. I saw it," he said.

"I'm good with the shooting; what I'm not good with is you keeping shit from me."

"Why do you think I'm keeping anything from you?"

"Morales showed me a picture of a girl. She used to work for Torres at LARO. 'Bout six months ago someone broke into her apartment and kidnapped her. They found her out in the woods near Joe Pool Lake, on a fucking spit. Raped, tortured, killed, and barbequed. Only, no one's really sure what order it was in."

"And *they* think that has something to do with this?" He asked. The thing was, when he said it, there was a change in his tone. That made the hole in my gut grow deep and wide. It made the axe blade in my head bury itself deeper. It made the voice, that of a shadowy figure long locked in the back of my head, whisper sweet nothings in my ear.

"*They* don't know. Officially, *they* suspect she might've encountered some *wetback* psychopath who chose her out of all the pretty little grad school blondes that think they'll save the world doing non-profit work. *I,* on the other hand, have to wonder if it's just one more thing you're not telling me. Like you knowing Torres," I said, letting the anger in my voice rise appropriately.

"I didn't know either of them. Not like you mean. I saw Torres on the circuit a couple of times. We played cards against each other. We didn't become friends. It's not really that type of environment."

"And I'm supposed to believe you didn't know anything about the girl either? That you didn't feel the need to bust out the cape and pull a Captain Save-A-Ho?"

"Man, fuck you," he said. He stood to leave.

"Yeah, that's fine. I'm good enough to do your goddamn killin', but I don't deserve any answers," I said.

"Is that what you think? Really?" he asked.

"That's what I feel; it damn sure is," I said.

"You realize, when you talk about how you feel, you sound like a liberal," he said, staring at me like he was making a point. I stared back and took a drink.

"My instincts, and your bleeding cunt, ain't the same thing," I told him.

"And once again, you're an asshole," he said, his voice rising as he came out of the oversized loveseat.

"I'm sorry you had to kill two men," he said.

"Don't be, I'm not. The thing I'm sorry for is not knowing why," I said.

"None of the answers I'd have to give would be good enough, Jeb," he said. I didn't reply, letting the silence descend around us. He excused himself to go sleep with his demons, leaving me with mine.

CHAPTER 20

I was lying on the couch, staring into nothingness, vast and dark, when my cell buzzed on the coffee table. I swung into a sitting position and took a drink before answering.

"Hello?"

"Bam Bam?" Redwood's voice hissed over the line, using my old call sign. I wondered what time it was in Lugano.

"Yeah, man."

"Why the fuck are people looking into you right now?" He meant Morales and his questions. If he wanted to know, so would people who knew me to be trustworthy. These were the kind of people you don't want thinking you're not trustworthy.

I told him everything that happened, just as it had happened. We'd served together, running recon when everything was still the wild, wild fucking west, and then again after I killed my marriage, and after he'd put the word in for me. And, on the Task Force, when we'd stepped through the looking glass. I'd spent a lot of time doing a lot of dumb shit with the man.

"That's all?" was all he asked when I was done, which meant someone had been worried, which would be bad. This, however, could be checked out for what it was before anyone got scared, or did anything everyone would regret. It was largely for this very (big) reason I had decided not to go any further down that particular path. When people get paranoid, they don't even trust the people they know they should, afraid of who they'll have to answer to every few years.

"'Fraid so, Bubba. How are you doing?" I asked. There was a long pause while he thought over what to say.

"So what's up with you? You need any help?" He asked, instead of answering.

"No, this shouldn't be a big thing."

"What about that other job coming up?" The other job was actually just another security contract. I'd been thinking heavily on it, and while it looked like a standard gig, I was leery of bumping into people who made the profession look like everything the media made it out to be.

"I don't know man. Gotta finish this first."

"I'm off the next couple of months. If you need the cavalry to come calling, just yell."

"Thanks, brother," I said.

"Don't thank me for that, man, you're all the family I got." Then he hung up, and I sat in the dark, thinking of all the places I'd been, and the things I'd done. Even in doing a job I loved and believed in, a job I had an aptitude for, I always felt so very much alone.

I knew hoping for sleep was now completely useless. I took my glass into the kitchen and freshened it up before sitting at the glass topped table, alone with my thoughts. The first six months downrange as a contractor I ran the roads, protecting convoys while getting goods and people to their destinations. Then, the company's close protection team took a hard hit, and I got moved up to the big time. Six months after that, instead of taking R&R, I came back to the States just long enough for sniper/counter sniper training. Six months after that, everything went completely insane, and I saw a side of the war effort I wished wasn't there.

The scrutiny placed on those tasked with keeping America safe only increased the need for men like myself. It was safer to outsource certain work to people loyal to their country, yet unburdened by the demands of law, career, or a set of murky, easily changed rules. Men outside the system who literally couldn't care less about senate subcommittee hearings. Men without families to speak of or pensions to ensure.

I hated the overwrought melodrama so often involved in the work when you crossed that line, the lies and deception, and the ever-increasing paranoia. I'd loved being a soldier at war, but hated the army, especially in garrison. The mind numbing bureaucracy that ate away at your soul, stubborn career driven men who thrived in garrison life, only to show their fear and cowardice in the face of bravery, as nineteen-year-old kids with drug problems saved their lives. In many ways, being a security contractor was everything I loved about soldiering with less of the things I despised about uniformed service: more freedom, less bureaucracy, much better pay.

Working with the Task Force, a lot of lines had gotten blurred.

I didn't like games, I didn't like playing cat and mouse with people who enjoy deception for deception's sake. Rather, it was the layers upon layers of lies people in that world threaded together, telling themselves it was for their own protection that bothered me. I hated that.

I hated being lied to, and I despised myself for doing the same thing, even when it was necessary. I'd met a great many people in that world who, as far as I could tell, had no code whatsoever, which made me hate them, and my own involvement with them, even more than my enemy. When we got to a place where I could leave, I did so. Of course certain people still held certain markers, but they trusted that I had no desire to be anything but hired muscle, and was not a threat. I hated spies, at least the pretentious Yalies and Princetonians I'd known and their world, but Redwood, my old friend, found a place where he could thrive, and I'd found another place I didn't quite belong.

CHAPTER 21

The next morning, I skipped thoughts of exercise for coffee and a big glass of water. While cooking breakfast sandwiches of crumbled sausage, scrambled eggs, onions, peppers, and lots of cheese for Cornelius and myself, he stumbled in and fixed a Bloody Mary, mumbling something only he could decipher. Probably reconsidering his worldview due to my brilliant articulation the night before of the overwhelming benefits of personal freedom and free market economy over the failed bureaucracy socialism inevitably brings. Or some such shit. Maybe that was just me being hopeful. At least he wasn't pissed.

He found his Copenhagen and put his morning dip under his lip. He sat down at the table, squinting at the sun's rays coming in through the pecan tree near his back fence. Sometimes the wind would pull the pecans into the pool, and it would be just one more thing to clean, but he liked having it there. I liked the idea of having a pecan tree in my back yard. I made yet another mental note that one day when I had enough money to buy land and build a home back in East Texas, it had to have a pecan tree. Probably several, along with pine, oak, and cedars, nestled within the odd mixture that marked our home county as the ragged edge of the old south. That was a long way away though, and the here and now was all I really wanted to think about.

Cornelius didn't have much to say until I stuffed his portion into a hollowed out half of Italian bread, and stuck it on a plate under his face. He smelled it while I went back and fixed my own before sitting opposite him. He placed his dip on a napkin and rinsed his mouth with some water.

"This shit smells good, dude," he said, taking a small bite. I grunted in return.

"How about I call your brother, see if he wants to take us out to the shooting range?" he asked. I started to make a snide comment about his politics or his manhood, something concerning the incident in the parking lot forcing his balls to drop, but fortunately I was too busy eating to make an ass of myself. I knew he'd seen violence in the Peace Corps, as well as growing up in rural East Texas, but in Africa it had been rare, isolated, and never directed at himself. Back home, if the violence he witnessed wasn't my fault, then I was invariably in the middle of it. The day before, not to mention the shooting at the bar, had largely been new experiences for him, and now he wanted to reassure himself that he was more than capable of taking care of himself. He didn't deserve me being an asshole by cheapening the events of the previous day, or his actions by belittling him. Besides, if I was honest, we'd been engaged in same political debate since before either of us could even vote. Odds were good I'd have another chance to have my say.

"Sounds good man," I said, munching away.

We wanted to make it to the range before the sun hit full broil, but that was just not in the cards. Joshua could take off work, but Maggie wanted to come, and she couldn't move until lunch. This gave me plenty of time to use Cornelius as a training dummy, allowing me to brush up on my skills as an instructor, while putting him through a dry range in the backyard.

He scoffed at first, not seeing the need to learn how to affect a quick magazine change, something about not being in a war zone. However, I convinced him it was for me, to work on my teaching skills, so he bore with me. He didn't gripe when I showed him how to work the various stoppages, or jams, and picked everything up without too much trouble.

We didn't come to a significant problem until he wanted me to teach him how to draw his handgun from concealment. A simple thing, like drawing your handgun from concealment, utilizes a specific methodology in order to do it properly. Anyone who carries a gun and doesn't recognize this is an asshole.

Unfortunately, for whatever reason, people who carry guns everyday are usually the worst offenders. Maybe it's just the law of averages. Armed citizens, people who take their own time and money to learn how to properly arm themselves, often have a better understanding of these things than the average cop.

Unfortunately, Cornelius was one of those people who got his concealed carry permit just to occasionally carry outside his pickup. His carry gun was a Sig 232 .380, and he didn't have a holster for it, content with just sticking it in a pocket with the lint. Maybe I had my work cut out for me.

By the time Joshua pulled his SUV into the driveway, we'd worked up a sweat. I still hadn't managed to convince him he needed to invest in some decent holsters. Cornelius drank water and I packed everything into their bags, while Joshua and Maggie met us on the back porch.

"Why you shaking your head, big guy?" Maggie asked, taking a swig from a bottle of designer water in her hand.

"Nothing babe, just trying to get him squared away is all."

"What's that supposed to mean?"

"He needs to invest in proper holsters, that's all. If the only gun he ever carries is a .380, he should at least carry it the right way."

"What do you have against his gun? It's what I carry," she said, baiting me. I always got the feeling she just barely tolerated me, though what she'd have against me, I wouldn't wager a guess. She'd never mentioned she carried a gun.

"Guys, let's go," Joshua said. He wanted to get there and secure a lane before everyone who didn't have time to shoot during the week got there that evening.

We loaded up in his SUV and headed south, turning off the highway at Beltline, and followed it all the way down to the river. There, we pulled Joshua's stands out, and posted targets onto the rubber backing and put on our hearing and eye protection, taking turns decimating our paper opponents.

Joshua trained like he was preparing for a competition, his hand a blur as it snatched his gun from the slanted, open rig on his hip, bringing it up to eye level and firing before it looked like he'd even locked out.

Despite the things we'd gone over, Cornelius shot with the square range, safety is the fundamental attitude that gets people killed. He held the gun out before him in a good strong Weaver stance, his footing solid and sure, and took deliberate aim with each and every shot. He made me want to drink.

Maggie shot one box of ammo in three rounds through her gun. First, she shot two handed deliberate, like C.W., then one handed, and then she practiced drawing her gun from the side pocket of her purse and firing. She made me want to drink to her. Since she was the only one of the three who actually carried their gun, I was happy to see her train for it.

We went back to Cornelius' and the three of us sparred in the back yard, two on one. Some things never change. We took turns beating the shit out of each other while Maggie ordered pizza and sipped a beer from the sidelines. At one point, Joshua had me in an arm bar, stretched out beside the pool, and Cornelius was standing above us, slapping me across the face. I was more than strong enough to fight the arm bar, but he had my back, and I was wedged. And C.W. kept slapping my face, which he knew pissed me off.

"Like that, tough guy? Like that, huh?" he snickered. I grunted, pulling my arm, breaking Joshua's lock. When I had enough room, I bent my arm and pushed my elbow hard into his inner thigh. My right hand got free and I pounded the outside of his right thigh, with heavy, thudding, blows. There's a bundle of nerves right there, bash those, you'll get left alone. As he folded I reached up and planted a hard blow into Cornelius' thigh. He cursed, and fell over. Maybe we should've been doing Tai Chi.

I crabbed my way to freedom and recovered fast enough to toss them both in the pool. This pissed Maggie off, but she didn't count. She had been sitting on the sidelines.

"Oh, that's good, get him all wet, thanks, I appreciate that."

"Sorry babe, didn't know you cared," I told her, shrugging off my gloves, and taking out my mouthpiece.

"Why wouldn't I care?"

"Honey," Joshua said, cutting her way.

"Oh, sorry, my bad."

"What's wrong? Did I miss something?" I asked, pulling a silver bullet from the cooler and popping the top.

"No, nothing," Joshua insisted as he and C.W. helped themselves out of the pool.

"Sorry, Jeb. It's just, whenever you drop in, he reverts into a teenager. Hell, they both do. Reminds me of my father, and why I left home."

"I remind you of your old man?"

"A little, and I'd rather my son be around the type of man I married."

"Maggie, what is your problem?" Joshua boomed, his wet shirt hanging from his hand. Everyone just sort of looked around, until the pizza guy knocked at the door. I took that as my cue to exit stage left, trying not to feel like too much of an asshole.

I took the pizza, giving the driver too much tip, but he'd had to go back to the car for the extra Parmesan and red pepper packets, so he'd earned it. I brought the pizza through the house to see Joshua pointing his finger at Maggie, clearly unhappy with her choice of words.

Cornelius joined me as I sat paper plates on the table and opened up the pizza and bread sticks. Maggie came through the door, saying her goodbyes, as Joshua stood outside, ringing his shirt out and staring up at the sky.

We sat, and went ahead and tore into the pizza, knowing he'd just make a scene if we didn't. "They having problems?" I asked, taking a bite of pizza.

"No more than usual," he said, eating the cheese-stuffed crust first. Joshua ambled in shaking his head.

"Did she apologize?" he asked.

"Sure," I lied. Maybe she'd be smart enough to play along with it.

"She's been under a lotta stress lately, with the kid and all. She acts funny sometimes. Sorry 'bout that, Jeb; you know I love ya'."

"I know that. Just like you know I love you guys."

"Yeah, hey, I'd better go check on her. I'll catch you two later, huh?" We said our goodbyes and chewed pizza in the silence.

"He's pretty pussy whipped, isn't he?" I asked, to no one in particular.

"I seem to remember once a bitch had you whooped worse than that. In fact, if memory serves, that bitch wrapped you around her finger on two completely separate occasions. In fact, I think you may have married the bitch as well."

"Do you really get to talk shit about that, you know, since you were in the Peace Corps then?"

"Oh, that's right, I forgot. My two years in Africa was somehow longer away and further apart than your four years in the army and the time you spent as a mercenary. I keep forgetting that."

"Why you gotta keep insisting on the m-word. Seriously," I said.

"Yeah well, we need to get cleaned up anyway, and go see Uncle Dearest," he said.

"I figured that might happen."

"Hey dude, you want his lawyers watching your back, the least we can do is stop in and say hi."

CHAPTER 22

We met Uncle Jack in his Preston Hollow mansion. His neighbors included several prominent businessmen, politicians, professional athletes, and George and Laura Bush. His Man-Friday, a massive behemoth of a man in a dark suit with both a small Navy SEAL Trident and the rainbow flag of Gay Rights on the corner of his lapel, greeted us. I felt tiny when he shook my hand.

He led us through the house, stopping only long enough to let C.W.'s aunt stop and chitchat over family gossip for a seemingly required measure of time before she bid us on our way, her lamentation about not seeing enough of C.W. floating through the air. Cornelius, for his part, wore a blue-collar chip on his shoulder he might've stolen from me.

"Thanks, Russell," Uncle Jack said to his right hand guy. Russell grunted, and asked if there was anything else. Uncle Jack excused him.

"That's my head of security, transportation, and facilities. Former Team 6 shooter," Jack said, beaming with pride. Russell did nothing to indicate that he was either bothered or pleased with the acknowledgment of his past life. Cornelius' mouth contorted as if he'd accidentally dropped in a foul hors d'oeuvres at a party and was too polite to spit it out.

I think Jack liked bragging about having a former SEAL in charge of his security more than Russell really liked being in charge. Still, if you're tired of getting shot at and blown to shit, there are much worse jobs to have than a well-paid baby-sitter to the obscenely rich.

"Busy keeping the cogs of the military industrial complex well oiled, Jack?" C.W. asked. Jack shook his head. I hoped Cornelius wouldn't fly off the handle with one of his wild theories about

Uncle Jack being in on the JFK assassination. I liked the idea of his lawyers making sure I didn't go to prison for saving his nephew's life.

"Goddamn boy, you don't ever quit with that old line of bullshit, do you?" Jack replied. He was of average height, but still fit and barrel-chested, with trim, ghost white hair in a no-nononsense brush cut.

"Just asking a question, *Unc,*" he said, folding into one of the deep leather chairs on our side of his uncle's desk.

I hadn't known Uncle Jack well growing up. I could only recall a few odd times being in his presence, notably at the family ranch deep in the pocket between Athens and Jacksonville. I remembered shooting skeet with the man, and talking football and the time he'd been shot down his first tour, his brief capture, and his E&E south. I didn't remember much else.

"Goddamn," Uncle Jack said, turning to me. "You grew up strapping, didn't you, son?"

"I just eat well," I told him. He smiled at that. It was a good smile, one I generally didn't believe men of his wealth capable of. That would be my bad.

"Can I offer you boys a drink?" he asked.

"We're good," C.W. said, answering for us both.

"I'll take one," I said. C.W. looked at me. I shrugged. Fuck him if he couldn't be sociable.

"What'll you have?" he asked, walking toward the wet-bar.

"Whatever the hell you're drinking," I told him. He laughed.

"A man after my own heart," he said. He poured us a couple glasses an unmarked crystal decanter and came back. He handed me the glass. It was bourbon. Ridiculously good bourbon.

He raised his glass.

"To the triumphant warrior… and those he protects," he said. I'd raised a glass to worse. Cornelius flinched in his chair.

It went down like sweet smoke rising off water, with just the lingering hint of something, something hard, but enticing. Like a dim light falling over the right woman's figure, shadows worn for lingerie.

"Goddamn that's good. Missing out C.W.," Jack said, bringing the glass away from his lips.

"Somehow I think I'll be ok," C.W. said from somewhere deep within his sulk. He was starting to piss me off.

"More for us," I said. C.W. shot me a sideways look, and I gave him one of my own.

"You two at odds a little bit over what happened yesterday?" Jack asked.

"Your nephew seems to think I should've waited for him to stun them with his chi instead of shooting them," I said. Uncle Jack smiled.

"Fuck you both," C.W. said.

"Goddamn boy. Man saves your life, you can't even bother being grateful."

"It wasn't so much that he shot them. I think he enjoyed it."

"Nothing wrong with a man taking pride in a job well done," Jack said.

C.W. didn't say anything. I took another small sip, just to stay even with Jack.

"So, you still looking into this mess, or is it over with?" Jack asked his nephew.

C.W. shifted in his seat, obviously uncomfortable at the request, or maybe just the thought that Jack felt entitled to ask it.

"Goddamn son, I didn't ask you to drive me home after shooting the President. I just want to know if you're still pursuing your investigation," Jack snorted, at infinite ease with the rumors circulated about him. Rumors that were so clearly relished by his nephew, his baby sister's son.

"Yes, I'm still pursing the investigation. Goddamn, I just started," Cornelius snapped at him.

"Slow your roll, son. Calm down. I was just asking," he told C.W., before turning to me.

"Jeb, my Jews,-oops," he started, smiled a shit eating smile from ear to ear just to piss off C.W. "My *lawyers* tell me we need to put you on the payroll if you're gonna keep protecting Cornelius here."

"I don't want money for that."

"That's commendable, but, it is your work. Besides, there are legal aspects to it, some mumbo- jumbo that doesn't mean shit to anyone but fucking lawyers."

"Neither one of us work for you," C.W. told him.

"Boy, I love you, I do. You always had more goddamn balls than you wanted to admit, despite your moonbeam politics. But you do work for me, in a sense. Not only are you a stakeholder in the family foundation, of which I am the head, I also own a few shares of that goddamn hippie rag you think you're gonna single-handedly save from extinction."

"Is that a threat?" C.W. asked, his voice hard edged and angry. Jack rolled his eyes.

"Goddamn boy, you are just straight up warped, aren't you? I'm trying to help you here," he said, shaking his head.

"Jack, that's fine. I understand how it is. If you're covering us with the lawyers, I need to cover you by signing some papers. It's all good," I said. If all I needed to do was sign some papers for his lawyers to make sure I didn't go to prison for capping some white trash that wanted to kidnap his nephew, so goddamn be it.

C.W. looked at me like I didn't know what I was doing. I returned it.

"I knew you'd understand. I'm afraid my nephew doesn't understand your work, even though the necessity for it should be obvious to him after yesterday," he said. He knocked back the rest of his drink, and nodded over his shoulder as he turned back toward the wet-bar. "Come on, kid. Drop that down your throat and I'll freshen you up real quick," he said.

I did as he asked, and came up out of the chair. He freshened our drinks, and then turned to walk me to a side door.

"We'll be right back, C.W. Don't bother looking for the original Zapruder film while I'm gone. It's being restored for my next Bilderberg meeting," he called over his shoulder as we walked out the door. I didn't bother looking back to see the look on C.W.'s face, but I didn't bother not smiling, either.

"You handle that shit pretty well," I said after the door had closed behind us.

"What…that tin-foil bullshit? Hell, kid," he said, shaking his head as we started down the hallway. "There's just enough truth to every thing that's ever been said about me to send that boy and every other bed-wetter into apoplectic shock. But," he said, giving me a knowing look as he took a sip from his glass, holding it with his thumb over the mouth for better control. "I just bet you know enough about the real world to know that, don't you?"

It wasn't really a question, so I didn't answer. I wouldn't have been able to think of anything appropriate to say even if I'd wanted to.

It didn't take long for us to come to the open door of another office, and he led the way through, rapping a solid, yet polite rap against the open door announcing our arrival as we stepped through.

Unlike Jack's spacious, uncluttered office that didn't appear to be used for anything but afternoon drinking, Russell's was small. The big man was behind his desk, with his suit coat on a hanger behind him as not to wrinkle it while seated. He wore a Galco Miami Classic shoulder holster with a custom 1911, complete with black maple grips with a silver "Gungnir," Odan's spear, inlay. Russell was a man with style.

The style of the office was that of a guy who worked a lot and got shit done. The desk and side table were cluttered with screens, papers, binders, and various other things. Tossed in a corner was a battered desert tan London Bridge Trading 3-day assault pack with college economics textbooks poking out the top. SEALs always got a lot of their nylon from that particular Virginia Beach maker, and expensive as they are, it would be too nice a bag not to use after ETS. Above him on the wall was a dark maple shadow box with his Trident, his gold Navy jump wings, and four rows of medals topped with a Navy Cross. Second only to the Medal of Honor, they were *very* careful with how they passed those out. Next to it was a plaque from the Pink Pistols.

"Jeb's on board. Get him squared away, will you, son?" Jack said. Behind the desk Russell sat, his suit coat hanging off a hanger behind him.

"Absolutely, sir," Russell said. He stood and offered me a chair in front of the table.

"Goddamn, Jeb's family, you don't have to insist on that 'Sir.' bullshit in front of him," Jack said, laughing. "Get him squared away. I gotta go try to talk some goddamn sense into my idiot nephew."

Jack left, drinking his ridiculously good bourbon as he skipped merrily down his marble hallway. Russell looked at me across the desk for a long moment. I smiled, and drank some of the good bourbon. He opened a drawer, and pulled a sheaf of stapled papers out. He leaned across the desk and handed them to me. I flipped through them.

"Do you need a gun? I know they didn't give your Glock back."

"I'm good; it's taken care of," I said. I didn't bother asking how or why he knew I'd used a Glock.

"What are you carrying now?" He asked, making small talk.

"Poor man's version of what you got," I said. I took another drink and kept reading.

"I got a guy out in Santo, does all my work. I'll introduce you, you want."

"Maybe sometime, I'm good with what I got for now," I said. The thing about custom guns, when they work, they're a dream. When they work. This wasn't the time to start fucking about with one.

I found the lines I needed to sign, and leaned forward, putting the paper atop the desk to write.

"You know, we have mutual friends," Russell said as I signed my name. I'd been wondering if we were going to go there. The whole wide world is nothing but a collection of sewing circles, and professional gun fighters are the cattiest bitches around.

"Yeah, that's been in the back of my mind since we shook hands," I said.

"You got a good rep, dude. Everybody likes you. Maybe not the chip on your shoulder, but since no one knows what the fuck it's from, they don't seem to mind it."

I didn't say anything to that. Just nodded my head and finished scrawling my name.

"My point is, Shaw," he said, searching for the right words. "I have my differences with Jack's nephew. It's a little insane that you two are such good friends. But, Jack considers you family. And mutual friends say good things about you. So, my point is, if you need something, all you have to do is ask. We have too many resources not to be used."

"Such as," I asked, handing back the papers.

"Whatever you need. We have a variety of business interests. Real estate, security people, investigators, all manner of things," he said.

"What about safe houses and dedicated security vehicles?"

"Of course, that shit's easy," he said. "Think you'll need it?"

"I don't know. I don't know if Cornelius would agree to it if we did."

"Why give him the choice," he asked. I shrugged. If only life were so easy.

Russell opened a drawer, pulled a card from it, and handed it across the desk between two fingers. "Here you go. Feel free to call that number at anytime," he said. I took the card, and slipped it in my wallet.

"What's with the biker schtick?" He asked.

"Walkabout. I'm supposed to be on vacation," I told him.

"That sadness in your eyes, bro? I've seen it before. You might want to take a break from the life. Maybe find a semi-permanent gig."

"Like you got here?" I asked.

"I like where I am. It's steady, and I can trust the man I work for. You don't get that by being *ronin* your whole life."

I shrugged. I'd heard it before, and from men who knew me far better.

Behind me, I heard a cough, and followed Russell's eyes over my shoulder to see C.W. poking his head in.

"You done here?" he asked.

"Yeah," I said. I downed my drink and stood, setting it on the desk. Russell didn't seem to care. We shook hands, and I joined Cornelius on the trek down the marble hallway.

CHAPTER 23

We were debating what to do for dinner when his phone rang. He had to set his bong down to go pick the house phone up off its hook in the kitchen. A moment later he tossed it on my chest and sat back down. I covered the mouthpiece with my hand and asked him who it was. He just grinned at me.

"Hello," I said into the phone.

"Hey, it's Rosie," came the voice on the other end. I sat up, as excited as a puppy with a rib bone.

"Why hello, Officer McCrummin, and how are you this evening?" I said, winking at Cornelius. He stared at me in disbelief.

"I hope you don't think this is too forward, but I was hoping you might want to take me for a motorcycle ride."

"There's no such thing as too forward, darlin'," I assured her. She gave me her address, and I told her I'd be there shortly. I sat the phone down on the table, and grinned at Cornelius, who was eying me like he couldn't quite believe it. I stuck my tongue out and flexed, laughing maniacally.

"Oh, go ahead, rub it in. You're going to go get laid, whoopdie-do. Bet you she won't let you use the cuffs."

"We'll see about that," I said, jumping on him, fake-humping him like a dog.

"Oh, God, oh God, get off me! Ahhhhh," he squirmed, laughing in his chair.

She rode with her hands gripped to my torso, her large breasts pressed firmly against my back, pulling me into her as we rolled smoothly down the road. Traffic was light enough to permit a little throttle, but there was no point showing off, at least not too much.

She didn't want to be seen having dinner with me, so we went out 67 to Cedar Hill, to a little Mexican place I knew in the open air mall, Matt's Rancho Martinez. We sat in the bar, and I drank sweet tea while she tossed back margaritas on the rocks and Tecates. We ate chips and salsa and made the usual small talk people make when they're feeling each other out.

As a rule I despise small talk. It so rarely means anything, yet is so often necessary in daily life, especially on first dates. She either had a gift for it, which was unlikely given her profession, or she was genuinely interesting, and for that matter interested in me.

If she hadn't been interesting, I wouldn't have had any trouble faking it. She was gorgeous, with that old school, thick muscular body that takes so much work to keep from fattening. Every year, more and more women waste away to the point where only gay pedophiles could find them attractive, but alas, she had a body I liked very much, and I wanted to get to know it much better.

"So, you like what you do, your job?" she asked, sticking a chip, overflowing with green stuff into her small, shapely mouth.

"Yeah, it suits me," I told her, hoping the evening wouldn't take a nosedive.

"Killing people?" she asked. Pilot to co-pilot, we have engine trouble.

"That's not what I do," I said, drinking sweet tea, crunching on ice. Lying through my teeth.

"But it's a part of it," she insisted, her dark eyes warm and lustrous, invitingly fueled by the alcohol in her system. She was one of those. She probably didn't even like me, just wanted a bad boy. Oh well, at least she wouldn't want a commitment.

"Sometimes," I said. "But it can be a part of what you do, too. Ever think about that?"

"All the time." Oh yeah, she was one of those. The green-zone had been full of models turned network reporters who practically preyed on contractors. It'd always made me a little sad since most, if not all, of them were married. But, I'd been hung up on my own failed marriage then, so I wasn't in a position to judge anyone.

"Can I ask you something?" She asked. *Here it comes*, I thought.

"Sure," I said, scooping a chip into the famous Bob Armstrong dip, named after a politician.

"Does it bother you at all?"

"Nope."

"That's all you have to say about it?"

"Yep."

"You killed two people yesterday, and now we're on a date."

"Yep," I said, hoping no one sitting nearby had heard her.

"Is something wrong? I didn't mean to upset you, really."

"Nothing's wrong, there's just no point in talking about it," I said. She shook her head in agreement. "What about your partner, what's he got a chip on his shoulder about?" I asked, switching topics. She smirked.

"Fuck if I know, man. He's just a peckerwood that never gets laid. He has a lot of pent up aggression. I think maybe he's trapped in the closet or something."

Our food came, and we ate. She drank more margaritas on the rocks, and I drank more sweet tea. I was worried I might have to enforce my rule about not sleeping with women drunker than I was, but she knew just exactly what she was doing.

She asked about where I grew up. She'd never been to East Texas except to drive through on the way to the coast.

"It's not exactly far away, babe," I told her. She laughed, called me a smart-ass. Said she'd never been this close to a real life redneck before even though she'd lived in Texas her whole life.

She'd grown up in a large Catholic family, felt bad when she went too long without going to church, and her family gave her shit for not only being a cop, but being twenty six and still single and childless.

"That's a little rough, isn't it? They just expect you to stay barefoot and pregnant your whole life? What about your career? Enjoying your youth?" I asked, pleased with what obviously lay ahead.

"Exactly, I work hard for this body. I damn sure want to enjoy it while I can, ya know?" she said, a little too loudly for candor. A couple of college-aged boys stared until I looked at them. I didn't look at them hard, but they turned away just the same, and I tried not to smile too broadly.

"So how 'bout it, cowboy? You gonna help me enjoy this body or what?"

"Only one way to find out, darlin'," I told her.

We rode home with her legs wrapped around my waist, her hands hooked inside my jeans, her fingers mere inches away from my working brain. I pushed the bike as hard as traffic and sobriety allowed. As we pulled up to her apartment building, she asked if I wanted to go make out by White Rock Lake. I didn't really. Make out, how old were we? But I wasn't going to say no.

She took me to a place I hadn't seen before, a little place above White Rock Lake, a piece of Dallas lost to most of its residents, and entirely to everyone else. We groped and kissed, laughed and flirted, all while drinking from my flask. I felt like a teenager, only better at it this time around. The lake below us shimmered beneath an incandescent moon, its short waves chopped by the wind while fireflies fluttered around us.

It reminded me of my youth, of campgrounds beneath piney woods, the smells of tree sap, and deer feeders full of corn, of cold rain and iridescent lake-water.

It reminded me of even earlier times, before we lost the farm. The connection we had to our ancestors, as we chased lighting bugs through the garden with nets and Mason jars, of evenings spent cooling on the porch with sweet tea and watermelon and homemade Junket ice cream made in ice cube trays.

It reminded me of a life, and an enthusiasm for it, that should last forever.

"Have you ever been here?" she asked, coming up for air, as I put the flask to my lips. I took a big drink just to keep her from getting too far ahead.

"No. I've been to the lake, but never from here," I said, telling her the truth. My voice spoke of wanting to be with her while I despised the concrete and urban sprawl the lake contrasted. The conformity of civilized life.

"Do you like it?" she asked, taking a drink.

"Very much so," I told her, doing my best not to sound as corny as I must have looked. I did like her, after all.

"Not me, this place."

"Honey, I wasn't talking about you. I don't like you at all," I said, smiling at her. She blushed, and responded by lightly biting my lower lip. I let her bite while one hand snaked inside her jeans. And that was all it took, just a touch, and she exploded.

She smiled through the sheen of sweat on her face, looking at me the way you always want to be looked at.

"You better take me home, Jeb. I can't get caught doing this, not here."

"Yes, ma'am," I said, licking my fingers.

I walked her up the stairs to her apartment, where, once inside she excused herself to the bathroom, advising me to help myself to the liquor cabinet. Which I did, *post haste*. I have this rule about sleeping with women drunker than myself. I don't have many rules, and very few morals, but that's a big one. I'd tried to explain my code once to a friend. He'd told me I was insane. Deep down, I knew he was probably right, but I didn't care.

I found a bottle of Jim Beam, and a can of Pepsi and made myself a large drink. I drank quickly, refilling as necessary. When she came out of the bathroom, she was nude, the soft muted light falling over her firm gorgeous body like a sleeve. She walked toward me, her hips swaying with a natural swing other women spent their whole lives trying to figure out.

"Your clothes are still on," she said running her hands over my chest, pulling me closer.

"Not for long."

It was nice, slow at first, yet without the awkwardness first time lovers usually impose upon each other. We started right there in the kitchen. She helped me out of my clothes, and we took turns on our knees. I held her against the wall, her thighs wrapped around my head and over my shoulders, her hands pushing the back of my head inward. I couldn't for the life of me figure out why girls didn't like that. Of course I didn't have to fight a gag reflex. Probably helped out. There was a harsh, angry ferocity inside her, and I am antagonistic by nature. By the time we made it to the bed, the symphony of our bodies resembled a grudge match more than it did safe harbor.

She was all thick, comfortable muscle that would turn to fat the moment she let it. But not then, not in that moment. In that moment she was all heat and power and raw aggression. Her high, firm, beautiful rump bouncing hard off my hips, thrusting back into me. She smiled deliciously over her shoulder, commanding me. Harder, faster, don't stop. Pull my hair.

When she came her whole body shuddered, long and hard, before she shot off me.

"Oh, shit," she murmured. I watched her glistening body relax for the briefest of moments with a sigh, then swing one athletic leg over, and coming up on her knees to face me. She kissed me then pushed me down.

"Lay down, buddy."

"Yes ma'am, Officer."

She mounted me, smiling.

I slept heavily, and woke to the sight of her buckling her duty belt. I shook enough of the fog from my head to find the clock on the bedside table. 7: 15. I was supposed to fix her breakfast.

"I thought you were off today?" I asked, rubbing the sleep from my eyes.

"Yeah, so did I," she said matter-of-factly. She picked her Sig 229 up off the dresser and press checked it, before hitting the de-cocker and slipping it into her holster.

"I got called in," she continued, her voice not quite even, almost confrontational. I sat up in bed, grimacing, my body aching from the soft bed and our workout the night before. When I moved, I could feel long scabs running down my back tear away from the sheets. Her claw marks ran from my shoulder blades to my butt, and they didn't begin to describe the vicious rounds we'd finished up with.

"What's wrong with you?" she snapped, sounding like a pissed off Drill Instructor.

"Nothing babe, I've just got a lot of metal holding me together," I said, wondering if she was always so pleasant the morning after.

"Well, that's your job isn't it?" she snapped. I told myself she was mad at being called in. I was about to ask her if she had time for a quick breakfast when a horn blared outside. She scowled and picked up her bag.

"Listen, thanks for last night. I needed that. There's coffee made. I trust you're not gonna steal anything, so like, please just lock the door on your way out, ok?" She said coldly, and walked out without even a kiss goodbye.

I nearly called out behind her, wanting to ask if I could call her. But I didn't. She had my number, and if she wanted me to have hers she'd have given it. Self-consciousness and awkwardness are never welcome in those moments.

I stared up at the ceiling, wanting a cigarette, and then I heard the door slam shut. I pulled myself out of bed, and limped stiffly through the front room. I peeked briefly through the blinds from the side, not wanting to be seen looking out.

I watched her slide into the shotgun seat of a patrol car, her partner, Shavers, eyeing my bike behind mirrored shades. The scowl on his face could have cut iron. I padded back to her bathroom, relieved myself, then walked back into the kitchen. I poured a cup of coffee, and cut it with the Beam, needing to numb my aching body, I stood in her little kitchen naked, and for some bizarre reason, wondered if I hadn't done something to piss her off.

I kept thinking about it. I set the coffee aside, poured Beam in a glass with ice and Pepsi for my pick me up, and drank it. Then, I drank another. Then another after it. They were short, quick drinks, and it took four turns to empty the bottle.

I drank the last one slowly, standing there, trying to work up the nerve to stretch the stiffness and soreness out of my damaged body, but no luck. All I wanted to do was drink and smoke and hope we saw each other again.

Finally, the fourth drink finished, I padded back across the carpet and into her bathroom. I turned the hot water on full blast and got the kind of response you think you should always have. I stepped into the shower and tried not to scream as it hit my back.

I watched the water running over my feet turn just slightly purple, and didn't care why she was mad, or who she was mad at.

CHAPTER 24

Later that day I was hanging out with Joshua, playing *Gears of War* on the Xbox. The smells of Maggie's cooking filled the house, and we were busy blasting alien scum to hell when we were interrupted with a hard, heavy knock on the front door. It cut through our gaming and laughter as well as the smells of Maggie's cooking. She called from the kitchen, and asked if one of us could answer the door. Joshua shot me a look, and swung himself out of his chair, and went to answer the door. He was pissed because I kept getting chomped to death by a set of giant alien worm teeth on our passage to destroy the beast's heart. I pled the fact that we were playing a game, instead of doing for real. He scoffed at that.

I drank ice water, wondering briefly how long it would take for Cornelius to get there, so we could all eat here, before walking back to his house and the booze that awaited me there.

"Jeb, someone to see you," Joshua said, walking back into the room. I pulled the glass from my lips, and watched Conyers step in behind him. I sat the glass down and stood, wondering just what in the hell this particular idiot wanted.

"Detective."

"Shaw, how's it going?"

"Was a lot better, right about two minutes ago."

"You talk like a con."

"How the fuck would you know?"

"I'm a cop, that's how."

"Whatever. You mind if we do this outside?"

"I like it in here, actually," he said then turned to eye a picture on the wall that Joshua had done. "Smell's wonderful."

"What do you want?"

"Oh, just wanted to check up on my favorite mercenary."

"Security contractor," I said, trying to correct him. He laughed. "Look, whatever it is you have against me, these guys don't deserve to be a party to it. Why don't we just step outside," I said, in what I assumed was a reasonable tone.

"I said I like it in here."

"Officer," Joshua bellowed from the kitchen, his child in his arms. "This is private property. Please, say your peace and be gone, sir."

Conyers took a step back, and I felt a jolt of pride in my baby brother.

"Huh," he said, and sucked on a tooth, his hands in his pockets. "Fine, we can go outside then, biker boy," he said, then spun on a heel and walked back toward the front door. I followed suit, shaking my head, wondering where he was taking this.

I stepped outside and lit a smoke.

"Do you have to?" He whined. I sucked in nicotine and looked at him. He coughed, while I blew smoke. This scene was getting all too familiar.

He stared at me hard for a moment, and then turned away. "What do you want, Conyers?"

"I want to know just what you think you're accomplishing by fucking a police officer?"

"An orgasm or two. You'll find out what that is after you hit puberty," I said, flicking ash. He stared at me for a two count, which was just how long it took for him to turn his frown upside down. Into a sneer. Guess he needed to work on his happy face.

"How long have you been back in the States, Shaw?"

"Couple months," I answered, wondering just what it was he wanted. "Is there a reason you don't like me, officer?" I asked.

"Who said I didn't like you?"

"Maybe I just assumed it, the way you've treated me," I said. He dropped his chin and looked at me over the rims of his Ray Bans. He snapped the thumb and forefinger on one hand.

"Think you're a smart guy, huh?"

"What do you want?"

"I'm trying to figure you out, Shaw," he said, pacing, making a show of it. He was all alone this time.

"There's really not that much to think about, man," I said. It was the truth. I worked hard to simplify my being.

"You're smart. You know the law, and you keep yourself covered," he said, shaking a finger at me. I wanted a long, strong drink and a deep hard drag, and I wanted to pretend I'd never met this man before.

"But then you go putting your dick in places that are off limits."

"That's not really for either one of us to decide," I said. Only a woman can decide who she'll sleep with. All an honorable man can do is try not to talk himself out of some pussy. I find not talking so much helps.

"Don't come here and piss on me because you can't claim territory for your own self. Your failings have no damn thing to do with me," I said. Rosie was a fine woman, and one sure to be sought after. A woman in full, in a male dominated profession, she'd have to make her choices more carefully than I had ever cared to.

"You got some business here or what, big man?" I asked.

"That's it? Really? You're gonna play it like that?"

"Who's playing?" I asked.

"I want to know what you're doing in Dallas."

"Trying to get to know my family," I said. He rolled his eyes.

"That's just a cover, isn't it?"

"What?"

"It's just you and me, so be honest. You're working for Agency, aren't you?"

"Did you OD on conspiracy theories last night?"

"No, but I know all about people like you. Go where the money is, right? Did your friend's uncle hire you? I know he's tied into the Complex."

"The complex?"

"He gives money to every Republican cause he can find. He's on the CFR."

"They gave you a badge, really?"

"You shouldn't make jokes."

"I'm not joking. You're an idiot," I said. Then I turned, and walked back into the house. He said something about not giving up, but I just shook my head.

CHAPTER 25

Several days passed. I worked out, swam in Cornelius'
bachelor pad pool, drank lightly. We ate dinner several times
with Joshua and his wife. I played with my nephew, threatened to
take him to the mall and use him to pick up chicks.

I mowed my Grandmother's lawn, hung out with her. We
watched Fox News and John Wayne and Clint Eastwood movies
and bad mouthed liberals. It was like church, only I enjoyed
being there. I took down some of her recipes to add to my
repertoire. I called Rosie, but she never answered or called back,
and for some reason I cared. Cornelius hit a wall with his
investigation. He couldn't find the old man who had capped
Torres and the biker. The surviving biker of the trio who made
the kidnap attempt hadn't been given bail, and refused to talk.

Their club was under surveillance, and the threat to Cornelius
seemed minimal, so I decided to give him his house back for a
few days, and tore off toward our hometown, to help move
antiques for my mother. Of course, I ended up driving to
Corsicana, in my dad's old Ford, to pick up a couple of pieces,
large pieces of thick, heavy oak. My back was killing me as I
rolled the dolly strap back around, ignoring my mother and her
best friend as they scoffed at my tattoos. They'd been scoffing at
them for two days, and it was getting old. Oh well, like the song
says, you're always seventeen in your hometown, I guess.

I took the bandana I'd been wearing for a skull cap off and
wiped my face when my cell buzzed. It was Cornelius, and he
was frantic, again.

"Dude, you gotta get up here! Fuckers attacked us, man," he
said.

"What? Attacked who?" I asked, pissed I hadn't been there.

"Fuckers jumped us, man. Broke my nose, knocked some teeth loose, but, man, the guy hit Joshua in the gut with a bat. They were going to break his hand, his drawing hand, when Maggie shot the one with the bat. They ran off after that, but Josh was coughing up blood pretty bad, man." His voice was past breaking; he was angry and nervous and scared. I tried to stay calm, but I'd never in my life been calm when my little brother was in danger.

"Where are you at?"

"Emergency room at Baylor. Morales and Fuck Stick are on their way."

"So am I."

I didn't bother going to my mother's for my bike, I just pushed the old Ford hard up Highway 175, cruising into Baylor Hospital and parking in a handicap space. I was directed to surgery, and found Cornelius and Maggie sitting in a waiting room. Maggie was rocking my nephew back and forth. She'd been crying, and looked like she might again. Cornelius was beside her.

"Where's Joshua?" I asked, my baby brother all that mattered. Maggie's eyes filled again, but she held firm, concentrating on rocking her son. Cornelius stood, walking with me to the hallway.

"He's in surgery, Jeb. One of his ribs' punctured a lung," he told me. I stared at him.

"We got here in time. He's gonna be ok. It was pretty scary at first, though."

"Who did it?" I had to know. I had to know so I could do what needed to be done. So they wouldn't be able to hurt the people I cared about again.

"Man, who else? Gotta be the bikers, man."

"Can you id them?"

"Naw, man, they were wearing masks. But she shot one of them, cops are prowling all over every emergency room in town as we speak."

"How's she doing with that?"

"She's not as ok with it as you are, but she's not going to lose any sleep over it," he said. I nodded.

We went back and sat down and tried to console her. She didn't say much. I felt guilty, even though I knew it wasn't my fault. I'd sought out violence my entire life, relishing it. Yet here the people I loved, whom I wanted so very badly to shield from it and from the worst in me, were suffering because of it.

I went to the restroom and washed my face in the sink, practiced some three chamber breathing, trying to clear my mind. It didn't work. It never does, not for me. When I opened my eyes, the only things there were worry and rage.

When I walked back into the waiting room, Morales had taken my seat. He was speaking into Maggie's ear, holding her hand. His eyes were wet, yet professional. Conyers was hovering over them, nodding his head, his face contorted in a smug scowl. As I walked up he turned to face me, pointing a finger at me.

"How do you like this, you bastard? See what you've brought into an innocent person's life?" I didn't say anything. Truth be told, I didn't think much either. I didn't know what his problem was, but he chose to become mine. My world was dim and red, but somehow I managed to act like a grownup. Then he put his hands on me.

My hand shot out, clamping around his neck like a vise. I turned, lifting him off the ground, and ran into the wall. He gagged, trying to get some air, but I just kept squeezing, kept smashing his head against the wall. A hole formed where I rammed his head, cracks shot through the wall. Electricity jolted through me. I refused to let go. Conyers kicked in my grasp, the electricity running through us both. I turned to see a wisp of a cop, all red hair and freckles, holding onto a tazer with both hands. I was wondering when they'd let Strawberry Shortcake join the force when another set of prongs hit me, and I dropped to my knees.

Cornelius was yelling at me, and finally I realized what was happening. I let go of Conyers, whose face looked like a swollen blueberry. We both gasped for breath, writhing on the floor. Only they let Conyers writhe. They rolled me over and cuffed me before I could move again.

I looked up at Maggie, rocking her son, my nephew in her arms while his father, my brother, lay on an operating table just down the hall. I felt guilty for losing control, giving her even more grief. Then Conyers scrambled to his feet, yelled something in what I assume was gutter Klingon, and kicked me in the ribs. Hard.

I looked up at him, the uniforms trying to decide what to do, when Morales came into view with a quickness his age and bulk did not suggest. He backhanded Conyers so hard it sounded like a rifle shot echoing through canyon walls.

Conyers looked at him, tears streaming down his cheeks, blood running from his lips. He started to say something. To make some excuse, something to save face, but Morales wasn't having any of it.

"No! You shut your mouth! You embarrass me, you embarrass the badge, and you embarrass your family! Just shut your mouth. Shut up!" He said, his face an inch from his partner's. Clearly he'd been holding that in a while. Conyers' mouth moved a smidgen and Morales raised his hand again. Conyers flinched.

"Get out of here, go! Vamoose!" he ordered Conyers. Conyers stepped past me. Morales looked down at me. "Can you control that goddamn temper of yours?" He asked. I said I could.

"Get him up, get those cuffs off him," he ordered. Conyers spun on his heels, flushed.

"You're not even going to arrest him?"

"For what? Self-defense, you twit? You put your hands on him, in front of people. People who don't need this shit," he said, his voice dangerously calm.

They insisted on helping me up before un-cuffing me. If they'd un-cuffed me first I could have just picked myself up, but I counted my blessings anyway. Strawberry Shortcake looked at me with wide eyes, slipping her cuffs back into their case. I wondered what she made of my little show.

"Thank you, ma'am," I told her, and she blushed beneath her freckles.

"Flirt later," Morales said. I turned to see him apologizing to Maggie. Then he turned, and led me away.

We stepped outside. The air was warm, with a slight breeze, and night birds already chirped in the trees.

"Do you have smokes?" he asked. I handed him my pack. "Menthol, thank God!"

He lit his cigarette and handed me the pack. I didn't feel like smoking, so I just slipped them back in their pocket.

"Goddamn, that was something; two fuckin' guns, man. Shit, you're a bull," he said, a little jittery. He didn't seem like the jittery type, and I wondered what was coming, if he had to play good cop and bad cop all in one since his partner only played fuckup. He sucked smoke down and looked at me.

"Walk with me."

We walked down the sidewalk a little ways. I looked up at the sky, a brilliant blue over orange, streaked with thin white clouds, the day's cherry fading into purple at the edges around the downtown skyline.

"Look kid, we both know, hell everyone knows, I got a partner whose a straight runnin' fuckin' idiot, and if there's any justice in this world, he'll be outta both our hair soon enough."

"He shouldn't be in it to begin with," I said.

"No, no he shouldn't. But he is. Only he's finally fucked up enough to get himself in real trouble. Trouble his family can't get him out of," he said. I watched him suck on the cigarette some more, wondering where he was going.

"Only what he's done, if it gets out, makes everyone look bad. We don't need that kinda heat, not from the press. None of that. Hell, this city's never more than one bad cop story away from a full-on goddamn riot."

"He lost the security tape from the bar," I spoke evenly. That's the only thing it could be. Morales nodded grimly.

"That's why he's been hounding me, he wants to think I had something to do with it," I said. I took a deep breath, trying to get control of my rising anger.

"I know its bullshit, but it's all he had to go on after it came up missing. You didn't help matters any by running your mouth."

"That's a poor excuse for shoddy detective work."

"He's a poor excuse for a cop. Don't like it, join the force."

"I'm not really into uniforms anymore."

"Yeah, I don't blame you," he said, flicking his butt into the street.

"So what do you want me to do?"

"Listen, the kid's done for. If he keeps his badge, it'll be to do drug awareness seminars at elementary schools. His family might have enough pull for that. But that's only if we keep it quiet, you don't press charges for that little stunt in there, and we keep it and the disappearance of the tape out of the papers."

"Why would I want to do a goddamn thing like that?"

"Because then you'd have not only myself, who's a senior homicide detective owing you a favor, but also his uncle, who's a goddamn assistant chief of police. Think it might be nice to have those markers to call in?"

I thought about it. It didn't take very long. If the cops didn't find the men who hurt my family, I would. Those markers would come in handy.

"What about this shit, huh? What's gonna be done about it? You gonna get the fuckers that did this? Can you at least put some uniforms out front of their houses?" I asked. I'd decided to stop trying to control my anger. I watched him breathe in, the expression on his face not one you expect from a homicide detective, not one you want to see on a cop.

"I can put uniforms out front, at least for a while. Have them drive by at intervals. We'll check it out, but you should know, we've kinda hit a wall anyway,"

"What wall?" I asked. He looked away, rubbing his chin. I asked again. I didn't like the look on his face. Then it hit me.

"Can I trust you, son? Can you keep this shit to yourself?"

"Trust me, you're the one asking for favors, shit."

"IA's been sniffing around. They want to know how the video just disappeared."

"They're not the only ones."

"Get in line," he snapped. I looked at him, wondering if maybe he'd forgotten who'd asked whom for a favor.

"Look kid," his voice softer. "I know you guys just stumbled into this thing by accident, I appreciate that. But you need to convince your friend in there to sit on this. Whatever the key to this thing is, extra pressure's not going to flush anyone out. I need to do some real police work, and we need to let IA do their thing. Between the two of us, we outta be able to figure this out, even without the tape. Losing the tape's bad, but it's just the tip of something else. Whoever took it is smart enough to know they can't risk doing anything else right now. They're gonna lay low. It might be months, or years before they pull something else."

I calmed down enough to light my own cigarette. I blew the smoke out my nostrils, and looked up at Morales.

"What d'you say kid, gonna play ball with us on this?"

"Not much of a choice," I stuck out my hand.

"That true what you said, about the favors?"

"Long as you don't waste 'em on parking tickets." Then I realized what he meant by favors.

As they gathered their things to leave, I took Cornelius to the side, away from the spectacle.

"What did he say to you?" He asked, looking over my shoulder like he had good sense.

"Don't do that, man, be cool," I told him. He looked at me in disbelief.

"What do you think he said? He wants you to sit on the story."

"Fuck you both."

"Just the bit about me and Conyers, let him save some face."

"Why would I want to do that?"

"Listen, I'm going to talk to him. Conyers just fucked up, but Morales needs the chance to do something with him without stepping all over his family's toes."

"What are you getting out of it? I know you don't want me to sit on it for political expediency."

"He's gonna see what he can do about getting some people on your homes, but he's gotta do that quietly too."

"What else?"

"Once he does something with Conyers, then he can come at this from a different angle."

"You want to explain to me why in the hell I'd want to do that?"

"Information," I said low, into his ear.

"Whatever he says to you, I better fucking hear it," he said.

"Absolutely."

CHAPTER 26

They didn't let Joshua leave until the next morning. Cornelius took Maggie and the baby home with a police escort. I stayed through the night. He was out for most of it, leaving me alone with my thoughts.

It wasn't a question of legality. One in which over-educated sharks in designer suits argued from law books written by them, for only them, in language only they could understand, before a jury of mind-numbed simpletons who could barely read the TV guide well enough to figure out when they had to be in place for American Idol. It wasn't a question of revenge, although pride certainly begged it.

They'd attacked the people I loved. They'd brought violence upon people who should have been able to live their whole lives without having to face it. Joshua, Josh-*a-boy* as we'd called him way back when we still lived on the farm, was an artist, painter, graphic designer, and comedian. His goal in life was to create beauty and make people laugh.

We'd known Cornelius literally all our lives. He was family as far as anyone was concerned. Another little brother I had always protected. He spent two years in Africa digging wells and explaining condoms to villagers illiterate in two languages, for fuck sake.

They were not up to dealing with these kinds of people. Until that afternoon, when masked men approached them in a parking lot, violence had been largely an abstract thought, and it should never have been otherwise. I knew how to deal with these kinds of people. Violence was not an abstract thought in my world. The path before me was simple and uncluttered.

I would find the ones who did this, and then they would do no more harm.

I was staring into the void, the static hum of nothingness as loud as a jet engine in my ear, the first thin streams of sunlight trickling slowly through the blinds, casting their ubiquitous slatted shadow across my little brother's face. Slowly I returned into myself and stood, walking to the window to close the blinds. I didn't want him to be disturbed by something as petty as the sun.

"Hey, Bubba," he whispered through parched lips at my back. I turned, tried to think of something perfect to say, then picked up the cup of water from his tray and held it to his face, the straw close to his lips.

"My arms aren't broke, Jeb," he said, his voice scorched with cottonmouth, his eyelids flittering as he tried to wake.

"You could probably use a drink."

He took the cup from my hand, shaking his head. Clearly, I needed to work harder on finding the perfect thing to say. He smiled.

"How do you feel?" I asked.

"Drugged. It's awesome."

He took a sip from his cup, waited a moment, then took a longer one. He repeated the process until it was empty. Somehow his stomach wasn't upset. My stomach always seemed to be upset after surgery. Maybe he just had better drugs.

"Where is everybody?" He asked as I refilled his cup.

"Home, with Cornelius and some cops."

"Keeping them safe, huh?"

"Yeah, they should be fine," I told him. I thought my tone was reassuring, I thought I was being positive. His voice hadn't sounded frail or weak in the least. But when I looked back at him, his eyes filled to the brim, soft tears leaked ever so slowly by the floodgates at their corners, trailing down his cheeks,. I moved closer, but he put a hand up. When he spoke, he looked down, toward his feet, instead of to me.

"Don't, don't touch me."

"Joshua,"

"Don't start your shit. I don't want to hear it. What you would've done. What you're going to do now. I'm the one who couldn't protect his family. I'm the one who got fucked up in front of his wife, Jeb. Not you. I'm the one whose wife had to save him. Me. I'm the one that's gonna have to live that down."

"He hit you with a bat," I said, pleading with him.

"No. Goddamn it…"

"Joshua," I pleaded.

"I want to be alone," he snapped, cutting me off. And that was that.

I walked back outside and fired up a smoke, wishing to God I had a drink. I would have sold my soul to have been able to trade places with my baby brother right then, even though I knew full well whatever soul I might have left was well spoken for, long ago forsaken for so many windmills that mattered not.

His physical injuries were nothing compared to the fight he faced inside his head. The hurt, the pain, the self-doubt. The deep scars of emasculation that now sat on top of the already strained relationship with his wife.

He'd been caught off guard, bested and busted up in front of his child and wife, who saved his life by bringing a greater level of violence to bear than the bad guy had expected. Hopefully that guy would bleed out slowly overnight, but I hadn't much hope.

I inhaled deeply, watching the sun rise over the city sprawl to my east, the early morning hues pulsating with vibrancy, the pale thin clouds sliding elegantly over a sky of already deep, deep blue, the air just as crisp and clean as modern, urban, life would allow. The leftover shrapnel that had been too small to bother with, the rods left in my back and leg, care of Uncle Sam, pinged, sending vibrations rippling just beneath my skin to all corners of my body. If only the bad thing coming was the weather.

I knew that whatever lay ahead, I would need help and information. With a heavy heart, I pulled out my cell, dialed a secure number in rural Illinois. It would ring on the desk of an old gray beard known as Champ, who knew everybody that had ever made a name for themselves in a particularly tough business.

>─┼─◄▶─◄─◆─►┼─◄

At Joshua's house, Strawberry Shortcake sat in the shotgun seat of a patrol car, her partner, a senior officer with the dark complexion only purebred Italian blood can offer watched the world impassively behind mirrored shades. We parked in the driveway behind the minivan, and lumbered out, Joshua under his own steam, entirely. He didn't want help.

We walked slowly to the front door, the officers silently watching from their car. We entered the house to find Cornelius in a corner, sitting in my mother's antique rocker. The house was filled with the sounds of cooking, a thin trail of smoke coming around the corner from the kitchen. It smelled of sausage and frying eggs and sweet maple. The baby was asleep in his play crib in the middle of the floor, and on the couch were several open bags, in various stages of being packed. Each looked very nearly full.

Maggie looked around the corner, dressed in the same jeans and t-shirt she'd been wearing the night before. She had dark circles around her eyes, and her hair was tied back so tight it looked as if her scalp might split in two.

"You guys hungry?"

"What's with the bags, babe?" He asked through gritted teeth. She leaned against the corner, her fingers rapping against the wood trim.

"I think we should go home, for a little while, Joshua. Get away from the city for a bit," she said. Maggie had grown up in our home-town, but they'd barely known each other growing up. She was a couple of years younger than Joshua, and they hooked up when they blundered into each other in a bar while in college. Where I would've have parlayed the chance encounter into a one night-stand, they'd found love, a relationship, and eventually a family. Her father owned a wrecking company, which he'd built up from one ancient truck to one with several drivers, and two full-time mechanics. He and her uncles were all roughnecks and rednecks, hunters and trappers. When she brought home what they thought of as a citified, fancy, limp-wristed artist, it hadn't helped that he'd grown up in the exact same place she had.

When they realized they knew him, and myself, with the reputation I had, they considered him a traitor to a way of life that seemed to be hanging from an ever more fragile clothesline, fluttering away in death's wind.

"Do I have say in this?" he asked.

"Please, Joshua, let's eat first. There's plenty of food, enough for C.W., and Jeb," she said, then turned and went back into the kitchen. Joshua took a deep breath, and turned around, walking past me.

"Gotta piss," he said, then walked toward the back of the house. I looked at C.W. sitting in the rocker, a spit cup in his hand, watching the baby sleep. He shrugged then spit in his cup.

I stepped around the corner, into the kitchen, where Maggie was stirring milk into a pan with flour and the grease from the sausage. She looked at me, her face without emotion, then turned back to the stove.

"Do you mind if I have some coffee?"

"Of course not. Help yourself, Jeb," she said, her tone no nonsense, all business, the one I'm sure she'd used a hundred times discussing finance with her clientele before maternity leave. I fixed a cup of coffee with the pink powdered cancer and sat at the dining room table, at what I hoped was no one in particular's chair. When Joshua came back in, he had his two-tone Browning cocked and locked, in a leather belt slide holster. He fixed a glass of ice water, and sat down across from me.

Cornelius got up from the rocker and joined us, spit cup in his hand.

"So what are you going to do?" he asked then spit in his cup.

"We're going home for a little while to let Joshua heal up in peace," Maggie said from the stove, stirring the gravy. When she was done, she ladled gravy out and walked to the table, sliding a plate heaped with eggs, biscuits and gravy, and sausage before him. He didn't look very hungry.

"You talk to Morales yet?"

"No, not yet."

"That's bullshit. I'm supposed to sit on that stunt Conyers pulled, and he's flaking out on us. Fuckin' pigs. man," he said, *The Cause* creeping into his voice.

"No, sometimes things take time. He's got to talk to some people, and then he's going to call me."

"And what are you going to do?" Joshua asked. I looked at him, and thought about trying to play it off, but didn't. I'd never been able to lie, and if I tried, he'd see right through it.

"I'm not sure yet, but I'll figure something out."

"Yeah, like you did before you left home last time?" C.W. said, scoffing.

"We're a part of this, too," Joshua said.

"Yeah, that's the problem. Just let me take care of this. I know what I'm doing."

"We're not kids. It's not your place to fight our fights for us."

"Don't make it sound like that."

"That's what it is," he said through his busted lip and blackened eye. Every time I looked at my little brother's face, I heard the monster in the back of my head laughing from the box I'd fought so hard to put him in. He wanted to come out and play. I wanted to let him. I took another drink. I tasted the dark, sweet coffee, and wished it was Jack Daniels.

"Big, bad Jeb, gonna kick ass and take names, no matter what. Isn't that right?"

"Bubba, you got a family to think about," I said, using my old nickname for him, trying to make a point.

"That's right. And I can protect them. Without you getting killed because you just have to swing your dick," he said.

"That's not the way to go about it, dude," Cornelius said, his voice bitter with many things.

"What the fuck do you mean, that's not the way to go about it? You don't even know what I'm going to do."

"Oh, I think we can guess, motherfucker."

"What's that mean?"

"What do you think it means? Jesus, Jeb, we know you. Think we haven't spent the past few years trying to figure out why you just had to leave home again?"

"Bear tell you something?" I asked, though I knew if there was one guy I could trust it would be him. I couldn't ask him for another favor, but I could trust him to keep the old ones under his hat.

"Bear didn't tell us shit. That's not the point, we know how you are, how you think. You just can't go around killing people because you think they need it."

"You don't know that I'm going to kill anyone."

"Shit," Joshua spit, a shallow, humorless laugh. C.W. shook his head in agreement and stared at me.

"Listen, we don't have to wait on Morales. The guy with the bat had a tat on his neck. We can check into that. We can ask around about Torres to some people I know, see what shakes loose," he said. His eyes were gleaming, the light in them dancing with the possibilities before him.

I picked up the water I'd poured with my coffee and took a long drink, then held the cool glass against my head, trying to numb the seed growing inside. I wanted to find an end to this, and if that meant killing another person, or a hundred, fine. I didn't want them to hurt the people I cared about. Yet they seemed to want to taunt them, searching for proof they shouldn't have ever had a need to acquire.

"Go with Cornelius, Jeb. Keep doing what you're doing, protecting him. Just like the parking garage. Wish you'd been there to protect *us* yesterday," he said. His voice was strained and weak, from the deepest kind of hurt, and I hated the world just as goddamn much as I ever had.

"Let the cops handle everything else. It's their job," Joshua said. He had a point, but the problem was so far the cops hadn't been doing their job. They only had the job so people wouldn't have to take responsibility for doing what needed to be done.

"Who the fuck are we going to ask? And what are we going to ask them?"

"Spamson Martinez," he said. I tried not to roll my eyes.

Spam Martinez had been one of the area drug dealers from the time we were in junior high on. He was a huge beast of a man, half Mexican, and, according to him, Samoan, which nobody believed until his cousin relocated to East Texas from Hawaii freshman year. Growing up, all he did was smoke pot, watch WWE and sell anything you wanted. The last I heard, his cousin owned a beauty salon/ home cleaning business/ mystic bullshit fortuneteller shop on Cedar Creek Lake. I knew this because the last time I'd seen him had been when I was working bail enforcement. I'd had to ask his cousin where he was, which she wouldn't give up without reading my palm and talking all kinds of crazy shit about my path. Crazy ass broads.

"Spam's not gonna want to talk to me, not if he holds a grudge."

"Man, that shit's old news. He's clean now," C.W. said, grinning. I looked at him. "Ok, ok, he's clean for Spam. Still, he knows the score man. He's helped me out before. Come on, this is the better thing, the right thing. Maybe you won't have to kill any more people," he continued to plead. I felt older than I was, battered and weary.

"This isn't a war zone Jeb. Whatever it is you think you need to do, you don't. You don't have to go on the aggressive," Joshua said. My baby brother. My poor sweet baby brother. Damaged in front of his wife and child. The things that ran through my mind, everything I would gladly go to hell for, in order to keep them safe and well, I could never burden them with these thoughts. So few people ever deserve to know that.

"What do you think, babe, think I ought to just sit back and do nothing? Let everything run the course its been on? Or should I go on the aggressive, huh?" I asked Maggie, who strode to the table to refill her husband's coffee mug. It wasn't a fair question, and I was an asshole for asking. She hadn't said anything about the shooting, occupying as many moments as possible fretting over Joshua and Cornelius, and over her son. She refilled my cup, looking me square in the face.

"It's what you're good for, isn't it?" She said, then turned matter-of-factly back to the kitchen. Joshua looked at her, his mouth trying to form around words his mind couldn't find, the pain in his eyes, the recognition of hurt and conflict behind it, and the choices before you when your biggest concern is the safety of your child.

"Go, home, rest up a few days. I'll hang with Cornelius, keep him out of trouble while he does his thing. You go home, give yourself some time to heal. Give it a few days, we'll link back up, see what we have, then go from there," I said, hoping I'd have it done by then. I could see Maggie's back and shoulders tense as the words sank in. I agreed with her, but I'd be goddamned if I was going to sit and see such great pain cloud my baby brother's face and not do whatever I could.

Fucking women.

"Ok, ok, fine," he said, looking at me, his pride not yet mended, but a little closer yet, with this brief reprieve.

CHAPTER 27

Cornelius went to order at the window. I slid into a bench with my boots on the seat and smoked a cigarette while I watched traffic pass by. I looked up and down the Hines, and remembered when I'd come there to blow off steam, first as a young roughneck, loose in the big city with 90 days pay, and then again after I'd mustered out, when I worked the door at one of the strip clubs and drank myself out of school.

Back when I'd been confused about myself and my place in the world.

"He'll be along shortly," C.W. said, taking a seat and sliding the two bags of food down between us. He handed me a bottled water and two foil covered tacos.

"Here," he said, I took them, sat the tacos on my thigh, and twisted the cap off the water. I drank half of it then sat it down beside me without capping it. I un-wrapped the first taco, and saw it was filled with skirt steak, onions, peppers, and cilantro, but no sour cream, or guacamole. They might not even have those things. I tried to smile at my whiteness, but could only think of my little brother, his injuries, and the uncomfortable anger his wife felt toward me. I ate anyway. It was delicious without those customary American trappings, despite my heavy thoughts.

"Yeah, real Mexican food," C.W. said, trying to notice something besides my anger. I took another bite and squinted at the sun and watched him wipe sweat from his forehead and put the straw from his cup to his lips.

"What're you drinking?"

"Orchata," he said, making sure to pronounce it properly.

"Good?"

"The best in town," he said, and stuck the straw back between his lips.

"He's not gonna be happy to see me."

"Oh, hell, he won't care. That shit was years ago. It's all good. You worry too goddamn much."

I ate my taco and watched a cab, a well-worn Ford Taurus, driven by a Hispanic man so obese it sagged on one side as it bounced into the lot. C.W looked up and smiled.

"Sweet," he said, and pulled himself from the picnic table.

"That him?"

"Well, yeah," he said, picking up the second sack of food. I picked up my water and followed as I un-wrapped my second taco.

The cab turned a wide circle in the lot around some parked cars, and pulled to a stop facing out. The driver was huge, in the way Samoans are huge, fun fat over hard muscle, and one huge arm hung out the window like Magilla Gorilla. He had a thin dark moustache over his upper lip; the kind that looked disgusting on everyone but him and Clark Gable, and his hair had been cut by someone who hadn't realized even Billy Ray Cyrus had finally let the rest of it grow out.

"Spam, what's happening, dude?" C.W. greeted as the cab swayed on its hinges after the brake.

"Don't 'what's happening' me, motherfucker," he snarled. He was speaking to Cornelius, but watching me. I took a bite of taco and chewed slowly. "What's that motherfucker doing here?"

"Chill, dude, he's with me."

"That motherfucker ain't with nobody but the devil. He's not even real. He's a fucking ghost story white trash back home tell their children so they won't smoke their rock," he said, pointing a finger at me. C.W. looked back at me. I shrugged. It'd gotten bloody, just before I left home the last time.

"Why be that way, big man?" C.W. pleaded with him.

"I'm missing fares to come here. That's money out of my pocket, and you haven't exactly been a regular customer lately, you know?"

"Shit baby, it's all good, here," he said, handing him the plastic sack of food. "Your favorite."

"This shit ain't my favorite."

"Goddamn, I'm sorry. It's still lunch, isn't it? You're still gonna make a little bit for your trouble, aren't you?"

"Yeah, what exactly is my trouble, son? Why you still running around with the angriest kid on the block?"

"Man," C.W. said, an edge creeping into his voice. "Stop being a little bitch. You got lunch, you're getting paid. What else do you want?"

"*Man*, what is it you want?"

"I'm looking for Boudreaux, any idea where he is?"

"Man, I ain't that coon-ass's keeper. What you want him for anyway," he asked.

"Need some info," C.W. told him. Spamson looked past him at me. I took another bite and chewed, nonchalant.

"Yeah, you're good?" He asked, one thick eyebrow cocked in disbelief.

"Of course man, that shit's all old news, bro," C.W. said. The cabbie rubbed his chin in thought. He brought the sack up through the window and set it in the seat beside him.

"He cool?" he asked, nodding at me. I took the final bite of taco and wiped my hand on my jeans.

"Man, this motherfucker is the coolest, trust me," C.W. assured him. Spam eyed me through well- honed slits, and then turned back to C.W.

"Wassup, dude? You scared 'bout that shit the other day?" he asked, an eyebrow cocked at C.W. like he'd never been scared.

"Oh, you heard about that, huh," C.W. said, brushing it off.

"Did I hear about it? Shit man...some dude walks into a bar, and straight up ghosts a Hermano and a Hound during a meet, the whole damn town knows about it."

"Yeah, I guess they do, don't they? Anyway, that's what we're here for. You remember Jeb's little brother, Joshua?"

"Yeah, sure. He was the *good* brother. The artist."

"Yeah, well, some guys jumped me and him. They hit him with a bat. Messed him up. They were covered up, had masks on, but they didn't wear gloves. A couple of them had the same tat right here," he said, indicating the spot between his the thumb and forefinger of his right hand. "Of a rosary and something else, looked like an ink blot."

"Yeah, that's the Hermano tatt. Torres' crew. The spot on their hand ain't no motherfucking inkblot. It's supposed to be a picture of the Southwest, merging with Mexico. They're real big into all that *Reconquista* bullshit. If Texas ever goes back to Mexico, my brown ass is heading further north."

"You have any idea where we can get a line on them?" C.W. asked.

"To do what?" Spam asked right back.

"I'm working the story, Spam. Jeb's just tagging along."

"Some *vatos* beat on Josh Shaw, and all Jeb's gonna do is tag along?" he laughed, so hard the car rocked around his bulk. "Shit," he finally continued, shaking his head. "Man, what you wanna fuck with that shit for, huh? Man, those people aren't people you go looking for, man."

"Spam, can you help us out or not? We'll take it from there."

He looked at C.W. a long moment, before reaching to his visor and pulling a cell phone from a little holder clipped there. He flipped it on, punched a number, and held up a finger. I finished my water and tossed it in a trash bucket.

The cabdriver spoke in Spanish and C.W. stepped away and turned back toward me, nodding his head. I scanned, more out of habit than anything. The pavement was bright, reflecting the sun-scorching heat back toward the infernal lamp in the sky.

One line kept turning over and over in my head.

Yeah, that's the Hermano tatt. Torres'crew.

I reminded myself to Zen out, to stow my emotions, and to wait on word from Champ. Champ had never let anyone down. Champ knew shit God had doubts about.

"Ok," the cabbie said, snapping the phone closed and sliding it back into its holster on the visor. C.W. turned back while the cabbie pulled a pen and scribbled an address on the piece of paper. When he was done, he dropped a hand atop the door, the small piece of paper held between thumb and finger. C.W. reached for it, and the cabbie snapped it back, out of his reach.

"You forgetting something, motherfucker?" he asked. C.W. looked at him like he didn't believe him, then reached in his pocket and pulled out a small fold. He peeled off a twenty and held it forward. The cabdriver just looked at him. He peeled off another and reached forward, a little more forcefully.

The cabdriver exchanged him paper for paper, and they both settled back, unfolding their rewards. C.W. read what was on his note and looked flustered.

"This is what you give me?"

"It's what you asked for, Boudreaux's there, it's his office."

"Man, fuck," Cornelius huffed, kicking at the pavement.

"What's your problem?"

"That club ever open back up?"

"Not yet. You there when that shit went down Christmas?"

"Yeah," he said, flicking the paper in his hands.

"You need some weed or something, dude?"

"No," Cornelius said, taking a deep breath.

"What about you, big man?" he said, nodding at me. "You need some juice or something?" he asked.

"What you got?" I asked.

"Man, I got anything you need. Winee, Deca, HG, whatever man," he said.

"No, forget it, he doesn't need any of that shit," C.W. said stepping between us. I stared at him. Spam shrugged and pulled a card, extending it toward me. I stepped past C.W. and took it.

"Thanks, dude," C.W. said. Spam looked at him, then me, then back at him, and shrugged before sliding the clutch into drive and pulling away.

Cornelius drove us to a neighborhood in West Dallas, way up high on the side of a hill made of hard white rock overlooking the Loop 12 / I-30 mix master. The neighborhood consisted of narrow, pot-holed side streets with small plots of eighty year old tract homes setting atop barren yards of hard scrabble crab grass and shale, the dirt driveways soaked with oil and transmission fluid. The main thoroughfares were two full lanes, on either side of which sat ancient buildings made of cement blocks, their storefront signs proclaimed them as taquerrias, lavandarias, and various mercados, while the dumpsters to their sides overflowed with refuse.

The vehicles that filled the narrow streets varied greatly, from clap-trap work trucks and rusted out mini vans filled with screaming kids, to thugged-out rides with expensive paint jobs that either hugged the ground on shallow rims or sat higher than normal, their suspensions lifted for the Southern Comfort gangsta look.

We parked before a short, squat, cinder block building painted purple, with thick stripes of yellow and green running across at the top. The building contained two businesses, the first of which was a locked door before an empty room, which sat dark through the windows, suggesting a neighborhood bar. The other was a narrow storefront on the opposite end, which advertised calling cards, along with assorted and sundry snacks, household items, and basic hygiene supplies. The advertisements were in Spanish, of course.

We pulled ourselves out of the truck and I followed Cornelius through the creaking door with its dirty, stained glass, into frosty, Freon produced air. A thick layer of dust coated the patch-worked linoleum floor, the aisles contained boxes of various American and Mexican made candy bars, mostly Mexican, and in the coolers were American made soda in cans and Mexican made soda and fruit drinks in big glass bottles and cheap American beer. Behind the counter's glass partition, a thick Hispanic woman maybe three feet off the ground stared at us blandly through thick, speckled eyeglasses. She looked to be dressed in faded maroon sweats and wore her thin black hair in a short, raggedy not quite beehive.

Cornelius introduced himself in English and she stared blankly back. He asked again, this time using a mixture of both English and Spanish, and she nodded vaguely in return. When she did so, the huge glasses nearly fell off her head, and the hair stacked oddly on her head waved front to back.

He asked her something, still using the border half speak, and she came back with the ubiquitous, pervasive, self-defense ingrained in her DNA.

"Qué?" she asked, her head cocked to the side, a thin, mocking smile crossing her lips. He took a deep breath, his eyes moving behind his glasses, looking for the correct words.

"I thought you had an in," I asked him, looking back out the front door, through the dirty glass.

Finally, she relented, and waved us through to the back of the shop. I followed him up the narrow stairwell, wondering where it was all going, where he was leading me. I tensed as he knocked on the door at the top of the stairwell. The door swung inward and a hard middleweight Hispanic with rec. yard muscles, dressed in chinos with suspenders and an undershirt, stared at us. He asked C.W. his name, then shut the door. A minute later the door reopened, and I followed C.W. inside. The office was a large, open loft, with wood floors, a low slung leather sofa against the far wall, across from an ancient metal desk with maybe three feet of paper stacked high atop it without any appearance of organization.

"Been awhile. You placing a bet?" a beer fattened mulatto asked without looking up. He had the soft, easy accent of southern Louisiana.

"Maybe. Need to ask you something first," C.W. said, sitting in the chair across the desk like he belonged there. The mulatto finally looked up to briefly stare at him over the stacks of paper, and then turned his attention toward me.

"Who the fuck is this you bring up in here, not asking first?"

"He's a friend. I hope there's not a problem. He's a good friend of mine," C.W. said, trying to be diplomatic. I stepped to the side of the desk and leaned against the wall, looking out the window.

"So? He no friend o' mine. Hell, I barely even know you. How long since you had some action wit' me, anyway? Since you went to a game? I was thinking I might not see you no more, maybe you got someone else to give yo' action to. Maybe that fuckin' kike down by the fairgrounds, huh? You givin' him yo' money, 'stead yo' friend Boudreaux?"

"Shit, man, I been working my ass off, which is what brings us here. I was hoping maybe I could ask you a couple questions?"

"What the fuck I look like to you?" Boudreaux asked.

"Hey, man, I ain't asking about anything to jam you up. I just need some information on a dead man named Miguel Torres. He was hooked up with some guys across the river."

"Yeah, and I seem to recall he got hisself shot in the head not too long ago. Don't sound like the kinda conversation I want to have me. 'Specially not with the motherfuckers watched him get shot, then turned 'round and put it in the paper. No that don't sound like a conversation I want to have, not at all," he said, then lit the Swisher with a butane lighter.

"Got any money? I got some dog fights. You interested in that? Manny there," he said pointing toward the leather couch against the wall, where the Mexican who'd opened the door for us sat. "He trains the champ, got this one pitt/rottie mix that's just hell on wheels, man. He's a goddamn sure thing," he said, like it was something to be proud of. C.W. watched the heat flash over my face, and raced to find something to say before I started in.

"You outta t'ink 'bout it, you. He a goddamn beast," he said, slipping the cigarillo between his lips.

And then, something deep inside me, that certain thing…snapped.

"Motherfucker, we look like the kind of goddamn white trash pieces of shit that'd want to see a motherfuckin' dogfight?" I asked. He stared at me. "Well, do we?" I asked again. C.W. hung his head. He just couldn't take me anywhere.

"Man, who the fuck you think you are, come up to my office, talkin' shit? I don't even fuckin' know you."

"Yeah, well, you don't tell us what we want to know, or I'm gonna put that out in your eye. You'll get to know me real goddamn quick then, won't you?"

He stared at me as if I'd struck him. C.W glared at me, shaking his head in disbelief. Manny just grinned expectantly at me from his perch.

Boudreaux shot Manny a look, and then waved his little cigar my way. Slowly, grinning, Manny stood from the couch, rolling his shoulders like a prizefighter warming up. C.W. nearly turned around in his seat, watching the scene unfold.

"Hey, man, what's with this shit, man," C.W. asked, like he could talk everyone away from where this was headed.

"Yo' friend needs to learn some manners. Manny gonna school him… real quick like," Boudreaux said, grinning through the smoke from the Swisher. "Wanna place a bet on that?" he asked, grinning around the little cigar.

"Man, come on. This shit's not cool," Cornelius said, his hands out, leaning against the desk.

"Move, C.W. Get outta the way," I told him, watching Manny move, dancing on the balls of his feet, sizing me up. He moved with a gracefulness I'd never been able to achieve. He saw that about me, knew my strength was my power and that his quickness would carry the day. He smiled at that, then squared off, standing with his hands to the side, like a gunfighter in an old movie, and then he opened his right fist and a straight razor glinted at me from between his fingers. I took a deep breath. At least he didn't know how to hold it properly.

I stood there like a big dumb bull, and he didn't even bother to feign with his left before spinning on the ball of his right foot, the right arm extending out, bringing the razor toward my face. I took one-step forward, caught his arm at wrist and bicep, pulled him toward me, and, pushing hard on my toes, threw the top of my forehead into his nose. Cartilage snapped, opening the floodgates for blood to pour out, but he didn't make a sound, and I didn't give him time to think. I brought his arm up, and then down on the edge of the desk. The human elbow is a one way hinge, unless you hit it hard enough the wrong way. I did.

He howled with the snap, falling to the floor, and I slammed his head several times into the corner of the desk.

"You know what I think? I think you need a haircut," I said, coming up with the razor. I'd worn my hair long once, when I still had enough hair to get away with it, and I knew the pride men with long hair took in that particular statement.

I wrapped his ponytail around my hand, as I opened the razor and brought it to bear. He cried out as I did so, reached up trying to grab at my hands, and I bashed his head again into the corner of the desk with a bang. Then I cut the thick rope of it off behind the rubber band, and he fell to the floor unconscious, bleeding from his nose, and eye socket.

I looked up at Boudreaux still setting in his chair, now holding a nice old snub-nosed Smith and Wesson model 66 .357 Magnum with some nice old Ajax black pearlite grips, his fat hand shaking with fear. I tossed the bundle of hair onto the stacks of paper, and stepped around the desk toward him, folding the razor over my knuckles the way people did when they fought with them on a regular basis.

"Jeb," C.W. yelled behind me, trying to yank on my leash. I didn't even bother to acknowledge it.

"You stay the fuck away from me, you," he said. His thumb reached up to cock the hammer back, and when he did so, I reached out, grabbed the gun, wrapping around the cylinder, forefinger beneath the hammer, and twisted it away, punching him several times in the chest and gut using the straight razor as brass knuckles. I slashed his wrist, then turned the razor in my hand, and ran the blade across the back of his hand. I doubted the blade cut deep enough to actually sever the tendons, but figured it was worth a try. He let go of the gun, his weak mind telling him to, then I hit him with the butt, slamming it into his face, hammering him with it until he fell from the chair in a bloody, crying heap.

I looked down at him, and tried to catch my breath. Cornelius stared at me from the seat he hadn't the time or foresight to vacate.

I folded the razor closed and slid it into my back pocket.

"You're fucking crazy," C.W. muttered, staring at me. I shrugged, turned the gun over, holding it in my hand, and swung the cylinder out, checking the load. "You're not going to kill him. I'm not going to let you fucking kill him."

"C.W., what the hell makes you think you have a say in the matter?" I asked, and snapped the gun closed. Boudreaux was on his back, staring up at me, blood running down his face, his blood soaked shirt glued to his body. I hovered over his body, grinning. He shook his head, trying to backpedal.

"Stop it, you're not going anywhere," I said.

"Hey, man, come on now, you don't wanna do nothin' can't be undone, man," he begged.

"How the hell would you know what I wanna do and what I don't?"

"Man, I'm fuckin' sorry! Please, baby. We got off on the wrong foot, man."

"Oh, you think?" I asked.

I reached down, grabbed him by the collar, and jerked him up against the wall.

"Man, what is this shit? What kinda guy are you, man?" he asked. I held him against the wall, my forearm in his throat, the barrel of his gun, right before his eye.

"The kinda guy will blow a motherfucker's head off with his own gun. That's what kind," I said and eased the hammer slowly back. C.W. reached out, grabbing at the .357.

"Stop it," he said, his voice hard with determination.

"Fine," I said, dropping Boudreaux to the floor. "You talk to the piece of shit."

I turned and walked back to the desk, pulled his chair up off the floor, and sat down, going through his drawers.

"Hey, man, come on now, just talk to me. Nothing else is going to happen."

"Keep that motherfucker away from me," Boudreaux bellowed as C.W. helped him to his feet.

"It's all good, he's not going to hurt you anymore," he said.

"Oh, I might," I said, almost under my breath, and C.W. glared at me. I watched him walk the fat bastard to the couch and rolled my eyes. He just glared at me. I went through the desk. There was a box of shells in one drawer, along with a cheap lock back pocketknife, along with reams and reams of paper. I didn't even try to go through it. I took out the box of shells and emptied it into a pocket of my vest. Next, I pulled a Swisher Sweet from the pack on the desk.

Cornelius pulled a roll of paper towels from the bookcase beside the couch, and tried to help him clean up. Boudreaux watched me through narrow slits, and I watched right back, sitting behind his desk, slowly unpeeling the cellophane from his cigarillo, lighting it with his butane lighter. Cornelius looked at me, shaking his head for the umpteenth time.

"Man, you didn't have to do all that. Look at Manny, man," Boudreaux whined from the couch.

"Shut your fuckin' mouth, bitch. He's the one came at me with a razor, you're the one, came at me with a gun. How fuckin' sad are you two? Shut the fuck up and answer C.W.'s questions, or I'll cut both your fuckin' throats and leave you here to rot," I said and stared at him, smoking his cigarillo.

"Man, I don't know shit. All I know, is sometimes he brought me some business. That's it. That's all."

"Come on now. There's got to be something else."

"Man, I met him not long after I settled in, after Hurricane Katrina. He was just outta the service."

"How'd you two meet?"

"Alejandro. The lawyer man, he owns this building, man," Boudreaux cried. C.W. shot me a glance that said he didn't feel like hearing it.

"Man, you didn't know Torres, man. He was into some heavy shit. He knew some scary dudes, man."

"Who was he working for?"

"Man, I don't know. Just some heavy motherfuckers. Motherfuckers that move shit, man. Weight. They do something, they do it big, you know what I mean? People, guns, dope, women. If they move it, they go big, or they don't go at all. The kinda people you don't want to fucking cross, man."

"We look scared to you?" I asked from behind the desk.

"Man, I'm fucking scared, man," he whined.

"Yeah, but you better be," I said, and pointed a thumb and forefinger his direction and dropped the hammer on him with a kiss. C.W. scowled at me and turned back to him.

"Look, can you give us something we can use? Anything?"

"Yeah, man. When I met him, he was hanging with a guy tended bar on the roof of the Malibu bar, man. That was one of his main guys. I bet they were still working together."

"Guy gotta name?"

"Yeah, man, it was a white dude, man. Name of Kendrick. Big, floppy fuckin' carrot top hair and shit, man."

"No, shit?"

"Yeah, man, no shit."

"Ok, man. We appreciate this, man. I'll make it up to you, man," C.W. told him as he stood to leave.

"Fuck him," I said, standing from the desk.

"Forget you ever met me, man, and that'll do," he said, sulking from the couch.

"You better damn well do the same," I said. They both glared at me. I slipped the .357 behind my back.

"You're taking my gun, man?"

"Yep," I said, and walked past C.W., who sounded as if he were apologizing for me defending myself. Typical.

We drove home without speaking, a mixed cd of 90's songs filling the cab the truck. "The City Sleeps" by MC 900 ft Jesus, The Butthole Surfer's "Pepper", Slobberbone's "Broken Down and Barrel Chested", and Primitive Radio Gods' "Standing Outside A Broken Phone Booth With Money In My Hand" were songs he kept going back to. It was like a flashback to high school.

Cornelius drove, looking straight ahead, and I drank a Mexican Coke with peanuts, and listened to the cd. We needed to go home, regroup, and change. Maybe eat some lunch.

"Did you have to take his gun, Jeb?"

"Did you have to apologize like a little bitch for me defending myself?" I asked. He shook his head.

"What was I supposed to do?" I asked.

"You picked the fight."

"You're mad at me, because I defended myself against a bookie and piece of shit that fights dogs. Are you fucking kidding me?"

"I'm just saying it didn't have to go there, is all," he said, then spit in his cup. "You like that shit. You like hurting people."

"Maybe that's where we differ. I don't consider those two pieces of shit back there actual people," I told him.

"I can't believe you took the gun. And the razor. After you carved them up. That's so fucking stupid, man."

"Fuck 'em," I said.

"Fuck 'em? Fuck 'em? More like fuck me, asshole. This is the first world, you prick. You don't just keep evidence. Dirtbags drop dimes on each other all the time. You should know this shit, man."

"You want me to get rid of them? Pull off the highway, I'll toss the shits," I snapped back.

"Oh, no. You keep your trophies, great warrior. Asshole," he said, laughing a shit headed laugh. I wanted to say something but knew he had a point. Keeping the gun and razor had been a bush league move on my part, one driven by ego as much as my desire not to leave my enemies weapons.

He stared straight ahead, his hands tightening around the wheel, and started to say something else, only to be interrupted by my cell.

"Brother Bam-Bam, we good on your end?" The voice on the other end asked. The voice, that of a spooky, herb soaked old hippy masking an old pro and deadly operator, a legend in the most dangerous circles, long gone to semi-retirement, a mentor to a precious lucky few of my generation in the business. He was asking whether my phone was secure, which it wasn't.

"No brother, it's really not."

"No problemo, dude. Did you get my letter?" He asked, referring to an encrypted email he would have sent to an email address only he and two other men knew of.

"Not yet, I'll check when I get a chance."

"Sooner you read it, the better. And brother, be *chill*. The man's family. I vouched for you, and now I'm vouching for him, *dig*?"

"With a fucking shovel."

"I knew you were righteous. Should I make preps for a reunion?"

"Don't know yet."

"Well, let me know if I do. Family sticks together, hoss," he said, sounding much like Ro had a few nights before, and hung up without another word.

CHAPTER 28

The address I'd been given in Champ's email turned out to be a mailbox in an old motel in Oak Cliff. Someone had long ago renovated it and turned into apartments. I found the corresponding numbered door, but no one answered. I looked around, sucking in nicotine. I didn't want to leave empty handed, but this wasn't the kind of place you go asking about someone uninvited.

In the small courtyard jutting out into the parking lot, children splashed in the pool, attended to by short, thick, watchful women who had categorized me the moment I pulled in. Most of them were Hispanic, and they ignored me the second they decided I wasn't official. The few whites eyed me through thin narrow slits. Their eyes betraying the walled off, angry look country people give outsiders even after they've left home in search of work within the city's wilds, afraid I was a dealer here to lead their men back down the road to ruin. There were even fewer black faces, despite the neighborhood, and they shared their white sisters' sneer. The inner city and the deep country are a lot alike that way. You pick yourself and your family up a little bit, keep your man on the straight and narrow, you'll do anything to keep from sliding back down. At least they found something in common. That's always nice.

I walked across the street to a Mexican dive, and sipped slow beers until dusk, watching the apartment building. When he finally arrived, he was driving a pristine classic El Camino. I finished my beer watching him carry a load of groceries up the stairs to the last apartment on the second floor. The walkway was wide enough to contain a porch swing on a tubular metal stand with a canopy, but instead he pulled a chair outside, where he could watch the kids in the pool, and took his seat, opening up a newspaper. I noticed he left the door open.

I finished my beer as a dark blue Toyota Land Cruiser driven by a mocha colored goddess with a short brown almost- Afro pulled into the parking lot. If I hadn't had business to take care of, I would have stayed in my seat and drooled over her when she walked in.

I left the empty bottle next to the ashtray full of smoldering menthol and walked outside into the bright, baking afternoon sun. Heat simmered, shimmering off the pavement in waves, and felt like an iceberg compared to the lasers that bore into my flesh from the chair on the second story balcony. I could feel his eyes on me the whole way, though he pretended to read his paper. I walked across the street, through the parking lot, and up the stairs. I approached him with my hands clearly to the side, not wanting to spook anyone as quick as he was.

"Might skittish, ain't ya?" he asked, scoffing, as I neared.

"Just bein' careful, old man," I said, telling him the truth. A thick chocolate pit with gray streaks on her muzzle and chin padded out and lay easily in the doorway, eying me like a snack.

"That's a beautiful dog," I said.

"Yep," he said, still not looking at me. He picked a dixie cup filled with crushed ice and what smelled like gin and tonic with a lime twist from the other side of his seat. "Call me old again, I dare you." He smirked. "I hear you're a good man," he said after a brief pause, turning his glass up.

"I have my moments," I said.

"Don't we all," he muttered, as he chomped on some crushed ice.

I leaned against the railing and waited.

"The man's recommendation is better than gold," he said, then cast a sideways glance toward the stairs. A little Hispanic boy, about seven, maybe eight, bounded our way, a foil covered casserole dish in his hands. The dish looked twice as big as he was.

"You a drinker, son?" he asked, eying the boy out the corner of his eye.

"Waitin' on you to ask, old man," I said.

"Go inside and fix yourself a drink, gotta take care of somethin'," he said, nodding his head toward the little boy at the top of the stairs. I looked down at the bitch lying in the doorway.

 "Don't worry, she's had dinner."

Very carefully I stepped over the dog and into a massive studio, and found the wet bar in the kitchen area. It looked like two apartments combined, and there was a set of stairs indicating he had both floors to himself. I found the bar, and fixed myself a stiff one with the gin, tonic, and lime that was already sitting to the front for use, on the rocks with crushed ice.

I watched the pit slobber lovingly as the little boy patted her head before walking away. As soon as the child left, she swiveled her head back to me, her eyes unmoving, her head cocked to the side as if in curious thought.

"I think I'm in love with your dog," I said as I stepped over her and back to the railing.

"She's got that effect on people. Big as you are, I hope you got an appetite. This is his momma's way a tellin' me she's short this month."

"I'm sure that gets old," I said, like it was any of my damn business.

"I don't mind, hell I don't need any more *goddamn* money, anyway," he said, a certain viciousness to his words. He sat holding the casserole dish in his lap. He folded his paper up and laid it across the top, and then pulled a work of art out from under the dish and sat it on top of that. Not threatening, he wasn't the kind to waste time with bullshit posturing. He probably never had been. He scratched behind an ear with the barrel of a beautiful, Colt model 1917 .45ACP, cut down, half Fritz special, with ancient Franzite fake stag grips.

"You know we're bein' watched right now?" He asked, only it wasn't a question. It was a test. I had to force myself not to turn around.

"To die for black girl driving a dark blue Land Cruiser?" I asked, thinking about the goddess I'd seen pull into the parking lot across the street.

"You noticed?"

"She's kinda hard not to," I said, thinking maybe at least now I'd get a look at her figure.

"Did you notice the grubby guy in the tan sedan up the street?" He said, standing.

"Ah…," I stuttered.

"Don't worry. When I was yo' age I thought with my dick first, too," he said, laughing.

"You know who they are?" I asked.

"Yeah, couple of private investigators. They work for a man whose path used to cross mine some back in the day. Haven't figured out what they want yet, and it ain't worth bracin' 'em," he said, standing slowly.

"Come inside 'n help me eat this. We'll jaw about this shit we're in," he said over his shoulder as he walked inside. The pit followed, and I followed her.

"You want me to shut this door?"

"Yep," he said, setting the dish on his small breakfast table, and going into the kitchen, bringing out paper plates and plastic forks.

"Sit down, son, shit. I don't hold for formality none."

I took my seat, wondering where this strange evening was taking me.

"So, what's –" I tried to start before he cut me off.

"You're the first goddamn recon man I ever met didn't have patience the good lord gave a whore with a habit," he said, shaking his head as he laid a huge, steaming portion of enchiladas and rice on to my plate. I just shut my mouth and stared at him, as he spooned a much smaller portion for himself onto his plate. There was a knock at the door.

"Give me a moment," he said, picking up his cut down revolver and heading to the door. The bitch kept her massive head calm on its pillow, her eyes roving back and forth with practiced ease. I would've killed a man for a dog like that.

I heard him speak better Spanish than he did English, with a distinct Salvadoran accent. I'd run the roads with some former Salvadoran Rangers, and they were fierce, loyal warriors. Great in battle, and even worse at cards than I was, which says a lot.

He walked back in, shaking his head.

"We got tamales, too. Everybody is short this month—damned economy. I spent half my life killin' communists, now they're in charge," he spat, placing the dish down next to the enchilada's, and then forked some onto my plate. Maybe he wanted me to die of a heart attack.

"You spent some time down south, too, I hear," he said, like it was an afterthought. I wanted to ask him how he knew so goddamn much, but kept my mouth shut. He'd tell me when he wanted to. He clearly wasn't a man anyone with any sense wanted to piss off. Besides, if Champ had vouched for me, he wouldn't have been so rude not to give him some particulars. His telling me that about Champ was confirmation I could speak as freely as I wanted.

"I don't want to be rude, sir," he shot me a look over his glasses that said he was more offended by that than the old man comment. As if I couldn't tell he'd been an NCO, "but I generally like to shake hands with the people I sit down to dinner with." He unpeeled some tamales onto a small paper plate and leaned over to set it on the floor. When he did so, he didn't say a word, simply looked at her, and she brought herself over and sat on her haunches. She didn't touch the plate, not yet. Finally he extended his hand. I took it, and immediately began to wonder how many hours, for how many days, for how many years, he'd been working it. For a small statured guy, he had huge, thick hands. Old- school gunfighter hands. Callused from all kinds of work.

"Joseph Travis Pine. I go by Travis. Friends call me Trav."

"Jebediah Shaw. But you know that anyway, right?" I asked. He smiled at me. At least he had a sense of humor. When he sat down, the girl on the floor coiled up between us and stuck her muzzle on the plate. The three of us ate. The conversation was bare. The food was a religious experience. It was the kind of food that would make a restaurant famous. The kind that couldn't be made for money, only love.

"What sort of name is Shaw anyway? English, or short'ned Po-lock?" he asked.

"Shortened Pollock," I said. He shook his head, like that made all the sense in the world.

"Champ said you were cursed with a poet's soul," he said. I shrugged. "How bad," he asked, hard, his eyes boring through me.

"I don't regret anything I've done, or my reasons behind it. But the people I worked for, and their reasons, well…maybe I think a little differently about them," I said. He nodded only slightly, seemingly satisfied with that.

"He said you had a temper too. Said as stubborn as you are, you could get out of hand."

I shrugged again. I deserved it, I guess. As hard as I worked to attain Zen, when I saw that flash of red, that's all there was. All there would ever be.

He just stared at me a long moment without speaking, before taking another small bite off his plate.

"Yeah, that happens. Eat up." He nodded toward the casserole dishes on the table between us. I shook my head.

"No thank you, I'm full as a tick. If I stay off my feed much longer, I'll weigh nine hundred pounds in no time," I told him, trying to be gracious. He shook his head like he knew just exactly what I was talking about.

"That's what you get, liftin' those goddamned heavy weights."

He unpeeled several more tamales on to his plate, then dropped it on top of the one on the floor.

She inhaled them.

He leaned over enough to look at her when he spoke.

"She likes enchiladas, but she cain't have 'em. Not wit' her ass," he said. She tilted her head upward and gave him a playful growl. It sounded like a purr. For the briefest of moments, his eyes held a distant, melancholy glint. Then it was gone.

"What do you know about me, son?"

"Well, you were a tunnel rat. You let people pay the rent with food, and you killed three people in a bar a couple of days ago. They had the drop on you, but they were still outclassed. You seem to know an awful lot about me, which would normally make me suspicious and uneasy, mainly because what interaction I've had with spooks has generally been negative. But the man who vouched for me, vouched for you, and I know him well enough to know he doesn't just give that shit away. I know you speak Spanish with a Salvadoran accent, which is a little unusual, but someone who had a mind to, might try to fill in a blank with that tidbit." He looked at me for a long second, then back down at the bitch. He snapped his fingers once, lightly, then patted his thigh. She raised up on her haunches and laid her head down for him to pat. He looked to her as he spoke.

"What you think, girl? Pretty smart, huh? Well, I was there long enough, wasn't I?" Like I wasn't even there, just him and the dog. "Son, I been in yo' line a work since long 'fore you was born. I been in this town, off'n on anyway, since before that, when I realized I wasn't welcome on the *rez*," he said. He moved his gaze up and held it on me. "It's a small world, and I know lots a people. I'm sorry 'bout your friend, and your little brother. Sorry things happened the way they did. Hope they heal up. But we can't go back now, and you know that, don't you?"

"Yes, I do."

"And you want to do something about it, right? Make sure it's over with, and they're safe, for good. Right?" he asked.

"Pretty much," I told him, tossing back what was left in my glass. He did the same.

"Why don't you be a lad, fix us another one," he said, handing me his glass.

Sure. Why not?

I took our plastic cups into the kitchen and fixed them strong. Cherry and chocolate aroma hit my nostrils, trying to mask the unmistakable hint of Mary Jane, and I returned with our glasses to find him puffing on a pipe. I handed him his cup and reclaimed my seat as he took a drink.

"Goddamn," he said, covering a cough as he averted his wet eyes away. "You don't fuck around, do you?"

"Moderation ain't exactly my strong suit, old man," I said. He stared off in the distance, at some point between the table and another plane, and nodded slightly.

"Good," he said. He stared at his drink a long time. "You know what they did to my little girl?"

"Yes. I saw the pictures," I said. He recoiled at the thought of someone else seeing her like that, and tossed back half his glass. When the glass came down, I saw two clear trails streaming down his face, while his eyes flashed so hot they burned blue.

I looked at him without staring, without shame or pity. I felt neither for the man. He deserved both his anger and his sadness. I was there to help him make it right. If we did that, we could keep the people I cared about safe.

As close to right as an innocent girl butchered can be made right.

"She'd be twenty-five come August. Ah," he looked away, briefly taking a drink, before putting the pipe back in his mouth. "Her momma didn't tell her 'bout me. Or me her. The work I was doin', she didn't think I'd live long enough to be any kind of father. Hell, I didn't either." His voice softened just a hair. The pit at his feet whimpered, ever so slightly.

"Anyway, she was going to SMU when her mother passed. She was goin' through her things. Found some letters, and pictures and such. Found her diary. She lived her whole life less'n ten miles from here," he said, one thick fingertip knocking soundly against the table's surface. "So, she found me. Showed me everything she had, didn't want any money. She was plain mule headed 'bout that. Wouldn't let me help her with school, nothin' else. Just wanted to get to know me. Huh, we…ah, we had a few good years together. It was nice. Been a long time since I had family to speak of. And then, one day," he said, and made a quick brushing movement with his hand, as if he were trying to cast away a foul smell.

"And then one day they took her from me. They did shit they wouldn't a' even done in El Sal. Skinned her, raped her, put her on a spit. She was my rock, my reason, my heart. She didn't have a mean bone in her body," he said, shaking his head in disbelief.

"All she wanted was to help people. And they took her from me," he continued, the tears flowing down his face at full speed. He paused to wipe his face with a bandana. "And now your people are caught up in this shit, too. I'm so goddamn sorry about that, kid, really, I am. If I'd caught their trail sooner, maybe it wouldn't have come to this," he said, more to himself than me. He wasn't used to visitors, and he certainly wasn't used to someone he could talk openly with. I imagined he'd flipped a switch deep inside himself to auto pilot a long time ago.

"I been…out of it awhile, kid. I'm old, slow. Fuckin' decrepit," he said.

"Torres," I started, and he looked up, focusing on me through wet eyes. "He was running his old crew, wasn't he? They're the ones who did it."

"Yes…yes, and no," he said. I didn't reply, just waited on him to explain.

"He ran a crew. Some were from his old set. Others, he picked up along the way. They specialize in home invasions, kidnappings, gun fighter shit. He kept himself insulated from 'em. He thought he was management, more interested in making money. He really believed that *Reconquesta* bullshit. He got tied into the *Zetas*, and was trying to finance a guerrilla force with drug money. That was his goal."

"You id his crew?" I asked. He shook his head.

"Somewhat. The fuck had excellent compartmentalization. By the time I got to looking, they were all laying low. The jobs the crew did were a separate function from his other operations."

"What else did he run?"

"He had a piece of just about everything. Huge chunk of drugs, ran some whores, gambling. Except for the drugs, most of the rest of that was just his intelligence gathering apparatus and beer money fund."

"Why....your daughter?" I asked. He shrugged.

"She must've found out about it. They were…dating," he said, his face turning sour with disgust. "If that's what you call it, I guess. They were fuckin'. Nobody dates anymore. Nobody courts. Nobody gives a shit," he said, no longer looking at me, his voice and stare both trailing off in the distance between us.

I tried to think of something to say while he stared at the spot on the table and thought, absentmindedly patting the dog's head.

"Why'd you kill him when you did? In public? In front of witnesses?" I asked.

"I needed to force the hand of the man behind him."

If Torres had simply disappeared, it would've left a smaller footprint, one the people he worked for could more easily manage. By executing him in public, it drew the public's attention, the press, and of course, the police.

"Uncle Alejandro," I said, expecting a nod of acceptance.

"Fuck no, not Uncle Alejandro. That motherfucker's got a bird's nest on the goddamn ground. Why would he want to risk it by tying into the shit Torres had going on? Fuck, Uncle Alejandro told me the little fucker wanted to kill him. That's why Torres was meeting the biker."

"That explains the range card," I said, trying to change gears and get my mind around the new information.

"Range card?"

"Yeah, I found a range card in his apartment. In a notebook with plans and sketches of the parade route for Cinco de Mayo," I said. He nodded his head, tilting it back to take another drink.

"Thing is," he said by way of explanation. "Thing is, they had a falling out, Torres and Alejandro. Torres wasn't down with the status quo."

"And he was going to have Alejandro assassinated so he could take over," I said. He nodded my way in acknowledgment.

"Bingo."

"Did it work?"

"What?" he asked.

"Killing him in public."

"*Shee-it*," he said. "So far, all it's done is bring you and yours into it."

"How long did you follow Torres?"

"Couple months. I didn't know where to start. At first, I bought the statement the cops put out, about it being a random kidnapping. Hell, it took me nearly a month just to work up the courage to pack her shit up. I'd go over there, and just… be. Just zone fuckin' out. She didn't have anybody but me. Her momma's folks are all gone. Finally packed up her apartment, gave everything her friends didn't want to charity, and brought a couple boxes of personal stuff back here. I set them beside my desk, and then stayed drunk for a couple months," he said it matter-of-factly, and not with shame, but not without regret.

"Then, finally, I got to lookin' through 'em, and things started to click. Maybe if I hadn't fucked off, I would've got to him sooner, and your people wouldn't be hurtin' right now. I'm so goddamn sorry about that, I am."

"Don't worry about that. It happens. I understand needin' a high lonesome. I was workin' on one when we fell into this myself," I said. He nodded.

"You ever hear of a man named Kendrick? Timothy Kendrick?" I asked.

"Nope," he said, shaking his head.

"Bartender. Supposedly he was tight with Torres. I think Torres was his supplier."

"That makes sense. Torres didn't bother with ghetto shit. He was uptown. It allowed him to profile people for his crew to take down. Bartenders can be great intel sources."

"We're supposed to track him down this weekend. C.W. wants to talk to him."

"Can you keep your boy on a leash, and out of our business?"

"I can try. It'd be best if I had a bone to throw him, preferably in a harmless direction."

"Then make sure he gets that bone."

"After that, what's our next move?" I asked. He grinned.

"Follow me," he said.

I picked up the drink fixings and followed him down the stairwell. When he flipped the switch at the bottom, I saw that he'd taken two apartments on both floors, stacked on top of each other, as his own. The top floor had been his living quarters, the bottom his, well, everything else. If he'd been married, it could've been called his man cave, or personal space, but since he wasn't, he didn't have to call it a damn thing to justify it. In one corner was a bench, rack, weight pile, heavy bag, speed bag, and treadmill. There was also a wooden Wing Chun dummy, escrima sticks, and small mat. Most of these things seemed to be collecting dust instead of resting from the hard use of a man training for revenge.

In another corner was an equipment-laden workbench, beneath a shelf of manuals. I saw three different reloading presses. Next to it, sat three large gun-safes. Against the rear wall, two targets were stapled to extra thick rubber. When I noticed the targets, my eyes searched the walls and ceiling, trying to judge thickness. It would be bulletproofed all the way around, as well as soundproofed. Finally, against the corner opposite the workout stuff, was a wall-less cubicle-like workstation, festooned with monitors, high speed computers, maps, photos, and newspaper articles pinned to the wall.

"Goddamn," was all I could say. I now officially had a new hero.

"You like it?" he asked, taking another drink.

"Like it, old man, I hope you fucking-well adopt me," I said, honestly. He smiled at that.

"Don't worry kid. I'll get you tricked out proper before you leave," he said. On the way to the workstation, he stopped at a table that sat facing the targets on the wall. On it were several guns, semi-custom 1911s, and Browning High Powers, a scoped, tricked out version of a M-14, and the newest gun, an H and K .45 caliber in UMP with an integral suppressor.

"Take a seat, kid," he said, indicating an ancient, low-slung brown leather-like couch facing the wall just offset from the cubicle space. I took a seat, balancing an ashtray from the battered coffee table in front of it on my thigh.

"This is what I have on his crew. It was made up of guys from his old set, plus a few hard cases he'd met here and there after he'd come home. They're hard motherfuckers, tough and mean. Some have been to war with Uncle Sam, others down south. All of them grew up in the streets. I know some of their hangouts, some of their homes of record, but it's still a work in progress.

I'm still gathering intel, trying to put the pieces of the puzzle together."

I flipped through the pages, looking for anyone I recognized. They all looked familiar, in the way character actors all look familiar when they play essentially the same role movie after movie. I recognized none of them, but they all had the hard, cold look of men who had long ago accepted violent crime as their vocation. Their eyes were empty, the bodies covered in intricate ink and scar tissue, and, like criminals, whatever code they subscribed to was one precious few of them ever actually lived up to.

"What do you know about Torres' drug operation? What should I look for?" I asked, trying to focus on the task at hand. He shrugged.

"Pretty standard, he's one step down from wholesale, working his way up. Chances are if you get it in a club, in Dallas proper, it's come through him."

"What are the chances we stumble around and step into some shit?" I asked.

"Well, they're a lot better now after you fucked up the wetback at the bookie's office. Word of that will get around, son. But other than that," he shrugged. I didn't like that answer, and he could see that.

"I doubt you'll get anywhere more than you've gotten. I doubt anyone will talk to you, and if you do find this bartender, I doubt he'll say anything without you taking it to the next level."

"In which case, I don't take it to the next level."

"You're pretty smart for a knuckle dragger," he said, taking a drink.

"We're real thin here," I said, staring at my glass.

"That's the problem. They have a broader support system than the Viet Cong, and we have none. It'll sure make life a lot easier if you can steer your friend away. There's no telling how bad it's gonna get."

"I'm gonna try to keep him occupied, hopefully we'll find just enough tonight and tomorrow to veer him away," I said. He didn't reply, just narrowed his eyes in thought.

"Do we have an actual plan?" I asked, hoping for at least some broad strokes.

"We still need more intel. I figure whatever will happen, will happen fast once we initiate. We need to find a weak spot to slip in. *Lift* someone in middle management or higher, and get the information from him," he said, using an old school British spec-ops term for kidnapping, or taking a prisoner. "Think your poet's soul can hold up to asking someone the questions we need to ask?"

"It's holding up pretty well so far," I said. "We'll need a whole lot more than just me and you to storm this motherfucker."

"Yeah, I got some *hands* comin' in. Plus, you should know, Eric's sending out invites for a reunion," he said. My face betrayed the fact that I'd never heard Champ's given name, and that I had refuted his offer of calling a reunion.

A reunion is gunfighter speak for a personal op., where you call up all your buddies from the bad old days to right some wrongs and go out like Butch and Sundance's older, bigger-dicked, ballsier brothers. It was a myth, a tired old joke among drunken contractors, the stuff of paperback novels and bad action movies. It didn't happen in real life.

I had declined his offer to call one, and had no intention of asking for one. I wanted to keep the work I did as far away from the people I cared about as possible.

I took another drink and tried to hide my feelings.

"It's my call, son. I'll cover the expenses, and we'll figure out a split for whatever's on hand there after it's over with."

"There'll probably be enough there to pay off the national debt," I said, and took another drink.

"That's not even counting the gold guns," he smiled.

"What kind of time frame we looking at?"

"We're looking at a week, minimum, just for travel, set up, and preliminary recon," he said, and nodded toward a pad and pen on the coffee table in front of me.

"Go ahead, write me down some contact numbers, and locations you think you might fall back to if you can't stay out of some shit. I'm not going to be around for the next couple of days, but you can leave me a message. I'll call and leave you the location of a clean vehicle, and the RV point. If you need me, call this number and leave a message," he said, handing me a card.

"What are you going to do?"

"Preparations, son, preparations. I'm going to talk to some people. Call in some favors. Get the lay of the land, whisper sweet nothings, get some gear squared away. You just worry about keeping your boy safe," he said.

"Here you go," I said, setting the pad and pen back on the table.

"Good, now I need you to do me a favor."

Evening descended as I walked across the parking lot, two foil-covered plates of enchiladas, rice, and tamales in my hand. The sun's last rays mixed with the moon's pale incandescence and bathed the world in soft yellows and blues. Across the river, downtown Dallas sat tall and gleaming, like its own island, like a castle overlooking a kingdom.

Birds fluttered in air scented with lavender and honeysuckle, and cicadas cried their song. I walked through the parking lot and across the street. Instead of climbing back in the truck or heading back into the bar, I continued walking around the building.

Leaning around the corner I saw the rear of the Toyota sitting, still and cold, the driver lounging to one side, her head cranked toward the front of the bar. I could've have crouched down, crabbed my way beneath her vision, but I wasn't trying to scare her. As it was, I didn't need to try. I was looking in her window, the plate in my hand when she turned to see me with my offering. She dropped her note pad, her hand shooting to a vanilla gripped semi-auto clipped in the box between the seats. I couldn't see what it was, but it was it had dark rosewood grip on a black frame.

"You owe me dinner, beautiful," I said, sliding the foil-covered plate onto the hood of the truck and walking away.

CHAPTER 29

Her partner was good. He knew what he was doing, and if I hadn't known he would be following me, I wouldn't have known he was there. As it was, he had no idea where our long meandering trip would take him. There was no rhyme or reason to the places I went. He waited outside a porn store while I stocked up on some essentials, then he followed me to a liquor store, where I found a bottle of Macallan I'd promised myself I would buy before I ran out of money. I didn't even try to lose him until I found a light just yellow enough to gun it without being obvious. After that, it was nothing.

I used my key to let myself in and found Cornelius sitting at his kitchen table, scowling at me from behind a stack of empty beer cans. His house bottle of Herruda was sitting there as well, and it had taken a good hit in my absence as well. Probably didn't want to smoke up with the boy in blue outside.

"Fuck you, motherfucker," he greeted me from his near stupor. I handed him his own foil-covered plate before taking my own seat with a small glass and the scotch from my sack.

"So where the fuck you been?" he asked, slurring his speech, badly. "Out crippling another lead, maybe?"

"Checking something out," I said, telling what I could of the truth while he unfurled the foil from the edge of the plate. When the smell hit his nostrils, he visibly lit up.

"Oh, damn that smells good. Where'd you get this?" He asked.

"From a friend," I said.

"What friend?" He asked, freeing a tamale from a corn husk. When I didn't answer he looked over the stack of empty cans at me with a cocked eyebrow.

"You know what'd be great?" he asked, trying hard not to smile.

"A cold beer?" I asked, pronouncing cold beer as one syllable. Hoping he'd forget about the questions.

"That'd be a number one awesome, man. A fork would be nice, too," he said as I walked past him to the kitchen. I left the whiskey on the counter, pulled a fork from the dishwasher, and grabbed two cold beers from the fridge. I handed him his fork and beer and took my seat on the couch.

"This smells awesome."

"You'll like it."

"Where'd you get it again?"

"My grandma's neighbor fixed it," I lied. I popped the top to my beer and took a long drink. I watched him eat the food the old man had insisted I take, and I looked at the empty beer cans on the coffee table, and the little pile of burnt hash and resin in his pipe, and I wondered how long he'd been at it.

"How fucked up are you?" I asked.

"I'm good, bro. I just had to take the edge off after your goddamn stunt this morning. Like we need to be making enemies right now," he said, shaking his head indolently as he used the edge of his fork to cut into the food.

I didn't say anything. Just like with the two in the garage, in his mind there would be one more chance, one last measure, one more line drawn for the enemy to cross, before taking life was justified. With him, a moderate response was always called for. Even if it got him killed.

"Not going to say anything for yourself?" He asked. I shook my head, and stared at the snub-nosed .357 I'd taken off Boudreaux sitting on the table. I slipped the Mexican's straight razor out of my pocket, and dropped it beside the gun.

"It's a match set, *Homes*," I said, and stood, draining my beer. Gently, I set it down on the table, and went to clean up. While I did so, I prayed, for the first time in a very long while, that C.W. would get too drunk and stoned to learn anything as we went about our business later in the night.

CHAPTER 30

Outside the ring of ambient light every city possesses, just outside the neon glow, was a darkness deeper than Satan's heart staring in at us from the crisp air from just outside the wire, as we came to the top of the stairs and stepped out onto the roof. We made our way through the sparse crowd to the bar, and ordered drinks. The bartender was a cute blonde with a swimmer's profile, her midriff looked like hard, flat rocks, and her jeans clung to the long muscles of her legs and rear.

She handed us our beers and C.W. paid with a ten, telling her to keep the change. She smiled in return, sliding the bills into the jar by the register, and then he asked if Kendrick was in.

"Sorry guys, he doesn't work here anymore," she said, her voice going hard, as if she didn't want to talk about the man. C.W. grunted in return.

"How long's it been since he worked here?" I asked.

"Few months. Why?"

"Any idea where he is?"

"I make it a habit not to keep in touch with his kind."

"And what kind is that?"

"The kind that makes the environment a little less safe for girls to cut loose and have a good time. Why are you looking for him?"

"Honey, I'm a reporter. I work for the Dallas Morning News," C.W. said, pulling a card from his wallet. "You got something you want to share, maybe?"

"Oh, I don't know about that," she said, and took a step away from the bar.

"It's confidential babe. You don't have to worry about getting in trouble. But, if you can help me with this story, it would mean a lot," he said, giving her his crusader for social justice tone. She took the card, and looked at it, then back up at him.

"You're really a reporter?"

"Yes, ma'am."

She looked at me, and both of us knew what she was thinking. The years of heavy weights, augmented with the occasional, judicious use of certain performance enhancing substances, the various tats and scars. You take one look at me, and you know exactly who I am, or maybe more appropriately, what I am.

Pleased to meet you. Hope you guessed my name.

"This is my friend, Jeb. He's here to make sure I don't get hurt."

"What, you're the brains, he's the muscle?" She asked, one eyebrow cocked, the pretty little sliver stud standing out. That's me: always the muscle; never the brains.

"If you were me, would you want to go around asking people the things I need to ask, without some handy?" C.W. said, trying to be charming.

"What's this about?"

"We need to ask him about a missing girl," I said, a hard edge to my voice, playing my role to the hilt. I don't know what C.W. had in mind, but the look he shot me over his shoulder was one that told me he'd had something else to play.

She stopped what she was doing and looked at him for a hard minute, thinking. She bit her lower lip, but she wasn't trying to be seductive, maybe for the first time in forever.

"He serious?" She asked C.W. He shook his head.

"Waffle House, Spring Creek Road, take 75 to Richardson and take a right. Can't miss it. I get off around two. Meet me then, ok?"

C.W. started to say something, but stopped.

"Sure, see you then," he said, and we turned, and walked back down the stairs.

We made our way down the stairwell, C.W. in the lead. At the bottom of the stairs, he looked at me, said he had to piss, then went to the bathroom. I stepped to the bar and ordered a double shot with a beer back, and lit a smoke with my old Zippo.

A waifish blond with either too much padding or ill-fitting implants coughed intently. She was halfway down the bar, and talking to a cocaine thin man with a faux hawk and Che t-shirt. The kind of modern metro wonder who would neuter himself in an effort to attract girls. The kind of guy who'd weep at the drop of a hat and openly express his own post-partum depression. The kind of guy I hated on principle.

I tried to put them out of my mind. I had far more important things to worry about.

The bartender, a red head with large natural breasts and the sly smile of one who'd seen everything behind the tap handed me my drinks. I gave her too much and told her to keep the change.

She smiled, and it might've made my day had it been any other.

I was mad at myself. For escalating the tension at Boudeaux's, taking the hard road out of honor instead of compartmentalizing my feelings like a professional and letting C.W. coax the information out of him. If I had just done that, we wouldn't be looking for a Carrot Top lookalike that slipped girls roofies, and I'd be able to gear up, train up, and do the damn thing right with Travis.

The Robert Donahue Band sang "Tattoo" over the speakers, and it was maybe the saddest song I'd ever heard. Didn't help my disposition, that.

The two halfway down stared at me in the mirror behind the bar and I stared back, blowing a long stream of smoke from my nostrils like a flame.

"Excuse me," the metro wonder scoffed from his perch. I tried to ignore him. I tossed back my shot and drew in some more smoke. I watched douche bag come off his stool and walk toward me.

"I said, excuse me," he said, a little too close for my comfort.

"You're excused," I said as C.W. took the seat next to me. I motioned to the bartender for another round, plus one for C.W. and she nodded my way, eying the man next to me.

"Hey, motherfucker, your smoke's bothering my girl."

"I believe this is a smoking establishment," I said, as calmly as possible. El Doucherino stared at me, huffing, working up the nut with each breath.

"Can I smoke in here, ma'am," I asked the bartender as she sat my next double and C.W.'s drinks down before us.

"For now, though the city council's talking about outlawing it," she said, putting our drinks down. I gave the same amount as last time. It wasn't as big a tip, but she didn't seem offended.

"Outlaw smoking, in a bar? That's a goddamn shame," I said, wondering what the world was coming to. I took a slug from my beer, and looked at the douche who hadn't moved.

"Well?" he asked, bouncing on the toes of his feet.

"Fuck your mother," I said, then took another slug from my beer and turned toward C.W. Douchebag put his hand on my shoulder, and C.W.'s face dropped with worry.

I took a deep breath and turned around, staring at him.

I put the shot glass to my lips and dropped its sweet amber down my throat.

"I'm not scared of some goddamn roid monkey. I'm a mother-fucking black belt, bitch," he said. Of course. Not just a douche, but one of *those* douches. A socially conscious, emasculated, dojo tough guy. Probably got their panties wet by talking up revolution while voting for a bigger, stronger, more powerful government.

Fuckballs.

"Dude, seriously," C.W. said, looking past me, finally deciding to chime in. "You really just want to leave us alone," he said. Douchebag cackled beside me.

"Tony, stop it. Take your seat or leave. There's no need for this," the bartender said, leaning on the bar.

"Yeah, sure," he said, then plucked the butt from my hand and tossed it at the side of my head. I spun on the stool, one hand shooting out and snatching his throat. His eyes went wide. I held him there a second, the room going quiet, then pulled him to me. I whispered softly in his ear, and then I let him go.

He turned and ran out the front door. His girlfriend stared at me.

"Does he have friends?" I asked. She shook her head yes. I finished my beer and slipped off the stool.

"Sorry," the bartender said.

"Don't worry about it," I assured her, then turned to C.W. He was shaking his head while he pulled on his beer, like he just couldn't take me anywhere nice. His shot sat untouched on the bar. I helped myself to it. He shot me a look, gunned his beer, and then we left.

We were stuffed in a booth, drinking coffee without speaking to each other when she came in and slid down beside C.W., across from me. She asked if we minded if she ate, and we said no, of course not. She got Diet Coke with a patty melt, and I ordered a chop steak and eggs, sunny side up, with onions and cheese, hold the hash browns, to go with my coffee and chocolate milk. Cornelius was full of self-righteous indignation, so he dined on that alone. Maybe he was still full from the food I'd brought him from the old man, the one man he'd give anything to find.

She took a large slug from her Diet Coke, then covered her mouth and let out a barely perceptible burp.

"Excuse me," she said, in a syrupy sweet little girl voice. Neither C.W. or I said anything, and a thin, vaguely uncomfortable silence fell over us. She looked at us, from one to the other, the question obvious on her face. Neither of us picked up the ball.

"You guys having a lover's quarrel or something?"

"No, honey. Don't worry about it. You know that old line about brothers fighting, right?" I asked.

"Oh, sure. What are y'all fighting about?" she asked. Cornelius looked at me without speaking.

"Let's just say, we have vastly different investigative techniques," I said, and drank some chocolate milk.

"Not just that trouble at the bar?"

"You know about that?"

"Shit. You should go back. Sam'd probably jump your bones, way she was acting afterward," she said, bobbing her head like she was jamming to some old school rock. I smiled, but Cornelius' frown sat in cement.

"What do you have for us," Cornelius said, finally speaking.

"It's not much, I'm not even sure I should say anything."

"Why not," he asked. She shrugged.

"I don't really want to spread rumors, you know?"

"Then why'd you agree to meet us?" he asked. She shrugged again.

"It's just that…Tim was suspected, a couple times, of slipping mickeys. He was one of those, always had some party favors, always knew who had some. He liked to act like he was tough, like he knew people, you know? I thought he was full of shit, but sometimes girls leave bars, and no one sees them again. No one even knows to be scared for a couple of days."

"You think maybe he was into something worse than handing out party favors?"

"I don't know. I think he was capable of it, you know?"

"Do you know where he is now?"

"If I tell you, how do I know this won't come back on me? He has some dangerous friends." Her tone was as soft as the muted autumn dusk, her eyes darting back and forth, as if searching the horizon for safe harbor.

"No, he doesn't," I said, softly hard, never wanting to see that look of fearful submission in a woman's eyes. She looked at me, as if for the first time, through the muscle and the ink and the bullshit, the realization of just exactly what I meant, finding what I hoped to be a comfortable embrace, one my dear friend seated next to her refused to accept about the world in which we lived. The simple fact that some people just need killing.

"He liked working raves—goth shit. Last I heard he was working a converted warehouse down off Industrial. Vlad's. Some pseudo Russian/Goth/vampire shit. Not my scene," she said, moving her glass out of the way for the waitress to slide our plates down. "Does this have anything to do with Michael Torres?"

"Can you tell us anything else about him? What he drives, where he lives?" C.W. asked, ignoring her question.

"I never went home with him, but his car made me wet. He drives a bad ass old Mach I, everybody knows it," she said, nibbling a fry.

"Did you know Torres?"

"Enough not to feel bad when he got killed. He was Tim's hookup, where he got most of his shit. I think he got him the job at Vlad's."

"You said Vlad's is a Goth club, we gotta dress in dog collars and shit to get in?" C.W. asked.

"Dress however you want. Just know the vibe. They have Southwestern-Russian fusion menu that is supposed to be something else," she said, then nodded my way. "Be sure to take your friend. I'd like to see the looks on the faces of all those mascara wearing pussies when someone who really does hate the world shows up. That'd be fucking priceless."

C.W. asked her some more questions, and then he asked them again in a different way, and she kept giving him the same answer. She either wasn't smart enough to know what he was doing, didn't care, or wanted him to think either of the two. Somehow I doubted it was the last one.

"If you guys go there, be careful. Vlad's is supposed to be a front for the Russian mob."

"Oh, really?" I asked. I hadn't expected to hear that.

"That's what they say. But, that might just be their press, ya know?"

I stepped outside, lit a smoke and punched Morales's number into my cell. It was late, but he answered before the first ring even finished.

"Morales," he said, as a greeting.

"This is Shaw," I said, leaving it at that. I didn't know how much he wanted to talk about over the phone, so I needed to let him take the lead.

"There's a dog park, on Mockingbird, at White Rock Lake. Can you meet me there in an hour?"

"Yes," I said, and closed the phone. I checked my watch, then smoked my cigarette in silence.

CHAPTER 31

I was sitting on the tailgate of my father's old Ford, smoking another menthol, and sipping from my flask when his headlights flashed coming into the parking lot. He pulled to a stop in the space next to me, and ambled out dressed in chinos, well-worn Tony Lamas, and an overflowing guyubera. He looked like he didn't mind being there, though he clearly had better things to do.

"What you got in there?"

"Maker's Mark," I said. A girl I had known while convalescing at Walter Reed Army hospital had given the flask to me as a gift. She'd shown me the eastern seaboard, and I'd shown her how to get drunk and puke in new towns and how to let one lost love taint every future relationship. In honor of her, and a special night, I only poured Maker's in it.

"Well, goddamn, you gonna make me beg?"

I handed him the flask, and he took a long pull, nearly coughing when it left his lips.

"Shit, that's good stuff," he said, wiping his lips with the back of his hand, before handing it back. "C'mon, let's take a walk."

There were two fenced off areas, the smaller one to the left for smaller dogs, the larger one to the right, for big ones. I followed him between the two, then through a gate, and down a narrow trail where the water lapped up on shore. There was a place for water dogs to frolic, but, like the fenced in areas behind us, it was far too late for any to be out. He turned, and looked at me for a long moment. The moon reflected off the water and cast a dull purple hue over his face, and I knew he was thinking maybe he'd made a mistake in trusting me.

"What do you need kid?"

"Information," I said.

"On what?" he asked.

"A man named Timothy Kendrick. Supposed to tend bar at a club named Vlad's off Industrial. Supposed to be some Tex-Mex-Russian Industrial Gothic fusion place."

"I know Vlad's. It's where the rich kids go to act like they're in league with Satan," he said. He watched like a hungry wolf while I drew in a lungful, until I finally offered the pack. He snapped it up and helped himself.

"What's this Kendrick have to do with anything?"

"Looks he was dealing for Torres," I said. I didn't mention the rumors about the missing girls.

"Talk to him yet?"

"No, I'd like a little more information," I said.

"Yeah, I bet you would," he said. I looked at him without speaking.

"Lotta rumors about Vlad's. Word is, from the intel guys, is that it's all bullshit. He probably started them himself. Helps the club to have street cred," he said. He took another drag, and rolled the smoke over his tongue without thinking.

"What kind of rumors?"

"The usual shit; every club owner that ever was wanted the public to think they were mobbed up."

"Can you be more specific?" I asked. He took another long drag on his menthol, and stared at me through the smoke, his cop eyes focused.

"What're you looking for?" he asked. "What'd you hear?"

"Rumor we heard was that girls sometimes had a habit of disappearing around Kendrick and Torres."

"Where'd you hear this?" he asked.

"Same place we got Kendrick."

"And that'd be?" he asked. I didn't answer. He frowned in the silence.

"Anything I could tell you, your friend the hotshot crime reporter should be able to," he said. "Unless of course, he's incompetent," he added.

"Big talk from a man that can't solve the rape and barbeque of an innocent girl," I spat.

"Fuck you! This is how you ask for a favor?"

"I'm calling in a favor, *puto*, not asking for one, remember that?" I said back. He stood rail stiff and straight, looking down at me, and I realized he was taller than I'd thought.

"Remember that shit? C.W. keeps the bit about your partner being a complete fuck up out of the press, and you give us a little something to work with, remember?"

"This is what you want to use that on? Really? You want to waste your marker on bullshit," he said, shaking his head. "Maybe I misjudged you, Shaw. I thought…," he trailed off, not willing to finish his sentence.

"First order of business is keeping my people safe. Everything else is second to that," I said. He turned away and smoked some more before flicking the cigarette into the lake. I watched it flicker like a drunken lightening bug, living free for two short seconds of flight before drowning in the lake.

"I need to know what we're walking into tomorrow," I said.

"I'll see what I can find out. It's going to look suspicious as hell, but I'll see what I can do. Brunch, tomorrow; John's Café on Greenville. I'll call," he said, and then turned and left.

I sat down, and leaned against the fence. I heard his car start up and drive away, but I did not move. Instead, I sat, and listened as the small waves splashed against the bank, and stared out at the dark, endless sky above the lake. I thought about what all those missing girls meant for my good friend, the fervor, the heat, the raw nerve that would provide an energy greater than a thousand suns, and I feared the road ahead.

Though my flask was near my heart, I did not drink.

CHAPTER 32

I was rolling down Mockingbird, back to C.W.'s, and caught the light where Greenville cut across it. Traffic was still on the heavy side, but starting to thin, everyone leaving the bars up and down Greenville.

I looked to my right, at the famous Dr Pepper sign on the corner, all that was left from the beautiful old art deco Dr Pepper plant that had sat there for years. Now it was a grocery store, gas station, a drive thru burger joint, and an apartment building that was sort of faux art deco. Across the street the strip mall that housed Campisi's, where Jack Ruby had eaten the night before he killed Oswald, sat almost unchanged straight out of 1963.

I had the window rolled down. I was listening to Hayes Carll sing "Bad Liver and A Broken Heart" live at The Handle Bar in Greenville, S.C., and I was trying not to think about where I was, or where I was going. And then my cell buzzed in my vest.

This line of work, no one retires, he sang, and I tried not to recognize the relevance of that line in regards to my own life.

"What are you doing?" C.W. asked from his end.

"Nothing," I said. "You?"

"I'm following our boy Kendrick, that's what I'm doing. I watched him load a comatose bitch into his car, and now they're pulling out the parking lot at Vlad's. You need to catch up with us."

Shit. Fuck. Goddamn it.

We'd made the decision to check out the club the next day, after we'd gathered some more intelligence, but apparently he hadn't been able to let it die. I should've known better.

"Are you moving?"

"Yeah, we're pulling out now."

"Stay back a-ways. Don't let him see you."

"I can handle this, Jeb. I just need you to move your ass. I'm doing all the goddamn work," he growled.

"Where are you at?" I asked, gritting my teeth.

"We're rolling up Inwood right," he said. That meant he was going north. The club was on Industrial, and south of that it crossed the river and turned into Hampton. I thought of three paths toward them, each having its merits depending on traffic.

"Ok, we're turning right at Cedar Springs. I'll call back. Hurry your ass, bitch," he said, and snapped the phone closed.

The gate was closed when I got to the apartment building, and I punched the number Cornelius had called me with into the keypad. After the gate creaked open, I pulled through, making my way to the building in the back corner. I saw the silver and black 1971 Mustang Mach I the bartender had described backed into a corner space, C.W. standing beside it, one hand in his pocket.

I parked beside it, on the grass, and unlimbered myself from the old truck. I walked around the back of the truck, and saw, inside the car, a young woman, in her early twenties, Gothed out in black plastic and dog collar with a choker chain, her multi-colored hair short and spiked, laying unconscious, splayed out and slumped in the passenger seat.

Cornelius was standing beside the driver side door, bouncing on his feet with nervous energy, a thick dip under his lip. I could see the grips of the .357 I'd taken earlier in the day wink faintly at me from the bottom of the hand hanging outside his pocket. He stared at me, his eyes wild with anger, the fervor they betrayed at its most intense.

I looked at Kendrick, his thick mop of curly red hair loose atop his head in a style stolen from Bart Simpson's nemesis, Side Show Bob. His hands were tied to the steering wheel at ten and two with zip ties. I looked at C.W., who for the first time, in a very long time, radiated raw anger. I tried to remember the last time I'd seen him in that state, if ever I had. I imagined an Indian kid in a bad leather jacket, crumpled and bleeding on the pavement.

"Man, you can have the bitch, ok?" Kendrick said, his hands moving beneath their bindings. Cornelius snapped, reached out, popping him off the eyebrow with butt of the Smith. Then, he kept hitting him. I let him go for a minute, thinking he'd tire himself out, but he just had too much steam. I grabbed him by his shoulders, pulling him away. He turned, quickly, his hands up in some martial arts form, and I swiped the gun from his hand while it was loose. Didn't want him accidentally letting one go.

He got control, holding his hands up, and I handed him his gun back. He took a long, deep breath through his nostrils, then another, and turned, staring at Kendrick, who looked back at us, his face bloody, his eyes tearing. Those eyes found me, and he asked, "Who are you, the good cop?" He asked more hopeful than sarcastic. Then, C.W. laughed, shallow at first, then great, big belly laughs. Kendrick didn't quite know what to make of that.

"Where are his keys?"

"I got 'em, right here," C.W., said, pulling them from a pocket.

"Why don't you go open it up for us?"

"Yeah, sure," he said, he said, still struggling with control, probably a little embarrassed by his lack of it. I watched him walk toward the nearest apartment, in the bottom corner of the last building.

"Do you have an alarm?" I asked Kendrick. He shook his head no. "If you're lying, I'll kill you," I said, snapping the big folder open and placing the edge against his throat.

"1971," he said weakly. I reached in and slapped his face, then, when he was stunned, grabbed a handful of hair and bounced his head off the steering wheel. C.W. turned with the horn's blare. I repeated the code to him, and he shot a thumbs up back to me.

He let himself into the apartment, turned on the lights, and a moment later, walked back outside, leaving the door open.

I cut the zip ties binding Carrot Top to the steering wheel, then opened the door, and stood behind it. When he didn't move, I reached in, grabbed his earring, and pulled. He followed pretty quickly, then.

"Get him in the house, I'll carry the girl," I said. Cornelius nodded, and I shut the door, pushing Kendrick ahead.

He couldn't stand it. At the first chance to run, he was off, trying to run right over C.W. The next thing either Kendrick or I knew, he was on his back, clutching his chest and wheezing. I hadn't seen the move, but whatever it was, it had been small, quick, and powerful. Maybe he'd used his chi. Or some such shit.

I picked Kendrick up and leaned him against the car. I slapped his head and he whined, still trying to catch his breath.

C.W. herded him into the apartment, and I picked the girl up and followed.

Inside was a little more personal than Torres' apartment had been, if only because it was more low rent. Standard bachelor as furnished by IKEA, Target, and Wal-Mart. The date raper as yuppie hipster. I carried the unconscious girl to the bedroom and laid her on the bed, took off her boots and choker, made her look comfortable, and then joined the other two.

Cornelius had him in the little dining room, hunched over in a chair, his hands zip tied to the little pieces of wood that ran from leg to leg. Cornelius was sitting in a chair near him, and every time he spit, he did so onto Kendrick's face. He was also holding a stun gun. I don't know where he got it, but he liked tapping it, and holding the thin blue current just past the end of Kendrick's nose.

I stepped past them, into the kitchen, and found a bottle of Three Olives chocolate infused vodka, held it up to show C.W., and he grinned back. I dropped lots of ice in glasses, grabbed a couple cans of Dr Pepper from the fridge, and made my way back into the dining room. I took the chair on the opposite side of the table, moved it next to C.W.'s in front of Kendrick sitting in his chair, and poured our drinks.

"What's this about?" Kendrick asked.

"You doin' bad. That's what this is about, Timmy," I told him, adding flourish to his name, imitating the cartoon *South Park*.

"Why haven't you called the cops?"

"You gonna be real lucky if we call the cops, boy-o," I said, handing C.W. his drink.

"You're not gonna kill me," he said. We just looked at him. "If you wanted to kill me, you'd have done it already."

"How do you know what we're gonna do? You tell us what we need to know, you might get lucky."

"Lucky how?" he asked.

"Lucky you might live, motherfucker," C.W. snapped, spitting a large wad onto his face. Kendrick contorted, the glob running down his cheek.

"We can do this easy or hard. You can live or die. You have 'bout five seconds to decide," I said, taking a drink. Chocolate vodka and Dr Pepper was actually kind of tasty. I'd probably have diabetes before the night was out, but it was tasty. Damn tasty.

"What do you want?"

"I want you to tell us everything there is to know about your friend Torres, and your boss, Vlad."

"He's dead," he said. C.W. reached over and backhanded him. It sounded like whip cracking.

"You waste time telling us the obvious, we're going to assume you want it hard. Torres, you were dealing for him?" I asked.

"Tell us about that. Who's in charge? Vlad? Did Torres work for him. too?" Cornelius cut in.

"At first, man. Torres was trying to branch out though, you know?"

"How so," C.W. asked. Kendrick shrugged like he didn't want to go there. C.W. leaned forward and put the taser on his knee.

"Ok, man," Kendrick started in, but C.W. zapped him anyway. Kendrick convulsed the moment the juice ran through him.

"Yeah, you like that, motherfucker? You like that?" C.W. said while Kendrick tried to catch his breath.

"What the fuck'd I ever do to you guys, man?" he asked, his voice nasal and whiny. C.W. smiled, a cruel thing he wouldn't recognize in the mirror.

"Tell us about the operation," I said.

"What's to tell? Drugs and wetbacks come north, money goes south."

"Where's Torres's crew come into it?"

"We started using them for muscle. Vlad doesn't have a lot of people. He's more hat than cattle. Playing gangster more than anything. He wasn't shit until he brought us on. We hustled the right kind of business, and Torres got his old crew for muscle when we needed it. It was golden."

"How'd that work out? Torres left the life ten years ago. How'd his old crew react to him showing up with work?" I asked. He laughed. I punched him in the mouth.

"Goddamn it, what was that for?" he asked as blood leaked from his lip and he worked his tongue over his teeth.

"Laughing, fuckhead. Now, what's so funny?"

"You are, if you think he left the life," he said.

"What about the girls?" C.W. asked.

"That's his crew man. They picked that up working with the cartel. Torres scouted them out at the club. We get a lot of poor little rich girls in there."

"Torres scouted them out? You helped him with that, right?" C.W. said. He was trying real hard to remain calm, but the snarl betrayed his anger.

"No way man, I wouldn't do that," he squirmed. C.W. reached over and hit him with the stun gun again. He jerked with the jolt, and gasped in its aftermath.

"They ransom the girls?"

"The ones from money, yeah."

"What about the ones that aren't?" I asked. He shrugged.

"They go south, man," he said, looking at the floor. "Who knows where after that."

"Vlad in on that shit, too?"

"Fuck no. You think he wants the kind of heat that would bring down? Fucker's half oblivious, man. All he thinks about is blow, cock, and his fuckin' image, man. He don't want to be in nothin' that heavy, man."

"Really? He doesn't even suspect? All those girls gone missing, surely someone would link them to the club?"

"Torres wasn't fucking stupid. He'd scout them out a bit before he took them. By the time they disappeared, no one would even think to tie them to the club."

"And Vlad didn't know anything about the girls?"

"Fuck no, man. Goddamn it. I keep trying to tell you, no. Vlad was the money-man. That's it. Michael used Vlad's money to buy from his contacts."

"How often do you guys take girls?" I asked.

"We try to keep it spaced out, but his crew gets greedy. They like the rush. They like the idea of bossing rich *gringas* around. Sometimes they get a little rough with the product; it's a real fucking headache."

I reached out and slapped his ear, open palmed. Hard. He recoiled with a yelp.

"No, that's a headache. You call the girls *product* again, I'm gonna lose my goddamn temper," I growled. I drained my glass, trying to calm down. It didn't work so I made another drink.

"Are there any girls in the pipeline right now?"

"Fuck no, man. If there were, it wouldn't have been too good for them, all the shit that's come down here lately. Motherfuckers are real goddamn paranoid."

"What's happening on Cinco de Mayo?" C.W. asked, and I had to catch myself before I showed a tell. Still hoping my plans with the old man were salvageable.

"Fuck, I don't know," he said, shaking his head like he meant something else. Because he did mean something else.

"Explain yourself, or we're about to get full retard up in here," I said. He looked up at me, his head hung down.

"You don't understand," he said. "These guys, Michael's people, they're not businessmen. They're not gangsters. They think they're soldiers. They think they're at war, that they're going to take back Texas, or some shit. They live and breathe that shit, man."

"The fifth, Timmy," I said. He looked up at me.

"Man, I don't know," he yelled. C.W. reached forward and gave him a jolt right on his crotch.

"Keep your voice down, fuckhead," he growled as he slid back into his seat next to me.

"You fried my dick, man. Why would you do that?" He cried. We listened to him sob for a few moments until he caught his breath.

"You weren't going to use it tonight anyway," C.W. said.

"Who does Vlad have in the police department?"

"Man, I already told you. Michael handled all that shit. He was the one with the contacts. You two are the first bubble we've had."

"Do you know how he linked up with Vlad?"

"Started with his uncle, man. That's all I know. They had an arrangement of some kind with the boys down south."

"Did Torres ever say anything about his uncle?"

"That guy's a fuckin' joke in their eyes. He's nothing but a white man to them."

"He doesn't have anything to do with this?"

"Fuck no. The girls are all Michael's crew, man. That's their thing. Think they're impressing their friends down south."

"What happens when they pick up a girl? Where do they go?"

"I don't know that shit, man. I just got a finder's fee for locating prospects. Michael did the rest."

"How long have you been doing this?" I asked.

"Couple years."

"How many girls have you picked up in that time?" I asked.

"I don't know," he said, with a shrug. "Nine, ten. Not counting a couple that got brave."

"How do you live with that shit?" I asked.

"What? Are you serious? Man, they're all whores. Everybody's out for themselves, man. Think they're not?"

I thought about that, trying to do the math, wondering how many other crews were working with them, in how many cities, when C.W. leaned over with the taser extended and touched him on the side, just below his chest.

Kendrick convulsed as the electricity shot through his body, his mouth open, the only sound that of the current and his grasping for breath and thrashing body. C.W. was smiling.

C.W. withdrew, his face pale and ashen. Whether he was simply drained from effort, or horrified at his pleasure, I didn't venture a guess.

"C.W.," I said, drawing his attention. He turned his head slowly, looking at me with wide eyes. "Do you have your recorder?"

"Yeah," he said, shaking his head, and pulled it from a pocket.

"Go over it again, Timmy. Everything you just told us, anything else you think of that we need to know."

When Cornelius pressed the button on the recorder, I swear it echoed.

"You're not going to fucking kill me, right? You said you wouldn't fucking kill me," he said, when he was done, and C.W. had shut off the recorder, rewinding it. He wasn't crying, but was well into pleading. Cornelius looked at me, the fire still in his eyes, then turned back to him.

"Motherfucker," he said, his voice breaking, his body shaking. He stood to his feet with a quickness that made Kendrick flinch, and walked out the front door, trying to get control.

I looked at Kendrick, took a drink, and followed him.

"Keep your fucking mouth shut, bitch," I told Kendrick on my way out the door.

I found Cornelius, leaned over, puking in the shrubs. I walked up next to him without speaking, and lit a menthol. He looked at me, his face flushed with shame. At that moment, I did not envy his sense of humanity. If he could have lived with it, I would've found satisfaction in killing the piece of shit.

"Should we kill him?" he asked, then puked again, sick from just the words.

"It's what I would do if I were working this alone. But not now. Now, it's not smart. We're gonna need him for the cops, but we can't turn him over yet."

"Because we don't know who Vlad has with the police, and city hall," he said.

"We don't know a lot. We need to put him on ice until then, but we can't kill him. Plus, there's the girl," I said.

"Jesus," he said. "What the fuck do we do?"

"We call Russell, see if he can do something with him," I suggested. C.W. didn't like that idea.

"God," he said, holding his stomach, flinching at the thought of asking Uncle Jack's man Friday for help.

"He's a good man," I said, and he looked at me. "And so's your Uncle Jack," I said.

"You got his number?" he asked, clearly not happy.

I nodded.

"Ok, then," he said, and walked back into the apartment.

CHAPTER 33

The next morning I was browning bacon and sausage in a huge skillet, about to take it out before whisking in the flour and then the milk, when the girl struggled around the corner, her eyes wide and uncertain. She didn't look as scared as she did confused. In the morning light, she looked even younger than the eighteen years her driver's license claimed. Not even old enough to be in a bar. She had just a little roll of baby fat left, right between her hips and belly button, and I swear to God it was so goddamn precious it hurt my heart.

"Who are you?" she asked, not quite confused, not quite scared, but a little worried.

"My name's Jeb, sweetie. Are you hungry?" I asked.

"It smells good," she said, standing up on her toes as she nodded her head. Curious, but still scared. I wondered how much she remembered from the night before.

"How do you like your eggs?"

"Hmmm..., sunny side up, please," she said, looking at the dishes I'd laid out, the glasses of water and OJ. I turned on the burner under a smaller pan, and coated it with a spray of canned butter.

"Why don't you have a seat; I'm sure you've got some questions. Afterwards I'll take you wherever you want to go," I told her, raising my coffee to my lips.

"Yeah, I'm sorry, but I don't remember coming home with you... Jeb," she said. I thought back to my days stationed in Germany, when I used to wake up in strange beds, not remembering the girls who'd taken me home. Often they'd sleep or pretend to while I rummaged unskillfully for my clothes, but they'd always made the choice to bring me home. I'd never once lied about who I was, or what I wanted. I hoped not many of them ever regretted it.

Even then, I'd had the rule about not sleeping with women drunker than I was. A warrior had to have a code, after all, and that was a part of mine. Chivalry, even in the briefest of relationships, being the hallmark of a knight errant. My buddies all laughed at me, saying, Jeb, why do you think they're still in the bar drinking? Logic told me they were probably right, that sometimes women wanted the animal sweat, fury, and release just as much as we did. But in that moment, looking at the sleepy-eyed girl who had no idea how lucky she was, I was never more glad to have lived up to that rule. I have so few, after all.

"That's because you didn't, sweetie. A bartender at Vlad's brought you here. This is his place. Timothy Kendrick, slim guy, looks like he needs to eat, a whole lot of bright red hair."

She squinted, and looked like a girl looking for her glasses. Finally, she started to nod her head just slightly.

"I came home with that guy? Ugh, I must have been wasted. He was so creepy. He had a bad vibe," she said. I nodded, then realized I shouldn't have after she caught it.

"I swear, I only remember having a couple drinks, and my head is killing me," she said, cautiously, almost a question.

"That's because he drugged you. He's a very bad man. But don't worry. I showed up, just in the nick of time."

"Where's he at?"

"He had something to attend to," I said. Right at that moment, he was bound, in a van, and being driven to a safe house owned by one of Uncle Jack's companies. C.W. and Russell were with him. C.W. wanted to see it firsthand. He was crossing a line, and he felt obligated to know exactly which one. It would've been so much easier just to kill the fuck.

"Wow, I woke up, still dressed…you know, and thought," she stuttered a bit, looking for the words, "I passed out on you. Wow," she said. She picked up the OJ and took a small sip.

"No kiddo, not me," I said.

"This isn't a religious thing is it? You're not gonna, like, start preaching to me, are you?" She asked, worried, looking down at the cup in her hands. I laughed, but tried not to make it too loud.

"No, it's not a religious thing. I'm not going to preach to you," I said, grinning as I shook my head at the thought, pulling the meat from the skillet to start gravy.

"Did my father hire you?" she asked.

"No."

"He's got a lot of money," she said.

"I don't give a fuck about his money," I said, harsher than I should have, harsher than I meant to. I was whisking the flour into the grease for the gravy when she started sobbing lightly. I looked up, hating life.

"Do you wanna fuck…me?" she asked, her voice cracked and frail, still staring down at the glass in her hands.

"No, sweetie," I said.

"Then why'd you help me?" she asked, timidly. I wondered how anyone could come to ask such a thing in such a way.

"Because it needed to be done. You don't owe anyone anything. Please, sit. Breakfast will be ready in a minute," I said, checking the heat on the smaller pan. I turned the heat under the mess down to a simmer, then looked up to see her, shaking slightly.

"Do you think I'm a whore?" she asked, her voice cracking. I walked over to her, and put a hand to her shoulder. She looked up at me, tears streaming down her cheeks.

"I think you're eighteen years old, sweetie. I think you want to have fun, and cut loose, and be your own person. And I think there are bad people in the world who would take advantage of you, because of it," I told her. She looked at me, then put her head on my shoulder, and cried.

When she was done, she laughed weakly, wiped her tears, thanked me, and sat down. I went back to the stove, coated another pan with butter, cooked four eggs, sunny side up, and finished the gravy.

CHAPTER 34

Two of the goons before the door held metal detectors, so that meant the guns stayed in the car. I slipped the Spyderco P'kal inside my boxers, beneath the hunk of pewter Kool-Aid man belt buckle and climbed out of the truck with Cornelius. I'd gone shopping earlier in the afternoon and was now clad in dark gray Dockers slacks, a loose fitting black v-neck tshirt, and had freshly polished and buffed my boots. Cornelius wore a short-sleeved silk button down and brown ostrich Tony Lamas.

They let us in without any more eye fucking than necessary, and we stepped through the doors and paid our dues, before joining the crowded dance floor. The place was actually billed as a macabre escape, and the décor fit. It was all dark wood and stainless steel; walls made of stucco and painted some dark mixture of red and orange. There were little metal cacti on the tables and artist's renditions of events in Mexican and Russian history were placed unobtrusively, almost subliminally, along the walls.

The men wore various clothes in black and gray, and the women mostly black and red. There was a decent smattering of light BDSM gear, collars and chains, but nothing heavy. And no one bared their fangs or hissed.

Despite the fact that I hate crowds and music too loud to carry on a conversation, I'd been to my share of clubs, and occasionally I even enjoyed myself in them. So long as I could afford to get drunk in them, and the women made no pretense of why they were there, I could always have a real good time.

Everyone is exactly the same the world over. It doesn't matter what type of music they play, especially since most of them sample the most generic pop bullshit anyway. The goal is the same in every club, the purpose of its patrons the same. To drink with your friends until you're brave enough to let go, and then give into every temptation you can find.

The music is always loud, there to provide rhythm and tempo for the foreplay on the dance floor. The drinks are cheap enough to encourage even the most cash strapped to pay for rounds with girls he doesn't know and who wouldn't give him the time of day elsewhere. There is the unmistakable smell of perfume and cologne, sweat and liquor that only intensifies as the night rolls on.

And most importantly, there's the absence of light, which provides the customers with the most important of ingredients: a sense of hope, equality, and freedom, no matter how false. Because beyond the bouncers guarding the doors like gargoyles at the castle gates, and the free flowing liquor that lubricates the maker-merry, the shadows of the night are the true rulers here, with good reason. Their shade holds more power than those who enter ever want to admit, for with equal measure they may dull a sharp beauty, or hold a favorable obstruction over another's imperfections. As the hours tic away, everyone slips ever more feral until there is nothing left but the needs of the animal inside all of us. The ones who do not accept this are the saddest of all.

We made our way through the bump and grind to the bar, where a bartender who missed her calling as a runway model took our drinks. Cornelius got the first round, so I did not know what I was getting until I took the first sip. Rum and coke, which was a semi-nice relief from my steady diet of bourbon, scotch, and vodka.

Trying not to spill our drinks, we zigged and zagged to a corner near the end of the bar, as far away from the crowded bar and dance floor as we could find. The club was in a converted warehouse, and there were two levels. The first one was the main dance floor and bar, the second contained the office and private rooms. On one wall, near what looked to be a service entrance to the kitchen, was a private elevator, sunk into a narrow abutment from the wall. Below a wall of tanks filled with exotic looking fish, there were stairs leading to the second floor, and there were a pair of thick goons at the bottom of it. So far, they didn't seem to pay us any mind. Whatever we were going to do, it would undoubtedly be world class stupid.

"Jesus, you having second thoughts yet?" Cornelius asked, drinking his rum and coke. He didn't really mean it.

"You're doing all the work, *pardna*, I'm just along for the ride," I smiled. I lied. I looked for exits, and enemies and signs from God. I didn't find any of the above, but I'm sure they were all there.

"Shit," he shook his head. Maybe be was looking for exits, too.

We settled in, drinking and eying over tonight's menu as it presented itself toward us. I was wondering if at the end of the night, any of these girls would not get to choose where they went, or who took them there. I saw the sadness in what they came here for, the pressure to be so many things, and to still be themselves. This was a part of that too, but this was also a release, the payoff, where for being so good, they got to sow their wild oats. They got to drink in excess and ingest fun substances, and have wonderfully dirty sex. They got to be young and have fun. I had sown my share of wild oats, but felt unbearably old at thirty, and it seemed like I had missed out on much. Guess that's what happens when you spend a good chunk of your twenties getting blood on your hands for nothing.

We watched people enter and leave. We watched them on the dance floor; we watched them come and go from the bar, and the stairs across the way, the elevator and service door beside them. We watched people come and go from the restrooms down the wall from where we sat, as well as the service door that shared its space in the wall. We watched a girl who might have been 18 ask us if we wanted another round. We did.

Shortly after the waitress brought our next round, Vlad walked out of the elevator beside the service door on the far side of the dance hall, and walked around the perimeter of the dance floor, along the elevated level above the dancers. Occasionally, he would stop and talk to patrons, smiling and shaking hands, a confident yet conscientious host.

In tow, but not dramatically close, a lean man in an honest-to-God sharkskin suit followed. His coat was open, and so large it hung off his frame in such a way that brought images of horrendous 80's fashion to mind. His gait was sure-footed but easy, his shoulders and hips set so that the coat would not print or telegraph or give an indiscreet peek at the hardware beneath it.

But that's not what I noticed. When it comes to protective work, especially if the principle is a shady-ass Russian nightclub owner, it's not too hard to find gang muscle or even ex-military to carry too much firepower, flex their muscles, and sneer at people. It's almost S.O.P. for Russian gangsters to act like they're in a bad movie. This guy on the other hand, though clearly heavily armed, did not sneer or emanate raw machismo. He even slid to the side to let people pass him. He just hung back, floating, letting his boss do his thing while he did his. And he did it without doing the characteristic fighter pilot head- swivel.

Instead he left his shoulders relaxed, increasing his sphere of vision, only turning his head to focus on something in particular, before carrying on. He did not waste movement by constantly moving his head, and didn't draw attention to himself by looking like a bodyguard to the uninitiated. He just hung loose. And when he saw me, and saw the things I saw in him, he did nothing. He didn't speak into his handset, didn't nod his head, and didn't blow me a kiss. He just kept floating behind his boss, calm and easy, as if Russian industrial techno-salsa-rock, or whatever the shit was we were listening to, soothed him.

Finally, Vlad slid into an empty booth not far from the bar, his pet shark at rest nearby.

"What do you think?" C.W. asked, turning his glass in little circles on the table.

"I think we should leave," I said. I meant it. I meant it so much I very nearly prayed aloud for it. I meant it so much, I thought about telling him the truth. That I'd found the old man from the bar, and that we were going to kill a bunch of people, and that it looked like Vlad and his friends clearly needed to go on the list, because I didn't buy for one goddamn second what Kendrick or Morales said about him being small time and harmless. However, I did buy that was exactly what he wanted them to think.

C.W. shook his head.

"You know, for a hardened mercenary, you're an awful big pussy," he said, grinning. I didn't bother correcting him.

We watched an extremely fit Hispanic couple walk out of the dance floor and to Vlad's booth. The man was average height, stocky, with close-cropped hair and a well-groomed beard.

Oh look, it's a goddamn party. Goody.

The woman was about 5'4, about 125, all of it muscle. The slit in her dress revealed a thick, toned thigh. Both scanned the room, but neither did so with the economy of motion Vlad's man had. He didn't bother to frisk them before letting them slide into the booth with his boss.

"Goddamn," C.W. said next to me.

"I know, that's a helluva thigh," I replied.

"You said it, bubba," he said. He raised his glass up and waitress reappeared.

"You two finally ready for another round?" she asked.

"I am," C.W. said, and dropped a card beside it, along with a twenty. "Would you please do me a favor, and give this to your boss, let him know if he could spare a few minutes when he gets a chance, it won't be a waste."

"I'll see that he gets it," she said. She refilled C.W.'s glass, took the card, and gave it to a passing waitress to give to Vlad. She looked briefly at us, rolled her eyes at the cheap ass bribe money, and continued on her rounds.

"Important man. Probably gets that a lot," C.W. said, a knowing smirk rolling low across his face.

"Sure," I told him.

I watched the server hand the card to the pet shark, before speaking briefly with Vlad and his guests, taking their orders. She came back by and asked us to wait. She told us we should order an appetizer, compliments of the owner. She said the caviar nachos were to die for.

"Sounds good," C.W. said. I looked at him like I didn't believe him, but didn't say anything.

Keep hoping, bitch.

Fuck you too, I told the voice in my head.

I ordered another drink, both to put up a front, and to shut him up.

C.W. had a third, and then a fourth. I scanned the crowd, looking for more players, but found none other than the odd bouncer. How many of them were on his real payroll, and how many were football players making some side money before going back to college in the fall, I had no idea. Though it threw the odds further out of our favor if something went down, I hoped none of them were.

The caviar nachos came and went. Little wedges of freshly made tortilla chips, with a sliver of foie gras for a bed beneath a tiny spoonful of caviar, drizzled with some kind of southwestern chili avocado cream sauce. I didn't see the point of eating caviar and not tasting the ocean, but then, I didn't see the point of eating it without vodka either.

"What are you so worried about?" C.W. asked, chomping away on the last nacho. He hadn't bothered smelling it, noting the presentation, or chewing it slowly. He hadn't said a word about the texture. It might as well have been stale tortilla chips covered in chili and Velveeta, with a sprinkling of pickled jalapenos atop it as far as he was concerned. And I was the Neanderthal?

"I seriously think we should leave, homeboy. I don't like this...got a bad feeling," I told him, playing up the intuition. Maybe I just told myself I was playing it up. I could feel a case of cold shakes coming like the hangover after a long awaited dry drunk.

Twenty minutes later, the heavy with the nicely groomed beard and his nicely muscled companion left, and Vlad leaned out of the booth looking our way. His face gave nothing away as he spoke shortly to his bodyguard, and then he disappeared back inside the red leather. The bodyguard lifted his hand to his mouth and spoke.

And then nothing happened. The suspense of him looking back at us just hung in the air.

"I wonder who the fuck they were," C.W., pondered next to me. There was an agitation in his voice at not getting to meet Vlad.

"Beats me, dude," I said, thankful nothing had yet happened.

"I gotta piss, be back in a sec," he said, and slid off his bar stool to go to the restroom. I sipped at my drink, and hoped he would resign himself to another day.

I sat, sipped my drink, and watched the crowd. I watched the girls come and go. I watched some douchebags from a frat house do shots. I watched a woman pretend to seduce a man into bringing home a pet. I watched Vlad leave the floor with his pro in tow. I watched the pro lean in, and listen to a bouncer as he passed. And my Spidey-Sense pinged off the rails.

The heavy wasn't giving an order, or telling someone what to do, he was being told the result. My hand clasped around my glass. It started to crack, but did not break. I took a deep breath, and looked around, and had violent thoughts. I took another deep breath, and tried to get control.

I looked at my watch, and cursed myself for not making a time hack when C.W. had left.

Some pro you are.

Go fuck yourself, you fucking fuck, I said to the voice of my own personal demon.

I scanned everything I could see and rose from the table, leaving the glass where it was.

He wasn't at the urinals, and he wasn't doing coke with everyone else in the stalls. The people in the stalls didn't much care for me stepping in for a look, but they didn't make an issue of it either. When I stepped back through the restroom door, two of the bouncers were waiting on me.

The first one was one of the pros. Not Sharkskin, but another one, who reeked of smarm and date rape. The other one looked like a mutant of a middle linebacker. Smarmy was leaning against the wall with his arm extended, so that his suit coat hung open wide enough for me to see the top of a stainless steel semi-automatic. It looked like a Walther P99, but I couldn't be sure. His friend the mutant held a collapsible baton in his hand like it was his dick, and it was the only thing he'd ever had to play with.

"Mr. Bam-Bam," Smarmy said.

"I've been called that, yeah," I said. He gave me the lazy, unimpressed look someone gives when they really want you to know how unimpressed they are with you, which usually means just the opposite.

"Please, follow me. Your friend is this way," he said, nodding over his shoulder to the door behind him, marked Employees Only.

"Sure," I said. I didn't know where C.W. was, and I needed a way to even the odds. I hoped following him would accomplish at least one of those things.

I followed Smarmy through the door, into a small kitchen. The handful of illegals scattered about at their stations ignored us.

I doubted the goon behind me was armed with any more than the collapsible baton he played with, like a teenager with a hard on. He'd be the one who would have to deal with cops, as they picked up the rowdy drunks. He'd be in and out of the crowd all night, dealing with angry, jealous boyfriends. It would be stupid for him to have a gun. I hoped he thought so as well.

I took a deep breath and tried to get my heart rate under control. Smarmy opened a new door, and hot air slapped us hard across the face as we stepped out into the night, into the alley behind the club. I could hear the dim thump of music inside the converted warehouse, and smell the stagnant stench of the river past the chain link fence and over the levee.

I resisted the urge to put my hand on my knife, not wanting to pull it until I knew I was going to have to kill them both. The bouncer behind me might have just been another moonlighting college football player. It didn't seem likely, but it was possible.

We stepped into the alley, our shoes trampling the loose pavement, where years of pounding by heavy trucks had turned the cement into tiny bits of loosely packed gravel. The air was hot and humid with musk, soaking us in sweat before the door had slammed back on its hinges. Beside a dumpster, several vehicles sat empty. When Smarmy turned, spinning on his heels to face me, I confirmed my suspicions about his firearm when I spied the grip of a Walther P99 with a stainless slide tucked beneath his waistband, the thin metal clip of a holster just another extra loop on over his belt.

"Where's my friend?" I asked, pretending I was surprised he wasn't there. Smarmy shrugged.

"I don't know," he said. He pulled a cigarette from a silver case and lit with a matching lighter.

"Maybe, you'll see him later, with your Mexican friends. Manuel said something about…introducing you to his dog," he said, smirking around the cigarette as he pulled in a lungful.

"My Mexican friends," I asked, my anger building. I told myself to remain calm. It didn't work. "I'm gonna kill every one of you fucks," I said.

Smarmy flickered an eye of command to the man behind me, and I heard the baton click open.

I turned as he was bringing his arm up over his head. I stepped forward, bringing my arms up in a classic Crazy Monkey defense position, bringing both arms in, leading with my elbows as I ducked my head and stepped forward, trying to close the gap as fast as possible. As fast as I could ever hope, faster than I'd ever done in training. Just not fast enough to keep from getting hit.

I was low, my left arm coming up over his shoulder when the baton glanced off my right lat. Even for a glancing blow, he'd had a lot of power behind it, obviously going for the kill shot when I moved. I pushed through it, wrapping my arm around his shoulder and wrenching down as I delivered four hard, fast cradle blows to his throat in rapid succession.

He made a loud wheezing sound, the baton dropped, and his free hand went to his throat. I dropped him, trying to push myself through to the next target, wanting to keep the momentum rolling. I was spinning on the ball of my foot, as if I were throwing a discus, my hand finding purchase on the Spyderco, when a starburst exploded behind my ear. I fell to the ground in slow motion, seeing Smarmy raise his gun even while I was falling.

As my back slammed into the hard cement, I rolled back on my shoulder blades, then twisted my hips violently, kicking Smarmy's legs out from under him, bringing him down to my level. I scrambled to mount him, my left knee pinning his forearm to the ground, keeping the gun away from me. He stuck his fingers in my eyes, and I let him, snapping the Spyderco P'kal out from beneath my belt reverse grip, edge in, and going to town.

I don't know how many times I stabbed him, but I moved that blade just like an ice pick working away at a block of ice. Fast and hard, until there was nothing left but little pieces for my drink. When it was over, when I looked down to see lifeless eyes above the matching gapes of his mouth and neck, I rolled off him and sat on my haunches for the briefest of moments. I could hear the big goon who'd tried to kill me with his metal dick slowly suffocating beneath his crushed larynx.

I picked up the Walther, press checked it, then checked the load in the mag. A .40 S&W. It was a gun I liked in a caliber I didn't. Still, it damn sure beat going back inside with only my dick in my hand.

I patted Smarmy down and found a single loose magazine inside his coat pocket, and a set of keys in his pants. Not much, but it beat a sharp stick. I took his money clip just for meanness.

I hit the button on the key fob, and the lights of a black suburban not far from the back door flashed. I wiped my blade off on his pant leg, stood, picked the baton up off the ground, and brought it down hard one final time on the big goon's bloody throat. I snapped its length closed against the brick wall and walked back into the kitchen, the Walther held just behind my thigh.

When I entered the kitchen, covered in blood, the wetbacks stopped ignoring me.

"Vamoose," I told them, and they vamoosed, out into the alley and elsewhere.

I went back the way I'd come, through the service hallway, and up the narrow staircase we'd passed at the back of the club. On the second floor, I could see through the fish-tank windows to the dance floor below. I made my way down the hall to a room marked office, and stood with my ear against the grain, the pistol in my hand. When I heard the sound of flesh being slapped and the curse of the defiant, I knew he was there, and that violence of action and the element of surprise were the only things that would get us both out of there alive.

With the panorama vision only enjoyed with massive amounts of adrenaline, I opened the door, and saw C.W. tied to a chair pushed back from the front of the desk, Sharkskin standing before him. Behind the desk was a fat man I hadn't seen before. He was lighting a cigar.

Past C.W. and Sharkskin, there was another man leaned up against the wall opposite the desk, one arm wrenched above his shoulder and resting atop a file cabinet moving a cigarette back and forth from his lips. Behind them, setting on a low-slung sofa against the far wall, sat two more men.

Sharkskin was hovering over C.W., his coat off, revealing a large reverse two-tone 1911 under one arm, his sleeves rolled up revealing blue tats, and a custom bowie knife in his hand. The knife was stuck through C.W.'s pants leg to the chair. Sharkskin looked up at me, his eyes wide with surprise, his cigarette falling from his gaping mouth. I shot him in the face.

He dropped over C.W., the chair toppling under their weight, and they fell to the floor.

As they fell past the end of my gun, a man of average height, with the wiry build of a prize fighter came up from a low slung couch against the back wall, bringing an AKSU-74 up, and I got jumpy. The first shot nicked his shoulder, and in my haste, I pulled the trigger as fast as I could, raking my fire across his chest until he fell down.

I shifted, firing into the third man, who was trying to pull a handgun from beneath his coat. My bullets tore through his crossed arm and into his chest and face. The man leaning against the file cabinet had forgone any weaponry on his person and lunged at me. I sidestepped back, bringing my elbow down and back, locked into my side for retention, and shot him four times in the chest.

I spun, the fat man behind the desk trying to bring a huge, beefy, snub-nosed Ruger Alaskan to bear when he looked in my eyes, and dropped the massive piece on the desk. I shot him in the head.

My ears rang, but only slightly, thanks to the adrenaline, and my heart thudded against my chest in heavy blows. My body felt numb from the rush of adrenaline, and I forced myself to focus. Cornelius was talking to me, but I couldn't hear what he was saying. I wrenched the bowie knife out of his chair, and cut him free.

The knife was a custom job, one I hadn't seen before, with a medium length blade, deep belly, stainless bolster and S guard. It had been carried in what I recognized as Mike Sastre's famous Southern Comfort sheath on the table. I slipped the knife back in its scabbard, and slipped it behind my hip. I pressed the de-cocker on the Walther, performed a tactical reload, and slipped it behind my belt before checking the AKSU-74 , or Suchka (little bitch), as it was known in Russian, and handing it to Cornelius.

"Keep your finger off the trigger," I told him. It was important for him to keep his finger off the trigger, because I'd left the safety off, not wanting him to forget it in panic. I didn't have time to teach him how to properly use it, but he damned sure needed a gun. He nodded his head, still staring at the dead men.

He stood stoop shouldered and wobbly beside the chair, slowly accepting our place and time. It had happened suddenly, violently, without warning, but we didn't have time for him to catch up. We had to move, and we had to move right then.

I peeked out the door, listening for the sounds of people running. There was nothing. I stepped forward, and looked through the fish tanks, and below to the dance floor flooded with people that hadn't stopped dancing, thanks to the soundproofing. I turned back, and Cornelius was right behind me, the AK held tightly before him, his knuckles white around its grips.

"Listen, we're gonna go right back out the way I came up, okay?" I told him, then through the door opened at his heel, I saw the bank of video receivers in the far corner, no doubt for the surveillance cameras at the front door and throughout the bar. We needed intel, and we needed to cover our trail.

"Hold up, hoss," I said, guiding him back inside with me. I locked the door, and asked him to stand in the corner near the desk, on guard. He did as I asked, but he wasn't happy about it.

There was a laptop on the desk, and beside it a large heavy duty-nylon bag for it. I shoved the laptop and its power cord into the bag, along with the big ass Ruger Alaskan, and then checked each man for wallets and weapons, transferring them to the bag. From the man who'd lunged at me, I pulled a compact, stainless 3rd Gen Smith and Wesson 9mm with a bobbed hammer in a clip holster from the small of his back. I handed the holstered gun to C.W., telling him to clip it inside his pants, before moving on to the next guy.

The gun Sharkskin had carried under his arm had been a custom 1911, with a stainless frame, black slide, and compensator, in 10mm. My respect for him as an operator dropped a few points. I wrapped the rig around itself, stuffed it in the case, and moved on.

I found a small Colt .380 on one of the remaining two men, and nothing on the other one. "Pussy," I said, to the corpse, as I kicked it in the ribs. Who carries a .380 as a primary gun on the belt? I mean, really.

"Jeb," C.W. pleaded.

"Yeah, okay," I said, still pissed at the armament situation, as well as nearly professionally offended.

I opened a wall locker, and found another Suchka, a 30 round magazine ready to go locked in place, and on a shelf, several more were stacked together, including two clipped together. Next to the spare mags was a single fragmentation grenade.

On hangers below the shelf were several sets of ballistic vests, with plates.

"Fuckin' sweet," I said. I slipped a vest on C.W., and then myself, took the AK, switched out the single mag for the dual stack, placed the spare one in my left rear pocket, and hooked the frag onto my belt. Everything else went into the bag.

"Keep watching the door, bro, just a little more time," I said. I moved to the bank of monitors and began pulling out their drives.

"What the fuck are you doing?" He asked, his voice filled with worry, nervousness, and anticipation.

"Chill, motherfucker. Just watch the door," I said. I'd done this exact thing, on two different continents. Lot of people need killin' in this world.

When I was done, I crammed them into the laptop bag with everything else. Practice makes perfect.

"We're gonna walk out this door, down the back stairs, and out the kitchen. I'll lead the way. You watch our six, do you understand?" I said.

"Yes, goddamn it, now let's get out of here already," he said. I handed him the laptop bag to shoulder, then led the way.

I led him into the empty kitchen, stopping at the back door and taking a quick breath. Outside was no man's land.

"Just follow me, and do what I say, okay?" I semi-asked, semi-ordered. He wobbled his head. Guess that meant yes. I pushed open the door and stepped out, the gun up, turning a full 360, looking for any threats. Outside, the night was still just as hot and musty as I'd left it, the smell of death not yet finding its purchase.

I looked at the black Chevy suburban parked near the door alongside the other vehicles. Realizing at least one of us might need to change our appearance, I yanked Smarmy's sport coat off, and found his newsboy style hat lying on the concrete.

"Jesus, Jeb," Cornelius said, as the door closed behind us

"They were going to kill us both, what the fuck you want?" I asked, not wanting to take the time for dumb shit.

"I just, I don't…"

"We'll talk about it later," I assured him still pissed at myself for letting it go this far.

"Get in the backseat," I said, as I slipped behind the wheel, and turned the key, lowering the windows and turning off the radio. C.W. slipped in behind me, and I had him move over, so that we could cover all sides a little bit better.

Weapons at the ready, we rolled out of the alley, and crept past the front of the building. At the end of the parking lot before us was Riverside Drive, or what I still thought of as Industrial Blvd. Beyond that, safety, freedom, security.

That's when it always happens. Just when you think you're home free, that the day is yours after all, that it's nothing but warm apple pie and big-tittied homecoming queens from there on out, that's when your ticket gets punched.

Out in front, at the valet station, beside a pimped-out, pastel-colored, lowered, extended cab mid 90's Chevy pickup truck with running boards and ground effects, Vlad was talking to the Hispanic man we'd seen him with inside, his girlfriend, and my friend Manny. Behind the truck I could see two more ghetto fabulous rides, and behind them, two serious looking black Cadillac SUV's. All of them filled with people who wanted us dead. Every one of them turned and stared at us while we slowly passed, every one of them lost in that long pause people have when they ignore the simian part of their brain, waiting on their intellect to catch up.

This…is when I opened fire.

Vlad and the others standing dove into the parking lot seeking cover. The ones in the vehicles were sitting ducks. When the AK went dry, I yanked the pin on the grenade, and tossed it. It was sort of a flimsy, weak, underhand pitch out the window, only half-assed aimed in the direction of the leaders who had taken cover inside the filled parking lot, and stood on the gas as the first rounds of return fire cracked off from their position. We rocketed out of the parking lot.

I took a hard right, going East on Riverside, as the grenade went off behind us, and throttled past cars, warehouses and businesses, through a red light, for a quick two blocks, before I took a hard left onto a side street. We cruised another block, before I turned down an alley, drove halfway down the block, and stopped just long enough to take quick stock and reload.

I flipped the magazines in the Suchka, rolling my hand to place the fresh mag in the well, before reaching up to work the bolt. My preferred method of working the bolt was to simply roll the gun, in my firing hand, over so I that I could see the bolt and be able to diagnose any problems, but when flipping mags your hand is basically in position to go ahead and work the bolt, so I worked it.

I looked in the rear-view at C.W. His breath was rapid and shallow, his eyes were wide, and his hands were so tight around the grips of the unfired little machine pistol they looked like white gloves.

"You ok, bro?" I asked.

"You just opened fire on them," he said, like he couldn't believe it.

"You're goddamn right I did," I told him.

On an arm extending off the dash, there was a laptop computer on a stand, similar to what some police have in their patrol cars.

Somewhere along the way it had turned itself on, and showed a map with a red arrow marking our location.

I ripped it off and tossed it out the window. There could be other devices, but I might have to get under the car and pop the hood to find them. Getting gone took precedence.

"Why the fuck did you do that?"

"Dude, it's their vehicle. It might be synched into the GPSs in their other trucks," I said. He looked at me, his eyes wide with disbelief.

"Just be cool, bubba," I said. "Hardest part's over with. Now, we just gotta get out of Indian Country."

We rolled easy to the end of the alley, catching our breath and listening to the city sounds. Sirens were already wailing behind us. We turned left at the end of the alley, onto the next major street, and took it to the I-35 on-ramp.

As usual, the highway was filled with traffic, but it moved at a steady clip, and we sailed evenly past the many hotels that catered to the business convention crowd. I thought we might have it home free, until the next exit, across from the famous waterfall overlooking I35, when I spotted Manny's pastel colored truck. The corner of its bumper was torn, nearly touching the ground, it's paint job marred with burn marks and debris. Following it were another G ride and a black suburban. They were staring at us.

"You got your seat belt on?" I asked C.W., a little pissed at myself for not making sure of it already. It's always the basic shit that gets people killed.

"What?" He asked back.

I looked in the rear-view and saw he didn't. "Put your goddamn seat belt on, now," I barked.

"Oh, shit," he said, as a shooter leaned out the rear window of Manny's truck, leveling a Mac variant at us. Needing both hands on the wheel, I dropped the little AK in the shotgun seat and took my foot off the accelerator, letting them overtake us, hitting it again and swerving into their rear bumper as they passed, spinning them around.

The impact caused the Suchka to fall out of the seat and into the floorboard.

Fuckballs.

"Fuck!" C.W. called out amid the screeching of tires and the crunch of metal as people crashed behind us, rolling across the back seat as I tried to straighten up and punch it off the X.

Traffic near the scene either stopped or slowed, some vehicles in the further lanes swerving to the right as they hit their brakes, while the traffic behind us stopped entirely behind the wrecked vehicles, creating a nearly empty lane past the immediate obstacles. I moved onto the shoulder and accelerated hard past until the right lane was clear, then moved over and pushed it just as fast as I could while keeping the bitch under control.

The pimped out Cutlass was right behind us, and behind it, I could see Manny's grotesque pickup push its way out of the mess, leaning to the side and billowing smoke like a pissed off rhino.

I did not see the black suburban loaded down with what I assumed to be cartel shooters. It was as if they had simply evaporated in mist. At least for the moment we just had the two vehicles full of comparative amateurs to deal with, instead of a suburban full of hardened, professional operators. Thank God for small favors.

As we passed the American Airlines Center and neared downtown, traffic picked back up, and I watched several vehicles enter the Woodall Rodgers on-ramp. I knew if I didn't do something about the two vehicles full of assholes following us, if I didn't control the field, they would, and they would do so without care or thought for innocent life.

I slowed, following a Lexus sedan onto the two-lane on ramp. The sedan was creeping slowly up the middle of the ramp, occupying enough space on both sides to keep from safely passing.

The Cutlass roared up, bullets pinging off and through the metal of the SUV. I swerved hard into them, pushing them against the concrete wall, and scrambled for a gun when C.W. leaned out of the window and fired the little AK. It was the sweetest sound I'd ever heard.

"Fuck yeah! Hell yeah, baby!" I yelled, elated, as the Cutlass came across the last lane of traffic and crashed into the side of the on ramp. I looked in the rear-view, saw the charging rhino coming for us, and pushed further up the ramp.

At the top, a little past halfway up the ramp, I swerved to the right and then back across, stopping hard without skidding, the suburban angled across both lanes, and brought the Suchka up to bear, aiming it at the bend in the track behind us.

As soon as the limping rhino came around the corner, I opened fire, in not so short bursts, and the truck crashed into the concrete wall, spinning sideways, wedging itself across the ramp and blocking further traffic. When the AK went dry, I yanked the spare mag from my waistband, used the floor-plate to hit the magazine release, knocking the two empties to the floorboard, rocked it in place, ran the bolt, and emptied the final mag in one long burst into the sideways truck. When it ran dry, I dropped the gun in the seat next to me, and steered toward the end of the ramp.

"Oh Jesus, oh Jesus, what the fuck, what the fuck," C.W. was saying as he tried to reload his own weapon.

"Is that some kinda prayer? 'Oh Jesus, what the fuck?'" I asked, hitting the gas as we came onto Woodall Rodgers.

"Fuck you," he said.

"I know, I know," I said.

We got on Woodall Rodgers and then took the next exit, before taking side streets and alleys around the north side of downtown and stopped at the red light under the mix-master. We rolled beneath the overpass, and took the next, down a street that led toward Baylor Hospital, and ran parallel to the historic Deep Ellum neighborhood, where my getting drunk had started all this.

We crossed the metro tracks, and I saw the Elm Street Station, a few passengers mingling in the opening, waiting on the next train. I began looking for a place to ditch the suburban. I had no idea how many of the traffic cameras were working, and all the sirens I heard were in the distance, but I knew they'd be running through them, trying to locate the vehicle.

"What now?" C.W. asked.

"First we're going to ditch this vehicle. Then, we're going to get someplace safe, take stock, and figure out our next move," I said.

"Are we going to call the cops? Morales?" he asked.

"No, not yet, anyway. We need to go to ground," I said. We needed all kinds of distance, but we needed to do so as safely and anonymously as possible. I also needed him to do what I told him, without giving him time to think. Letting him think had gotten us into this goddamn mess.

"Do me a favor, put on that sport coat, please. And pass that cap up here," I asked. He did so, forgetting to un-sling the gun beforehand. It would be going in the laptop bag.

"Unsling the gun, homie. We're putting it in the bag," I said. He nodded his head, and did so, his movements slow and uncertain.

"Hey," I said, raising my voice just a notch to get his attention. He looked up at me, his glasses crooked beneath his ball cap. He'd never fired a weapon in anger, never experienced combat, never been so close to being tortured. I did not need him going into shock over it. The past half hour had been eventful, even for me. For him, he might as well be on another planet.

"You did really well, bro. You're hot shit with that choppa," I said.

"Really?" he asked, as if I were lying.

"Fuck yeah, you saved both our shit, home-boy. Big time," I said, emphasizing the truth.

He smiled at that.

The light turned green, and I rolled through it.

Across from the metro station, I saw a short narrow path, more of a driveway than an alley, and I pulled in. There were fences on both sides, everyone employed by the businesses gone for the night. I parked in a dirt lot owned by someone who either didn't know what they had, or had decided to hold out for more money.

I killed the engine and we climbed out, and C.W. made a show of taking deep breaths, his hands crooked beneath the straps of his vest, pushing out to relieve the tension on his chest.

"Oh, Jesus, fuck, shit," he said.

"You're doing good bro, be cool," I told him. Going for reassuring.

"That was insane," he said, leaning against the side of the truck.

"Yeah," I said. I pulled out my cell and called Morales.

"You got some fucking nerve," was how he answered his cell phone.

"What can you tell me?" I asked. On the other end I heard heavy breathing, behind what I assumed was intense thought. Morales did not strike me as a man who did anything lightly. Whether it was killing himself with fried food and doughnuts, working a homicide, or helping a friend in need, he struck me as a man who walked heavily upon the earth with each and every step, and I respected him greatly for that.

"All they have is a description of the vehicle, I'll call you on this phone if there's more," he said, and hung up without another word.

I closed the phone and put it back in my pocket and thought about our situation. I thought about the metro rail across the street, but I was also covered in blood, wearing a ballistic vest I didn't particularly want to take off, with someone I needed to protect, carrying with us a bag of guns and raw intel we needed to process.

I didn't see the train ride being worthwhile.

I strained to listen past his heavy breathing, as the city lived and breathed around us. The traffic on the streets, the sirens in the distance.

I looked at my friend, the worry on his face, his breath shallow yet heavy with tension. The thoughts on my mind were as heavy as any had ever been.

The smart thing was to dump the vehicle; however, that might mean dumping weapons and protective vests in order to blend in. If it were just me, I might not have thought twice about it. Not with C.W., though. I was responsible for him, whether he liked it or not, and I didn't like the thought of pulling him out of that goddamn vest.

I pulled out my cell phone, and punched the number for Uncle Jack's man Friday.

"Tell me this isn't you," was all he asked.

"We're ok, we need a pickup, though," I said.

"Where you at?"

"Just outside downtown. Across the street from the Elm Street Metro Station."

"Tell me you're not taking the rail."

"No, but we need to move."

"Copy that. I'm not close, but I'm on my way. You need to find a secure RV and hit me back," he said.

"Gotcha," I said, and pressed the end button.

"Who was that?" C.W. asked.

"Russell," I said, scrolling through my phone until I found the cabbie, Spamson's, number, pleased I'd had the foresight to add it from the card he'd given me the day before.

"Who are you calling now?" he asked.

"A ride," I said, punching the number.

"Yo, this is Albert, what can I do for you?"

"Spamson, this is Jeb, can you come pick up me and Cornelius?"

"I'm on my way to another fare, dog. Gonna have to wait."

"Drop it, we'll make up the difference, and then some."

"Shit, that don't keep regular customers happy, know what I mean?"

"Spam, it's important," I told him, trying to keep an even tone.

"So are my regular customers," he said. C.W. watched my nostrils flare, and then reached out and grabbed the cell.

"Spam, this is C.W. We'll buy the night, homeboy, just come the fuck on," he said, and then paused, before he gave him our location.

"Be about fifteen minutes," he said, handing me the phone.

"Just gotta know what to say, hoss," he added.

CHAPTER 35

Spamson was game. He had a place near where we'd come from, on Riverside, in an empty concrete lot just behind the Lew Sterrit jail. We sat in a deep corner of the lot, nestled in some weeds, the back end touching the bushes and trees along the slope of the old train grade that ran behind the jail. The car sat at an angle behind what I assumed at one time had been the end of a loading dock. Some skateboarders had fashioned a ramp against it. The nose of the cab was facing out, the windows were down, the A/C was off, and we were listening to the low steady traffic of Spamson's police band, the traffic on the boulevard a couple of hundred yards away, and the faint but steady hum of sirens a few miles to the west, on scene at Vlad's.

I didn't really like being that close to the scene of the crime, but Spamson assured us he wasn't the only cabbie that pulled into the lot for a quick nap, and that cops generally left them alone.

"You're covered in blood," C.W. said. I didn't like his tone, wanted to ignore him out of spite, but he was right.

"Hey, bro, you got some baby wipes, change of clothes maybe, anything in here?" I asked Spamson. He reached for the dash, hit a button, and the trunk opened. He nodded, unmoving, his ears tuned into the police band almost exclusively. He hadn't asked where we'd come from or what we'd done. We'd grown up together, and though he and I had never really been that close, all my friends growing up had been his friends, and that was enough. I'm sure being a foot over society's imaginary, bullshit line probably helped his thought process, but he had no reason other than our history to help us. Sure, it was a job, but the risk of getting caught up in whatever shit he could guess we were in, could not have been worth the price alone for a man reformed in every way that mattered. God bless East Texas and tribal ties.

I pulled myself out of the cab, found the baby wipes in the trunk, and closed the trunk to kill the light. Next I pulled off the vest and then the blood covered shirt, and began giving myself a babywipe bath. It was just like the 'Box, all over again.

We were in the shadow of the arc, the first building blocks of the grand bridge that would supposedly transform downtown when finally built, making Dallas a downtown city, like New York, Chicago, or LA. They'd been talking about flooding the Trinity and making it navigable since before I was born. The plans to do so had been nothing but boondoggle after boondoggle, the latest being a carpet bagging mayor's legacy to her adopted home town.

Maybe it's true of every city on earth. Those in power only ever cared about what they wanted, even if no one else seemed to agree. Maybe because no one else wanted what they did.

The sad thing is, even if everyone did want it, all they would've had to do was legalize gambling, and private interests would've taken care of it. But hey, I guess that's what tax money's for.

I listened to C.W. say something to Spamson, before scooting across the seat and opening the door. "Bring the bag with you," I told him. He paused, looking at me, half out the door, and then leaned behind him and grabbed the bag and the Suchka.

I stopped what I was doing, and put the gun on the hood of the trunk, within easy reach.

"You really think we need all that? Haven't you killed everybody in town?"

"Shut your goddamn mouth," I snapped, cutting a look at Spamson still inside the cab and ignoring us as hard as possible.

He started to say something else, but caught himself.

I pulled another baby wipe out of the box, and went back to work, staring at him, through him, toward the entrance of the lot and the lights of passing traffic.

"This shit's fucking crazy," he said, shaking his head.

"Yeah," I said. When I was done, I dropped the baby wipe atop the bundled up shirt with the other one, and grabbed the bag and moved it to the trunk.

I gathered the wallets from the bag, and then pulled the cash, working it into a thick stack. I guess Vlad's guys hadn't joined the plastic revolution with everyone else in the first world.

I counted it, thumbed it into halves, folded one, and slid it deep into a pocket of my slacks. I folded the rest, and stuck it in the opposite pocket. I looked at the toy 10mm, the little .380, the silly ass Ruger Alaskan, and the two spare mags for C.W.'s little AK. I stuck one mag in my left rear pocket, top down, facing the same way I'd carry spare mags on my belt.

"What are you doing?" C.W. asked.

"What's it look like," I snapped.

I took two steps and squatted down, my head just above window level. I pulled the fold of money and handed it to Spamson between two fingers.

"This is for bringing us here. You can take off now, no one will hold it against you, but if you stay, I'll triple this," I told him. He took it from me, unfolded it, and looked at it. As he realized how much I'd given him, certain things flashed in front of his eyes. It would be trite to call them dollar signs. I knew they weren't. What he saw was what he could do for his wife and young child. I could remember when similar things flashed before my own eyes, and I hated myself for playing on those needs.

"Fuck yeah, bro, I ain't no bitch. You know that, *homes,*" he said, throwing me a fist bump, oblivious to the earlier antagonism.

My cell buzzed in my pocket, and I fished it out.

"Flash your lights, asshole," Russell said.

"Roger that," I said, before telling Spamson to flash the lights as the big truck pulled in. Russell flashed once in return, and veered toward us.

"What now?" Cornelius asked.

"You go with him. Fuckin' duh," I said.

"And what are you doing?"

I took a deep breath, and tried to ignore the righteous indignation creeping into his voice.

"I'm going someplace else," I said.

"Where? Maybe I want to go with you," he said, his voice firm and curious.

"No, you don't get to go with me," I told him, trying to gain distance, as I studied the headlights of the big truck weaving its way through potholes toward us.

"Hey, goddamn it, who the fuck put you in charge?" he snapped, spittle flying, his voice rising, stepping so close I could feel the heat and booze and adrenaline sweat on his breath.

"You did—the moment doing it your way stopped working," I told him, trying to remain calm. The last thing I wanted was for him to cause a scene in an empty lot behind the jail, down the street from the night club I'd just shot up.

Russell cut his lights as he pulled the big truck around the corner and alongside us, so that C.W. and I were between it and Spamson's cab. Dirt rose in the air as he came to a stop, and the exhaust from his diesel clung to it in the hot, still, dark night air.

The rumble of his engine held the sounds of sirens in the distance just below a still surface.

"Why do you look like you just stepped out of a Madonna video?" Russell asked.

"My shirt's a big 'ol no-go. You got anything? What about a go bag?" I asked.

"I got a nasty ass stankin' workout shirt that's probably still soaked."

"Fuck it," I told him, with a shrug.

He reached behind him and pulled a gym bag from behind the seat. He opened it up, and tossed it to me. It was gray, and drenched with stank sweat. It did, however, fit.

"You gonna regroup or go proactive?" Russell asked.

"I'm going to try to keep the momentum in our favor as long as possible," I said.

"I don't have any clean weapons on me, that shit takes notification, *son*. I got a spare blow-out kit you can have though."

"Fuck yes, that'd be great," I said.

The not-so-merry giant shambled out of his oversized truck and stepped past us. He walked to the rear of the truck, a Ford Expedition, and opened the rear doors.

"I'm going with you," C.W. said.

"No, you're not."

"You don't get to tell me what I'm going to do."

"I can tell you you're not coming with me," I said.

"Fuck you, Jeb," he yelled, rising up, grabbing the shirt I'd just pulled on, trying to pull me closer.

I was trying to be reasonable, but anger is not something I've learned to easily let pass. Past a certain point, it stays for hours, sometimes days or even weeks, the wounds inflicted, real or imagined, festering, as hot as magma. The only things that have ever seemed to satiate the need to inflict damage upon the world, other than violence itself, were the touch of a woman who would never love me again, and sweet, sweet liquor. I had no plans to ever talk to the first bitch again, and I needed a clear head for what lay ahead.

"I'm not letting you go alone, Jeb," Cornelius said, standing before me. His feet spread at forty-five degrees, in some sort of stance. Whether it was Tai Chi, or Kung Fu, or one of the other bullshit, mall-ninja dojo scams he studied, I had no idea, but I wasn't in the mood. I had to go on the offense, or at the very least, instigate a proactive defense. I didn't have time for his bullshit.

"Get the fuck out of my way," I said, the warning in my voice obvious. I stepped forward and he sank his hips, centering himself. If he was going to make me move him, I was going to make it good and painful. I didn't want to have to do it more than once.

I stepped forward again, and his hands found my chest. For a moment I thought I felt the power, the energy that ran through his body; the energy that gave him such confidence. I took a deep breath, hoping I could control myself. I'd studied a mixed bag of violent arts since before it was cool. I'd been lifting weights since puberty. My best bench is five hundred neat. I have to work twice as hard to develop any finesse, but I hardly ever need any. I'd spent the last several years at work as a gun hand not because I was imbalanced from the war, or because the military had brainwashed me, but because it was the only work I'd ever cared to suit myself to. I was a warrior, in the strictest sense of the word, and it was all I'd ever wanted to be.

And I wanted him to get out of my way, and to stay that way, but I didn't want to hurt someone, who for all intents and purposes was probably a more welcome member of my own family than I was.

I brought my hands up and over, slamming into the tops of his wrist. Because he was centered, he didn't fall forward off balance, but he couldn't get his hands up in time to prevent me from slamming both fists into his chest. He fell too quickly to gather his balance.

I watched the pain wash over his face, the recognition of the line we'd just crossed, and it broke my heart. But that wasn't the worst of it. No, the worst of it was when I leaned over as he sat on his haunches in the dirt, the air around us hot, and rank with sweat and the stench of the river and the exhaust of Russell's diesel, and slapped him, open palmed, letting him know he was out of his league, and there was nothing he could do about it. I slapped him again and again, all the way to the ground. He tried to put his hands up, but instead just stared at me as I did so. A thin trickle of blood slipped and ran down from the corner of his mouth.

"Know your place, bitch," I said.

"What the fuck's wrong with you two?" Russell asked as he slammed his doors shut and stepped towards us, holding out a nice fat medic bag. I took it, opened the door behind Spamson, and tossed it inside. Russell helped C.W. stand, and put him in the big diesel before turning to look at me as I handed him the laptop bag.

"Couple pistols in here, plus a laptop, wallets, and cell phones. The drives from the surveillance feeds might have some intel in there."

"You really just rode around in a cab with this shit?"

"Yes," I said. I had done nothing wrong. Taking the laptop, phones, and wallets might be suspect to a cop, but I would've said I simply took it to give to the authorities. If the cops had arrested us, I'd have had far worse problems anyway.

"How's Kendrick?"

"Locked up tight and happy to be there," he said, a certain uncertainty, one I knew well, creeping at the edge of his voice. Kendrick was in a weird place. He was helping us, because he didn't have a choice, but he was comfortable with it because he thought of us as the good guys. The problem was, things were escalating at such a rate that might prevent us from contacting the police. Which meant Kendrick, a known criminal, and not your regular, dime-bag pickpocket, but a genuine bad guy, one involved in human trafficking, knew way too much about everyone involved on our side, not to mention Russell's setup with Uncle Jack.

"He's my problem, if it comes to *that*," I said. He looked at me a long moment, the corner of his lip turned up slightly, in such a way as I couldn't tell the difference between smug and snarling.

"If you're dead, he's my problem, now ain't he?" he asked, before climbing back into his truck.

I grabbed my shirt and the used baby wipes, and walked behind the cab into the bushes at the base of the train grade, dug a small hole, and placed them there. I covered it up, and went back to the cab, grabbed the box of baby wipes and Suchka off the trunk lid, and told Spamson to open it again.

I placed his baby wipes back where I'd found them and paused. I looked over the top of the trunk at the lights on the boulevard, as if I could see the future if I just searched hard enough.

I thought for a minute, and then walked back up to the cab and leaned in Spamson's window.

"Do the back seats fold over?" I asked.

"Yeah, dog," he said.

I opened the door behind him, grabbed the vest, and placed both the vest and the Suchka down right behind the back of the left rear seat.

I slid in the cab, closed the door, and scooted over to behind the passenger seat. I found the tab at the top of the seat cushion, and pulled it down, reached into the trunk and readjusted my gear, and folded the cushion back up.

"Where to, boss?"

"We need to go to the gayborhood to pick up a car. Take the long way around, though. Get us away from the sirens, bro," I said.

"Not a problem, hoss. Not a problem."

We rolled out to the boulevard, and waited for a break in traffic.

"You want some music?" Spamson asked.

"Fuck, yes," I told him. He punched a button on the dash, and we caught the tail end of an ad. As we pulled out into traffic, Bleu Edmonson sang "Echo", and I scrunched down low in the seat, and scanned the perimeter as we moved. I looked out the window at the traffic and bums, liquor stores and stop lights, squad cars and street walkers, and did my best to ignore the song.

CHAPTER 36

I sat in the dark, drinking Russian vodka from the bottle and waiting on Vlad to return home. On the table were the Suchka, and the baton, already extended. I wanted it ready, no flashy action-movie cool shit, snapping it open when I need to use it. If I was gonna crack someone's skull, I didn't want them to have a warning.

I had developed a little game, to help with the wait. Every time I thought about the way Cornelius had looked after asserting my dominance, I took a drink and thought about how much fun I was going to have hurting Vlad for that when he finally got home. I was drunk, and tired. Therefore, I thought hard about the coke I'd found in his bedside table, but I didn't touch it. Maybe later, I told myself.

A full third of the vodka was gone by the time I heard the whine of a high-powered sports car on the street outside, and then the garage door opening. I stood from the table, slipped the Suchka's sling around my neck, gun in my waistband, picked up the baton, and moved quickly to a position near the door to the garage, just inside a laundry room.

There were two of them, and I was surprised I could hear them above the beating of my heart, and the vodka-laden wheezing of my breath. Silently, I cursed myself for a rank amateur, doing stupid rookie shit like getting half-drunk while waiting on a mark. I moved the AK to behind my back, held the Walther in my left hand and the baton in my right, and tried to get in the groove, using the alcohol in my system to my favor instead of against me. Sometimes, a stimulant's a stimulant.

I moved as quickly as silence allowed, into the hallway, behind the two men. I could see a big goon before me, a Ruger SR9 in one hand. He stood in the doorway, right behind Vlad. Now was the time, the magic moment. I took long, sure strides, bringing the baton up high, and then down, as hard as I could on the big guy's skull. It cracked like a melon on a stage, and he dropped, so much dead weight. Vlad turned, shock registering on his face as I brought it down on his clavicle. The pistol in his hand dropped. Next I hit his thighs, several times each. He fell, scrambling on the crowded floor. I saw his good hand reaching for the little gun he'd dropped, and I smashed the baton into it, driving it into the tile floor, magnifying the force and destructive power. He howled in pain.

"Shut the fuck up," I told him. If he heard me, I couldn't tell. I slapped him a few times to get his attention, then rolled him over, using the furry cuffs I'd found in the box of toys under his bed. Next I reached into the bag, and pulled out a bath towel I'd balled up and duct taped, with lengths of tape extending off it. I stuffed it in his mouth and taped it down. He really didn't like that, and when he started to kick, I brought the baton down on the tops of his feet, just hard enough to cause some fractures. He'd be able to walk, but man, it'd hurt. He deserved worse.

I picked him up over my shoulder and carried him into the living room, where I tossed him on the couch.

"Chill, motherfucker," I said, and walked back to fish the wallet out of the dead guy's pants pocket.

I took his money and tossed the wallet back down. He knew what he was getting into. I picked up the bodyguard's SR9 and then picked up the small .380 Vlad had been holding, a Smith and Wesson Bodyguard. I checked the load and slipped it into a pocket.

I picked the bottle of vodka back up and walked into the living room where Vlad lay, twisting on the couch. I took a swig from the bottle then dropped another on his face. He tried to dodge it, but he didn't have much luck. I took another swallow and grabbed an ankle, turning him around, and letting his feet drop to the floor. I pushed him up into a sitting position, and tore the tape from his mouth without ceremony. He didn't scream. In the movies, they always scream. He just snarled.

I sat down on the coffee table and took yet another drink, trying to control my blood lust, the desire to do the man harm. I needed to find a balance before I ran out of vodka. We stared each other down for a long, weary minute. Our proximity and the nature of our actions leaving no doubt as to who or what we were.

"You want some vodka?" I asked. He looked at me like he couldn't believe what I'd just asked.

"Sure," he said, slowly nodding his head. I lifted the bottle above his head and poured some in his mouth, without letting the bottle touch his lips. He swallowed it in a large gulp, and coughed as I took the bottle away.

"Know why you're alive?" I asked.

"Because you're a fool," he said.

"You can do better than that, c'mon. What's coming down the pike May fifth?" I asked.

"Oh, that," he said, blood dribbling out his lopsided grin. "Call your superiors. I want to come in."

"I don't have any *superiors*," I said, imitating his accent. "But we're both pros. You tell me what's happening, and I'll leave you alive. It won't be pretty, and you'll be in pain working yourself free to use a phone, but you'll be alive."

"You lie for shit."

"I'm going to hell for a lot of shit I won't apologize to God for, but I never lie," I said, telling him the truth.

"You stupid fuck!" he spat. "When I say you lie, I mean I know who you are. I know you work for the Man from Champlain," he said, and my blood ran cold.

Vlad wasn't a gangster. Well, he wasn't *just* a gangster. Vlad was a fucking spook.

"Yeah, you understand now, don't you?" he sneered.

There had been sort of an unwritten truce between the superpowers since the end of the Cold War. We both still hate each other, and we're going to keep spying on each other, but if we kept from whacking their guys, they wouldn't whack ours. It was tentative, one Russia barely held up its end of, but it was real. Mostly.

Unfortunately, for Vlad, I hated fucking spooks. With a passion.

"I understand it explains the go bag, laptop, and sat phone behind the fake vent in the dining room," I said.

I'd be lying if I said I didn't enjoy watching the recognition that he really wasn't getting a pass spread across his face.

"Fuck you. My people will square this. They'll kill your brother, rape his wife, and eat his son," he scowled.

"No, they won't. I'm gonna kill all of them, too," I said, snapping my wrist, bringing the baton hard into his throat. He didn't believe it, even as the last thing he saw was me—drinking his vodka and smiling.

I checked my watch. In another time and place, I would have taken the time and care to dispose of the bodies properly. I thought about it now, but time and circumstance led me to believe that would be a bad idea. I didn't know what his night had consisted of after the shooting at the club. If he'd talked to cops, what he might've said to them, if he'd ignored them altogether. Whom he might've talked to, reached out to on his side of it. He would be on a lot of radars. I needed distance more than anything.

I capped the vodka, gathered my things, and left.

CHAPTER 37

The world was already baking beneath the mid-morning sun when I watched Boudreaux, transplanted coonass bookie, criminal wheeler-dealer, and general all around low level scumbag, park his Southern Comfort modified Saturn. Yes, a jacked up instead of lowered Saturn, complete with gold rims and trim, which he parked in the space in the alley near the dumpster behind his building before letting himself in the back door. No doubt, with a long day of scumbaggery ahead of him.

I left my shade, and made my way through bright heat of the alley to the door. He'd left it unlocked, for which I was thankful, and I slipped in soundlessly. The Walther hanging loose along my leg, I listened, letting my eyes adjust to the dark stairwell. I heard the sounds of shuffling, as cooler doors opened and closed, then more shuffling as Boudreaux stepped before me.

His hands were filled with his breakfast of soda and candy when he saw me. He stopped, his mouth open, his eyes wide. He stuttered around words he couldn't find. I motioned up the stairs with the pistol, and he nodded. I followed him up, three steps behind, watching the tenseness of his body posture for signs he might get brave. I doubted he would, he seemed like the type that would always have someone else do the heavy lifting, but you never know. Desperation breeds many things.

He fumbled with the lock. "Sorry, man," he said. "Why you here, anyway?" he asked.

I stepped up behind him and placed my free hand on his shoulder. "Not yet," I said softly. "Just open the door."

He shook his head, muttering what might've been a prayer under his breath. Finally he got the door opened and let us in. I had him lock the door behind us then made him take the heavy steel bar from the side and put it in place. He had to set his breakfast down to do it, but he didn't seem to mind. Guess he knew better than to bitch about it. When he was done, I walked him over to the couch and told him to sit. He sat.

"Are you armed?"

"Thirty eight in my boot," he said.

"Leave it there," I told him, then walked around the desk, grabbed the chair, and rolled it around the desk, so that I could sit and watch him without peering over the mounds of paper. I folded a leg over a knee, and rested the Walther on my thigh.

"Eat, man," I told him. He looked confused, which I understood, given my previous behavior, but I really didn't feel like doing things the hard way. I'd had a long, unpleasant night, and it weighed on me. Focusing on the task at hand had kept me from dwelling on my actions, but now, the bloody work, coupled with the lack of sleep, not to mention too much vodka, had left me drained and completely without energy.

"All that shit went down last night, that was you?" He asked. I didn't answer. I rubbed my sore eyes with a yawn, and looked at Boudreaux staring at me, his soda and candy in his lap.

"Man, I ain't done nothin' to nobody. Why you come here now?"

"Man, eat. I just want to talk. Toss me one of those Cokes, too," I told him. He tossed me a Coke and I popped it, draining half of it. It was ice cold with that Coke bite that used to taste so good on a hot day spent mowing yards or hauling hay. Normally, I was always a Dr Pepper kinda guy, but it was a little sweet for morning pick-me-ups and hard labor. The can was ice cold, and I held it to my head.

Boudreaux eyed me, slowly unwrapping a chocolate something or other. He still didn't believe me. In truth, I was still thinking about it, but didn't want him to see that. He was a scumbag, sure, but he wasn't a direct threat to me or the people I cared about. I didn't give two shits about him providing access to drugs or gambling, or even working girls, provided they were there of their own volition. We'd be better off as a society by having a real discussion concerning the sanity of prohibition.

The dogfights I took a much harsher view of, though not nearly as much as the smuggling of girls into slavery. If he were a part of that, I didn't know what the immediate future held for him. I didn't particularly want to kill him, but if he were a part of that, I would.

I also knew there was no way in hell he knew anything about a planned terrorist attack on downtown Dallas or anywhere else. He didn't have the stomach, brains, or balls for that. If he'd have caught wind of it, he wouldn't have lived long enough to tell anyone about it.

"What do you know about last night?"

"Man, I just came from da' flophouse, *Homes*. Manny called me up, told me to go get the doctor, bring him over. You did that all by yourself."

"Doctor?" I asked.

"Street Doc, guy had a habit. Now he takes care of people can't go to no hospital."

"Where's this at?"

"Shit, man. They got a whole building, down on Jefferson. Next to the steakhouse. There's a Taco Shop on the first floor. Got some cribs in the top floor, where they keep some trim."

"How many people are there?"

"What's left of da' crew, plus some of those mean motherfuckers from down south you shot up last night, too."

"Guys from down south? They're here?"

"The ones could get away. They're all fucked up, man. After I took Doc Hap there, they made me hang out and help while he did his thing. I don't know Spanish too good, but they were pissed, man. I don't know how you did all that shit. Just crazy to think one man did all that."

"How many people are there right now?" I asked. He stared at me, the fear growing in his eyes. I tried to remind myself to tone the fervor down a notch.

"Come on, Boudreaux, you helped 'Doc Hap' fix them up. How many?"

"Doc Hap didn't fix any of 'em. They said they didn't trust him. They just wanted him to stop the bleeding, hook 'em to the IV's, and knock 'em out till he got back with some more drugs. I think they're waiting on a larger crew to get here. Bringing real doctors with 'em. Like I said, they're real fucked up, man."

"Boudreaux, you're wearing on me here, man. Come on, now. How many?"

He shook his head, trying to think it through.

"There's three *vatos* downstairs in the taqueria on guard. Always three. That's their job. Johns got to go thru them before they can go upstairs on a normal day, you know, not like today. Upstairs, there's six rooms, three on each side. There's," he counted on his fingers, "four or five motherfuckers you chopped to bits last night hooked up and doped to the gills, just waiting on back up." He paused. "You really not gonna hurt me?"

"I hope not, Boudreaux, I surely don't," I said, the can cold against my head. "That depends largely on you. You expecting anyone?" I asked.

"Not for a couple of hours. Mamma Conterras be in 'bout an hour or so, open up the sto'."

"Where can I find Manny?" I asked.

"Man, I don't know. Truth is, he move around. Gotta place he stay with his girl, another crib somewheres he keep to bring *strange* his girl don't know 'bout, 'nother one, outside town he keep his dog, an old farm house he and Miguel bought cheap. That's where I took him after we took Doc Hap to the flop house and got those boys squared away."

"Directions, Boudreaux, to the farm house.

"Goddamn, take 35 like you going to Waco, turn east on Belt Line. It's down there, not far from the river, man."

"What about the taco shop. It open for business today?" I asked.

"No man, those three *vatos* are still there though," he said.

"Tell me about them."

"Victor. Bout my height, little chunky, silver stud in his eyebrow. He opens up the shop every day for the girls that work there, cookin' downstairs. He holds court there, keeps the dining room closed 'cept for crew business. Usually a guy watchin' the door behind the counter keeps a shotty underneath it. Couple other guys for security, maybe some prospects to hold their straps, and run errands."

"Ok," I said, trying to take it all in, trying to visualize the taqueria and the flophouse above it, as well as the safe house where Manny kept his prized bulldog and the routes to each.

"Tell me something, Boudreaux, what was Manny doing here the other day?"

"You mean when you and C.W. showed up?"

"Yes, when me and C.W. showed up," I asked.

He shrugged around a mouthful of Moonpie.

"Wanted talk to me about makin' sure some pamphlets or some shit got passed out during the Cinco de Mayo parade."

"Pamphlets?"

"Yeah."

"During the Cinco de Mayo parade?"

"Yeah, big mon'," he said, his native Creole creeping in.

"Do you have any of these pamphlets?" I asked. He shook his head no.

"Nope, he just wanted me to make sure to have people in place to spread them out. Supposed to be helping some of Uncle Alejandro's people."

"You mean from LARO?"

"Yeah, the college kids," he said. I stared at him while I thought about that, and the notebook I'd seen in Miguel's apartment.

"Lay down, Boudreaux, and get comfortable," I told him. I took the duct tape from the drawer and used most of the roll binding his hands to the arm of the couch. I took his cell phone, but left his gun.

"When Mamma Conterras comes in, she gonna make her way up here, to check on you?"

"Yeah, man, if I don't come on down, she'll be up," he said, softly, still not believing what was happening. I took a small pillow and propped it under his head, so he wouldn't get a stiff neck.

"Boudreaux, you tell anyone about this, anyone, you'll regret it. Understand?"

"Yeah, man, sure," he said, tears flowing slowly, silently down his cheeks.

"And Boudreaux," I said, and he just stared at me, an entirely captive audience. "Get outta the dog fighting business. I won't tell you again," I said, then left him to his silence.

CHAPTER 38

I sat in Kendrick's 1971 Mustang Mach I, listening to the big 351 Windsor engine rumble like a prowling beast, my gloved hands flexing around the steering wheel as I watched the back of the strip mall that housed the taqueria and the brothel above it. I was losing time, and it was killing me.

The problem was I didn't have any idea how hard of a target the building itself was. It was a flip of the coin whether or not the back door was reinforced, if it had a steel bar going across it, if it was even locked. I didn't know, and I needed to know.

I had risked a drive down the perimeter, noting the three sentries on guard downstairs, but nothing else. The thing that got me was, though they were supposedly on a five alert goddamn lock down, I watched people come and go without so much as knocking or unlocking the backdoor. I was afraid Boudreaux had fed me a line of shit.

I thought back over our conversation, everything he'd said, his tone and body language. The worst thing would be to walk in blazing on a bunch of innocent people just trying to open up shop for the day.

Everything I could remember about Boudreaux as he'd talked rang of truth. There was always the chance these simply weren't the brightest criminals. I decided to go ahead and do it. If I didn't like what I saw inside, I simply wouldn't pull the trigger.

I pulled the ballistic vest I'd liberated from Vlad's night club the night before off the seat next to me, and shrugged into it, strapping it down tight.

Next I pulled the little Suchka up, checked the chamber, and draped the sling around my neck. I had it and one spare magazine, Smarmy's Walther with one full mag and a partial, the

Ruger SR9 I'd taken from Vlad's friend the night before, and Vlad's little Smith .380. I also had my Spyderco P'kal clipped inside my pants, and the big custom bowie I'd taken from the nightclub the night before.

It wasn't much, but it was a start, and I knew I'd pick up something along the way. All I needed were dead men.

I swung the door of the taqueria open and stepped through, bringing the Suchka up as I moved forward. There was a chunky one sitting in a booth halfway down the wall, his back against the brick wall, a toothpick in his mouth, and a cell phone in his hand. There was a stainless Colt Python with a 4-inch barrel and big, blue, faux marble grips with big finger grooves at the end of the table. He didn't look up from his phone, probably thinking I was someone else.

To the left were two men past the end of the counter. One of them was talking to a child in his early teens, talking to him in Spanish and pointing at the closed sign on the door. The kid looked like he needed a bath and a fix but not necessarily in that order.

The fourth man was standing at the counter, but facing the outside with his friend, the grip of a semi-automatic pistol sticking out of his back pocket.

I kept walking forward, my front sight finding the bridge of the nose of the one sitting in the booth as I took up the slack on the trigger. His face exploded with the three round burst, and I continued moving forward. The next one, the one at the end of the counter somehow managed to entangle himself as he tried to turn and draw his weapon at the same time. My burst stripped across his chest on the way to the third man, who had ducked down behind the counter.

I moved forward down the length of the counter. A big chrome 1911 A1 stretched over the top of the counter, and I fired through the counter below it, not stopping until I came around the end of the counter and fired another short burst into his face.

The big one writhed on the floor, his hand on the Hi Point 9mm he'd been trying to pull from his back pocket. I fired a single round into his head, and then pulled the mag from the gun, stuck it in my left rear pocket, grabbed the reload from beneath my belt, and inserted it in the gun.

The chrome .45 had a stove pipe and I might've chosen a sharp stick over the Hi Point, so I left them both where they were. I could hear heavy feet scrambling on the floor above me. I picked up the fancy Python along the way, and stuck it in the small of my back.

I moved up the stairs at the ready, listening to the fearful scramble of trapped animals above. I had more feeling for livestock in cages.

I saw the barrel of a sub-machine gun poke through the door at the top of the floor, the man behind it not having the training or common sense needed to properly slice the pie. I fired through the door jam and wall as I moved up the stairs. The gun dropped on the landing, its owner screaming as he fell back.

I did not go through the door. As I neared the top of the stairs, I went low, sliding across the landing at the top. I saw a young kid, maybe seventeen, crabbing down the hall as he held a bloody hand.

I was lining my sights up with the back of his head when a hard case, naked except for bandages and gauze stepped out of the nearest room to my right with a cut down pump shotgun and fired into the plaster above my head. White dust and paint chips hung in the air, filling my eyes and obscuring my vision. I fired through the billowing cloud of paint dust and gunpowder, feeling more than hearing the satisfying thunk of bullets slapping flesh, and then the heavy thud of a body and a gun hitting the floor, separately.

I turned back, found the escaping man, now in the middle of the hallway, scrambling madly for an open door, and fired. His brains scattered across the wall beside the door he'd been trying to crawl through, just out of reach.

I came to a stand on the move, going to the door across the hall from the naked, gauze wrapped man I'd just killed, and stepped through, finding two men in a bed, IV's hooked to their arms, stuck in a drug induced sleep paralysis, their eyes fluttering, some portion of their being aware of what was happening.

Helpless.

I fired a short burst into each of their heads. I wished I'd used better fire control coming up the stairs as I pulled the partial mag from my back pocket, hit the mag release with the floor plate, and inserted the partially spent mag, before working the bolt from beneath the gun.

I cleared both sides of the hallway, before moving across, to the room the man with the over under had come from. There was another man, dressed to his waist, his chest, arms, and half his face covered in gauze, sitting on the edge of a mattress, trying to pull a handgun from a holster. I put the end of the barrel between his eyes, just to see the recognition flash in the good one, and pulled the trigger.

I stepped back toward the doorway, and heard scrambling down the hall, and the metallic click-clack of weaponry being readied, and shifted the Suchka to my left shoulder, going down to one knee as I leaned low out of the room.

A man on the other end fired a Mac variant of some sort, but his bullets sprayed around me in an overhead arc, and I poured my own into his chest.

He dropped the Mac, falling in a cloud of blood against the door jam, and slid to the floor. He sat up, leaning against the door jam, staring at me before looking for his weapon. I had to respect the man for his mindset, even as I took careful aim on the bridge of his nose, and pulled the trigger. The final bullet in the mag zipped out, and painted the scene behind him with blood, brain, hair, and bone.

I dropped the Suchka, and pulled the Ruger from my waist, shifting it to my strong hand as I moved across the hall. Before I got to it, someone stepped through the hallway, gun in their hand, and I fired a nice controlled pair into his chest, and a single round into his head as I moved forward.

In that room, I found two more men dressed in gauze, one rolling around on the bed tangled in wet sheets, the other on all fours in the floor, trying to get up. The one on the floor had a cut down O/U in one hand, and was trying to gather the wits and strength to mount a defense, so I put two bullets through his crown, before shifting toward his friend tangled up in the bed.

I stepped over the dead man, put a knee on the edge of the mattress, fired several times into the what looked like the face of a drowning man trying to claw out of the sea.

A closet door flung open, and a chica ran towards me screaming. The Ruger was empty, so I punched her in the face with it. Rugers are real good for that.

She dropped to the floor in a heap, and I kicked her; once in the gut, and once on the chin. It didn't break, but it turned her lights out. Thankfully, since I needed the ammo.

Bullets began zipping through the walls from all directions. I dropped to the floor hard enough to knock my breath out. Half a minute took a lifetime, lying in the floor next to the unconscious woman, and the dead man, bullets zipping through the thin walls, splinters thick and sharp, nothing but shrapnel tumbling in the air, searching for a home.

Then the ominous sound of silence, and the frantic metallic clanking of a slide or bolt being unjammed across the hallway. I ripped the Walther out, rolled over, in the prone, looking over the top of the pistol. Across the hallway, standing in the doorway, was a banger, wearing pants and an open shirt, trying to unjam a Draco.

I shot him twice in the chest, and he just looked at me, working the bolt on his stupid AK pistol as he did so. I took a more careful aim, as he cleared the jam and came toward me, firing. I found myself lost to the moment, and all my training and experience went out the window, and I fired until the slide locked back.

I stood, using the middle finger of my strong hand to work the Walther's mag release, drove the partially spent magazine home, and worked the slide.

Then, I stood there, for the briefest of moments, listening, before holstering the Walther, and picking the O/U up off the floor, checking its load, and moving on.

No one met me as I came across the hallway, and into the room across the hall. There I found a man, pale white, wrapped in gauze like the others, sweating and mumbling, somewhere between this world and the next. I extended the shotgun out with one hand, against his head, and pulled the trigger.

A large man came screaming through the door holding a tomahawk over his head. I fired the second barrel into his torso, but it didn't stop him. I blocked his downward swing with the shotgun, sidestepping while I tried to deflect his momentum, and he simply spun like a top, coming at me again, swinging the tomahawk in side arc this time.

He swung down twice more. The hard, powerful blows made the shotgun reverberate in my hands as I tried to parry, backing up.

He came back down a third time, and this time pushed the shotgun low enough to cut the top of my eye socket with the skull crusher on the back of the blade as he reversed direction.

It stunned me something fierce, and he laughed at me, behind the cover of star-bursts in my vision.

"Amigo, I'm going to enjoy killing you. You can't stop us," he said, with a voice long scarred by cigarettes and tequila. I shook my head clear as he brought the tomahawk back up. I stepped forward, closing the gap, and clinched up with him, pulling him close as he picked me up and ran forward, slamming me hard against the wall.

It knocked the wind out of me. He was bigger and stronger, and knew it, and squeezed me harder than anyone had ever squeezed me before. A wall of blood poured over my right eye and down my face.

My hand found purchase on the Walther, and I pulled my elbow as far up and back as I could sandwiched between the angry giant and the wall.

"Amigo is a Caddo Indian word for friend. That's Texas shit, fuckhead," I said, and began firing. The first shots impacted his hip, legs, and stomach. He loosened his hold some after that, allowing me a wider range of motion, and I stuck the barrel deep into his armpit, the gun turned horizontally. I would like to say I had the presence of mind to do so in order to minimize the possibility of jamming the gun, but really that's just the position my wrist found itself in.

I fired three times fast, and I swear I could hear the bullets ripping right through the width of his chest, feel them shred his heart to puree.

He let go of me fully then, and stepped back, staring at his chest.

And then, he looked back up, his hand tightening on the hatchet for one last try, and I brought the Walther up and shot him just below the nose, a straight shot right to the base of central nervous system.

I wheezed, trying to catch my breath, and looked at the gun in my hand, empty with the slide locked back, and dropped it, wondering if I could get back to the car and gone before the cops arrived.

I stepped toward the hallway, only to be met by the end of a stainless Taurus 92, in a pair of hands that were connected to arms at full extension.

I grabbed the wrist of the strong hand, pushing it away from me as I pulled him toward me, a small statured Hispanic with long greasy hair who might've been a hard fourteen or young twenty one came in with it. I didn't give him time to think, just snapped the Spyderco P'kal out and open, acquiring the proper reverse blade, edge in grip, and stabbed him in the throat, working the blade back and forth until I'd cut all the way through his windpipe.

I grasped the gun as he slid down the door jam, streaking a dark bloody smear as he went.

I closed the knife and slid it back into the pocket of my jeans. I cycled the slide just to make sure there was a round in the chamber, losing the one that had been in there. I just wasn't in a press check kind of mood.

I stood there a moment, looking into the blinking eyes of the man-child I'd just killed. A man who would never take another drink or laugh at a friend's joke. Or feel the soft, warm flesh of a woman in his arms ever again.

The realization of where we were, the narrow plane on which we stood, I could see the recognition of such in his eyes, the brief lingering last light as he could feel the blood gush from his throat and over his hand in its futile effort, until finally he dropped it to his side.

This moment, shared with a man dying by my hand, was a mistake.

For no reason other than that, I wasn't prepared when the next one stepped crouching through the door, a cut down pump gun in his hands, firing as fast as he could into my chest.

I don't remember backpedaling as his rounds hit my vest with their heavy thuds. I did notice I was being shot, and I remember thinking how nice it was when his gun clicked on an empty chamber, even as I found myself falling through a window, and onto the roof of the next building.

And then I hurt too goddamn bad to care about having been shot, because I landed on my back, the Python I'd forgotten about right on top of the bolts the army had put in my spine as a parting gift.

All I saw was blue lightning. All I heard were the sirens in the distance, and above them, the crackle and electric flame of nerve damage. My fault for putting a gun there.

Way to go, dick.

I rolled over, trying to get mobile, and then an anvil fell on me, feet first. On me and my goddamn damaged spine.

I tried to catch my breath, and hurt so bad I didn't much care if I sounded like a little bitch doing it.

I felt something punch my right forearm, and when I looked blood was running out of it. I felt the Python yanked from my waistband, and was almost glad to be rid of it, and then I got kicked in the temple, which is about what I deserved for thinking such a thing, and rolled back over. I looked up to see a hard old man spit in my face, as he stuck the Python into his waistband.

I was confused by that, and then I saw a brilliant whirling glimmer, and I barely got my arms up in time to shield my face, as I kicked as hard as I could into his gut.

He cursed and spat at me, and then I felt the bottoms of my forearms slice open and then I heard him yell as he raised the machete back over his head.

Great, now you're in a sword fight, dick, said the voice in my head.   .

"Fuck you!" I yelled, to both of them, and managed to get a hand on the handle of the bowie at my side. I brought it out, reverse grip, edge in, not really the preferred grip for a knife that size and length, but I was going on pure reflex. Besides, I was just happy the goddamn arm was working. He could have taken it, instead of playing with me.

I managed to bring it up and roll as he was coming down with the machete in a long chopping motion, narrowly avoiding the blade. He came back again, this time harder, with more power, and I managed to avoid it, and tag him with the tip, dragging the edge down his forearm.

He yelled in surprise and rolled off me. I managed to work myself into a standing position, and flipped the big bowie around, with the edge up, like we were fighting on The Sandbar.

He stood, the sirens coming closer, and raised the machete high. He didn't give two fucks about the cops. Prison was probably more home to him than the streets. Honor was more important to him than freedom ever had been.

I drove forward, meeting the machete with the back of the knife, driving it down to the hilt, and trapping it hard in the guard. I smashed my forearm into his bicep, controlling the arm and snapped the bowie up and into his face. The machete fell from his grasp, and out of the bowie's guard, and as he tried to backpedal I snapped a fierce back-cut into his face.

He took two steps back, his eyes focusing on mine as blood ran down both our faces, each of us remembering the Python in his belt.

I stepped forward, turning the big blade over in my hand and came down, fast and hard, severing his arm at the wrist with the swedge, and thrusting straight back into his stomach.

Blood was everywhere. My head was covered in my own. Scalp wounds are notoriously bloody, even if they look worse than they really were.

The hard old man stared at me, blood running from his lips, defiant to the last. I slashed his throat wide open, nearly decapitating him.

I could hear sirens approaching, the sounds of traffic breaking. I picked the Python up off the hot tar paper roof, and gimped my bleeding ass away, with as much quickness as I could muster.

CHAPTER 39

I sat comfortable in the undergrowth overlooking the small frame house. It appeared empty, but I could see a starved mongrel caged in the back. Just outside the cage, two small puppies whined for their mother's attention. She was dead, her carcass lying nearby. It didn't seem to be bloated, so I doubted she'd been dead very long, but she was clearly dead.

I'd found this spot high up on the hill behind the house. There was a white rock road that ran down behind the hill, probably for the power company, and I'd parked off it, out of sight.

I was shirtless, having pulled into an alley to clean myself as much as possible with Russell's shirt and a couple of bottles of water. I had mended my wounds with QuikClot gauze and bandages from the blow out kit Russell had given me, but I could feel the wrapping starting to loosen from blood and sweat. I knew I needed to do something about that. They were mainly superficial, somehow, though they cried for stitches. I felt a strange tightening when I made a grip with my right hand, and I worried a tendon or two might've been damaged.

Quit your bitchin', you lucky fuck.

I knew he was right, so I didn't say anything back.

I sat in the shade while the raw, earthy scents of my youth in the woods surrounding me, and watched the small house. I hoped there might be first aid, maybe a fresh shirt inside. A properly set up safe house should have enough supplies stockpiled to keep a small group buttoned up for weeks, if not months at a time. I knew what I'd put in the ones I'd set up.

I was starved for information, but I didn't want to risk turning on my cell, let alone call anyone. I'd scoured the radio in Kendrick's car, only to find sensationalist coverage of the events that had unfolded, along with a rehash of the previous night's events, and speculation connecting the two.

No shit, they're related. You killed a bunch of fucking people. Dick.

"Seemed like a good idea at the time," I said before I caught myself.

I shook my head, pissed off that the guy was back. He'd been gone for so goddamn long, too. At least I hadn't heard my name, or description, or the description of the car I was driving on the radio. Thank God for small favors.

When dusk came I would risk approaching the house, but not before; it wasn't worth it until then. Unless someone came and left, then I might need to follow them. Only no one came.

So I waited, which I hated. I'd had enough of waiting when I ran recon. I had lots of practice, I could do it, find that place inside where stillness simply breathed. I just didn't like it.

Time passed more slowly than I can describe. I watched the pups in the dirt, the monster in his cage. His little pen was just a very narrow corner of a larger one, and inside the larger one, sat an old oak tree. From the oak tree, a length of chain hung, swinging ever so slightly in the breeze.

Attached to the end was a device, made of leather and metal, which a man might attach to the head of a dog, before suspending them in the air. They did it to build the neck muscles.

Looking at the evil thing hurt my heart.

I was pleased when darkness finally started to fall. I've always felt more at home in the dark than beneath the harsh light of day. I made my way through the undergrowth to the side of the house. I stood beside a window and listened. Nothing.

I could still hear the puppies whine, trying to suck on their dead mother's teats. I felt ill. I let myself inside and searched the house in darkness. It was pretty bare, but functional, the cupboards filled with canned foodstuffs. I found canned milk and poured it in a bowl for the puppies.

I stuffed their mother in a garbage sack, and walked her into the wood-line. It wasn't smart to leave signs like that, but I couldn't stand to let the poor things hurt anymore, and didn't like the thought of them trying to suckle their dead mother.

The safe house probably hadn't been set up by a pro. Manny might've taken whatever weapons and medical supplies that had been there when Boudreaux had dropped him off, but I doubted it. As far as my wounds were concerned, I'd have been better off going to my grandmother's. I set the Python on the top of the toilet's tank, and filled the sink with scalding hot water. I threaded a needle with dental floss, took a long pull off a bottle of Jose Cuervo I'd found in the cupboard, looked at myself in the mirror, and decided I might as well start with the eyebrow. Go ahead and get the bitch out of the way first.

I sterilized the needle and anesthetized myself with the tequila, squeezed my eyebrow as back together as possible, and started.

The eyebrow cut was the worst. It was jagged, and gaping, a little patch ready to be torn off. Somehow, it didn't hurt nearly as much as I expected, but the anger might've negated that. Or maybe it was the tequila.

There was a short slash on my cheek, and I couldn't remember how or when it'd been put there. The slashes on the bottoms of my forearms were deeper, but only the one on my right worried me. I was having trouble fully closing the bottom two fingers when I made a fist. Of the wounds on my arms, the stab wound to my right forearm looked the worst. It had bled a lot, but after I'd gotten that under control it hadn't been much of anything. It could have been much, much worse.

The bottom of my right forearm took the longest, because of the loss of dexterity in my weak-side hand. I was so goddamn lucky it wasn't even close to funny, but I hurt. Bad. And nothing hurt as much as my back, where I'd landed on the stupidly placed gun atop an old injury.

I pulled the plug, took another slug from the tequila, and watched all that water, thick with blood, a deep, dark red in color, empty down the drain. I ran another batch, just as hot, and used a washrag and a bar of soap to give my half-naked self a bath.

When I was done, I pulled my knives from their scabbards, and rinsed them off before replacing them. Then I picked up the Python, checked the load, six +P hollow points nestled in the chambers of the beautiful gun, and walked through the house with it hanging in my hand at my side.

Somewhere along the way the Smith .380 I'd taken off Vlad had disappeared from the pocket I'd stuffed it in. I only mourned its loss because of the situation. As good a gun as it might've been, as far as I was concerned, a .380 was really just a bad ass brass knuckle.

One handgun, six bullets, two knives, a bottle of tequila, and a rampant id ready for bear. One bad motherfucker. If only.

I stood in the kitchen for several minutes, listening to nothing. I wondered how long it would take Manny to return. I wondered if he would. I wondered how long it would take me to grow bored with the wait, when I couldn't take any more of listening to the pups whine outside, or the voice in my head, or the worry I felt for my friends. I wondered if I could risk using my cell. I wondered if I should. I wondered what wondering about it said about me. Protecting the people I cared about was the whole goddamn point. Fuckballs.

In the front room there was an ancient, dust covered television set in a wooden box, a Curtis Mathis number probably built in my home town before the plant closed. It didn't work because it didn't have a digital converter. It looked like some grandmother's house, and I guessed probably had been before someone had bought it furnished from her estate, and never bothered to toss her stuff. I slipped the Python beneath my belt, at the front this time, above my appendix, and slowly, almost leisurely, began searching the house.

In the closet in the master bedroom, I found some clothing. Most of it looked to be Sunday go-to-meeting dresses for an old woman. They, and the house, reminded me of the farm, the old home-place, and my Aunt Opal. In the back of the closet, I found a man's denim work shirt, so faded the blue had worn to near white, and it felt softer than cheesecloth in my hand. I slipped it on, just to see if it fit, and let it hang open while I continued.

A couple of hours later I draped my new denim shirt over the back of a kitchen chair, dropped a pair of folded cotton khakis that would make do in the seat, and sat in another, the bottle of tequila and the Python before me.

I needed to contact C.W. but, I didn't feel like fighting that battle yet.

I punched another number instead.

"And it's the luckiest motherfucker I ever met in my entire goddamn life," Russell asked when he answered the phone.

"How's C.W.?"

"How the fuck should I know?" he asked.

"He's not with you?" I asked. Captain Obvious, here to save the day.

"Does it fucking sound like he's with me? Goddamn. Given your rep, and the people you've worked with, I expect a little more from you, you know that?" he said.

Neither of us said anything for a moment after that. He had to go *there*. Just like Vlad.

"Look, he's safe for now," he said. "He's at home. He talked to Morales without a lawyer. It looks like your cop talked some sense into him. He managed to put a couple people on the house, too."

"You checked it out?"

"Yes, I checked it out," he said, the agitation in his voice growing.

"Just like I showed up at the worst RV ever, just like I took him to a safe house, and then let him burn that safe house so he could talk to Morales in private. Just like I took him home, and kept him safe until y'all's friend, the bail bondsman, showed up. Just like I did it all with a smile on my face the entire time I had to listen to his sniveling, insulting, lib-tard idiocy. I don't much like being treated like shit to help out assholes that look down on everything I've ever done, you know?"

I didn't say anything. Not even at the mention of Bear Wallace, my old friend, partner, and employer. An ex-narc turned bondsman who'd earned some hard stripes in a bad way as a man of the law. I thought about the circumstances that had led to me leaving the small East Texas town myself, Bear, C.W., and my baby brother Joshua had grown up in. I hated myself for Bear being dragged into this, even though it wasn't my doing. He deserved better, and always had. They all did.

As for Russell, in truth, I often felt the same way, but it was obvious there was something else, a much deeper pain between them.

"Look, we're keeping tabs. So far neither of your names has appeared in connection to all this. It's kind of amazing. Do you know how many people you killed the last couple of days?"

I didn't say anything to that either. What was I supposed to say? I was just glad he hadn't laid on me the whole 'Jack calling in favors' bit.

"Where are you at? Do you need anything?" he asked.

"I'm waiting. I need nothing right now. Thanks," I said then ended the call.

I stared out the window of the back door, at the pissed off mongrel in his cage, and the pups whining in the dirt as the day died and darkness descended, and hated so very much of the world.

I drank the tequila and listened to the pups outside cry for their poor dead mother, their psychotic father snarling, rattling his cage all night long. I wanted to go ahead and put him out of his misery. I wanted so badly to take the poor pups somewhere else.

I kept waiting.

I listened to the steady whimpering outside and cried with them in the night.

Each moment I felt worse for leaving them out there, but I couldn't risk moving them. Their absence would alert someone aware enough to look, and I needed the element of surprise. I prayed for them to live long enough for me to do what I'd come to do, and then I would take care of them.

A hundred years ago, pit-bulls were known as the Nanny Dog. They were revered for their gentle, protective nature. They were America's mascot during the First World War, symbolizing both our slow to anger nature, and fierce dedication once committed.

And now limp-wristed, twat-waffling do-gooders everywhere reacted to the real problems of animal abuse, over-breeding, and dog fighting by suggesting the dogs themselves were the problem due to an inherently violent nature, instead of turning their anger toward the real reason behind the problems. Banning, even euthanizing a helpless creature that would do nothing but reciprocate the love it has been shown, instead of the subhuman scumfucks responsible for their behavior.

What truly tragic bullshit.

I listened to the pups, and heard the monster growl in his cage. I could not wait for *Manuel* to arrive.

When I got tired, I helped myself to a couple lines of Vlad's coke. I told myself it was just to stay awake.

I thought about a lot of things. Thinking always gets me in trouble.

I thought about what happens when people came to the U.S. in exodus, escaping where they had been to find a better life. I thought about what happens when we treated them with the bi-polar duality only modern America can really pull off. Little more than slaves, while simultaneously offering a system easily exploited for their needs, and being shocked and offended when they take advantage of it.

I thought about what happened when we didn't respect ourselves enough to insist people from a country and culture without a history or understanding of liberty assimilate and find a fragile grasp of the ideals of a republic for everyone's benefit. How, in not doing so, we doomed everyone.

I thought about all the people who profited from their plight— on both sides.

I thought about what happened when you created black markets through prohibition, and how everyone with three working brain cells thought it was a bad idea nearly a century before, yet now people believed the government's fairytale of its worth.

Its worth.

Its worth.

Its worth could never be calculated in earthly numbers.

I wondered what it said of us as a society to allow the de facto enslavement of a people because we were too kind and compassionate to enforce our own laws and borders. I wondered how much longer a society could last, when it had so little respect not just for itself but for the people who came to it clamoring for liberty.

I thought of Joshua, his wounded pride and strained marriage. How I'd fought every fight that had ever come his way.

I thought of our good friend, Cornelius Winston Ellsworth III, always searching in his way for his long-dead sister. Always having to prove to the world he was better than his piece of shit father.

I thought of the wife I'd once had and the life I'd once wanted. Both lost forever: my great failure. Mainly, though, I tried really hard not to think about the poor, poor pups crying outside.

And as I always did, when my thoughts turned their darkest, I thought about violent men without a code, who cared for nothing but personal gain and self-aggrandizement and the domination of those weaker than themselves. Men who enjoyed seeing fear in innocent eyes.

I thought about the only way to stop men such as this.

And how much I enjoyed seeing that same fear in their eyes…just before I spilled their blood.

I thought about all these things, and I tried to keep each in perspective.

But I could not.

And when the automatic gate opened and the old farm truck pulled inside with Manny behind the wheel, I was nowhere near sane.

I forced myself to stand firm, watching the crippled Manny emerge from the driver's seat and limp over to the cage, his face bandaged, one arm in a sling. Stuck in his waistband, I saw the butt of an engraved, chrome plated 1911 with carved ivory grips. He was all alone.

I watched him pick up the little bowl I'd poured the milk in, and toss what was left out. I watched him taunt the already enraged pit trapped in the cage by bouncing the bowl off his scarred, dented head. Then he noticed one of the pups pissing on his boot, and he went ape shit. He picked it up by the scruff of its neck and tossed it at the pit, whose jaws snapped on it in midair. The bloody red mist hung in the air like a slow fog.

I was going to wait until he came inside. I was going to calmly ask him my questions. I wasn't going to let my anger get the better of me. But I didn't do any of those things. I wasn't calm, I wasn't cool, and I certainly wasn't collected. I went ape shit in return.

I rushed outside, his head turning, the recognition twinkling in his good eye as the screen door slammed shut behind me. He went down quickly, his frail, drug-abused body without strength. Meekly, he tried to pull the pistol from his waistband, but he couldn't get it done. The little pussy bitch.

I was lost outside myself, my steel-toed boots stomping and kicking. Grinding his bones into powder, pulverizing his organs, shredding his skin into useless, bloody tatters. He reached again for the gun and I took special delight as the bones in his hand snapped with loud pops beneath my heels.

I looked up, and caught the pit's eye; his jaws working slowly around his bloody meal. I screamed through tears, shaking with rage, and went back to work, connecting leather covered steel to flesh, completely lost in the moment.

That's a goddamn lie. I wasn't lost. I knew just exactly what I was doing, and I enjoyed it. Fucker had it coming, and I was happy to be the one delivering. I just wish I'd gained control of myself sooner. I was afraid he might die before he could answer my questions, the little pussy bitch that he was.

When I was done, I looked around, catching my breath, dizzy from exertion, lack of sleep, booze and two lines of a dead man's coke. We were all alone, just us poor dogs. Quickly, I searched what was left of his body and took a thick roll of bills bound with rubber bands from the pocket of his chinos, as well as his cell phone.

I scrolled through his cell, through the recent calls and then the text messages. They were all in Spanish, all of them leading up to the last, which said simply "noon". I checked the date and time it had been received, and tried to do the math in my head. If they were sending a team of heavy hitters to make sure it was done right, I figured it'd take them a day at the most to assemble, then two days' travel time. If they were coming from the other side of the border. If not, then I had no way of knowing.

At my feet he wheezed, not quite dead. Trying to move though both arms, now broken in several places, were useless. Maybe he had some answers left in him, after all, I thought with a smile

"Manny, Manny, Manny, what am I going to do with you?" I asked, looking around, thinking.

Then my eyes settled on the terrible device hanging from the tree inside the cage, and just… knew.

"This is just not your day, Manny," I said with a laugh, and then dragged him inside and went to work.

It wasn't easy. The device was made for a dog's head and neck, not a man's. So... it took a little creative engineering to get it to fit and work. He cried the whole time, his bones broken far too badly to mount resistance.

"Ok, Manny, you hear me?" I whispered in his ear. He whined a yes. "You're in a lot of pain, right now, aren't you?"

"Si," he said, this time a little louder, but not much.

"You want the pain to end, or you want to hang here and bleed out all day long? It's up to you, man," I said, nuzzling the cold barrel of the .357 against his battered skull.

Rule Number One: when asking someone the Hard Questions, never lie. Ever. They'll see right through it, and you won't get fuck all for actionable intelligence. Tell them the truth, and the certainty of the situation crystallizes for them. When given a choice between the long hard path and the quick exit, precious few feel the mad stirring of the warrior poet deep in their hearts.

"Shoot me, man! Have mercy. Please, mercy, *por favor*," he said, knowing the score.

"Mercy? Like when you and your *vatos* jumped my little brother the other day?" I asked calmly.

"Man, that wasn't us man."

"Bitch, please. Fuck you," I said, pushing his head to the side with the barrel of the gun. He wheezed, whining inside the horrible, ill-fitting iron mask.

"No, seriously. This came straight from *Juarez*. They said to leave you be. Said we didn't need the heat," he spoke slowly and deliberately, but there was nothing in his speech that was erratic or searching. He was telling the goddamn truth.

"Who passed you the information? Who told you to leave my family be?" I asked.

He shook his head, unwilling to answer. His bones were broken, his body torn, his organs ruptured.

"Look at me, Manny," I said. He sputtered and spewed, twisting at the end of the chain. "Manuelo, man to man here, all that shit. I'm telling you, you're going to die today. There is no way around that. Right here, right now…it's just us. Me and you. You can have it easy, or you can have it hard. You can go in pain, or easy like Sunday morning. No one will ever know. And God, my friend, if He does exist, isn't going to care one way or another. No one knows I'm here. I can draw this out. You feel me, *homes*?"

I leaned back, and looked him in the eyes.

I didn't want to spend another day there, but one way or another he was going to give me something useful.

"Look at me. Do you want mercy? Do you want me to end this?" I whispered in his ear, as heartfelt and meaningfully as I could muster.

He grunted, his mouth full of blood and what had been his teeth. His jaw broken, and wired tight inside a foreign device designed for use against one of God's creatures.

"What's that, Manny? I can't hear you."

He mumbled some more.

"Well, that's real goddamn interesting, Manny," I said. I turned to leave, but he thrashed, demanding my attention.

I pulled out the bowie, slid the big blade inside the leg of his chinos, and down his thigh. The sharp blade cut through the soft material like butter. I repeated the steps, and let the pants fall to the ground.

I ran the back of the blade up the inside of his thigh, and rested the tip behind his scrotum. "Ask yourself if I'll do it. Ask yourself if you really want all your homeboys to know I cut off your *huevos*," I said.

"No…please… I can't," he whimpered, struggling with it.

"Why the hell not?"

"My soul," he said, his voice weak and pleading.

I left him hanging there, and walked away.

In the truck I found the remnants of a fast food meal, a cheap nylon wallet with a Velcro fastener. It held more cash, a driver's license, credit card, and gas card all under another name. They were good fakes, too. If I hadn't known who he was, I might not have noticed.

I looked back at him, hanging from the tree, strapped in the device he'd used to torture so many animals now. I looked at the beast in the cage, prowling and snarling at us both and at the whole wide world. I tapped the wallet against my open palm, looking at the blood dripping across the crucifixion tattoo on his left breast.

My soul. My soul.

I slid the wallet in my pocket, and walked back inside the dog pen.

"It's the goddamn priest, isn't it?" I whispered in his ear. He finally started to cry a little.

"Does he know about the girls? The ones you kidnap and hold for ransom? The ones you rape and put on spits?" I asked. I grabbed the chain at the top of the mask and shook it like a motherfucker. *Manuel* howled beneath an angry wind.

I stopped, letting him catch his breath while I stared in thought.

"No," he spoke, his voice low.

"Bullshit! He probably got in on that action, too, didn't he?" I yelled, like I had good goddamn sense.

"No," he insisted.

I pulled out the gun and held to the side of his head.

"Last thing, *Manuelo*," I said, looking him in the eye. "This is your last chance if you want an easy out. What's happening come the fifth of May?" I asked.

"*Day of rage*," he said.

Well, fuck.

Day of rage was a term used by radical groups for widespread demonstrations, which would lead to chaos, anarchy, and revolution. It had originated in the 60's by radical leftists. The most recent had been the previous winter in Egypt. It was bad juju. And it was coming here. And it was all our fault.

I slid the Python back in my waistband.

"Mercy, please."

"Naw, man, I'm good," I said.

And then I drew the Bowie and sliced his belly wide open. His guts bulged out, his intestines hanging there, ever so slowly falling toward the ground. I worked the latch on the gate without opening it, and then stepped back outside and closed the first one just as the beast burst through to his meal.

I watched for a minute, kind of enjoying Manny moaning and screaming. I thought he might be in too much shock to feel any real pain, but his eyes went from me to the dog and back to me, and they told a different tale.

I walked back inside as he jerked on the chain, crying inside the mask. I cleaned myself with hot water and a towel in the bathroom, changed pants, draped the old denim shirt over my body, gathered the bottle and the towels and the soap I'd touched, and walked back outside. I dropped the trash in the grill, along with the pants I'd been wearing, doused everything in lighter fluid, and dropped a match on it.

I pulled the gun he'd carried from the dirt, a chrome plated, engraved Colt Commander in .38 Super, ivory grips with the Mexican eagle and snake carved. I knocked the dirt off it, cocked the hammer, and press checked it, before putting it on safe and putting it beneath my belt at the hip, but not over my spine.

Fuck a whole bunch of that shit.

I picked the last puppy up in my arms. Poor little guy.

I looked at his father, growling at us inside his cage, his jaws covered in blood. I looked at the monster hanging in the tree next to his cage, his eyes pleading with me to end him while bloody tears ran down his face.

I turned with the little guy tucked into my arm and walked back to the car with my new best friend.

CHAPTER 40

It was well past dark when we finally got back to Cornelius' house. He was sitting in his love seat, his grandfather's Luger in hand when I walked in carrying some provisions I'd stopped for, the puppy nestled in my arm. Behind him, extending around the corner of the kitchen and down the back of the wall, was a long sleeved denim work shirt, and at the end of it, a huge stainless, engraved, Smith & Wesson semi-auto, in what looked to be 10mm.

I wasn't sure, but the caliber fit. Bear, our old friend, and my old partner, liked weird, oddball calibers in large diameters. Knowing him, he probably had it stoked with full powered hand loads. So much gun for someone who didn't like shooting people.

"Don't shoot us," I said, shutting the door and throwing the lock. "We come in peace," I said, laughing at my joke. Bear shrugged, said something about me still being an asshole, and slid the gun into a leather belt-slide holster.

"Where the fuck have you been?" C.W. asked, climbing out of his love seat.

"Running some errands," I said, noticing a Winchester pump beside the front door, looking at me like an old friend.

"For two days?"

I just looked at him. I didn't know what to say, so I didn't say anything.

If I hadn't needed to stash the pup someplace safe, I wouldn't have even come then.

"And what the fuck is that?" He asked, indignant.

"A puppy," I told him, walking past him into the kitchen. Bear sat down at the kitchen table, behind a can of Coke and a game of solitaire.

"Why the fuck do you have a puppy?" C.W. asked, following me.

"He needs a home," I said, setting everything down on the counter. The sink was empty, for once, and I set the stopper, running lukewarm water into it.

"Well, he can't stay here," Cornelius said, trailing me into the kitchen.

"Why not? You need a puppy," I said. I put the little guy in and gently wetted his fur. He whined so very softly, and it broke my heart.

"Jeb, I'm allergic to dogs."

"No shit?" I said, gently rubbing the shampoo over the little guy.

"Yeah, no shit. Why do you think I never had one growing up?"

"I just thought you were a dweeb," I said, smirking.

"Oh that's funny; that's real rich. I need you to keep your angry, psychotic self around in case these assholes show up again, and you're off playing James Herriot."

"Relax," I tell him, soaping the puppy up. He did not like being wet, but they never do at that age. Cornelius went to the fridge and got a beer.

"You want something to drink?" he asked.

"Fuck no," I said, still pissed at myself for all the booze and coke I'd poured into my system like a rank amateur the past couple of days. Bush league mistakes I should've paid dearly for.

"I hope that shampoo's a de-licer."

"It's got fucking de-licer. It's name-brand shit," I snapped, glaring at him before I caught myself.

"Fuck it, fix me a drink," I said, changing my mind. No way I wouldn't need one before we were done.

"You want Coke, or you gonna drink it like a man?"

"Coke, I need the caffeine," I said. He fixed a drink and sat it beside me while I washed the little guy.

I helped myself to my drink, and then realized I had not eaten since the previous morning. I drank anyway.

"What the fuck are those?" C.W. asked, looking at my homemade sutures. The new ones were even more uneven and jagged than the old one, and he'd given me shit about that one.

"What?"

"Your forearms, man, what the fuck happened? Are those stitches?"

"Would you do me a favor and fix little man up with some formula in one of the bottles from the sack?" I asked. He shook his head in disbelief, but did it. He finished by shaking the formula in the bottle for several seconds before handing it to me. When I reached for it, he pulled it back.

"You gonna tell me what happened to your forearms?"

"Do you really want to know?"

"I could make a pretty good guess," Bear called, over his shoulder, sitting at the table. C.W. looked at him over his shoulder, before turning back to me.

"Yes, Jeb, I want to fucking know."

"An asshole didn't know what he was doing with a blade. That's what happened."

"That's about what I figured," Bear said.

"Did you kill this asshole?" C.W. asked, filled with the self-righteous indignation true believers always carry.

"What do you think?" I asked.

"I know what I think," Bear again, over his shoulder, his face focused on his cards.

"Bear, do you mind?" C.W. snapped. Bear turned around and spit in his Coke can. I thought he was going to say something, but he just stared at C.W. I grabbed the bottle from his hand while he wasn't looking.

"Hey," he snapped, turning back around, but it was too late. I picked the little guy up, and carried him and my drink to the table, sat the two handguns I carried down on the table, and sat down across from Bear. C.W. followed.

I held the little guy in the crook of my arm, and put the nipple in his mouth, and he began chugging away. I was so happy I thought I might cry. That was just what I needed, my rainbow for the fucking year.

"Ok, now that you've fed your new pet, will you please tell where you've been?"

"Don't you know?" Bear asked, shooting him a look that questioned his intelligence. I shrugged.

"I want to hear the asshole say it."

I didn't say anything.

"What now?" he asked.

"Well, I hope you'll listen to reason and go somewhere off the fucking map with Bear while I finish this shit up."

"Oh, no. No you don't. Fuck a whole bunch of that. You don't just get to run around killing everyone you think needs to die. I can't believe you're not in jail. I don't know what kind of deal you made. There has hardly been shit on the news. I don't know how you managed that."

"I don't either. There should've been something. No one can run that kind of interference."

"The gang shooting on Jefferson, that was you, right?" He asked. I just looked at him.

"Motherfucker, I've swept for bugs. Talk to me."

I shrugged, and turned my attention to the little guy in my arms.

"What the fuck is this? Do you have anything to say?"

"Will you do me a favor?" I asked.

"What's that?"

"You got my .45 handy?" I asked.

"Yeah, I got your .45 handy. I got your whole bag of guns, asshole."

"Will you get it please? If you get my gun, I'll tell you everything I've done up till now," I said, wondering if it were, in fact, the truth.

"Ok," he said, and left the table to get my gun. Bear looked across the table at me and spit in his can.

"Hell of a way to have a reunion, huh?" I asked.

"I-magine," he said, not turning away from his cards.

"What're you carrying?" I asked.

"Pair of 10mm Smiths, couple back-up guns."

"I saw that. Never knew you to be much of one for barbeque guns."

"They were a gift from my woman."

"Your woman," I asked, looking up from the suckling pup. Though he had never been a womanizer, he had been a rather committed bachelor. He liked his space, and kept a distance from anyone he hadn't known since diapers.

"A lot can happen in half a decade, Jeb," he said, and nodded toward my new stitches. "Do those yourself," he said, but not asking a question.

"Was the only one there to do 'em."

"You do that other one too?"he asked, nodding toward the older one, just starting to fade.

"Yep."

"They're gonna be so fucked up they make that old one look good. Were you drunk?"

"Not when I got cut. Maybe a little when I sewed myself up," I said, paying more attention to the little guy in my arms. Bear shook his head and pulled another card.

"Same old Jeb," he said. I thought I could feel him staring at my extended pinky finger, not fully dexterous due to its injury, but that might've been in my head.

"Seemed like a good idea at the time."

C.W. walked back in, sat the empty .45 on the table in its holster down next to me, spare mags in their pouches, the one that should have been nestled in its grip beside them. Keeping the pup steady, I used one hand to slip the fully loaded magazine in place, and then pull the gun from the leather. I held the gun against the table, muzzle down, with the recoil spring flush against the tabletop. Pushing downward I racked the slide, which chambered a round.

I set the safety, and it held it my hand, pointing away from my friends. There was just something about it, something that felt good and true and an indelible part of me.

"There, you happy?" C.W. asked.

"I'm a little bit closer to it."

"You gonna fill me in now?"

"I'm a part of this, too, *now,*" Bear said, still not looking up. I wondered if he was still mad about the shit that had gone down before I'd left home.

"Ok," I said. "Here, goes."

I told them most of it, leaving out some of the more gruesome details. I shouldn't have, it wasn't smart, it went against even the most basic OPSEC, but I told them anyway. I did not tell them anything about Travis, our arrangement, or that Vlad might have been, in some capacity, a spook.

Also, I might've left out the part about torturing poor old Manny and feeding him to his dog. Neither one of them would have cared too much for that. Though I knew there was much C.W. still hadn't told me, I did not pressure him. He'd had enough, needed to adjust to the knowledge of what I'd done, and would still do.

"That's it?" C.W. asked expectantly.

"That's it."

"What next?"

"I'm hoping you pack up, and take a vacation. Some place off the map. I'm hoping Bear goes with you, and I'm hoping you're willing to take this little guy here, too."

"You have lost your fucking mind."

"I've heard that before," I said with a shrug. I hadn't had any hope that he might actually do it, but it would've been nice.

"What I meant was, what are you going to do next?"

"I know what you meant," I said.

"What's coming?" Bear asked.

"Not entirely sure yet. A whole lotta bad, whatever it is."

"You're not going to tell me what you're doing next?"

"I can't," I said. It was the truth. Whatever I did next, time was the most important factor. I needed to ditch the pup, find him a place he could crash, then head to the rally point. I needed to link up with the old man, and fill him in on what I'd learned. I also needed to get a few precious hours of sleep.

We moved everything into the living room. I undressed down to the waist, took my boots off, unpeeled my socks and stretched out back on the sofa, the .45 on the table, the puppy on my chest.

"Those stitches on your arms are fucking gross, dude. They're gonna be fucking ugly-ass scars," he said. He was laid out in his loveseat, wrapped around a long pillow, the Luger near at hand.

"Maybe," I said, softly rubbing the little man on my chest.

"You don't even care you're going to be disfigured?" He asked.

"Not really."

"That's fucked up. You got issues, dude," he said with a scoff.

I didn't say anything to refute that. After a few minutes of silence, Bear flicked off the kitchen light, walked into the TV area, punched a button on the stereo, and sat in the La-Z-Boy on the other side of C.W.

"Ballad of a Southern Man", by Whiskey Myers, a band from East Texas, who often sang about the same back roads we'd grown up riding down, filled the air with a low, melancholic buzz.

There was an M-1 carbine, WWII canvas mag pouches on the stock, leaning against the wall beside his chair. The metal held a dull, well-oiled gleam, and it took me back to another place, the same one the Winchester pump did, sitting by the door.

"If Joshua were here, it'd be just like old times. All of us camping out. We even have a dog," I said. In my head it sounded humorous.

"Boy, I wouldn't play that hand with him right now," Bear said with a whistle. "Your baby brother is ten kinds of pissed off at you."

"He'll get over it," I said.

"Shit," they both said, close enough to qualify for unison. I left that where it was. They would have just taken his side anyway.

"When are you taking off?" Bear asked.

"Tomorrow. Just need to crash for a bit," I said.

"Just like that," C.W. asked.

"Just like that," I said. He shook his head.

"Well, whatever your deal is, at least Morales put some cops out for protection," he said.

"Those aren't cops," I said. Before I had announced myself, I cased the place, and had found the same pair of private investigators that had been following the old man. If I had thought they were a real threat, I would not have risked stopping. I would've eliminated the threat.

"And who the fuck are they?"

"Private investigators."

"What the fuck are private investigators doing watching my house?"

"Waiting for Jeb," Bear said. C.W. looked at him, and then back at me.

"Is that true, waiting on you?" C.W. asked.

"I-magine so," I said. "Relax. If you want, I'll shoot 'em in the 'morrow," I said. Neither one of them laughed.

I felt the little guy's wet nose nestled against my chest, the shallow rise and fall of his breath, and I did not care about their feelings.

CHAPTER 41

The pre-dawn air was dark and cool, her elbow propped on the open window. She held her head in her hand, fighting sleep. She would shake her head every few minutes, then put it back down. Then in a moment, she'd let out a few soft, gentle snores, before picking her head back up and starting the process all over again. I had been standing there for what seemed like several minutes.

The clothes she wore may have been the same ones she had worn when I had sat the foil covered plate on her hood. I wondered if she had eaten it. Probably not, she looked like the type who was way too professional for that. She snored softly again, picked her head up, looked at me, then set it back down without registering my presence. I was glad she wasn't protecting my friend. She could have done some exercise to get the blood flowing, but maybe she didn't want to draw attention to herself. I wondered if she'd snort a little coke, but she didn't strike me as someone who consider that an option.

Then, everything moving extra slowly as she recognized what she'd seen, her head picked back up out of her hand, looked at me, her mouth wide with fear, shock, and anticipation. Then she remembered her gun. Her hands went scrambling for the console between the seats, but the comfortable grips of her Beretta Elite II weren't to be found. When she didn't find it, she looked back at me and her gun in my hand.

Her mouth formed an *O*, working itself around words that wouldn't come. I handed her the gun, butt first. She didn't know what to say.

"Can I buy you a cup of coffee?" I asked. Slowly she reached up, staring at me in disbelief.

The Beretta had a stainless barrel and slide on a black frame, with thin, dark rosewood grips, heavy slide, crowned target barrel, and Heine night sights. It wasn't exactly a rare gun, but it wasn't one you saw every day either. I saw the silver KIA bracelet on her wrist as she took the gun, and hoped she had chosen the gun after careful thought and deliberation, instead of it looking pimp.

"I'm a lot of things, but I'm not a danger to you. You have nothing to fear from me. I think we need to talk."

"Sure," she said, still unsure.

We sat at the kitchen table, coffee in our cups, and introduced ourselves to each other. I held the puppy on my chest where he slept. We'd walked in, and he'd been on the couch where I'd left him whining up a storm. Therefore, I picked him up, put him on my chest, and brought him with us to sit at the table.

"So," she tried to start, but the hand on her cup was shaky, her lips quivering. She blushed, her light milk chocolate skin accenting with cinnamon.

"How long you been up, Toni?" I asked.

"Going on seventy two hours now," she said, embarrassed at being caught unaware. I let that die a natural death.

"Who were you with?" I asked, motioning to the silver K.I.A. bracelet on her wrist, similar to the one on my own.

"Air Force. I was with the Security Forces," she said.

I was trying to establish a rapport, to let her find some comfort.

"So, maybe you could tell us what you're doing staking out my house?" Cornelius asked, the agitation and anger in his voice a rumbling tremble. He didn't give a shit where she'd been or what she'd done.

"Waiting on Jeb, here. After he ditched Larry the other day, we lost Pine, so we figured you were the next best place to wait. "

"What are you talking about?" he asked her, then turned to me. "What the fuck's she talking about? Who the fuck is Larry?"

"A guy I work with. We were staking out Pine, and then Jeb here showed up. He let me know he saw me, so Larry followed him, but that didn't work. When we realized Jeb distracted us, and that Pine was gone, I came here hoping he'd show up."

"So he could lead you to Pine? By the way, who the fuck is that, anyway?" C.W. asked.

"I found the old guy," I looked at him then back at the puppy. "From the bar, the shooter," I said.

"I'm sorry, what did you say? You found the shooter? You knew his fucking name and you didn't tell me?" He said, his anger rising. I don't guess I blamed him, although I think he was more pissed about his story than anything else. I drank some coffee and rubbed the little guy on my chest.

"It wasn't time," I said.

"When would it be time?" he wanted to know. I shrugged. I looked at Bear at the end of the table. He hadn't said anything, and didn't look he was going to. I looked at Toni.

"So, why are you following him anyway?" I asked her. She looked into her cup and took another sip.

"He asked you a fucking question," Cornelius said, pissed at everything by now. She shot him a look that could have cut steel. Bear just sat back, still pissed and silent at the whole episode. Probably thinking about drive trains and transmissions and how he'd be better off having never met either one of us on the playground all those years ago.

"I'm not sure what I can share with you guys. Christ-fucking-sakes, a reporter, the redneck bail bond king of East Texas, and a goddamn mercenary. It's like the Three Amigos on acid," she said, shaking her head as if in disbelief.

Maybe I shouldn't have given her the gun back. I was afraid if she called me a mercenary again, I might yank it out of her purse and make her eat the fucking thing.

I kissed my little friend on the nose and felt instantly better. Puppies rock.

"The girl on the spit was Pine's daughter. She worked with Torres at LARO. They were dating. She found out what he was into, they made an example of her," I said. C.W. glared at me.

"How long have you known this?" C.W. asked, staring at me.

"When Joshua was in the hospital, I called my rabbi. Guy is major league connected to people across the spectrum. I fed him what I remembered about the shooter, and by the time we had our talk with Manny and Boudreaux, he'd gotten me a name, an address, and an introduction. I was hoping I'd be able to throw you a bone in another direction."

"I can't even believe you," C.W. said, glaring at me, slamming a fist down against the table. Bear scoffed, a short, sharp snap, his sole contribution to the conversation thus far. I didn't say anything, just drank my coffee and held my friend.

"Ok, I know how Pine fits into this. He's after revenge. Why are you on him?" C.W. directed his question to the woman sitting at his table. She just stared at him. She was beyond beautiful, and her beauty probably went a long way when it came to time to sit and stare, but it wasn't giving us any answers.

"She's looking for a girl," Bear finally said, beating me to the punch.

"You betcha," she replied, fixing her deep blue eyes on me.

"You're looking for a particular girl?" I asked.

"That's right."

"How long have you been looking for her?" I asked.

"Does it matter?" She answered with a question.

"How long have you been following him?"

"Does it matter?" She answered with another one, her tone the still the same, her body maybe just a shade stiffer as she had to stuff the anger and frustration somewhere.

"Were you outside the bar in Deep Ellum when Pine took out Torres and the other two?" I asked.

"Oh, you mean when you two were stumbling around drunk outside flirting with that hot Latin number?"

"Yeah, then," I said.

"No, not then, I don't know anything about that. If I had been there, I would've been compelled to come forward with any information, dig?"

"Ah," Cornelius said, leaning forward, his dip fat under his lip.

"How did you know to follow him?" I asked.

"I did my homework. Just like you," she said, flat and even, staring me straight in the eye.

"I didn't do my homework. I cheated. I called a motherfucker so wiggy and spooked out he probably scares the shit out of the egg heads at Area 51."

"Cause that's just who you needed to hook up with," Bear said, and then spit in his can. I shot him a look for bringing up old shit, but he didn't care. I ignored him, but only because something finally clicked in my thick skull.

"It's the Senator's daughter, isn't it? Party girl dropped out of school to go to rehab. She's not really in rehab, is she? Someone has her and they're using her as leverage, aren't they?" I asked. Her face went white. C.W. took everything in. Bear looked from me, to her, to back at me, and spit in his cup, probably not as indifferent as he seemed. Probably not.

"Get the fuck out of here," C.W. said. Toni just stared at me.

"The rally's on the fifth. They want him to switch. To publicly change his mind, and declare he's voting against his own bill, or his little girl gets it," Bear said, filling in whatever blanks anyone had.

"She was friends with Pine's daughter. They were taken together," she said. When she said it, her eyes were not cast downward in shame because there was no shame for her there. Instead, they took turns on each of us, trying to figure out the fuel inside.

I'm sure each of us looked at her like she was the bitch responsible for it all.

"They were taken together. They used Pine's daughter as an example of what would happen if they didn't follow their demands," she said.

"You're doing K&R for the girl?" I asked Toni.

"Jaime, her name is Jaime, and yes, we're trying to bring her home," she said, her voice even and professional, only her eyes showing emotion.

The work I'd done in the K&R field had been limited to search and recovery, and, on occasion, reprisal. By the time we'd come into something, it was already a mess, all hope for a peaceful, monetary solution was over. The people I'd known who worked the other side of it, the negotiations, were a different breed than I was. I was glad I'd rarely been in a position where hiding my hatred, or the desire to do violence on those involved, was needed. Some people will tell you it's just a job, and don't get emotionally attached. And you know what? That's just more bullshit dreamed up by people who think life in LA is normal. If you spend weeks or months with a client's family, going back and forth with the monsters who are keeping them in a cold basement or a jungle cage, it's going to get personal. You're going to be emotionally attached. Someone you've never met or even talked to will be as real to you as anyone you've ever known. After weeks or months, the suggestion that recovery won't be made can be near crippling.

"Why aren't you working with the Feds or the locals?"

"The client's call. They think if they play ball they have a better chance of getting their little girl back. She's still local. They send proof of life every couple of days. A picture via encrypted email, usually against a backdrop of either the Dallas or Ft. Worth skyline, usually with that morning's paper. It changes every time so we can't pinpoint it. All over the fucking map"

"How can you not be working with them?" C.W. barked.

"There're more crooks undercover as cops in this town then there are cops undercover as crooks. Why do you think nothing came from the investigation into Pine's little girl? We knew Torres had to be a part of it. We didn't know how much of it Alejandro knows. We were trying to backtrack through them when the old man popped him in front of you two."

"That I believe," C.W. said and spit in his cup.

"Can you trace the calls?" I asked, ignoring his "down with the movement" bullshit vibe.

"Don't you think we tried? We have ex-NSA geeks working on this, with the very best gear available outside the deepest levels of the gov, and they can't hack the encryption," she said.

Nobody was better at electronic warfare and surveillance than the NSA. Assuming they were pros, and working with currently available equipment, and I assumed they were, the only things they couldn't hack would be recently developed software in use by the government. Or, possibly, another government. Or a third party with ridiculous amounts of money and influence. Like a drug cartel.

"Fuck," I said. It was all I could think of.

"Yeah. Which is why we need you to stop and let us handle it. Stop writing newspaper articles, stop killing everybody in your path. Just stop."

"Why would we do a thing like that?" C.W. asked.

"Our lawyers can help your friend here, if... anything...that's happened the past couple of days becomes an issue for him."

Everyone at the table laughed but her. There might've been the faintest threat in her voice, but I didn't much care. It's why we were laughing. I wanted to point out the hypocrisy to C.W., but didn't. It wouldn't have done any good, anyway.

"When it's over with, you get the exclusive. Everything, including interviews with all involved," she told him, and then nodded to me.

"But we're close right now. We're lining out a deal. We just need you to stop doing what you're doing," she said, pleading with herself as much as us to believe it.

"If you wait until the fifth, you'll die with her," I said, Manny's words reverberating in my skull.

Day of rage.

"Why do you say that?"

"Day of Rage. Revolution. That's what Torres was planning. He was using the militia to pull a false flag attack at the rally. If he could get it to happen right after the author of the most strict immigration/ border security bill ever written publicly confessed a change of heart, it would be madness," I said.

In truth, I thought it had the potential to be beyond madness. I thought about the notebook I'd seen filled with notes concerning the parade route, how he was planning on herding people into a giant kill- zone. I thought of buffalo crashing off a cliff.

Dallas, Assassination City, and then some.

"That's insane," C.W. said, staring at me, his spit cup in his hand.

I looked at Toni, who now seemed to hide behind the cup in her hands. Her eyes were wide with worry, searching for the right thing to say, the right place to go.

"Your best bet to save the girl is to go to the Feds. You don't have a chance waiting it out," I said.

Eyes watering, she shook her head and looked past me, at the sun's reflection shimmering off the little kidney shaped pool.

"No, that won't work. I've begged her father to do that already," she said.

"You can't go to the authorities because you don't know who you can go to, do you? Because whatever they're holding over his head, they're holding it over other people too, aren't they?"

"I swear to God, newspaper man, if you put any of this in print before the fifth, I'll kill you myself," she said. C.W. just stared at her.

"What are they holding over him?" I asked.

"Fuck if I know," she said, and took a drink from her cup. When she did so, her eyes flashed to the side.

"Oh, I think you do, bitch," Bear said, having caught the flash in her eye too.

"Who the fuck are you calling *bitch*, pecker-wood?"

"The bitch that's sitting at my friend's table, lying to us, that's which one," Bear said. He was enjoying himself more than I remembered. Maybe he just needed the release.

She turned her attention back to me, ignoring him.

"I don't know what they have on him. He's a politician, who knows what the fuck it could be?" she asked.

"Well, maybe you need to find that out," I said.

"We're working on it," she said.

"For five months?"

"We haven't been on it that long," she said.

"Then who the fuck was doing it before you came on scene?"

"Nobody. The family was trying to do it themselves, with their people. We've only been on it half that, and that's because the wife came to us after she left her husband."

"After two and a half months of negotiation?"

"I don't think there was a great deal of negotiation involved."

"How badly did they take it out on her? The shift to you doing the talking?" I asked. I did not suspect switching negotiators half way through would be taken positively. She looked away, but this time, steeling herself, her hard eyes watering with emotion, swallowing a thought, an image, a picture in her mind.

That couldn't have been a good sign.

"Not only is he gambling with his daughter's life, he used his influence to kill the investigation into Pine's little girl, didn't he?"

"That was before we came on. It was one of their first demands," she said. I stared at her a few moments, taking stock, and then looked out the window.

"What are you going to do?" she asked.

"That's none of your business," I said.

"We've already established that it is."

"We've established that there's a young woman about to die a very bad death, because your people can't do their job. It might not be their fault, but that doesn't save the girl, does it?"

"If you know where she is, tell me. I can work with that," she said.

"How the fuck am I supposed to know where she is? I just found out she was missing," I said.

"You must've gotten some intel the past couple of days. You know everything else."

"Leave me your card. If I come across the girl, I'll be sure to call you," I told her.

"What are you going to do? You and a broken down old man," she said, yelling, pleading, her voice rising. "Listen to me, you… you…*fucking redneck, roid-monkey, super merc, goddamn stereotype motherfucker*. Pine is dying. He's eaten up with cancer. It started in his colon and spread throughout his body. The fact the he's walking around is either a miracle or a testament to the power of raw hatred. Six months ago he was on his deathbed."

Her words hung in the air like napalm sticking to flesh. I thought back over my conversation with Pine, the meal we'd eaten, the food he'd barely touched. I wondered if six months was long enough to come back from that kind of place, for one last go round. One last chance to do bad things for good reasons, and help those too weak to do it themselves. To make an innocent girl, raped and butchered, right. As right as she could be made.

"She's almost home," she said, but we both knew it was a lie, bleeding hope.

"Leave me your card," I said. "When I leave here later, do not follow me. I'll call you," I said.

"Goddamn it, listen to me," she said, her voice straining. "We're professionals."

"So am I," I said.

"Then help us," she said. "If you keep it up, they're going to get scared. That's not good. We know people with the Fed. We're going to bring them in, their shooters on the fifth, the day of the rally. All we need is to get her there. They need her father to make his speech. That's a part of this. They need that. That's the thing that's going to get us the girl."

"Honey, come the fifth, this city is going to fucking explode. I'm sure whoever has her won't have a problem taking her downtown to watch the fireworks."

"It's all I've got, goddamn it. And I'm not going to have it much longer if you keep wreaking havoc."

"Leave your card. Do not follow me. I will call you," I said again.

"Why don't I believe you?" She asked, the tone of her voice more accusatory than questioning. Cornelius just looked at me, his eyebrow cocked, which was his way of telling me he wanted to hear this as well.

I thought of girls being kidnapped, snatched without warning, raped and brutalized before being sold into slavery. So much cattle on the hoof. I thought of my own family, innocents threatened by chance. I thought of the law, infinitely malleable, all too often failing to protect those it claimed to serve. And I thought of violent men without a code, and how best to deal with them.

"I don't know what you want me to tell you," I said softly, thinking of the girl, thinking something needed to be done about that once and for all. I also knew they wouldn't understand. They thought they did, sure. But in the end, they would entrust the task to the same people who had already failed. To agents of the law, people who served order instead of justice. People who thought stopping just short of what needed to be done made them better than the bad guys.

I stood, and then went outside to lay with the little guy in the hammock in the back yard.

I needed to relax, and wait on the old man's call, and plan my route so that I could leave C.W.'s without being followed.

CHAPTER 42

The night was dark, the air just starting to cool with the promise of rain when I rapped my knuckles against the dry motel room door. I saw the shadow move on the other side of the hole, and then heard the sounds of the locks being thrown.

"Get the fuck in here you goddamn madman," he said, almost a snarl.

"There's a girl being held hostage," I said, almost inadvertently. I had to get it out, to share, to know he felt the same. That whatever we were going to do must take that into account. That it was our first priority.

"I know. I know who she is, too. Now get the fuck in here so I can cuss your big ass proper like," he said, and turned and walked back into the dark room. I followed, closing the door behind me.

"What the fuck were you thinking?" He asked, under his breath.

"You're upset," I said, stating the obvious.

"Fuck, yes, I'm upset. I thought you were going to protect your friend. I thought you were going to throw him off the trail. Do you know how many people you killed the past couple days?"

"Never been big on cutting notches," I said.

"Oh, I could tell," he said, shaking his head like he couldn't believe he was having this conversation. "You're just a goddamn walking ball of chaos, you know that? You can't just get in rolling gun battles through downtown, and the next morning mass murder the survivors while they're hooked up to IV's in a goddamn whore house, and expect to get away with it. This is the surveillance age kid, and you should goddamn know better," he said.

Anger radiated off him, but it wasn't just anger. It was sadness, and desperation, and animosity toward the situation itself. I shrugged.

"I didn't have much of a choice. Cornelius is good at what he does. He moved faster than I thought. I had to go along with him. Both you and Morales thought we were safe going to the club. Shit went south real fast. I barely got us out of there."

"And the next day, at the flop house," he asked. I shrugged.

"Anytime I have a chance to strike my enemy while they're asleep, wounded, and drugged, I'm going to take it."

"I should've been there, should've goddamned bird dogged it," he said. Maybe he was a little mad at himself, for not being a part of the past days event's.

"What could you have done? It got taken care of. It's over with."

"Working girls deserve a stray bullet for selling some trim? Some kid there to buy a dime bag and a taco deserve one? Maybe the kid has a shitty home life, and the gang represents love and family and everything he doesn't have. Maybe he's hanging around in the hopes of being taken in. Are you numb to collateral, kid? Because I never have been, and I expect more from one of Eric's boys," he said. I didn't say anything, just let him have his rant.

People kept bringing up Champ, whom Travis knew as Eric, and what they expected from the people who worked with him. It was starting to annoy the piss out of me.

"You've got to learn some patience, kid. You're a fucking recon baby for Christ-sakes," he continued.

"It's in the past. The plays were made, and I had to react. At least I took a lot of players off the board."

"You didn't take shit off the board. Maybe half the goddamn B-team," he spat.

I took a breath and looked at him. He stared at me a long moment before continuing.

"The real players are already here, son. The cartel shooters he wanted to impress. The ones who gave him the go ahead to pop his old man. They're here, and they have the girl," he said.

I could see indentations on the far bed, so I sat at the head of the one nearest the door, and pulled a small glass ashtray my way. He shot me a curious look from the corner of his eye, and I wondered if it were test time.

"Did you get here clean," he asked.

"Yep," I said, inhaling death, taking my slow, sweet time.

He pulled a chair over to the far corner of my bed, straddled it, and pulled out a pipe and pouch from the ether.

"Got some medicinal here, mixed with some vanilla and bourbon. Want a turn on it?" he asked. I thought about what the gorgeous P.I. had said, the cancer eating away at him from too deep a place for anything of this world to reach. How him just walking around was a miracle. I shook my head,

"Fuck no," I said. "Sounds like a dick in the mouth."

"Shit," he scoffed.

"I got a bottle in my bag. Besides, I don't have the lungs to smoke that shit while I'm working," I said, the gentle, residual numbness of cocaine a fond memory. I almost wish I'd kept it.

"Suit yourself," he said, gently packing his pipe.

"You mind if I get comfortable?" I asked.

"Long as you don't go to sleep. We got a lot to talk about," he said.

"I ain't going to sleep," I said. I stripped down to the waist, sat the .45 close by, pulled the bottle from the bag, poured enough for me to sip on in a plastic cup, and stretched out on the motel bed, the ashtray on my chest.

"You ready for a debrief?" he asked. I shucked another cancer stick from the pack and monkey fucked it off the old one before nodding my head.

"Yep, if 'n you want it," I said, stabbing the old butt into the ashtray on my chest. He folded his lean arms over the top of the chair and puffed on his pipe. The ember glowed inside his pipe, and a strange purple hue cast around him. I took a sip, and smoked some more, and told him everything that had happened since I left his company.

I told him about tracking down Kendrick, and Uncle Jack's man, Russell, keeping him under wraps for us. I told him how it went down at the club, how we'd escaped, and how I'd left C.W. with Russell so I could go pro-active and keep the momentum rolling.

I told him about what Vlad had said, and how he'd asked for asylum, and how I'd killed him anyway, just for meanness sake. I told him how I tracked Torres's crew to the flop house, and then how by the time Manny showed up at the safe house I was a little far gone.

"What'd you do to Manny?" he asked when I was done. I smiled a little smile.

"I put the boots into him. I kicked him down to blood soaked strips over shiny bone, and then I hung him from a tree, in the same device he used to bulk up his dog's neck muscles. I put that on his head and wrenched him up, and then I took my knife and played with him some. And then, instead of giving him the bullet I promised him, I sliced his stomach open, watched his guts fall out, and fed him to his dog," I said. He just stared at me, his dark eyes shrouded, his face hidden in the darkness of the night and the room itself.

"Damn, son," he said, not sure what to say.

"That's exactly what I did."

Fuck it, I thought.

"And you left him like that?" he asked.

"Yep," I said. "I don't know how long he might've held on, but I bet however long it was he didn't much enjoy watching that dog eat his guts out."

"Kid, you ever worry about your soul, doing shit like that?" he asked, his voice shallow and heavy with worry.

"Naw," I lied, mainly to myself, for the dog's sake.

Behind me, the first drops of rain hit the window. Instinctively, I wanted to throw back the curtains and slide the window open a few inches. I wanted to look out at the parking lot and watch the raining night. To see puddles form across the crumbling blacktop, to let the sound of its relentless patter, the smell of fresh rain cutting through city smog, mixed with the beautiful blue ambiance of moonlight and neon, and let it wash over me.

I didn't though.

There were too many reasons not to.

"After that, what happened?"

"After that I went to Wal-Mart, got some stuff for the pup, and then I went to C.W.'s."

"Yeah, I bet that was a helluva reunion," he said.

"It could've been worse," I said with a shrug.

"Had a talk with your private detective, though," I said. He shot me a disapproving look.

"The bitch, or her partner?"

"The bitch. They're doing K&R for the girl's family. They've been on you longer than you think. She was on you that day you popped Torres," I said. He stared at me through the smoke flowing from his pipe.

"She said that?" he asked, like he didn't believe it.

"She said it, but in such a way as she could pretend otherwise," I said.

"She's the one that told you about the girl?"

"She be the one," I said.

I took a drink, and then another drag off my menthol, and looked at him sitting there, staring off into space.

"What, goddamn it?"

"She said they're coordinating with FBI SRT to be in place for the meet before the rally," I said, and watched his face. He nodded slowly in the vanilla scented marijuana fog around his head.

"She really believe that girl'll live if they wait that long?"

"Not really," I said, before continuing. "I got the impression her old man pulled rank on her over it."

"Sounds about like him. He was all suit and posture and by the numbers twenty five years ago."

I thought of things to say, but did not. I took a drink, and smoked some more, and watched his face. Most of the time, he watched me right back.

"She say anything else?"

"She wants us to play ball," I said.

He waved a long, callused hand at me through the smoke screen. "And stand down."

"Yeah, that."

"I suppose she offered you lawyers, too," he said, recognizing the old gambit for what it was.

"Of course she did. The thing is, I believe her. She means it. She cares about the girl."

"I ain't about to leave some poor girl to the same fate as my Kelly Jo," he said, nearly taking umbrage.

"Never thought that," I said.

"You better goddamn not have," he said, staring at me through the smoke like he might cut my throat.

"The fifth of May is right around the corner. It's another week, speed of fucking sound, before we even start to put together a serious op down south. And that's in a different goddamn AO. This shit's going to end before then, and that poor little rich girl and a whole lot of other people are going to die unless we do something to head this motherfucker off at the pass."

"I know," he said. His voice was firm, and solid, but steady. It did not rise.

"What do you think about that shit Vlad said?" I asked. He rolled his eyes.

"Every two-bit Cyrillic fuck-up that had a cousin or an uncle or a limp tried to pass himself off as a spy of some sort. His people might've done some contract work for their side. He may have even been a low level sleeper of some kind. Though, being a closeted gay pseudo-mobster probably wasn't a genius cover."

"Everyone thought he was a joke."

"Ok, well, maybe it wasn't so bad," he said with a shrug, and hooked the pipe into the corner of his mouth.

"Toni, your P.I., she said they had ex-NSA nerds working on breaking the encryption on the proof of lives, and can't get it done. That's a little more high speed than the freaks I've worked doing K&R."

He didn't say anything, just puffed on the pipe hanging in the corner of his mouth while he scratched his neck.

"They could get that equipment from the cartels," he said, finally.

"They could get it from the Russians, too."

"Kid, they could have gotten it from the Russians via the cartel. Fuck, they could have got it from China, or made it themselves, or even from D.C. What matters is they have it."

I wished my new friend, the pup I'd left with my old friends, was there on my chest. I hoped that, regardless of what happened, he'd have a good home and grow up to forget his beginnings. I knew the psychic scars lasted a lifetime in many humans, and I knew the same could affect his behavior, how he viewed the world and reacted to it.

Thinking about that, I wished I could kill Manny again.

After a few minutes of a heavy silence, I killed the aging butt in the little ashtray, and scooted up a little further along the headboard, so I could drink a little easier. I drank, and looked out between the curtains, and wondered what was next.

"How do you know about the girl?" I asked.

"Alejandro told me," he said.

"The P.I. said he wasn't being co-operative," I said.

"He's not, not with them, anyway," he said.

"If he's so goddamn co-operative, how come you're just now finding out about it?"

"Because he hasn't known about her that long. He wasn't in on it with Torres. He's been playing catch up on all this since they killed my girl. They reached out to him, told him to pass the word that if anything else happened, they'd roast her. So, he called me."

"I still think he's into it deeper than he lets on. He's says he's helping people, but all he's doing is getting rich. I think he just wants to protect his goddamn cash flow."

"That what you think, boy?"

"Yeah, yeah it is."

"Alejandro was the boy's father, not his Uncle," he said.

I took a drink and thought about that.

Alejandro had been a surrogate father figure in and out of his life, and had groomed him to be his successor. Every time Torres had struck out on his own, first with a gang, and then in the military, it had caused a rift between them, one Alejandro always managed to exploit for personal gain.

"Fuck," I said, thinking about it.

"Yep," he said. He smoked his pipe and leaned back in the chair, pushing with his feet on the end of the bed.

Rain rattled off the window, and we both listened to it for a while, alone with whatever was going through our heads.

"Believe it or not, Alejandro is trying to do right by the girl. Things went downhill real fast between him and Michael after what happened to my Kelly Jo. He knew something was wrong with his boy, but he didn't know what."

"He just gave you his own kid?"

"If everything goes off the way Torres planned it, this country is gonna be in a world of pain for a long time over it. And the people he's trying to help will be fucked harder than anyone. He gave me his kid, not to protect himself, but the people he's trying to help."

"I still say he's a paternalistic asshole."

"Yeah, and you just spent two days killing people because they *might* hurt the people you care about."

"Least there are a few less people between us and her," I said, my eyes hard, leaving something else unsaid.

Something neither of us wanted to admit. That we simply didn't have the time to wait and form a team of people at our discretion and do a proper train up. The girl didn't have that much time.

Lightning struck, and I felt cold run down my spine. The rain hit the window a little harder, a little faster, for a mad minute, before fading.

I tried not to think about how at that moment it was just me and a dying, broken down old man about to step forth into the breach.

I downed what was in my cup and debated another. I thought about it so hard, finishing the bottle would've had less of an effect. I sat the empty cup on the opposite side of my gun and left it there.

"What's our next move?" I asked. He smoked his pipe in thought without speaking.

"The key to finding her is their infrastructure. Ol' Uncle Alejandro hasn't been their guy for forever. It was probably Michael since he was a kid. They'll need someone else to take care of getting them documentation and all that," I said. He didn't reply. The smoke from his pipe billowed and hung over his head in blue hue, just visible against the dark of the room. I couldn't see his thoughts.

"I bet it's that fuckin' Priest," I said, disgust rolling off my tongue. He started to say something, but stopped.

"You got the papers you took off Manny?" he asked. "Sure," I said. "Outside pocket of my bag."

He reached over to my bag atop the dresser, ripped open the outside pocket, and pulled Manny's wallet out.

He flipped through it, and then sat and stared at me, holding it in his open palm.

"You torture a guy to near death, feed him to his dog, leave him hanging from a tree, and then you roll around with his wallet and don't think anything of it?"

"I wanted to show them to you," I said. He shook his head.

"I can see that," he said. "Hit that light, will you, kid?"

I reached for the lamp bolted to the wall beside the bed and turned it on. Travis flipped through the cards until he found the driver's license, and he held that close to his face for examination.

"This is good shit," he said.

"I know. That's why I wanted you to see it," I said, nearly snapping. Very nearly exasperated. It was the work of a pro. I wouldn't have bothered dragging it along if it wasn't good enough to notice.

"There's only a couple of people in the 'Plex this good. And I bet you I know which one did this," he said. He stuffed the cards back into the wallet, and unfolded the proof of insurance.

He looked at me, and then the paper, and then back to me.

"You've already driven past this, haven't you?" He asked, like he could read my mind. He reminded me of Champ, the wiggy old spook that had taken me and the Dink under his wing. I wondered how well they actually knew each other.

"Yep," I said. I'd cruised it on my way.

"Well?"

"It's not too big, really. Big, but not that big. It's occupied, but it doesn't look like it's in use as a ranch. Spanish style main house, couple of small guest houses off to the side, large barn in the pasture, away from the house. It didn't look empty, but it didn't look like they were holding the 9th Legion either."

"What kind of perimeter they have set up?"

"Got a big rock gate with a call box, and one camera, both of which were state-of-the-art just before I was born. Pipe fence around the property. Trees and scrub inside the fence. The acreage is on a corner, and when you turn that corner you get a pretty good view of the house and buildings from the side. There's an old railroad grade running through the back of the property."

"We'll check all this stuff out tomorrow, see what unfolds," he said then paused in thought. "And you said the P.I. said they got an encrypted video sent via email for the proof of life," he asked.

"That's what she said."

He stepped from the chair and moved it back to the desk. He then set his pipe down, turned off the light, took off his shirt and shoes, and laid out on his bed.

"The camera, the speaker box at the gate. They didn't even look functional. Could be, it's just another safe house. Could be it's not even that. But if they have the kind of equipment that can make ex NSA geeks scratch their heads, maybe they feel secure enough not to upgrade their physical security."

"That happens when you're dealing with amateurs. Someone gave them a souped-up cell phone or a laptop with a code and they think they're bad ass. If she is there, we need to figure out a way to get her before reinforcements show up, 'cause those boys from down south are going to be a whole different level of hard. We don't need any more of them ahead of us than we already got."

"We're running out of time as it is."

"Don't mind fuck yourself boy. You're too old for that bullshit, and I'm too goddamn old to nursemaid. We'll fucking draft people if we have to. Offer them something they want more than the girl if we can't. One way or another, she's going home."

I stared out the window and listened to the rain and didn't say anything.

"You never know, kid. Everything might just work out for us on this," he said.

"Be goddamn nice to catch a break for once."

"Preaching to the choir, kid, preaching to the choir."

CHAPTER 43

The sun's intense heat reflected off the blacktop with a broiling mirage. We cut through those simmering distortions as we turned into the parking lot of the Anchor Motel on Harry Hines Boulevard, Dallas, Texas, of some renown. I smiled as we pulled to a stop inside the parking lot. Once, long ago, I'd worked in a warehouse nearby with Joshua; two country boys loose in the big, bad city. Working girls openly plied their trade, and winos clustered beneath overpasses. On our lunch breaks, we'd cruise up and down the Hines, amazed at the spectacle of urban life. Later on, after I'd mustered out of the army and was drinking myself out of college the second time, I'd worked the door for one of the gentleman's clubs down the street. I once broke a pimp's arm after I'd decided I didn't like the way he treated his employees.

"You, be cool, follow my lead now, ya' hear?" the old man said, throwing it in park and opening the door. I let loose the belt buckle and stepped out, into the heat.

Shutting the door, I stretched, the rods in my back and leg, results from old wounds screaming at me. A latent Hispanic in Chuck Taylors, Daisy Dukes, cut off Dallas Cowboys jersey, and a hair net waved at me from behind a pillar. I shrugged polite indifference, and followed Trav up the stairs.

We'd made the block three times, taking three different routes, looking for surveillance, and come up nil, yet, now, I followed the old man as his head swiveled back and forth, searching everything within his field of vision for danger.

As we neared the door, he held a hand back at me, motioning me to stop and take position between the door and window. I did as he asked, leaning against the brick just outside the window, my hand on the .45. He knocked three times fast then paused before knocking twice more.

We waited a long ten count for an answer. Finally it came. The door opened up and a bear hug enveloped the old man. The man doing the hugging was a short, overweight Hispanic, his hair both long and thinning, dressed in worn chinos and a t-shirt from an old Pearl Jam concert beneath a long, heavy bathrobe. They seemed to have a history the old man didn't want to acknowledge.

"Goddamn it, get off me already," he said, stepping into the room. I followed, my hand still on the butt of the gun.

"Shit, kid, who am I? What is this?" he said, stepping back as the door swung closed.

"It's been so long, Papa," the rotund little man chanted, gregariously.

"And how many times do I have to tell you I ain't your damn Papa?"

"I know, I know, but, you know. Yeah, you know," he said, still speaking in his fast, happy little singsong. I cocked an eyebrow and the old man just shook his head. "How are you anyway, Papa?"

"I'm fine Umberto; we just need to talk is all."

"Well, come in to my home, have a seat," he said, and opened the fire door to the adjoining room. We followed him inside, to find an at least semi-permanent living space. Sitting on the dresser were several laptops, cell phones of various makes, a couple of different digital cameras.

The bed was pushed into a corner, and a plush leather sofa backed against the wall. The television against the opposite wall was much larger, much more expensive, than the others in the rest of the motel. There were a couple of low bookcases against another wall, and they contained various notebooks and foodstuffs. A hotplate sat atop one.

"Please, sit," he said, bouncing on one narrow ankle, turning like an elephant in a tutu. "You guys want a beer or anything?" he asked, hopeful. As if he hadn't had guests in quite some time. We both nodded sure, we'd take a beer. He wanted to give us one so badly, it would've been a sin not to.

He pulled three beers from the tiny dorm room sized fridge and we sat, Trav on one end of the sofa, while I took a corner of the bed. He handed us the beers and sat next to Trav. We twisted the tops off and took our first pulls. Trav wiped his lips with the back of his hand, looked around the little room once more and shook his head.

"When the hell you gonna move into a house or at least an apartment?"

"Papa, you know I like my freedom. My work requires I be able to travel light."

"You've lived here for fifteen years, 'Berto. Really think you're gonna need to pick up and move like that?" he asked. Umberto shrugged. You never knew in his business. Whatever it was.

He took another pull and looked at me. I held out my hand.

"Berto, this is my friend, Jeb. Jeb, this is my old friend and associate, Umberto," Trav said, leaving last names out of it. He took my hand and we shook.

"So, my good friends, what can I do for you?"

"First things first," Travis said. He pulled a small notebook from his back pocket, tore a page out, and handed it to him.

"I need you to throw a blanket on this address right here. Everything. Eyes and ears if you got the juice. We know they're hooked up to the net, and streaming video, but it's encrypted."

"Are these bad people, Papa?"

"Very bad, 'Berto. We think they have a girl who probably wants to come home in the worst way right now," he said. I couldn't believe he'd shared so much with the man, but 'Berto just stared at him through his impossibly thick glasses, with a concentration that could have sparked a fire at the bottom of an ocean trench.

"Absolutely, I'll get on it right away."

"Good, and I'm going to need you to patch it through to my laptop."

"Not a problem. What else?"

"I need you to look at something, and tell me if it's your work, ok?"

"Sure, Papa, anything for you," he said.

Travis handed him Manny's wallet.

"Ah, yes, I know this man," he said, holding up the fake driver's license.

"You knew Manny," Travis asked.

"Yes, Miguelito brought him by many times. They did good work, helped a lot of our people," he said, his voice sincere and honest. I had to check myself to maintain decorum.

"Torres brought him here? Michael Torres? Miguel Torres? Whatever fucking name he went by," Travis asked.

"Yes, Papa."

"What did you do for them?"

"Oh, you know. Driver's licenses, credit cards, social security cards, insurance papers. City paper work, you name it. Mainly just stuff for the people, you know? Help them live the American dream."

"Have you done any work for them lately?" Travis asked.

"Sure," he said. "All the time."

"Anything out of the ordinary?"

"Miguelito brought a hard case by here a few months ago, just to introduce him to me. He needed full packages for himself, several others."

"What do you mean, by hardcases?" I asked. "Gang-bangers, or military?"

"Oh, military, for sure. I remember thinking how strange it was that Miguelito seemed to want to make a good impression with the man. Usually, he walked around with a chip on his shoulder about life."

"Did you do the work for the man?"

"Yes, of course."

"Did you keep records?" Travis asked. Berto started to sway from side to side, physically hemming and hawing as much as he was vocally.

"Papa, you know my work is important to me," he said.

"It's not like that, Berto. Miguelito was caught up in some bad stuff. There are lives at stake here. Innocent lives, people that didn't ask to be a part of some real bad stuff coming down," Travis said. Berto looked at him, a dry sheen of recognition glossing over his eyes, before he gave a reluctant nod.

"Si, Papa. I can get you the information. It may take a day to pull it up. You know I only keep on hand what I'm currently working on. Everything else is stored safely elsewhere."

"I know, I know, Berto. It's all good. Listen, can you also do a rush job for me and my friend?"

"Of course, anything for you, Papa."

"Can it with the Papa shit, already. We need two works, double time."

"I can have them for you by tomorrow," he said.

"That's outstanding, Berto," Travis assured him.

We took turns standing in front of a digital camera, while Berto took our pictures. Berto had several different shirts on hand for us to change in and out of. He asked if we wanted to pick our new names. I gave him a pseudonym I'd written some articles under for various food and gun magazines. You never know what'll come in handy, and what'll pass for cover in weird corners of the globe. I couldn't remember birds or flowers for shit. Stick with shit you know well enough to bullshit. For me, that leaves guns and food.

We were changing back into our clothes when I thought about all the work Berto had done to help his people.

"Hey, Berto," I said. "Now that Miguelito is out of the picture, how will you go about, uh, helping your people?" I asked. Berto looked at Travis, and then back at me after Travis nodded his ok.

"Father Mitchell has been a big help over the years as well," he said. In his eyes I saw a great deal of fear, uncertainty, and anger, none in small measure.

"Father Mitchell, huh? You know him pretty well?" I asked.

"Of course," he said. "He has done much work with Miguel and his Uncle. He's going to help distribute pamphlets to the people during the Cinco de Mayo demonstrations."

"You're not planning on being downtown come the fifth, are you?" Travis asked.

"Oh, hell no, Papa. You taught me better than that. Too many cops, too many cameras. To hell with that," he said. "You know I don't like crowds."

"That's good," Trav said, slapping his shoulder. "One of us will be by tomorrow to pick this up."

S. A. Bailey

"Of course, that's no problem. This same time for sure, but I'm usually here anyway," said the man whose work required he be able to move at a moment's notice.

CHAPTER 44

We rolled down the windows and lit smokes, blowing beer breath and nicotine-tinged smoke out as we pulled out onto the Hines. Stopped at a light, I blew a plume from my nostrils and looked over at the old man. He pretended not to notice.

"Told you it was the Priest," I said.

"Yeah, kid, you did. I just think you enjoy it being him a little too much."

"Papa?" I asked. I just knew there was a story behind that. The old man shook his head in response.

"Fine," I said, like a sullen teenager. He took a deep breath, and let it out, staring at the light below the Northwest Highway overpass.

"His mother was a working girl, worked out of that very motel he's living in. I used to chase her down whenever she skipped bail, back when I did that work, between wars. I did her a couple good turns over the years. She needed 'em. She got the HIV, then she died. He was twelve, I think. I looked after him. Lived with me a little while, then I had to go back down south, so I put him in a prep school. The prep never took, but he got a full ride to some university out west. He designed a... a, hell, I don't even know what the hell it is. Some computer-widget-shit. Got richer than four foot up a bull's ass. Came home and bought the motel his mother whored out of. I remember when johns used to have to dodge his big wheel in the parking lot," he said, shaking his head with a far off look in his eyes.

"He owns a few more motels, some rental property. Sometimes he moves around, but not very often. He's got family here, blood. But they cutoff his mother, and, well," he said, not knowing exactly what to say, how to explain the situation, "they see each other, but it's tense. They try to bring him back in, but he thinks they want his money."

"If he's got so much goddamn money, why's he scratching out life forging documents for wetbacks?"

"Because his mother was a junkie who whored out of that motel and died of the HIV, and he never got over it, that's why."

"Ahhh," I said, and blew some smoke out the window.

"He's clued into Homeland Security," he said.

"What?"

"Yeah, contract work. Plus, they like having someone with his brain on the reservation, fat and happy. Some terror list suspects, from that thing in Richardson couple years ago, they came to him for papers. He turned them over to a Feeb he knew. So the local law dogs give him a 'reasonable pass'."

"What the fuck is a reasonable pass?"

"Let's just say, not all scumbags are equal. Let's just say, too, the people in the trenches have to use some common sense from time to time. Some low-level drug courier comes to him needing a driver's license? Not even worth cuffing him. Somebody that wants to get a job bussing tables, mowing lawns, or hammering a nail? *Shee-it.* He's known among certain quarters as someone that can be trusted."

"He's an informer."

"More like a conduit. He's the best there is at what he does, maybe throughout the South and Southwest. Dallas, for sure," he said.

"And he just gets a pass, on everything?"

"Don't tell me you hold that against him," he said, then turned and stared into my soul. The light changed, but he didn't move until I acknowledged the truth.

"Where to now, hoss? I said, putting the menthol back to my lips.

"We're gonna go talk to a holy man, son. That's what we're gonna do."

CHAPTER 45

It would be a lie to say I couldn't remember the last time I'd been to church. That had been my wedding day. Truth be known, I thought of it often. The warmth of the sun, the love in her eyes, the joy in her smile. The peace I felt by her side.

These things would only be mine, for such a short time. I see them now as a dream, always fleeting.

Beyond that, I couldn't remember the last time I'd been purely of my own volition. It always seemed to involve some event for which my participation was deemed necessary, no matter how reluctant a participant I might have been. At least this time I wasn't going to a funeral.

A priest met us in the foyer, and asked us nicely to wait near the altar while he fetched Father Mitchell. Travis lit a candle, and said a short prayer. I couldn't remember any, and wasn't willing to lie, so I sat in a pew on the second row and self-consciously flicked my Zippo until the old man shot me a look as he sat down in front of me.

It was a gift from Cohiba, my old team leader, the man that had led us through the looking glass, and introduced us to Champ. He'd grown up near the Pennsylvania burg where they were made, and had them inscribed for all of us that lived. It had the unofficial unit motto and task force symbol we weren't really supposed to have emblazoned on the front. Some secret squirrels we'd turned out to be.

I thought about my surroundings, and what the symbol on the side would mean to those I'd tortured and killed, and reminded myself not to dwell on old shit. The Great Mind Fuck has to be kept in check, especially when you're working.

When Father Mitchell saw us, he stood bolt straight, and stared for the longest few moments. When he regained his composure, he checked his surroundings, and walked toward us, his head down.

"What are you doing here?" he asked.

"You're involved with some very bad men, *padre*. You must have a great deal to repent for," Travis told him.

"Not as much as you," he said, nodding toward Trav, before turning to me.

"And you especially. Do you enjoy torturing people?" he asked, a hard edge to his voice. I wondered if someone had found Manny, and if word had gotten back to him.

"I guess that depends on what your definition of a person, is," I said. I probably didn't have to smile as I said it, but I had a hard time helping myself. "But sometimes, yeah, it's a blast."

"You're an evil man. Manuel—," he started, but I cut him off.

"Was a drug dealer, a pimp, and a murderer. He helped enslave his own people, and made money doing so. He tortured animals for fun. I did what I did with good reason, and I'm proud of it," I told him, my voice as calm and even as the next plane of existence.

"Monster," he barked, a low, vicious growl.

"Keep your voice down, *godda*—Father, we just want to talk," Travis said, correcting himself mid-speech, shooting me another look over his shoulder. I shrugged. I told myself to just ignore his abrupt change of speech.

"We have nothing to discuss," Father Mitchell said.

"Don't be so sure," Travis said.

"What do you want?" the priest asked.

"We want to keep a bunch of innocent people from getting killed. We're going out on a limb here, hoping you want the same. And we're taking it for granted that whatever you're involved in, you're involved in it out of faith, and because you genuinely think you're helping people. We just want to talk," Trav said calmly, while the priest eye-fucked me for good measure. I wondered if he'd found Manny and pieced two and two together.

Father Mitchell stood ramrod straight, his fists opening and closing in little balls by his side. He stared at us, seated in the pews before him, and had to think about what to say, and how to act. I wondered if he was thinking more about how he wanted to be seen. That might've told me something.

"And if I don't?" he asked.

"Then we leave. Maybe we get it done, maybe we don't. Maybe we don't get anywhere close. Maybe we die trying. Maybe I die in my sleep. Maybe then, this kid doesn't have anyone holding onto his leash anymore," he said, and I tried not to flinch with his metaphor.

Father Mitchell took a step back, staring at me with uncertainty. I blew him a kiss.

"What do you want?"

"Miguel was working with a cartel, planning what is known as a false flag. They were going to use some white trash to pull it off. He seemed to think the only way they would ever get anything really done, would be to spark a race war. He kidnapped a senator's daughter to force him onto the stage and publicly denounce his own bill."

"He also helped orchestrate the kidnapping and ransom of several young women," I added. Father Mitchell just looked at me, like I was no better than they were.

"He was running his old crew, trying to impress the cartel bosses. They put one girl on a spit, cut her up. Used her as an example," I said. I would say all the color drained from the man's face, but it was already gone. He was almost in a state of shock.

"Father," Trav asked, leaning forward in his seat. The priest swooned a little bit, then shook his head trying to regain his composure.

"Is that what you think?" he asked with a heavy sigh.

"Tell us why we're wrong," Travis said.

"Michael didn't have anything to do with what happened to Kelly. Neither did Alejandro. What happened to her was a warning, to them both, from the cartel. Michael blamed Alejandro for it as much as he did the cartel."

"Why?" I asked.

"Because they're evil," he said, as if it were that simple.

"You mean like me?" I asked, probably with a snarl. I could feel the bile rise in his throat as he clamped down hard.

"Michael ... had been uncomfortable ... with the things he was involved in for some time. He was always angry, even as a boy. Kelly changed him, changed his heart. She gave him the strength to get out of it. He went mad, after what happened to her."

"He fucking well deserved to," I spat. Travis sat silent, visibly bristling at my rage.

"He hated himself for what happened to her."

"He earned it," I said.

"They're both dead now. Why not let it die?"

"You think this thing died with them?"

"Why wouldn't it?" the priest asked, hoping and praying.

I cackled in laughter, the idiot.

"We've still got what's comin' the fifth of May, now don't we?"

"Is that really still a worry?" he asked.

"There's still a girl out there, lost, and wantin' to come home," Trav said.

"They're gonna kill her, no matter what. Even if they get what they want. We just want to save her, and keep something real goddamn bad from happening come the fifth of May. You can understand that, can't you?"

"I can't help you," he said. He stood from the pew, and looked at both of us with disbelief. "I'll pray for your souls," he said, and turned and left.

"Pray for your own, father," I called after him, my voice a little too loud. I wanted him to know I'd come back for him, that his place with God didn't mean shit to me.

Travis looked at me.

"What the fuck's wrong with you?" he asked. I shrugged. We left.

CHAPTER 46

We drove back to the motel, gathered our gear, and took separate vehicles to yet another rundown, shitty motel. The only difference being this one was closer to the ranch we suspected the girl to be in. The old man checked us in, and then I climbed in with him.

I smoked still another cigarette while he took us through town. It reminded me of every other small, dying town in America. We passed schools, churches, video stores, all of which looked to be on their last legs. Amid all the decay were the small family owned restaurants who struggled to stay afloat while the fast food chains moved in next to them, one after another, and could not sell their cardboard tasting shit fast enough to meet demand.

We stopped at a place that had plate specials, real home cooking with local ingredients. The type of place I'd eaten in all my life and seemed to be growing increasingly rare. Travis had the meatloaf with green beans and squash, and I got the chicken fried steak, mashed potatoes and fried okra: my dream meal. We both drank from huge glasses of sweet tea, and picked at the small salad bowls put before us.

I have a theory that there is some arcane cosmic law that states the better the home cooking in a small town diner, the cheaper the salad. This was proven once again, as a wedge of cold iceberg lettuce was dumped in a cheap plastic bowl that looked like wood veneer with half a pound of grated American cheese, soupy ranch dressing, and completed with some brick-hard croutons floating around for crunch. This was the green hand dealt before us.

We trudged through it toward the promised land of real home cooking without wavering. By this time I was starving anyway, and far too hungry to care how bland or wet the dressing was.

I tried not to watch as the old man picked at his with great caution. Finally, he dropped his fork into his bowl with disgust, and scowled at me.

"What the hell is it, kid?"

"Nothing," I lied.

"Son, don't lie to me. You ain't got the aptitude for it," he said. I shrugged, trying to find something to say.

"That bitch P.I. told you I'm dying, didn't she?" he asked.

"Yeah, she did," I said.

"And now what?" he scolded.

"Nothing," I said.

"You're goddamn right nothing. That little girl's the one that matters. Not my old ass," he said, and I nodded again.

The waitress brought our orders out. They were everything the salad had promised them to be, which was pretty much the opposite of the salad itself.

"That friend of yours, the ex-undercover hand, he a good man?" he asked, speaking of Bear.

"The best," I said.

"Skill-wise, what's he like?"

"Good, a quick study. Not a shooter unless he has to be, though. He's a great wheel-man, best driver I've ever known," I said.

He nodded his head, staring down as he slowly cut into his meatloaf with the side of his fork. "He know CQB?"

"He trained with county SWAT before he went undercover. Don't think he ever used it on the job."

"What about the giant queer?" he asked, speaking of Russell.

"He's an ex-SEAL," I said, obviously he knew how to shoot.

"Think he'll come in on this?" he asked, as if I'd answered the wrong question.

"Possibly. It might involve Uncle Jack though. I get the impression he's not looking to make waves."

"We might need Uncle Jack before this is over with our own damn selves, boy," he said.

"You give him a call when we're done here, and see if he'll come out and talk to us," he added, two slow bites later. I nodded. Neither one of us mentioned just how badly we were undermanned to be taking down a house, not to mention a hostage rescue. If we'd simply wanted to kill everyone, life would've been a whole lot simpler.

"What about the P.I.?" I asked. He made a motion like he wanted to roll his eyes, but then he looked at me, and shrugged.

"Your call," he said.

We ate in silence for a few minutes.

"The thing is…with Bear. If he says yes, we're gonna have to do something with C.W.," I said. He looked up at me in thought.

"Can he keep his mouth shut?"

"He's a reporter. He's working the story," I said.

He nodded slowly and didn't say anything. His cell buzzed and he fished it out of his shirt pocket.

"Yo, how's it going, 'Berto?...Gotcha, thanks," he said, closed his phone back, and dropped it back in his shirt pocket.

"You 'bout had your fill, Heavy Drop? Berto got the patch up. We need to *git*," he said. I looked at the gravy and leavings on my plate, the toast I was about to sop them up with, and nodded. I didn't need to eat all that anyway. I guess.

CHAPTER 47

"I don't fucking believe it," Russell said, staring into the laptop screen.

"There it is, boy, God's own honest truth," Travis said.

Berto hadn't just come through, he'd come through in a big, big way. Although the perimeter defenses looked like shit, inside was like a lot of better equipped drug houses. Wired up the yin yang. And the one hooked up to the internet, was hooked up to them all. The encryption they were using might have been state of the art, but that was it. That's only a small piece of the puzzle.

There were six cameras total. One at the front and back doors, and one aimed at the back of the property, one in the corner of a large main room, another above what looked like a security door, and another in what looked like a basement. We counted six men coming and going, with an obvious pecking order.

I'd taken down several houses, but much of my training was either on the job, or on the fly. A former SEAL, he'd had access to the best schools and a nearly limitless budget from SOCOM. So, what I'm saying is, you could say he knew his shit. He had enough experience, and architectural training to sketch out floor plans from the pictures we'd taken of the house and from what he saw on the video feeds. It wasn't that hard, we'd made similar sketches before he'd arrived, but compared to ours, his looked legit. Everything I draw always looks like the scrawling of a demented, club-fisted retarded child anyway.

"We still need the blueprints," Russell said.

"*Bam Bam's* gonna pick them up tomorrow," Travis said, cutting me a sideways glance, still giving me shit about the past couple of days.

"*Bam Bam, Bam Bam smash!*" Russell said, giggling, moving his own much over-developed arm in a hammering motion through the air.

A man that large shouldn't giggle. Ever.

The old man joined in his laughter.

"Fuck you both," I said, visibly trying not to smile, and lit a smoke.

"Bam Bam wants a fag in in his mouth!" Russell exclaimed, continuing the joke. I gave an exaggerated, full body shudder, and he laughed harder.

It was a good, good sign. It had taken less time than I'd ever experienced for us to connect as a team. It wasn't much, but it was a great beginning. Not for our sakes, but for the success of the mission. For the girl.

"How many shooters do we have?" he asked.

"The three of us, maybe the P.I., maybe she has some people she can bring in. Bear, too, but we'll have to do something with C.W."

"We could just make him act like a man," he said, his voice even, though it dripped with spite.

"What's between you two, anyway?" I asked.

"Between me and Cornelius?"

"Yeah," I said. He took a deep breath, a long pause, and then let out something he'd obviously been keeping in awhile.

"He's fuckin' Linus, man. His family's wealth is a security blanket. He acts like he doesn't want or need it, but goddamn, whenever shit gets hairy, he keeps crawling back. My best day? The day I graduated BUD/S. My father cried he was so proud. My worst day? The day I told my folks I was gay. I come home on terminal, healing up, dealing with *that shit*, and I figured, fuck, gay ain't no big deal. Goddamn war hero and shit. My father disowned me on the spot. I don't even know if the bastard votes, or can tell you the difference between the branches of government. I was riding bulls before I sprouted pubes. Hell, I've probably fucked more women than he has. I have a goddamn Navy Cross. Once I told him I was gay, that was it. Your BFF shits on Jack every chance he gets. For all Jack's right wing Republican bullshit, he's never treated me as anything less than equal. Fuck, he treats me better than anyone outside the Teams ever has, not to mention a good measure of the motherfuckers *in* the Teams. First day I met your boy, he'd just started working at the paper. Been back from Africa a couple of months. He was riding his high horse all over the place. Jack introduced him to me, and when he did it, he used one of his lines about me being the toughest cocksucker he knew, or some such shit. I don't even remember what it was. Like I care. First off, it's true, I suck a mean dick. It's a part of the whole 'being gay' thing. Second off, for Jack, it's just another tactic. He doesn't use it all the time, but it fucking well unnerves people. Not so much that I'm gay, usually, just…the crassness of it. And sometimes, sometimes if we're at a function or gala, he'll say it to a Bible Nazi, whisper it in their ear, just so I can see the look on their face. That little hippy douchebag has no clue what his Uncle is involved in, or how much good he does in the world. Part of it is Jack's fault. He doesn't give a shit about taking credit for fuck all. But the thing is, Jack keeps the lines open with other people just like him. People with lots of money, who know how to spend it smarter than the fucking government. He and Champ know each other for God's sake. That's just how small the world is. That's the kind of man Jack is. And fucking Cornelius doesn't have a clue. He's just another sheep that sees the world the way he wants to see it, instead of the way it is."

"Been holdin' that in a while, son?" Travis said, fixing his pipe.

"'Bout a minute," Russell said.

"What else, though?" I asked.

"You tell me," Russell said.

"Six months ago, there was some trouble. What happened?"

"Oh, that, shit. C.W. lost his shit at an underground table, and y'all's friend the cowboy had to shoot a couple of tough guys to keep him from getting killed. First place they came after it happened? That's right, Uncle Jack's sanctuary."

"He said he was working on a story," I said, still not believing it.

"Yeah, after it happened. Here's the scene: C.W. and the cowboy, your bail bondsman friend, sitting in Jack's office, C.W. freaking the fuck out, and the cowboy wanting to go home. He didn't even care about explaining shit to the cops, or fuck all else. He popped 'em, he got the package to safety, and he wanted to be done with it, since he wasn't getting paid to do dumb shit. He was pissed at C.W. for dragging him into it, without telling him everything, and the only reason he stuck around as long as he did, was to be sure C.W. would leave well enough alone."

They both eyed me in the silence that followed. I smoked, and pushed misshapen smoke rings toward the ceiling, and wondered what else there was.

"Having said that, is he up to this? The cowboy?"

"Yeah."

"You know that for a fact?"

"Yeah."

"I don't have a problem with your bondsman pal's mindset. He's got it. I just want to know how deep his base his. Working undercover is a different set of skills than taking down a house. Don't get me wrong, the guy is a fucking legend in his own right. He *earned* that shit. Still, it's a different skill set."

"Yeah, I get that," I said.

"How the fuck are the three of you even friends?" he asked.

"We grew up together."

"Must've been deep in Satan's taint. Jesus, what a group," he said, shaking his head.

He went back to his notes, thinking, scratching, and jotting. Travis did the same, keeping tabs at the computer screen, worshiping it like an idol. I smoked, and looked at my own notebook laid out down the length of my thigh.

"We're still short, for a job like this. Numbers wise, it's a little better, but, shit. It's still a little retarded. Not to mention your pal the hippy."

"C.W. can hold his own," I said.

"Yeah, if you'll hold his dick while he takes a piss," he said. I didn't respond.

"Ok, I might know a place we can stage out of. We set it up so it could be used for different things. We'll need to re-configure the shoot house to match the target location, and we need the blue prints to polish off what we have from the video feeds."

"You have a shoot house?" I asked.

"Yes, Jeb, we have a shoot house," he said, and then flicked his pen against his yellow legal pad, and blew air.

"It's left over. When I first came on board with Jack, he had some people kidnapped in Mexico. I was part of the team that brought them home. It's where we trained. After, he brought me on full time."

"How well's it set up?" Travis asked.

Russell looked at him out the corner of his eye like it was the dumbest question he'd ever heard. "Professionally," he said. He looked at his pad and rubbed his face and rose.

"I need to talk to Jack. If we're going to use his facilities, he's going to want to know what we're doing. He won't interfere with the op, but he's going to have to talk to the lawyers to see what we can do about keeping us safe on that end. Doing this kind of thing on American soil is going to be problematic, to say the least. He's gonna wanna talk to you guys, too."

"What time?"

"Call me after you get the blue prints, and we can get to work on the shoot house. Jack will make his way when possible. We need to be able to walk through it, try to feel it, and he'll appreciate the hustle on our end," he said.

When he left, a silence settled over the room. The old man lit his pipe, and I poured a drink and opened a fresh pack to go with it.

"He sure jumped into this awful goddamn quick," the old man finally said.

"Yeah, I know," I replied.

It'd been bothering me. I was glad to have his help, and Uncle Jack's resources, but I had the feeling they'd discussed this before I'd even thought to ask. Which might not mean anything, by itself. They probably spit-balled contingencies all the time. Jack knew C.W. was in over his head and that they needed to prepare for that eventuality.

In the back of my mind, I wondered what C.W. wasn't telling me, and if the problems he'd encountered six months before had anything to do with the task ahead. At that point, I wondered if it even mattered.

I took a deep swallow of whiskey and pushed the thoughts way away. I needed to focus, not dwell on trivialities and character defects.

I slid further down the bed, and closed my eyes.

CHAPTER 48

That night, my dreams came. My relative sobriety didn't help, but that was to be expected. I should've just gotten drunk for all the good not being drunk did me.

Half the dreams were about my ex-wife. Only in these dreams, she's not my ex anything. In these dreams, she's still very much in love with me, though when I'm awake I know that will never be the case again. If it ever was to begin with. Still, I like these dreams and very much so.

In these dreams I'm always successful and well adjusted, and whatever I do for a living seems to require that I wear a suit and tie. I seem to make an awful lot of money in a manner that does not involve violence. In them we have a family and live in a nice house with a front yard full of lush, thick St. Augustine. A rich man's lawn, in front of a rich man's house. Perfect for rolling through with the children who complete our life together. In these dreams, I have it made. In these dreams, I am happy and at peace.

When I wake from these dreams, I always feel drunk whether I've been drinking or not. I've had these dreams after being stone cold sober for endless months, and whenever I wake from them, I always, always have to think, to try and remember whether or not I'd drank the night before.

Afterward, when my wits have made their way back home, I usually lay curled around a pillow hoping that it hadn't really been a dream. That somehow in my sleep, I'd traveled through the astral planes, through a wormhole to some parallel universe where that version of us had worked out for the better. I never really believe it, but I want to so desperately it may as well be possible.

The rest of my dreams, the ones I remember anyway, aren't as nice. They're worse when sober. In them the monster in my head runs free. The long dark flames of his body flow brightly as he dances across a scorched landscape. He's not death, or life, or sex, or drugs. He's not violence or war. He's none of these things, at least by themselves. He is all of them in the excessive, psychotic amounts I'd fallen in love with. He's too much of everything wrong and bad. He's pride and greed and envy and lust. Above all else, he is my oldest friend, Anger, in all his glory. The one I have to fight every goddamn day of my life.

That night he came. First there was darkness, and then a dim red light snapped on, revealing a long hallway. I saw a door at the end, far away, and began to walk. I knew what was coming. The electricity humming through my body warned me, as it always does, but I knew I wouldn't wake until the dream had played out, whether I wanted it to or not.

I set forth at a normal pace, my steps loud against a wooden floor. Soon, their sound grew faster, and I picked up the pace, trying to catch the sound and outrun my shadow. The door just got further and further away. My breath grows thin and weak. Soon I'm wheezing and can't catch my breath.

I fail, in heaves and gasps, falling to my knees while he laughs at me without showing his face. I rise, drawing my pistol, and spin to face him. Only he's not there. There's nothing but an open field of knee-high St. Augustine grass, with patches of Blue Bonnets and sunflowers blooming brightly beneath the warm blue sky. I recognize the pasture behind the old family homestead, way back when, before the oil field went bust and the scum bags at the bank took everything my family ever had, breaking my father's massive heart.

I turned back to the door, as if the old farmhouse had been there to begin with. Of course it's not there, just more goddamn grass. I look up further, to see the old homestead, all of us sitting on the porch, eating watermelon chunks, laughing as the juice runs down our chins. I start toward the memory, its colors as rich and vibrant as the Van Gogh's I'd seen on leave in Paris.

As I get closer, people leave the painting. One by one, they make their good-byes. I sprint forward, hoping I can still catch the moment. I can see my father, dressed in his oil stained coveralls and work boots, fresh off the rig, leading us to his work truck to take us fishing, Snoopy fishing poles in our hands, a new puppy poking his gentle head out of the zipper of his coveralls.

At the foot of the farmhouse's sagging porch, it's just me and my dear old aunt who loved us so. Her head is down, her chin on her chest, a dress and bonnet, which she never wore in life, concealing her features. Without moving she tells me she has a gift for me. She asks if I want it. I say, yes, very much. She reaches behind her rocker and tosses her present to me.

It lands in my hands and I stare, fear's cold shudder running through my body. I stare at the box, its lock busted open. I look up to his grinning face, through the black cloak of flame.

See what you've done, Jeb?

Fuck you.

No, fuck you. I've been waiting soooooo long for a chance to come out and play, Jeb.

Get back in your fucking box, *bitch.*

Such tough talk.

He stood from the rocker, and danced in place, before skipping across the porch. Beyond him, I can smell something cooking. I can see the small living room, the colors of the rug on the floor just exactly like I remembered.

A bonfire in the middle of the floor, demons dancing around it. Maggie, my brother's wife, bound and helpless, as they took their turns. Joshua, my baby brother, also bound, forced to watch, killing himself against his restraints.

Want me back in the box, tough guy? Put me there.

My hand flexes around the pistol's grip, but instead of wood panels on a steel frame, I feel the bend and twist of cheap plastic. I raise my hand to see a lime green 99 cent squirt gun, the kind they have near the checkout lines of small-town grocery stores.

The kind I got almost every trip there.

I stare back at his laughing face, while the farmhouse bursts into flames.

Come get me, unless you're scared, bitch.

I cannot hesitate, I know this. If I hesitate, he will smell the weakness, and it will be that much harder next time, if there even is one.

I step onto the porch, the box in my hands. He stops his little dance, and turns, and I step into the flame.

I woke covered in sweat, wondering where I was. I saw the old man, setting in the middle of his bed and rocking back and forth, praying in the dark.

I sat up, and found what was left of my drink. In his hands was a battered, salt grimed Bible, and an ancient rosary. He watched me drink what was left in my cup.

"What are you doing, old man?"

"Praying," he said softly. I laughed, as hard and as mean as I've ever laughed. He slapped me with the back of his hand. I saw nothing but blue lightning, and heard its thunderous snap crack my ear drums as I fell back against the headboard.

I fell much further than that. I fell back more than fifteen years, to the first time I decided I was man enough to take my father. I could taste a thin trickle of blood wash over my tongue, but the only thing that hurt was my pride.

"Son," he said softly, then stopped, his eyes filled with pain, and looked around the darkened room, never finding whatever it was he wanted to say.

"I think I'm gonna step outside, and get some air," I said, and moved off the bed, swiping the bottle on my way out the door.

CHAPTER 49

I watched the sun come up, my bottle not much more empty than it had been when I'd stepped outside. I let myself back into the room, and showered while Travis lay in bed. We didn't say anything to each other as I walked to the bathroom, stripped, and showered.

He didn't say anything as I dressed in my usual jeans, boots and brown t-shirt under my leather vest. He just rose from the bed, checked his laptop feed, and stepped into the bathroom to shower. I stepped outside for my morning smoke.

I watched as a group of children willing to get up early enough to skip cartoons in favor of the pool's magical powers splashed happily in the wake of a cannon ball. I smiled, thinking about the group of friends I'd grown up with, and how rare it seemed that we were still so close, even though we were so very different and often far apart. I wanted the kids in the pool to have the same thing, and more.

I heard the door to our room open and close, as Travis stepped forth and tore me from my lament.

"Hungry?" he asked.

"Sure, what do you feel like?"

"Let's go to the diner down the road."

"Cool," I said. "I love a good diner."

We ordered both ordered coffee and water, and he asked for orange juice to go with it while I begged for chocolate milk.

"Chocolate milk, really, kid?" he asked, peering over his half rims.

"What's wrong with chocolate milk?"

"Shit's nothing but sugar," he said. "Keep it up, one day all that muscle's gonna turn 'round on you, boy," he muttered, shaking his head at his menu.

I didn't say anything. I was probably still glowering from the night before.

"Didn't say it was show muscle. If that were the case you wouldn't be here with me. Takes a lotta work to keep up, s'what I meant."

"I know," I told him.

"Good," he said, still studying his menu. The waitress came back with our drinks and took our order. I gave her one for steak and eggs, medium and sunny side up, forcing myself to forgo the hash browns and gravy, still feeling chastised. He ordered a western omelet with a bowl of mixed fruit on the side.

She wrote it all down and went to put the order in its place, leaving us with our thoughts. I put a dollop of choco milk into my cup, before adding the pink cancer. Because cancer tastes good. Travis shook his head and drank it straight black.

"I'm gonna call 'Berto, bring him in. We're gonna need someone to do comm's. Also, I want someone monitoring the feeds when we hit it, so you won't need to swing by there. He'll probably be here when you get back."

"You trust him for that?"

"Yes," he said, and I felt the slap from the night before on my cheek. "Given any more thought about bringing the P.I. in?" he asked.

"It might help. Having a female there might help keep the package calm," I said with a shrug, drinking my coffee. He nodded, his head lowered, deep in thought.

"Nobody just *has* a shoot house sitting around," he said.

"You don't trust them?" I asked. He took a deep breath.

"No, I trust them. I even trust that they want what is best. I know Russell does. He was in a pain last night when he talked about his father, and love when he spoke of Jack. The thing is, I know they're going to want the favor returned. And chances are you'll be the one that has to pay the toll, boy. Even if I live through this shit, I ain't got a whole helluva lot of time left."

"I'll worry about that when the time comes," I said. He started to say something else, but didn't.

We dwelled in abysmal silence, until the waitress brought our food. The silence hung heavily over us, a persistent cloud while we ate.

"You got a problem, old man?" I asked.

"One of these days, all that extra muscle's gonna turn to fat, if 'n you ain't lucky, *boy*," he said, repeating his earlier statement.

I gave him the eye fuck for a moment before I caught myself, and then shrugged it off.

"Never said it was show muscle. If that were the case, you wouldn't have the history you do, or be here with me now. I'm just saying, it's an unnecessary burden. That's all."

"Ok," I said, a little miffed. He didn't seem to have anything else to say, so I plucked the ashtray from the top of the napkin dispenser and lit up. He shook his head, yet again.

"You want one?" I asked.

"Fuck no, shit'll kill you," he said.

"You smoke a pipe."

"I'm already dying, boy," he scoffed, then stared out the window. I smoked away, my pride still bruised. Halfway down I killed the cancer stick, feeling like an ass.

He looked up over his fruit cup, his spoon in hand, and said, "You really should eat more fruit, kid."

CHAPTER 50

The lawyer had a big house in Steven's Park. A precious few miles south, off Hampton road, was my grandmother's little block near Ledbetter. A place that had once seemed like a sanctuary to me was so close. The air was warm but still crisp with dew. It was a big, well cared for house with the appropriate landscape.

Though later the sun would no doubt rise, taking away the morning's nice crispness, you could tell that no matter how hot it got it would, in fact, be a fine day.

In the crescent shaped driveway around the front yard, a silver Lexus sat, looking like it had only recently been down a lot of bad road. No one answered the bell, and the door opened when I tried it, so I let myself in.

I closed the door softly behind me, and my breath rolled like a fog over the Italian marble floor.

The house sat silent, and bad things, cold things, ran up my spine.

I slipped the .45 out, and tread carefully.

The receiving room, or whatever it was called, was untouched. Full of ornate, expensive furniture that was never used. The kitchen was a mess of hastily fixed meals, most of which, judging by the refuse, hadn't needed to be cooked.

I found him in the back of the first floor, in a long, narrow room that served as an office. It felt like a cozy apartment, compared to the unused spaciousness of the rest of the house.

A big, but not expensive desk set on one end of the room. The room itself was stuffed with file cabinets and book cases, in so untidy a fashion as to imitate a harried college professor's. Or, a garbage dump full of antique office furniture.

There were a few pictures here and there, newspaper clippings, whatever, but what caught my eye was a picture of him and Morales, nearly three decades before, graduating from the police academy together, both of them from the same neighborhood, both of them at the top of their class. At that time, headline material.

In the same case was another clipping, concerning both of them in a gang shoot out with some Jamaicans, in the late eighties. The late eighties had been a rough time for Dallas. The clipping mentioned awards for valor for both men, and several dead gang members.

The man himself was laying on the floor, next to a long leather bench he'd fallen off of. Bottles of beer and tequila sat around the room at various levels, and the stale acrid stench of burnt marijuana hung like a filter in the room. Next to him was a large, leather bound scrap book. It was filled with pictures of his son.

I slipped the .45 back in its holster, and nudged him.

He rolled over, his white dress shirt falling open, several small burn holes showing themselves in the process.

His eyes opened, like he recognized me, and then he started to speak, and then he rolled to the side and puked.

"There you go," I said, continuing on down the wall, looking at the artifacts of his life.

"I didn't know you were coming here," he said, his voice still heavy with wretch.

"That's ok, I didn't know you were a cop."

"That was a long time ago," he said, between heaves.

"Where is everyone else?" I asked.

"I gave the staff two weeks off, paid. God only knows what they're doing with it."

"Wife? Girlfriend?"

"My wife is at her apartment with this week's boy toy, I presume. I never bring my girlfriends here," he said, as if stating something I obviously should have understood.

"Well, glad that's working out for you," I said.

He let out a massive sigh, and rolled over, leaning against the leather bench.

"I thought we were meeting later," he said.

"I know."

"So, you come here anyway?"

"Yes."

"That doesn't make any sense," he said, shaking his head.

"It makes perfect sense," I told him.

"How does that make sense?"

"Do you have the blueprints?" I asked, ignoring him.

"Yes, of course," he said. "They're on top of the desk."

I walked around to the back of the desk, and looked at the prints and architectural drawings and photographs all neatly stacked in some semblance of order. Even during what I'm sure was a massive, soul searching, drunken, black out pity-party, he'd still kept everything nice and neat. It didn't say much for him, but it did say something about his intentions. I hated the asshole a little bit less.

"Leaving them elsewhere would've implied confidence in the situation," I said, implying all that needed implying.

With that statement, he looked at me in a new light, taking something else into account.

"You enjoy your work, sir?"

"At times," I said, putting the edges of the prints and papers flush together, so that I could roll them neatly.

"You enjoy killing people?" he asked. I ignored the question, and began rolling everything up. He nodded his head, and made a swishing sound with his mouth.

"Do you really think you can get her out?" he asked weakly.

"We're goddamn sure gonna try," I said.

"And the fifth? Do you think you can keep that from happening?"

"First things first. If we have the girl safe, then there's no reason not to scream it from the rooftops."

"Is there anything else I can do . . . *to help*?" he asked. His voice was sincere, filled with shame and worry.

"I think you've helped just about enough," I said. Nothing about the man made me want to coddle him, to give him a shoulder to cry on, to assuage his guilt.

He looked at me for a long hard moment, his eyes flush with a flurry of conflicting emotions. Anger, a prideful, sinful anger that would flash hot at the slightest insult. It burned bright but quick, fizzling out in a sea of fear, shame, and despair. He was in many ways a man at the end. He hadn't planned it, and in fact had probably started with the best of intentions. He may have still believed, or tried to at least, that the work he did was good, and that he helped people more than hurt them. That the excesses of his character were the minor, token flaws of a great man, understood and even expected defects of a man of position.

He nodded his head and looked away. No speeches about how he couldn't believe it had come to this, no *I was only trying to help*, no *but I meant well* bullshit. I didn't want to hear it.

I finished rolling everything tight and secured it with rubber bands.

"So, that's it?" He asked. I stood briefly, before the door, and looked back at him. I thought of things to say to agitate, to turn the corkscrews further in his head and heart. Things that were fueled by my own anger. I could have asked him how he liked being a modern plantation owner, or if he'd ever loved his son, but I think I knew the answer to both, and neither would've accomplished anything.

I couldn't think of anything comforting to say.

I'm an asshole that way, sometimes, with some people.

I turned and left the way I'd come.

CHAPTER 51

I pulled back into the parking lot and let myself in using the key card after knocking and announcing my presence. Travis was sitting at his work station, the glow of his screen reflected over his face. His pistol sat comfortably nearby.

"Where's 'Berto?" I asked, surprised he wasn't packed up and ready to move.

"On his way," he said without looking up from his laptop.

"Where's Russell?" he asked.

"At the estate, probably getting cleaned up, which is exactly what I need to do with my nasty ass," I said, peeling off my shirt. Stiff and sore from the road, and putting together the shoot house, stinking of stale sweat, I ambled to the shower.

The rush of hot water pounded my face, after a moment I turned, letting it spread over my permanently stiff back. I wanted to lay suspended forever in a pool of hot water. Instead I scrubbed myself clean. My skin felt raw, reborn and bloody. Looking in the mirror, I decided to shave later, and applied deodorant and Bay Rum. When I was done, I finished toweling off, and stepped out with the steam, to find the old man shuffling satellite photos and maps of the property.

I walked past him to lie down, atop the same bed I'd used the night before, clad only in the towel around my waist. The A/C was running cold, and I felt comfortable and sleepy.

"Don't you fall asleep yet, boy; you're gonna wanna see this," the old man coughed around his pipe. I'd just started to drift off, the edges of a dream beckoning forth. It was that good dream, the one where I lived with my ex-wife in the house with a picket fence around a yard of lush St. Augustine. I was cooking on the grill while she chased the kids and dog around the yard, as friends and family pulled up in the drive. The next scene would be us in bed, which was my favorite.

"I think I'm good with sleep old man," I said, falling further away, enjoying the vibrations drumming rapidly in my head. The volume on the television rose above them, high enough to change the dream I wanted into an impossible nightmare.

"—Authorities say to be on the lookout for this man, Jebediah Shaw. He is wanted for questioning in the assault and rape of Dallas police officer Rosie McCrummin, as well as the murder of her fiance. Subject is said to have been involved in the shooting in the bar in Deep Ellum earlier this month, which left three dead," the almost-model-worthy beauty read from her teleprompter before the screen switched to Conyers, his pompous sneer leering at me from the screen.

"This man is highly dangerous, and should not be approached. If seen, you should contact the police," he advised. I pulled myself up the wall, so that my back was resting against the headboard, and lit a smoke from the pack on the bedside table, placing the ashtray on my stomach.

"Ain't that some goddamn horseshit," Travis growled, he eyes red with rage. We couldn't very well prove to them that I hadn't done that, by telling them where I'd been when it had happened. That I'd been here with the old man plotting to kill several people. I wondered if Conyers was in on it, if he was dirty, or if he was just feeling the pressure, and wanted to see me squirm, instead of doing some real detective work.

"I could call Morales."

"That's the dumbest goddamn thing I ever heard. I wouldn't be surprised if they been playing you the whole time."

I didn't want to believe that, but knew it made some sense. Morales playing the harried old veteran, Conyers just being himself.

No, I couldn't believe that. Still, if his partner, El Doucherino, was able to throw this at me, even just the suspicion, things weren't going as well as they should on that front. If I met him, I'd need to do it without notice.

And just like that, something clicked.

"How do you feel about the press, old man?"

CHAPTER 52

I tried to sleep, knowing I needed a power nap, while the old man went shopping to get me some new clothes. But it proved all the more difficult. I trudged into the bathroom to shower again and actually shave. Since I hadn't been arrested or even processed for anything, the only picture they found of me was for my old concealed carry permit. I'd taken the course a few months after I'd mustered out, and my hair had been thick and long, my beard well on its way. I'd also been fat, with the months of inactivity before rehab began at Walter Reed, and the whiskey I'd sucked down. So I already looked a lot different, but they'd included a couple of still shots taken at the hospital, which were a little blurry and off center, but still gave a better picture.

Russell had called the motel room, assuming I'd already dumped the cell. He didn't sound like a very happy camper. He didn't much like my plan, but he did agree that it would be beyond retarded for me to go to C.W.'s house. He'd find a way to get Bear and C.W. He asked me nicely not to do anything stupid and get arrested.

When Trav returned, I was sipping a Dr Pepper and munching on a piece of cold meat lover's pizza when he let himself into the room. He sat the sack down on the bed near my feet, picked a piece of pizza from the box and sat down.

I tossed the hardened crust into the wastebasket and reached down for the sacks at my feet. Dressed in cheap khakis with plenty of room, a wife beater underneath a dark blue Hawaiian number with white palm leaves, and brown Skechers skater-punk shoes, I gave him the rundown.

"Russell called. He's going to find a way to pick up Bear and C.W. and bring them to the safe house. Wants to know what's keeping us."

"Still think it's a bad idea, what you're doing," the old man said, concentrating on his screen.

"We need information; we need to know what happened, when, and how. We also need help. I need to talk to the P.I., and I need to talk to C.W. and Bear. I'm not gonna do anything dangerous," I said.

"Just tryin's pretty goddamn dangerous. Stupid, too."

"I don't want to run unless I have to. So I go see what I can find out. I get pinched, you guys can pull off the op without me."

"You get pinched, we ain't gonna have any goddamn choice," he snapped.

I shrugged.

"Cuttin' it awfully close."

"Yeah, but I need to check on them anyway," I said, press checking the .45 and slipping it into a holster, before taking the newsboy hat I'd pulled off Vlad's guy, and pulling it on my freshly shaven head. I picked up the keys to the souped-up eighties model Chevy Malibu he'd squared me away with.

"You be safe, boy," he said as I walked out the door.

CHAPTER 53

My knees ached from the damp air. My nostrils were filled with the musk of dirt and newly wet pecan hulls. The rain had tapered off since I'd taken position beside the house, but I'd taken a fair soaking waiting on it to do so. I was crouched at the side of Morales's garage, still trying to convince myself it was a smart thing to do, when I heard the engine of his department issued Ford whine toward me as his headlights crested over the freshly washed cement of his driveway. I listened to him kill the engine and gather his things before opening his door. I waited until he was halfway out, with his hands full, before stepping out from behind the corner. He looked at me, his hands full, his eyes wide and searching. I showed him my hands, indicating I wasn't going to harm him, hoping he wouldn't force my hand by doing his duty.

"What the fuck are you doing?"

"Me? What the fuck are you doing? You want to tell me what the fuck is going on?"

"You fucked up, that's what."

"I didn't do it."

"That's not what it looks like. You were fucking her, right?"

"We spent one night together. I didn't know she was engaged."

"Yeah, well, you look awfully damn suspect, you know that?"

"What about Rosie?"

"She's in and out of consciousness. She took a pretty good beating. Whoever did it knew what they were doing. They made it hurt."

"Did they leave any evidence?"

"Yeah, as a matter of fact they did."

"What was it?"

"A thumbprint, on a expended shell casing from a 9mm."

"A hollow point, right? Federal HST?"

"Yep."

"Someone took a bullet from one of my magazines from the shooting. I've been carrying a .45 since then."

"Goddamn, you should be a detective. Exactly how do you plan on proving this?"

"I didn't rape Rosie, and I didn't kill her boyfriend."

"Yeah, well, someone's sure done a hell of a job of setting you up."

"I'm supposed to look suspect. They're trying to flush me out before the fifth," I said, as if that explained everything. Morales just stared at me.

"Are you any closer to finding the mole?" I asked.

"No."

"The mole is the rapist."

"Assuming it's not you, yeah, I guess it could be."

"Could it be your partner?"

"Conyers? Don't be dim. He's a twit and incompetent, but he's not the mole. He's not even smart enough to pull it off."

"He keeps fucking up cases that involve players in this shit. You tell me. You're the one's not holding up his end of the deal."

"We haven't been able to do anything but follow the mess you've made. You were supposed to give them a nudge. Christ, if I'd known it was going to turn out like this, I wouldn't have given you anything!"

"Well, it's a little late for that, isn't it? Maybe you're dirty? Been friends with old Uncle Alejandro a long goddamn time.

Couple of old school, ghetto gun fighters back in the day, weren't you? He left the force to find the good life. Maybe he slides a little taste of it your way every now and then?"

He stopped, and just stared at me. Every facial muscle, every nerve, every tic, totally calm. At the bottom of his eyes burned the hottest white light I'd ever seen, longer than a flash, but not much more, like black powder sparked, before fading away. Leaving in its wake what I can only describe as a profound sense of disappointment, deep hurt, and anger flaring like a tintype flash.

"What do you want from me? Huh? Now, get the hell out of here before I decide to do my job," he said, and then turned around and walked to his front door without so much as a glance over his shoulder.

CHAPTER 54

Toni Ashford, the high powered private op who was working it from another side, lived in Uptown, a small neighborhood of yuppie filled townhouses in the pocket of the mix-master just off downtown. The people who lived there were upwardly mobile, and largely had been birthed that way. They wore skinny jeans and shoes that looked like boots but were really shoes, and gelled their hair tight in faux hawks nearly ten years after that dumb, pretentious shit should have been cast away. Which is to say, they weren't my people.

I ate deep-fried chicken gizzards from a under a gas station heat lamp and remembered why I loved fried food. I swallowed it with a guzzle of frothy Dr Pepper from a can, and felt twelve years old again. All I needed was a campground, a dog, and a twenty-two pump.

I found myself thinking about the pup I'd taken from Manny, hopefully nestled up and comfortable with my old friends. I smiled, thinking, maybe, if everything worked out, and I didn't die or wind up in prison for crimes I actually *hadn't* committed, I might have a new friend.

I'd been waiting for a couple of long hours, and the prissy folks were starting to cast glances, when she finally pulled to a stop in front of her town house. I waited until I was sure she was alone before I put it into gear and pulled to stop beside her Land Rover. She looked at me, one hand firmly inside the front pocket of her purse, no doubt gripping her nine-millimeter.

"We know where the girl is. We're going get her. Do you want in?" I said, my voice as smooth, calm, and even as possible. She stared at me, her hand on her gun, the wheels in her head turning at warp speed and going nowhere.

"I didn't rape Rosie. They're trying to flush me out before the fifth. Only one thing is going to stop them."

"I have to get my go-bag," she said, pointing to the back of her truck. I nodded, and then watched her hips sway in the rear-view mirror.

Less than a minute later she closed the back door of her truck, and carried a rifle-bag, and separate backpack that looked like a book bag and tapped the trunk of the car. I hit the button, the lid popped open, and she placed her bags inside.

"Go," she said, slamming the door closed. "Get out of here before I have to explain you to my better half," she said.

I did as she asked.

CHAPTER 55

"This all the people you got?" she asked, raising her voice, shaking her head as if she just didn't believe it.

"It's what we've got," I said. She turned, and stared out the sliding glass door toward the large pool, shimmering in the afternoon sun beyond it.

We were sitting at the kitchen table, drinking coffee, and waiting on the old man to finish up with 'Berto, and for Russell to arrive with Cornelius and Bear. The safe house was huge, two-stories, made of red brick, with a dark tin roof and overhang. It had a wide, wrap-around porch, and was fully stocked and furnished. The grounds were freshly clipped, neat, lush, and well cared for. The huge four-car garage was divided up in equal parts gym, workspace, and stockroom. Shelves were filled with food stuffs, tools, electronics, reloading equipment, etc. The deep freezes were filled with food. The pool was huge, the hot tub beside it looked brand new and never used.

There were, however, absolutely no personal artifacts anywhere I could see. It looked like a model, if you wanted to sell to the ridiculously rich and fabulously prepared, and felt more like a barracks than a home. I thought about what Russell had said about how he'd come to work for Jack, and wondered if this had been where the team had trained for the mission.

When we'd arrived, Russell had been helping Travis and Berto set up a TOC. There was a ton of top shelf equipment there, but Berto had brought a van load of his own. We helped them unload it, without bothering with introductions, and then Russell showed us our rooms, the arms room, and gave us the code to the shooting range in a barn a couple of hundred yards to the side.

Then, Russell left to check on C.W. and Bear, Toni carried her bags into her room to change, and I made coffee. She came out barefoot in snug jeans and a gray t-shirt just as the pot finished brewing.

She'd wanted to check with Travis and Berto, but I let her know they were better alone. Travis was watching the video feed, like an addict with a jones, and Berto was setting up his equipment, and trying to connect.

So instead she sat with me at the table, and I finished catching her up to speed.

"His guy good? I can make some calls," she said, equal parts interest and power trip. She was as much a type A as anyone else in that line of work, and at the very least, a small part of her would be pissed at being bumped down the chain of command not once, but twice. Still, she'd got in the car, with a BOLO for rape and murder hanging over my head, knowing nothing else about me but my vibe. That bumped her up a few notches in my book.

"He hacked the video feeds your eggheads couldn't," I said. I hadn't meant it antagonistically, but she frowned at it anyway. One of these days, I'll learn how to talk to women, maybe even people in general.

I turned, and looked out the windows to the pool, and beyond, to a giant old oak way out in the pasture behind the house that looked like it had been there since buggy trails had littered the landscape. Deep down a part of me wondered and hoped that if I put my hand on it, it would share with me its wisdom. It had lasted as long as it had, weathered that many storms.

I stared out at the tree, and thought of the old homestead and of fathers and sons. I thought of my own father, a good, good man, who had meant so much to me even when we fought. Of Alejandro, who had tried to raise an heir instead of a son only for it to backfire in the worst way imaginable. Of Cornelius's father, no kind of man to think of, long since rotted away in a grave in some East Texas woods. Of Travis, the old man, an absentee father without the knowledge of his position. A hard-bitten soldier of fortune who picked up strays and let illegal aliens pay the rent with dinner; a dying old man who prayed at the side of the terminally weak and spiritually infirm.

I was staring out at the tree, and thinking of all these things, when my cell buzzed again. It was a call from Russell.

"We got mad problems, yo," he said.

"What's up?"

"I got three guys, just stopped at the curb in front of C.W.'s. They're wearing police windbreakers, and have badges slung around their necks. I recognize them from the video hacks," he said.

"I'm on my way," I said.

"Bring friends, motherfucker. They did."

CHAPTER 56

Toni and I readied ourselves in the back of the van as the old man drove. We were outfitted with heavy armor, and weapons. I had my .45 on my thigh, and the old Winchester 1200 Riot gun strapped over my chest. She had opened up her big rifle case to reveal a mid-length AR carbine of some custom build I was unfamiliar with, but had become as generic and ubiquitous to my generation of gun fighters as custom 1911s and P35s had been to another. Her Beretta rode solid in a thigh rig hanging off her "war belt", opposite a magazine pouch on her other leg.

On the floor was a gun I'd only seen in magazines and *Punisher Armory* comic books. A scaled down version of the old German MG-42, a CETME squad automatic weapon in .556 that could be broken down and stashed in a large suitcase. Travis had it, and spare box magazines, ready to rock. He'd had the thing stashed for a rainy day. For decades, evidently.

Travis was up front, driving, and talking to Russell on his cell, and giving us the what for. Not only were there three guys inside posing as detectives, but others had arrived. There was a carload on the street, and another around the block. We weren't sure where so many of them had come from, but there they were. Still, it was the three inside that really mattered.

The three inside were our biggest worry.

Bear had been a jailer, and an undercover narc. When he was twenty one, he'd walked into a bar to buy some meth from a local dealer, and before anyone knew it, a local case bumped hard into a Federal one, and he was steam rolled into the big leagues. He ran dope, horses, cattle, and guns; from Bogata to Alberta; by plane, truck, foot, horse, boat, and rail. And the case, like his career in law enforcement, had ended badly. He hadn't survived that long, that deep, with that little training and experience, by not having the very best bullshit detector engrained in his DNA. I consoled myself with the knowledge that he would know they were full of shit and not actual cops.

Travis stopped in the alley a couple of houses down from C.W.'s, and we climbed out. Trav drove to the end of the alley, to take position on the second set of shooters on the next block. They were rolling heavy for a reason.

Toni worked the lock on the back door of his detached garage faster than I'd have been able to, and let us in. We stayed back, away from the windows, and crouched low, assessing the situation.

Bear was leaning against a wall, his arms and legs crossed, looking like a tired cowpoke after a long day on the range. C.W. was standing, animated, and trying to talk to the man in the lead. Evidently, the fake cops were trying to play them for information before they took them. Which meant, if they got what they needed right off the bat, they could go ahead and kill them and be done with it.

I will swear, to the day I die, that I felt a cold bunching of tension at the top of my spine, and that Bear glanced one laconic eye straight at me.

"Fuck, let's do it," I said, moving down the garage to the door. The door opened up inside the back yard, just outside the vision from those in the house. So, we had that going for us.

"I should be on point," she said. I looked over my shoulder at her like she was crazy.

"You've got that stupid shotgun," she said. She had a point.

The shotgun wouldn't have been my first choice, had I had time to select and test fire something from Jack's arms room. However, if I have to choose between going to war with a shotgun I know works, and the latest, greatest, Capt. Billy

Whizbang Ninja Killer 2000 I haven't tested, I'm going with the beat up shotgun. Even if I hadn't used it in a few years.

"Ok," I said, nodding my head. I put my hand on the knob, and twisted.

"Ladies first," I said, and stepped back, opening the door as I did so.

She was fast, so fast she was already coming up to the house, her rifle up, as I rushed to catch her.

She fired even faster. So quickly that controlled pairs of semi-automatic fire seemed full auto.

Her bullets punched through the glass, spider-webbing it, knocking her target down with a misty red cloud hanging in the air. As the body fell, Bear extended one long arm toward the closest man and fired a very small handgun, several times right in his face.

Toni ran onto the patio, her rifle locked into her shoulder, when five heavy booms thundered inside the house, and the third one fell dead.

C.W. rose from his seat, the .357 in his hand, and stared at us as Toni stepped toward him, shifting her weapon behind her back to a non-threatening posture as she saw him.

Bear dropped the tiny hideout gun he'd emptied in the police imposter's face, and the M-1 carbine appeared in his hands. C.W. stared at me as if wanting to assign blame.

On the street behind us, Trav opened up with his CETME, and I turned and ran back through the yard and around the corner toward the front of the house.

Gunshots rang out in front of the house as I came abreast of the corner of the front yard, and leaned just around the house to see several Hispanic men, dressed like plain clothes cops, scattered in the front yard. Each moved as if pulled by a different puppeteer.

I opened up on them, as did both Bear from inside the house and Russell from down the street. The first one I shot in the back of the head, the second one turned as his buddy fell, firing a 9mm handgun, his bullets hitting brick and mortar, dust from C.W.'s house fogging my vision.

I racked and fired, racked and fired, too fast to count. I heard gun fire down the street behind me, and saw Russell, on the opposite end of the fire fight, dive behind a stationary sedan.

The shotgun was out. I moved it behind me as I turned toward the threat, pulling the .45 from the thigh rig, firing before I hit full extension. I fired fast, emptying a whole mag on the upswing, watching my bullets impact across the hood of a look-alike police cruiser, getting at least one good solid head shot on one of the men as he tried to level an assault rifle of some kind over the hood.

When my slide locked back, my support hand had already purchased a replacement from my belt, my strong hand bringing the gun in toward my face, my thumb hitting the mag release, watching, beyond the gun in my hand, the vehicle my remaining enemy was using for cover as I slammed the magazine home, and worked the slide.

I held the gun in front of me, focused on the remaining threat, as I moved forward.

A dark mullet appeared behind a G-3 battle rifle, and I put two perfect hits in the ocular cavity, steadily moving forward.

I heard the unmistakable, hearty boom of a .308, and then that certain awful groan, and then the sound of falling meat and flailing limbs. I looked to my right to see Russell in the middle of the street, looking through the optic of a Springfield M1A Scout, and then fired again.

I heard the sound of a hammer hitting a melon on a stage, and then he waved his hand in front of his face, telling me to cut sling load, before turning and running back to his vehicle. I ran toward Bear, who stood in front of the house jamming a fresh magazine in place.

I pushed him forward, transitioning back to my shotgun, and thumbing more shells down the tube as we moved. That's what happens, when you take a shotgun to combat.

We went through the backyard, past the little pool and out the gate just as the old man pulled the van to a stop. We worked the latch, slid the side door open, and piled everyone in.

Travis rocketed down the alley, slowing just long enough at side streets to keep from hitting anyone, before rolling smoothly through them. Sirens surrounded the block behind us.

He turned onto McMillan, and then, just after, took Monticello to the highway. He had a police scanner on, and we listened in silence the whole way. Somehow, there was no mention of a van as units careened onto the scene.

At once, and without warning, everyone let out a massive sigh as we crossed beneath the 635 mix- master.

"What the fuck was that?" C.W. asked.

"That was them saving our ass, boy," Bear growled at him, his M-1 carbine in his hands, a fresh magazine in place.

I was behind them, in the trunk monkey position, Travis's obscure relic of pure 80's awesomeness in my hands, fresh box in place.

"Please," Toni said, looking over her shoulder at them from the shotgun seat. "Let's just get home first, and then we'll catch everyone up to speed," she said.

"I just left home," C.W. said, to no one in particular.

No one answered him.

CHAPTER 57

We made it back to the safe-house without speaking, and unloaded without incident. Berto had freshly brewed coffee, soda, pitchers of ice water and sweet tea, and several stacks of pizza waiting for us. Russell and I devoured them. Toni and Bear both ate numbly. Neither Cornelius nor Travis ate, but for different reasons.

As we ate, we talked over what had happened, what the men had said to them, the cues both of them had recognized, and how we'd gotten lucky with Russell seeing them approach as he pulled to the house. Then, I told them our plan, and what we wanted from C.W.

"You want me to lie?" Cornelius asked. Everyone stared at him.

"He didn't do it," Toni snapped, like she knew me, dropping her slice of pizza to her paper plate.

"That's not the point. The point is he wants to bring me in now, when I can help him. He kept this shit from me, just like he kept Gramps here from me," he said, pointing a finger across the table toward Travis.

"You little fuck. All he's done is keep you alive," Travis said, then got up from the table and left, his eyes bright, wet, and red with rage.

Bear, his eyes as hard as stone, put a hand on C.W.'s shoulder, leaned over, and whispered in his ear.

C.W.'s disposition changed. His skin lost a little color, and his Adam's apple bobbed with a visible swallow.

"Ok, fine, I got your back on this shit. I'm just sayin' it's some bullshit, that's all," he said.

I shrugged.

Everyone else at the table picked at their food and listened to the heavy, uncomfortable silence of friendship tested.

>—I—◄►—O—◄►—I—<

"So, what's with you and that fucking shotgun," Russell asked. I shrugged. Everyone had gone to bed, and we'd sat up on the back porch, game planning. Evidently Russell was one of those that felt the shotgun was obsolete the moment the first Henry rifle left the factory.

But that was far from what really troubled him.

It's not that there were so many of them and so few of us. Not just that, anyway.

It's that they were all split up. There were probably scores of men in the house, with the higher ranking members on the first floor, in rooms along the hallway leading to the safe room the girl was housed in.

The rest were upstairs.

If we made a bee-line for the girl upon entry, the men in the first floor bedrooms could be taken out along the way. If the six of us stayed together, we had better odds of getting to the girl and getting her out quickly. Not to mention in one piece.

The problem with the plan was that it left the men upstairs, and one long, nasty, fatal funnel of a hallway to come back down with the girl.

Someone needed to go upstairs and take care of business.

And we didn't have enough people to ensure any sort of tactical advantage that wasn't built on surprise.

Naturally Russell wanted the job.

The thing was, he had more experience breaching doors with explosives than anyone else, and we were afraid that's what we were going to have to do.

I'll say this for Uncle Jack though, he spared no expense. Nothing but the best for his hired gunmen.

Russell, and Jack by proxy, was a big fan of H&K. I wasn't, but then H&K didn't hate anyone with Uncle Jack's money.

I was the only one not carrying a shortie 416 with suppressor. I didn't think anyone had that shit but CAG, but Uncle Jack had a rack full of them.

The arms room itself was located in the basement of the big house, which was surprisingly chill. I noticed the thickness of the walls and ceiling with the help of the bright, fluorescent lighting, the hundreds of guns, and the thousands of pounds of ammunition, food stuffs, and water, and realized it wasn't just a place for teams to go into ISO before a mission. It was Uncle Jack's safe house. Or one of them, at least.

I wondered how much it cost to build a house that big with a room like that on the flat North Texas Prairie, where no one else dared do such a thing. No one built basements that far southwest. Storm shelters and root cellars yes, but they had always been built away from the house itself, as if after thoughts, structurally and culturally.

This was the result of planning, dedication, and money.

So much unlike the safe-house where Manny had kept his dogs and the ones I'd used or set up in the past.

"I mean it, dude. What's with you and that fucking shotgun?" Russell asked. There was a hard, angry edge to his voice.

I shrugged and watched the smoke from my cigarette fall away in the surprisingly cool night air. "Dude, I like you. I do. I actually really like you. And I have respect for you as an operator," he said, his voice even and truthful. "That's why I just don't get it. I mean, I get the .45, hell, I'm carrying one. And the .38 in the back pocket. Old school cool like a motherfucker. But the fucking shotgun, man? What the fuck? The basement here is an operator's wet dream."

I took another long drag, and looked up at the stars, and wondered what I should say.

"The girl is the thing. We aren't going to be able to do this without raising the alarms. We need to get to her, as fast as we can. Getting to her, and securing her, is the first thing."

"And there's you, with your shotgun," he said, as if proving a point.

"Fighting her way out of there, with them distracted, would make things a lot easier," I said, and watched his face as it sank in.

"Do you want to die?"

"No."

"You are fucking insane," he said, shaking his head. I didn't say anything in return.

"Shotgun makes a big boom. It's one helluva rabbit. It occupies people's minds," I said.

"Rabbits get eaten all the time," he said.

"Not this one."

Toni couldn't do it because we needed her with the girl. She would most likely be in an awful state of shock, and Toni would be able to provide an instinctive level of comfort and support the rest of us were simply unable to.

Travis couldn't do it, because the only thing on his mind was the girl. Trying to place his focus on anything but getting to her and killing everyone in his path, would be a mistake.

Bear was tough and capable, but he didn't have the work history either I or Russell had. He was a shooter out of necessity, not trade. Besides, we needed him behind the wheel, watching our six, monitoring the radio traffic, and keeping C.W. in line.

Russell and I, the two of us, it was all we'd ever wanted to be. What needed to be done was work for a gunfighter, the kind who'd never cared to be anything else.

The door to the safe room was made of thick steel. We could see it in the blue prints, and its specs were in the papers Alejandro had given me.

There was a possibility it was unlocked, but it was also possible whoever was in charge wanted to keep the men away from her as much as possible. I had some training and experience with explosives, but it was nothing compared to the former frogman. Compared to what he knew, I might as well have had a satchel full of chicken bones and virgin blood, because what I knew was more alchemy than hard tested, scientific fact. At least that's the level of confidence I had.

I didn't tell him this in front of the others, but waited till we were alone and ruminating. I didn't wait to tell him out of pride, so much as not wanting to instill a lack of confidence in the rest of the team. We were already out-manned and out-gunned, and the rest of them didn't have enough experience to know we weren't outclassed.

Though we were on the side of the angels, we were still working outside the boundaries of law and normal society.

Toni was uncomfortable but dealing with it. Her father had a long career before going private. Because of his status, and the status the bulk of their clientele would hold, she had a good working relationship with people in all levels of law enforcement. Probably even some friends.

Bear didn't seem to care one way or another. He never said it, but I'm sure he felt like he was once again helping clean up my or C.W.'s mess, which I guess he was. Still the voice of reason, which probably said more about himself than those he considered friends. Or maybe I hoped that.

Russell was far more concerned about Jack's knowledge and involvement than anything else. Jack showed up with the Swenson customized Commander he'd carried on his second and third tours in a beat up tanker holster, mag pouches and Randall #15, a hollow handle and saw-backed survival knife still hanging off a strap, wanting to drive the van. I'd thought I might see him pull rank on Russell, but the big man had been diplomatic, a stone professional who obviously cared deeply for his boss.

I'd worked briefly in the EP field, doing gigs between various real jobs and for Champ. I couldn't remember protecting anyone I liked or respected as much as Russell did Uncle Jack.

Travis was silent, wound as tightly as a snake arming itself, the expression in his eyes a tragic mix. In them I saw the natural antagonism I knew I would feel in his place. His plans for revenge co-opted by necessity, the reason why more important than the people co-opting it. Instead of lashing out at us, he drew inward, and when I saw that in his eyes, I felt the cancer eating at him deep within my own chest.

To his credit, C.W. was no longer playing his usual little bitch self. He knew we couldn't go to the authorities, because we had no idea who was dirty, how widespread the corruption was, or even what side they were on. If they were working for the girl's father, it would be in their best interest to get her home safe. If they were working for the cartel, maybe not so much.

Yet, still, I could tell he wasn't happy with it. We were part of a society, one with laws and that whole bit.

His part in this was a paradigm shift most couldn't deal with.

Thankfully though, like Travis, he turned it inward. In some ways, they were more alike than not, and I could respect that.

"Fuck, I'm going to bed, you stubborn bastard," he finally said, standing from the table with a yawning stretch. "You gonna talk to *Timmy*?" He asked, putting the *South Park* polish on it.

"Yeah, I'll handle that," I said.

"We got a backhoe in the barn and hogs in the woods. You got options," he said, grinning, and walked in the house. I drank water, and wished I it was single malt.

I punched the combination into the key pad beside the door, and heard the locks open. I pushed it forward without stepping inside, and saw Kendrick lying on the bed in the corner. When he saw me, he moved to a seat on the edge of the bed.

I walked inside, closing the door without locking it. I took one of the chairs from little card table along the wall, and straddled it, within arms' reach of where he sat.

I looked at the table beside his bed, where a Bible that might have been Trav's lay on an open page. I could feel his fear permeating the room, wafting off his body in waves, a steady mirage of desolate prayer. I had experienced it hundreds of times in my life all over the world, but I couldn't remember anyone who deserved to have their prayers answered less. Maybe that was because I'd killed them all.

He stuttered, looking for words, but I cut him off.

"Shut the fuck up," I snapped. He shut his bitch mouth.

"Do you realize why you're alive?" I asked.

"Because.... because you need me, right?"

"No, *Timmy*," I said, pouring salt on the wound. "The only reason you're alive is because killing you would mark a good man's soul. I don't want him to carry a piece of shit like you around with him the rest of his life."

He didn't say anything to that.

"Life as you know it, is over with. Whatever happens after tomorrow, however it shakes out, whether we have to involve you in the story or not, you don't have any options. None. If you try to go behind our backs, I kill you. If you tell anyone about this conversation, I kill you. If you say or do anything other than what we tell you to say or do, I kill you. When all this is over with, you will never go back to another club ever again. Ever. You have a business degree from SMU, you fucking putz. You're going to work for a job we tell you to. It will be boring. You will be in a cubicle. You will hate it. You will be monitored. Daily. Someone will always be watching you. The rest of your life. You slip up, I kill you. Do you understand?"

He shook his head yes.

"Say it."

"Yes."

"Yes what?"

"Yes I understand."

"Yes you understand what?"

"Yes I understand if I don't do what you say you'll kill me."

"No, *Timmy*," I said, my voice soft and still like deep water. His lower lip quivered.

"This is not about me, what I say. This is about you. The life you've lived," I said. He didn't reply, just looked indirectly back at me with a nervous energy in his eyes. The smart thing was to make him simply disappear.

"Can you live with that?" I asked.

"I don't have a choice, do I?"

"No," I said.

I stood, walked to the door, and looked back.

"Also, I'm taking your car. You won't be needing to pick up chicks anymore anyway," I said over my shoulder as I walked out the door. I smiled as the locks slammed into place.

CHAPTER 58

We were up early the next day. I cooked a big breakfast for everyone that wanted it, and after we'd let it digest, we went to work. The plan was simple and basic, easily grasped by everyone. Even C.W., without training and experience, caught on.

Berto, the insane genius that he was, had managed to record several hours of footage from the hacked feeds, while creating (not finding, actually creating, though I'm too much of a caveman to know the difference) another backdoor in their software that allowed him to feed their security the recorded images while he kept eyes on the live feeds. God bless the chunky little man-child.

I, Russell, Toni, and Trav were the primary squad.

If we were both really good, and really lucky, we could extract her, and then worry about the bad guys later. I was thinking a healthy measure of high explosives would be very nice.

If we weren't that good or that lucky, worse come to worse, we could hold them off while Toni took her out a window and through the woods, leaving us a free fire zone in the house. If it got worse than that, we could use an explosive charge to punch through a wall and extract.

We drilled and shot all morning and into the heat of the day. Afterward, we ate a light lunch, drank ridiculous amounts of water, and game planned before turning in to get some sleep.

I woke early, before that day's sun had slowly died, and padded through the house in my shorts, dropping in the pool to float, enjoying the empty nothingness of the water and of being alone. In the pool I felt weightless and free, beholden to no person, thing, or ideal.

The thought of going up those stairs alone didn't trouble me, but there was a jealous streak somewhere deep that hated not being the one that would get to tell the girl she was safe and going home. I knew it was childish, and felt no small measure of shame for it.

A violent man chooses to live with a code, not to just satisfy the call to arms, and not just for the primal satisfaction of successful combat, but to protect the weak and the innocent. To elevate himself above those without one, and above petty, strutting satisfactions. To place their safety and well-being above his own. To place might behind right. A violent man embraces a code because he understands others won't.

At some point, Toni slipped in, and began swimming laps, cutting the water with a seriousness that would make anyone take notice. I pulled myself from the pool, lit a smoke, leaned against a brick support column, and watched her swim.

Eventually, she pulled herself from the pool, and stretched beside it, air drying, paying me no never mind.

She was taller than I, well built, and strong boned, for a woman.

She turned on the ball of one foot, stretching her arms out, and I saw the tats down her side. On her ribcage, was a dog-tag, known as a meat tag, with her name, rank, and social security number. And below that, hash marks, twelve of them, for confirmed kills.

"You're gonna need some more ink," I said, to break the ice more than anything else.

"Yeah," she said, and paused, before straightening up, and looking at me.

"You don't keep count?" she asked.

"No," I said. "I don't believe in cutting notches."

She rose up from her stretch, stood tall, and stared out over the pool. She nodded at something, just to herself.

"I do," she said, her voice as cold, hard and pure as Cimmerian steel.

She wore just tiny shorts and a sports bra, things which did nothing but showcase her body. Her *café au lait* skin was nearly polished bronze in the light of the setting sun. Her breasts were heavy and natural, the sports bra thick with their weight and water from her swim. There was grace and pride her in carriage, every movement mindful. A certain nobility I knew would always be beyond me radiated from her person. Lavender, and lilacs, and something else I couldn't quite touch, floated through the air with it.

"I popped my cherry pulling the trigger on three guys lobbing mortar rounds at us outside Kandahar. It was colder 'n shit, and winds higher than a motherfucker. 900 meters, three shots, three kills," she said, staring listlessly out at the giant oak, and obviously something much further past both it and the dipping sun.

Around her neck she wore a small custom knife, known as a HAK, on a chain. It had once been the "Sexual Chocolate" of knife fetishist operators, and was still a very good choice, if you understood the blade and its strengths and weaknesses. Something told me she understood those things very well.

"I still can't believe I made those shots," she said, her voice a little lighter, a little younger, a little further away. As if there was a little piece deep inside her, the Amazon, the warrior woman, that needed the touchstone of past courage to see her through.

Maybe that's what the hash-marks were. Not a macho, blustering vanity, but a constant reminder of what she was capable of. I knew my ink was much the same. Of course, I had many weaknesses.

She looked up, and caught my stare, and something sparkled with recognition.

"You like what you see, Whiteboy?" she asked, not angry in the least, but not particularly joyful or sad either. Like a woman who had long grown accustomed to how men think and act.

"Yes, I do. Very much, in fact," I said, telling the truth, like I had good sense.

She smiled at that, like she didn't believe me, and stared out at the setting sun.

"Sorry, you don't deserve that," I said, suddenly self-conscious. She shook her head, as if she were shaking off the water.

"Deserve, what?"

"For me to look at you like that," I said.

"And how is that?" she asked and turned to look at me as the sun dipped a little closer toward the horizon behind her.

"Like a piece of meat," I said. She looked back out over the flat prairie land, and that giant old oak between us and the sun.

"*That* was not...how you were looking at me. *That* was...something else entirely," she said. She said it matter-of-factly, without shame, or regret, or anything else.

She didn't elaborate further. Somewhere deep inside I wondered if I owed her far more for what she saw in my glance.

"Can I ask you a question?"

"Sure," I said, putting the cigarette back to my lips.

"What are you going to do if this insane plan of yours doesn't work? If they don't believe it?" she asked.

"It's the truth; they have to believe it."

"People go to prison all the time for *truth*."

"I'm not going to prison," I said.

"You going to run, if it comes to that?" she asked.

I started to tell her yes, but something caught in my throat. Everyone in my line of work has that ultimate contingency "get-gone-and-stay-gone" plan somewhere in the back of their mind, constantly turning. I had friends all over the world I could turn to. And a few enemies whose weak spots I'd memorized just in case I found myself in a spot and needed certain provisions.

Still, the words just wouldn't come.

She smiled faintly as she stared out at the setting sun over the prairie.

"I don't think you can run, Jeb. I don't think you have it in you. In fact, I think if you were all alone, you'd try to pull this crazy shit off by yourself. I think you're insane like that," she said, and turned on the ball of her foot and began walking back inside.

She stopped even with me, placed a hand upon my chest, and looked me in the eyes.

"Nobody ever got hurt just from lookin', Whiteboy," she said, matter-of-factly, just the barest hint of a smile crossing her lips.

I turned to watch as she finished her trek, and then looked out at the dipping sun, and tried to enjoy the last of my cigarette, and tried not to feel that old familiar ache.

She was wrong. A person could be hurt by looking at her a certain way. It just wasn't her.

CHAPTER 59

I was first through the door, like always.

We filed silently through the empty kitchen. In the right corner, we could either go right, into the entrance of the long side hallway, or through the entryway to the big living area in the middle of the house. I went, shotgun first, into the living area, moving off line and out of the way as soon as possible.

There was a man in there sitting on a couch, probably supposed to be on guard duty. There was a television on a Spanish channel, turned down low, and he was in the middle of a heavy lidded yawn, somewhere between asleep and awake.

He heard something, or maybe felt it, our presence, a rippling in his consciousness, whatever, and stood abruptly, his hand reaching for a weapon on the table. I stepped to the side, covering him with the shotgun, as Toni walked forward, a suppressed H&K 45c extended in her hands, and put one round through his skull.

I felt Russell and Travis both slide past me into the hallway, and a man stepped out of a door along the far wall, which led to the garage, shirtless, a pistol hanging in one hand by his thigh. I fired and pumped, fired and pumped, his chest opening up in fist sized, dark red chunks.

Toni paused, looking me in the eye.

As if it meant anything.

"Go get the girl," I said. She nodded briefly and kept moving forward with everyone else toward the objective. I thumbed shells into the tube, and ran away from them, toward the men who would now be awake and arming themselves.

I bounded up the stairs with the gun up. Between the shotgun blasts and the adrenaline, I couldn't hear my own footsteps on the thick carpet. I hoped my enemy couldn't either.

"B,- number 1, coming out now," Umberto whispered through the ear-bud, and I put my back to the rear wall of the stair case for a better pie angle on door number one, door number one swinging open and a bare arm holding an AK, it's stock folded, coming out.

I fired and pumped, fired and pumped, and then, instead of stepping back down the stairwell, I stayed where I was, shifting my focus down the hallway's funnel, and thumbed more shells down the tube.

I waited, for what seemed like forever. It always seems like forever, even though in reality it's only a few seconds. Adrenaline can be a big help if you're in a position to use it to your advantage. Tachypsychia can be a real bitch if you don't though.

I waited, wanting to look at my watch, to speak into my throat mic, to charge forward toward the enemy. The milliseconds passed slowly.

I heard yelling in Spanish, not the bark of command, but of men bartering. I stared down the shotgun barrel, waited, and wondered.

I wondered what was up with the rest of the team. I wondered how many men they'd encountered downstairs. I wondered why they hadn't yet breached the door. I wondered in what state they would find the girl. I wondered if a neighbor was calling the cops yet. I wondered who the next man I would kill would be and when he'd show himself.

I had all of these thoughts in a matter of seconds.

"Breaching," Russell said through the ear bud, just before I heard the muffled explosion downstairs.

Door 3 opened up, and a man came out low, firing. His shots hit the wall behind me, and mine landed in the door jamb above him.

I pumped and fired, hitting him this time in the side of the neck, and pumped again.

For some reason lost to even the gods, I bitch stroked it, and was staring at the jam wondering where my testicles had gone when Door 2 opened up.

A man came out, trying to push the barrel away with the bottom foregrip of his AK.

I punched him in the face with the barrel of the shotgun, and then came down hard on his near wrist, the one that held the pistol grip.

Using that momentum, I leaned forward slightly, rotating my strong hand under the gun, and shifting my hips, brought the stock up, in an underhand motion, against the side of his head.

I bashed him twice more, only to be tackled, and pushed down the stairs by another.

We rolled all the way down, everything flailing. I found myself at the bottom, my shotgun out of reach, and one pissed off Mexican on top of me.

He punched the side of my head a couple of times with what felt like brass knuckles.

I looked up, and watched him bring a two-tone Bersa .380 toward my face.

I grabbed his wrist with my dominant hand, wrapped my legs around his waist, and wrenched. He fell atop me, his shot hitting the kitchen floor a few feet away.

The air was thick with gunpowder residue and flakes of porcelain tile.

Shifting my hips, I worked my left hand inside the back pocket of my jeans, yanked the .38 out, and jammed the barrel in his ear and pulled the trigger.

Blood, brain, and bone fragments erupted as if from a geyser, spraying me from the chest up. I made a mental note to be sure to stick it in an arm pit if I ever had to do that again.

One of his friends stepped out onto the staircase firing a Galil, one round punching through my thigh, a couple more zipping through the dead body atop me, hitting the heavy armor on my chest.

I emptied the .38, wringing one round off a step, and the last three up his thigh and hip.

He dropped the Galil, sliding onto his ass, and down the stairs.

I dropped the .38, pushing the dead man off me as he scrambled for his rifle, and his friends came onto the staircase.

The .45 was in my hand before I realized it, my thumb disengaging the safety, my hands meeting in a solid thumbs forward grip, locking out at full extension as the three dot Novak night sights lined up on the chest of the first man, already firing his AK.

Everything was super slow-mo. Even the sound of his AK was a dull mute.

I fired four times, not in controlled pairs, but as fast as I could pull the trigger.

As he fell, I watched the last man duck back inside the hallway, and I emptied the magazine through the dry wall, the slide locking back on an empty mag.

I dropped the mag, pulled another free, and slammed it inside the gun as he came back through the door, bloody and pissed.

I hit the slide lock with my weak hand's thumb as I came back to a full extension, and fired twice, into his chest, and twice more into his face.

He fell, rolling down the staircase into the man who'd come out with the Galil, who now sat a few feet from me, three steps from the bottom, holding the leg I'd shot, swimming in shock.

I shot him in the head.

There was a lull then, one of those terrible silences when the euphoria of adrenaline takes its leave, and you have to force yourself to reach that higher level to keep in fate's good graces.

And then I heard the unmistakable sound of a spoon spinning away from a grenade, and stared down my sights and up the stairs, perfectly aware of the blood pouring from my thigh. And then a hand reached through the door, and in that hand a long canister type grenade. I fired carefully, at warp speed, emptying the mag, and reloaded as the white phosphorus grenade exploded at the top of the stair case.

There was the pop of the explosion, and the feint fizzing as the smoke filled the room and the fire caught. It spread quickly from the top of the stair case into the hallway, and around the top of the room.

I crawled backward finding myself against a wall, and recharged the .45. After so many years of using high cap nines, having half the mag capacity was kinda starting to annoy me.

I shoved the gun back into its holster, and began to administer aid to the opposite thigh. It was bleeding quickly, but not the mad spurting of arterial bleeding. It hurt, but I could move the leg, so I didn't think it'd hit the bone.

The fire spread quickly, along the walls and down the stairs, circling the room.

From the stairway above, I heard screams, and I smiled as I tied my tourniquet.

Toni came back into the room, all alone. She heard my laughter, and saw my cruel sneer, as the remaining men burned above us, and her face contorted in revulsion. I ignored it.

"You two fags stop playing Tango and Cash, and come the fuck on," Russell said, Trav right behind him with the girl in his arms.

"Can you move?" she asked, recovering.

"Help me up," I said. She helped me up, and then handed me my guns. She went to put an arm under my shoulder, and noticed the dark wet spot growing from beneath my armor.

"Don't," I said. "Just get me to the van."

"Got no choice, you fucking asshole," she said.

Bear had brought the van up and parked it sideways before the front door. C.W. was beside it, rifle in his hand, covering the house, the side panel door open for everyone to climb in. Travis was already inside with the girl, who clung to him with a wild eyed fever.

Russell was at the rear of the van scanning everything quickly, before moving to help us in the van.

"How bad are you hit, dude?" he asked.

"Could be worse, I guess," I said, the burning in my guts just starting to flare hot.

"Fucking asshole," he scoffed, like he cared, and helped Toni put me in the van.

"Anything on the bands yet?" Russell asked as Bear as he climbed in behind me.

"Nope, all clear. So far. Can't be much longer, with shit catching fire like it is," Bear said, master of the understatement like always. The house behind us was quickly becoming Dante's dream.

"Get out on that drive-way, and give me a minute, let me check the hero's wounds."

"Whatever you say, boss," Bear said, with an appropriated sing song.

The doors slammed shut, and Bear rolled us away from the rapidly engulfing flames, and onto the long driveway.

Russell hit a switch on the ceiling, and a flood light blinded us.

"That house is burning fast," Bear said, staring down the long drive way to the blacktop behind the gate.

"A minute's all I need to unfuck his dressings," Russell said. The dressing on my leg was more than adequate, but he was hovering over me, and shaking his head.

"That's some dark blood," he said, working on my leg, shaking his head. Toni leaned down, and whispered in his ear. He looked up at me as he finished what he was doing.

"Get the vest off, let me look at it," he said.

"We need to get out of here," I replied, the pain in my side growing. It felt like someone had cut me open and jammed a hot coal in my gut.

"He's got a point," Toni said, something in the house exploding behind us.

"Oh, fuck," C.W. said, looking ahead. "We got company."

Russell and Toni both strained their necks toward the front, to check.

"Cops," Russell asked, both he and Toni straining their necks forward to what was next. A round clanged off the windshield.

"I'm guessing not," Bear said, understated.

"Fuck!" Russell snapped, shouting hard. "Turn this bitch around, goddamn it!" he commanded, his voice bellowing.

He left me where I was, moving past everyone to the rear doors, where he hooked himself to a lanyard attached to a D – ring bolted to the floor, and picked up his baby, an M-60 E4, and hooked it to the bungee suspended from the ceiling, before looking back at us.

A few more bullets ricocheted off the windshield.

"Spread those kevlar blankets out, goddamn it," he said racking the bolt on the machine gun, and kicking open the rear doors, the doors locking in place.

Bear turned the van around, and straightened it up, facing back toward the house, and past it, and he punched it hard, so hard it took a second for the gears to hit, and a couple more rounds cracked as they passed. Then Russell opened up.

Hanging out the motherfucker by a thread, just him and his belt-fed.

The world seemed to pause as Russell yelled his war cry, and the rear of the van seemed to sink slightly just before lift-off as we felt the heat and fury wash over us.

The girl touched me, as if more concerned with my wounds than her own as the van rocketed forth.

Russell held tight on the machine gun, and yelled like a proper cowboy, bearing down hard the whole way.

I could feel the van pause and grip, finding traction, before lifting off. I looked past Russell, over his shoulder at the long stream of fire flowing from his weapon, past the trees. I saw past the cars in the driveway, the main house we'd just left, and the guest houses beside it.

"Where the fuck are you going?" C.W. asked, shouting.

"Shut up, I got this shit," Bear said, as if the last thing he needed was commentary.

"Shit," C.W. said, tensing, his tension filling the rest of the vehicle, only matched by the fury of Russell on the machine gun.

I felt the bump of unpaved earth and heard the crunch of rock and grass as we left pavement.

One of the vehicles behind us caught fire, and another crashed into the house.

And then Bear stood hard on the gas, and the front end of the van turned nearly skyward, as Bear steered us up the old railroad grade. We caught air at the top, Russell laughing as he bounced on his string, the van fishtailing as Bear turned us down the path that had once held track.

Bear punched it hard for half a minute getting out of sight of the house, and then slowed down enough for Russell to make safe his machine gun and unhook himself.

"How's he doing?" he asked.

"His leg's bleeding faster," Toni said, her hands bunched tight atop my dressings, her muscular arms hard with tension. I hadn't noticed how hard she was pressing my leg before.

"Get us to a blacktop, and sail us even and smooth away from this place," Russell said. And then he jammed a syringe of morphine into my good thigh.

CHAPTER 60

It wasn't the first time I'd been shot, but it was the most painful. That's for goddamn sure.

Russell had helped me out of my chest rig, and cut my jeans, and then applied the bandages and QuikClot gauze as Bear drove us back to the RV point, where C.W., Trav, and I had switched vehicles. I wasn't going anywhere near cops until the coast was clear, gunshot wounds or not.

"Hang tight, kid, we're almost there," Travis told me as he swerved through traffic. I didn't watch, just grimaced through the pain, my eyes closed tight, looking for that special place where I could go until this was over. Wherever it was, it was further away than it had ever been before.

"Hey, son, you awake back there? You stay with us, goddamn it!" Travis shouted from behind the steering wheel.

"Fuck you," I sputtered.

"That's the spirit," he said, then swerved again.

"Seriously, don't you know a back alley abortion doctor on *this* side of town?" Cornelius asked, only half joking.

"Son, now ain't the time for you to be runnin' yo' mouth."

We bumped along for what seemed like years. I risked a peak through heavy slits. Mid-morning traffic crawled before the Dallas skyline. Blood was starting to break through the adhesive. They say gut shots are the worst.

The next time I opened my eyes we were leaving downtown, and entering South Dallas, Erykah Badu's picture stared at me from the side of the Black Forest Theatre. I started singing to myself.

"Jeb, Jeb, you ok?" Cornelius asked, worried.

"Baaaa-du," I hummed.

"We're almost there," the old man said, steering the van off the highway and onto a neighborhood street.

"This is the place? This is where your doctor is? Jesus, man," Cornelius reassured me as we came to a stop in a dirt driveway beside an ancient, large, two-story house that had probably been something to look at...when my grandmother was in junior high.

"Relax, I'll be the one cuttin' on him. Hap's probably too drunk by now, anyway," Travis said, slipping the transmission into reverse and turning the wheel.

"Hap?"

"Short for Happenstance," he said backing us up nearly to the back porch, which was sagging and dilapidated. Cornelius shook his head in disbelief.

Great, I thought, a street doctor named Happenstance. One who was drunk before the rush to work traffic petered out. Fuck me, I'm dead, I thought.

C.W. jumped out and threw open the sliding door and helped me out. An obese black man who was just tall enough to not be a midget, stepped out onto the porch. He wore corduroy pants and a dirty, wrinkled, long sleeve paisley shirt that hadn't been fashionable since probably ever. He smelled of ripe body odor, talcum, cheap cigars, and sweet, sweet liquor.

He led us into a narrow hallway, and through a large kitchen. The place was covered in trash, and refuse. Crusty pizza boxes and moldy, grease stained hamburger wrappers, empty store brand soda cans and various empty liquor bottles littered the floor and counter.

We walked through a white sheet into what had once been a dining room. On top of the hardwood floor sat an immaculate, though ancient, operating table. Over it an arm held a halogen bulb and magnifying glass, and next to the whole setup was a small stainless steel table with instruments.

They laid me down and stretched me out and cut my shirt off. Travis positioned the light where he wanted it, then the magnifying glass. He slipped the scissors between my skin and the tape, but I didn't feel anything. The blood had eaten through the adhesive.

"Goddamn," he said softly.

I didn't feel anything as he worked. It didn't take very long. He made the incision, pulled the flattened slug, and sewed me up with a practiced hand. The last thing I remember was him letting me know I could go to sleep before he started on the leg.

CHAPTER 61

The first thing I saw when I woke was the ceiling fan. Its wood blades churned the raw, metallic odor of the room over onto itself, again and again.

I tried to sit up, and pain shot through the stitches pulling at my side. I was nude, except for the dressings and tape around my thigh and stomach. Everything was dark; the only light was the glow of the television in the living room, reflected off Hap's round face, his face blank in its wash, the sounds of the video game coming from the television.

"Hey, mystery man, you made it," Hap said cheerily, waving at me with a bottle of peach snaps in his hand. "You shouldn't move around though. That's no good," he warned, before turning back to his video game. I didn't see the old man or Cornelius anywhere.

Slowly, I swung my legs off the side and slipped off, careful of where I bared my weight.

"Where is everyone?" I asked, stretching as much as I could stand. Looking for some clothing, or at least some shoes to wear in the wasteland that was Hap's home.

"Mr. Travis left not long after he sewed you up, the other fella, he stayed all day, only been gone 'bout a half hour or so." Great, they left me alone with this loon, I thought. "Other fella said to tell you he left a message for you on the fridge."

I practiced walking, breathing, and grimacing all at once as I made my way through the hanging sheets and into the wasteland of his kitchen. On the counter was my bag, the pair of Sketcher top siders I'd worn earlier, and some jeans, my belt through the loops, the pewter Kool-Aid Man leaping off the front of it. The

.45 in its holster, and spare mag carrier were on top. I didn't see a shirt, and I couldn't find my cell anywhere.

The fridge was covered in take-out menus held in place with little magnets, and faded Garbage Pail Kid stickers. I didn't think anyone still had any of those things damn things.

On top was Cornelius's note. It was short, sweet, and to the point.

Jeb- Josh is home, and he's in trouble. Do not call the cops. They're at his house, and he recognized them as the men who jumped us. I took your cell, mine was out of juice. –C.W.

I had to move, had to get to the people I had to protect. I had to be able to move before I did that. I found a bottle of cheap vodka in the freezer, then a can of generic soda from the fridge. I tried the vodka first, then popped the top and drank a good measure of the Doc Shasta.

I slipped on the jeans, and shoes, buckled my belt, picked up the .45, press checked it, and slipped it behind my belt.

Then I picked up the vodka and walked into the living room, leaving the soda on the counter. "You got a phone here, Hap?"

"Sure," he said, missing the long jump on the 8-2 level of the original Mario Brothers game. I'd had trouble with that jump myself. When I was nine years old.

"You mind telling me where the fuck it is?"

"Ain't got no call be raisin' yo voice to me like that!"

"Just tell me where the fuckin' phone is," I said, my voice as even as I could keep it.

"In the hall, man," he said, turning back to his game, sulking.

I hobbled back down the hallway, to find an ancient rotary phone on a little shelf hollowed into the wall. Garbage Pail kids, rotary phones, and Mario Brothers.

Jesus fucking Christ, I thought, shaking my head.

I tried to remember the old man's cell number, but it didn't come. I had another slug of cheap vodka, and dialed Joshua's house, but the line was busy. I tried my cell, which C.W. had taken, but he didn't answer. I took another slug of vodka then remembered Travis's number. Of course it was turned off as well.

I would've tried Bear's cell, had I known the number, but it probably wouldn't have done any good anyway.

I found my wallet, then Toni's card. I dialed her cell, then her office number.

"Ashford Consultants."

"I need to speak to Rory," I said, dropping her father's name.

"He's unavailable; care to leave a message?"

"No, it's important. Please tell him it's Jeb Shaw."

"I'm sorry, but it's not going to happen."

"Listen, bitch," I said, but she hung up.

I walked back into the den, steadily sipping the vodka.

I looked out the back door, at the sun's light just starting to wane.

"How long was I out, Hap?" I asked.

"Whole goddamn day. I figure, man gets shot, he's gonna need his rest, that's what I figure."

"When did Cornelius leave?"

"'Bout half hour 'go, like I said."

"Hey, Hap," I said, getting his attention.

"Yeah, man?"

"You got a car, Hap?"

"Sure I got a car," he said, concentrating on his game.

"Where are the keys, Hap?" I asked, my voice as still and even as the water's surface on a calm spring day. He paused his game, to turn and look at me with his mouth hanging open in disbelief.

I stared at him, shirtless and bandaged; my gun in my belt, drinking his vodka.

CHAPTER 62

I circled the block once before turning onto their street. Hap's ancient, rusted Plymouth Galaxy sputtered and coughed with each turn. Two patrol cars were parked in front of Josh and Maggie's. In the first one, Shavers and Conyers sat side by side, like golems, ready for dusk to provide some relief.

In the second, two thick Anglo guys without necks, whom I'd never seen before, sat up front. Behind them, in the cage, Cornelius sat with his arms wrenched behind his back, his hands obviously cuffed.

I wondered how many of them I needed to kill, and if I could do it without harming anyone who didn't. Neither the situation nor the odds looked positive, but I had my priorities.

I pulled to a stop in their driveway, behind the same dark green cargo van that had delivered me to south Dallas that morning. I looked at Shavers and the other uni getting out of their patrol car, and took one last long pull of Doc Shasta and vodka before stepping out. I had borrowed Hap's ridiculous paisley button up to cover my gun, and the fingers of my left hand teased the bottom hem, ready to rip it up and out of the way for my right to pull my gun free. I swear I could feel the tendons rip further where I'd been stabbed on the rooftop. I just had a little bit further to go.

I saw Joshua's worried face through the glass of the garage door, and I heard it start to rise as I stepped forth to meet the officers.

"Hello, officers," I said. Maybe I could lull them into a false sense of security.

"Just try it, Shaw, just you fucking try it!" Conyers yelled, his department-issued Sig coming out of its holster.

"You must not've heard the news, Connie," I said, trying to buy enough time, letting him get close enough for me to do something, anything. Shavers just stood there, lost behind his dark shades, his hand on his gun.

"The only news I know, fuck face, is that you're going to prison. And I'm the one going to put you there." As he spoke, I watched another squad car pull to a stop the street. White men in ill-fitting uniforms stepped out holding AK variants. My mind processed that faster than Conyer's did.

I yanked my shirt high, my hand gripping the butt of the .45. I was bringing it out and up when the first gunshot exploded, and Conyers fell into me. I pushed him down, staring at Shavers, trying to redirect my arm's momentum. But he had the drop on me, and I saw the gun barrel flash three more times.

His bullets hit me in the chest, and I fell, C.W., still inside the back of the patrol car, beating the window. The .45 fell, my arm hopelessly outstretched and grasping for it.

I stared at it, its grips, oh, so close. I tried to stretch my hand out but my arm wouldn't move. I looked up, to see Shavers speaking. I couldn't hear what he said. I didn't give a fuck.

I couldn't let him win.

I couldn't let them hurt my baby brother or his family. Joshua was the good son. He deserved those things too much.

Shavers could kill me, and that would be fine as long as I took him with me. I'd spend my eternity in hell fucking him in the ass, reminding him he hadn't been able to hurt them anymore. He started to raise his gun and I swung over, with everything I had, crawling, clawing for my *.45,* in the grass just out of reach, begging the monster to come out. I was his, now and forever.

I was almost there when Joshua stepped out of the garage, his pistol locked tight in his hands, firing so fast the shots sounded like one continuous burst. I looked up to see his rounds tear through Shavers' face, turning it into so much bloody red pulp.

He fired so fast, and reloaded with such speed, one could hardly hear a pause in the string of fire. The cops from the second patrol car were still drawing their guns when Shavers fell beside me. Joshua granted them no quarter, recharging his weapon as he shifted on the move, firing before they brought their guns up. In my mind's eye, for some reason I saw footage of a Huey coming in on a hot LZ. His bullets tore large fist sized groupings through their faces, each round perfectly hitting it's mark.

"Jeb, Jeb, oh god, Jeb," Joshua said, rolling me over, pulling his shirt off.

"Iss ok, bubba," I tried to reassure him, as he pulled his shirt off and bunched it on my chest, trying to stop the flow of blood.

"No, no it's not!" he didn't think it was so great. Cornelius, having somehow escaped the patrol car, slid down with us and held my head in his hands.

"Everybody's ok? Everybody's ssafe?" I asked.

"Shut up Jeb, just shut up!" Joshua told me. He must have been busy; he didn't want to be bothered.

"Itss ok, is all good, guyss," I said, so very happy they were safe. That was what mattered.

"Jeb, Jeb? Jeb…," I heard my baby brother call softly in the distance, as I, for the second time in my life, embraced the comfort of the dark shroud falling over me.

CHAPTER 63

When I awoke, Joshua was sitting in the chair beside my bed. His hands were clasped in front of him, and he was praying. Neither one of us had ever been much for church, but there he was, praying at my side. I was starting to sense a pattern.

When we locked eyes, he stopped and stared at me. And then, tears running silently down his face, he leaned over and kissed the side of my head for what seemed like forever.

My baby brother, taking care of me.

When he finally let go, he found a cup, poured me some water, and gave me a sip.

And then he began catching me up to speed.

Shavers and the other two had been the ones who had jumped them in the alley. They had placed temporary tattoos similar to the ones Torres' crew wore in visible locations, as part of their disguises. They were the ones who had busted his ribs and threatened to destroy not just his drawing hand, but his ability to express himself through his art, and more importantly to earn a living and provide for his family. He recognized Shavers voice, as well as the builds and body posture of the other men. These things had burned themselves into his memory with a white hot flame, and, if things hadn't ended the way they had, would've surely laid there tormenting him through this life and the next.

No one knew just how long Shavers had been dirty, if he'd been taking orders from a particular person or group, or if he was merely a free-lancer, taking jobs as they came. I wanted badly for him to be a part of some greater agenda, but I knew the simple truth was that he'd done what he'd done for money, as contract labor. Though I realized this, something he'd said about family would always come back to me, from time to time, giving me pause, cause to stop and think and wonder if maybe he'd had a greater purpose after all. I don't know why I would bother with such frivolities. Violent men without a code do not deserve so much thought.

The men who'd showed up in the other squad car were identified as Russians, both with long criminal records. In fact, several of the men in Vlad's crew turned out to be wanted by Interpol, hiding out in Dallas, a place where the Russian mob had no known presence.

Conyers lived, and supported what C.W. told the cops. I did not hear of him again or see him for the rest of my stay. Thankfully.

A phalanx of Uncle Jack's super-powered lawyers met everyone at the hospital, while Jack made calls and called in favors from some people and threatened others before making contact with the girl's parents. Say whatever you want about the rich and powerful, it's always nice to have juice on your side.

The girl was in some serious state of bad shock from it all. Being kidnapped, watching her friend butchered, the months of captivity, the harrowing rescue, the fire. Toni stayed with her, and she clutched Toni like a stranded sailor clutches driftwood. Eventually the army of people trained and equipped to deal with rape and kidnap victims brought their transgressions, but Toni stayed with her the entire time.

After he'd removed the bullet and sewn me up, Trav had gone back to check on the girl and run interference. The plan had been for him to stay. We still had things to do, and we wanted to stay under the radar while Jack took care of his end of things.

In the end he figured the bullet was out, the bleeding had stopped, and I could take care of myself. He wanted to check on the girl. By that time she was in a secure room, cops, doctors, lawyers, and the rest outside, there to care for her, but he had to see her. He couldn't be there for his daughter, he could never make that right, even that score, bring her back, and that pain would finish the job the cancer had started, but he still needed the fix. As if the only thing that would ever abate his pain would be seeing this girl, Jamie, safe and sound and with her family.

Morales came by several times, but only three visits were official. On these he was accompanied by another senior detective, sometimes two, and they went over my story. I knew my story, because Morales and Jack had told me before they let the others come around just what my story was. I'd been enjoying the hospital pharmaceuticals the first time, so he came back a second time, by himself to make sure I knew what I'd been up to. Once he brought some brass, and I didn't find out why until later.

Joshua came every day. Sometimes he brought his wife and son, and sometimes not. Maggie was kind, in the way people are kind when they're know they're not entirely wrong, but also not entirely right. He brought with him my new friend, the pup. The little guy would lie on my chest or across my shoulder, his nose on my neck, and it was the most sincere kiss I'd ever felt. When he left him there, against hospital regulations, no one had the heart to say anything about it.

Of course, I also had a gun under my pillow.

The fifth came and went with nary a shot fired nor angry yell in Dallas. The parade downtown had been a sober affair, more of a wake than anything, and I turned it off, hit the sweet morphine drip, and faded back into the next realm.

Rosie came to see me after the spectacle died down. She was on leave and seeing a therapist. It wasn't her idea, but it was strongly suggested she do so if she wanted to salvage her career. She'd been warned to stay away, but she said she thought I deserved better than that.

Her bruises were no longer swollen, but had not yet started to fade. She wore comfy jeans and a gray t-shirt that hung tight to her body. She moved with a self-conscious stiffness that betrayed the nature of wounds both physical and mental. A cop who had tried to control every aspect of her life with a strong hand and had failed. One who had been raped by her partner before watching him kill her fiancée with a bullet he'd taken from my gun.

Everyone she worked with knew we'd slept together, whether it was their business or not.

Her fiancé had been a nice young man from a family that was close to her own. They'd dated off and on since they were teenagers. He had an accounting degree and a good job in a commercial real estate firm downtown. He had been planning on going to school for his MBA in the fall.

All he wanted out of life was to be a good man, and make lots of money to support the family he wanted to build with Rosie. It had been expected that they would marry, and either then, or upon her first pregnancy, that she would leave police work behind.

She said she knew she should have been flattered. He was a good, good man, with a brilliant mind, and he would have provided a wonderful life for their young family. And now he was dead, and everyone in both their close families knew she'd cheated on him with a vagabond gun hand just passing through.

An adulteress, doomed, forever burdened with the psychic mark of the scarlet letter in a family she would never be able to please.

Cornelius would often come in the evenings. The whole business would give him work through the summer and most of the winter. There was already talk of a book deal. His agent wanted to shop it around Hollywood in outline form.

He finally got his interview, but only because Jack convinced me that it fit into the overall tapestry that was being woven. I did my best to make contractors look good, and insisted they not use the M- word.

It was basically the truth, the difference being in this version, we had actively been working with Toni and her people for a lot longer than two days, and that the crew Manny had run had been taken out by a rival gang.

Afterward, when he'd taken his last pound of flesh, after everything had settled and I'd spent days navigating through a drug fueled maze to the truth, I realized what I'd missed.

"Did you love her," I asked, gently stroking the snoring puppy on my chest.

"What are you talking about?"

"Kelly. Your old yoga girlfriend. Travis's little girl. The one that left you for Torres. Did you love her?" I asked. It seemed simple enough.

"Fuck you, you prick," he said, without looking up at me.

"I'm guessing that's a yes," I said.

He didn't say anything. Just sat there in place, shaking, like there was nothing else for him to do. Like he'd been so close to not having to share that.

"It's all good, bro. Just, the next time you need me to kill a bunch of people, all you have to do is ask. I mean for real."

And then he looked up at me, his eyes as wet and furious as a storm about to burst, and at the bottom of their swirling depths, still pools of the deepest sadness I'd ever seen.

He gathered his notebook and left without another word. I kissed the little guy's nose. At least he got it.

Toni became my new best friend. Between her and my grandmother, I don't think I ate a bite of hospital food the entire time. On one of her visits, after she'd decided we were friends, she brought her lover, a spunky blond who tried hard for butch, but would always be too cute to pull it off.

I tried to convince them both to hop the fence for me. They both thought that was the funniest thing ever, then left me with platonic kisses cooling on my cheeks.

The bitches.

The next time she came, her father came with her. He'd been by before, but I'd been out. He was a tall, stern man, with graying hair and wire glasses, dressed in a three piece suit over a runner's frame. Any man who wore a three piece suit during the Texas summer must've just been a joy to work for.

The last time she came, the day before my discharge, she asked what I was going to be doing with my life. I told her I hadn't thought about it much, but it would be a long while before I was fit enough to go back to doing what I had been. She offered me a job. I said I'd think about it. I did have a puppy to care for, after all.

I woke one afternoon to find Russell sitting in one of the uncomfortable chairs, eating my Jello. Which was fine because I never really cared for it.

"How long you gonna milk this shit, hero?"

"Go suck cock in hell," I told him. He smiled at the thought.

"You really gonna stick around after this?" he asked.

"Might as well," I said. "Somebody has got to look after him, after all," I said, looking at the sweet hunter twitching in his sleep, chasing his prey while safely snuggled on my chest. So fierce.

"You really going into the P.I. business with them?"

"They need muscle. Besides, it'll make do 'til I heal up enough to go back to real work."

"About that," he said, scraping the last of the Jello off the sides of the plastic cup.

"We're putting something together. You have a place, if you want it," he said. He didn't elaborate. He didn't need to.

I didn't see Travis, though I was told he came several times when I'd first been admitted. He didn't send flowers, but a package of chocolate, and bourbon. I could have kissed him. The card said for me to come by anytime, which I did, the day of my discharge.

The sun's ember was dying, and night birds chirped in the air. He watched me step out of the cab, and walk up the stairs with my cane. He was sitting in his chair, munching on a cold tamale, his drink on the little table between his chair and the swing. His pit was relaxing in it, on her back, belly to the world, tongue hanging out.

I walked up slowly. He didn't smile, or extend his hand.

I stepped past him, and gently placed the pup down beside the thick neck of the older dog, and watched the tonal shift in her vibe as she wrapped him up in nature's most perfect, loving embrace.

"You a drinker, son?" he asked.

"Waitin' on you to ask, old man."